RISE OF THE CIRCLE

Tom Reynolds

ONE

The devastation was catastrophic, unlike anything the world had seen since The Battle all those years ago. Alpha Team fought to capture and contain the metas, which had been released from Silver Island, for days on end. Many of the escaped metas, the smart ones, chose to flee Bay View City altogether. Those that didn't and were captured were executed. There would be no place to hold rogue metas in Bay View City while Alpha Team was running it.

I wish I could tell you that I learned all of this because I was out there in the fight. I wish I could tell you that I'm only here telling you this now because, in the end, I defeated Alpha Team and returned home safely. That isn't what happened, though. For the past week I've had to sit and watch these events unfold on television, just like everyone else, everyone else who was lucky enough to be far away from the fighting at least.

No one could completely escape it, though. I watched in horror and helplessness as a member of Alpha Team ripped the head off of an escaped meta right in front of me, on the other side of our living room window on the forty-seventh floor.

The reason I couldn't do anything to help was a promise I'd made to a woman named Michelle, a woman that I had known as Veronica for the three months she'd been dating my older brother, Derrick, before revealing who she really is and asking me to agree to join her with little additional information. When she asked me to help her, I was on my back, barely clinging to life. She made me promise one thing: that I would not use my metabands under any circumstances until she returned.

I don't know if I made the right choice agreeing to that, not that I was in any shape to fight even if I wanted to. I've been forced to watch as my city tears itself apart piece by piece, helpless to do anything about it. The sad truth is that even if I disobeyed Michelle and powered up my metabands to fight, there is little I could do. Midnight is gone, presumed dead by many. All the other supposed *heroes* either left the city or found themselves lined up for execution alongside the criminals. If I wanted to power up my bands and fight, I would have no allies, and everyone from both sides would be out to get me. Any attempt at stopping the criminals or Alpha Team would result in little more than a momentary distraction for both.

Derrick is scared, the most scared I've possibly ever seen him, and that includes the time I was six years old and got rocks stuck up my nose. Maybe he's just been putting on a brave face since our parents died and he's had to take care of me, but seeing the city the way it is now makes it feel like all hope has been lost. Even if I hadn't promised Michelle that I wouldn't fight, it would be hard to go out there knowing just how likely it is that I'd never come back and that Derrick would never forgive himself for being unable to stop me.

The little that Michelle did explain before she left pertained to all of this being much bigger than me and much bigger than just Bay View City. If I engaged in fighting Alpha Team or any of the others, they would know that not only was I still alive, but that I hadn't left the city either. According to Michelle, they would stop at nothing to make sure I was put down for good. Even after that they wouldn't stop. She told me that they would find out who I really am, who Derrick is, and ultimately who she really is. She didn't tell me this out of self-preservation; she told me this because according to her, what she's working for is much bigger than any of us, and it could all easily come crashing down if the wrong people learn about it. Risking my life meant risking countless other lives for what she assured me would've been a suicide mission anyway. That didn't make it any easier to watch as everything I knew was destroyed.

I've never felt more helpless, sitting at home all day,

everyday, alone. Derrick stopped working from home and practically moved into his office. With people fleeing the city left and right, he had little choice. He had to make sure someone was there to keep his business alive. Ironically, business has never been better for him. Nothing draws public interest around metahuman stories like when a group of them decide to practically destroy a city.

In fairness to Alpha Team, as if they deserved such a thing, property destruction was minimal. After all, it's hard to try to convince the rest of the world that all other metas should be eradicated if you just go and destroy the city yourselves.

But by far the hardest part of the past week has been not knowing what happened to any of my friends. Midnight, Sarah, Jim, they are all unaccounted for. Only in the past few days has anyone outside of Alpha Team been able to get anywhere close to Silver Island to assess the damage. Reports are coming in almost hourly on the rising number of dead bodies being found, and that doesn't even count the rest of the city, where conflicts are still happening around the clock. Even if any of them did manage to escape, there are very few safe places in Bay View City.

Michelle has forbidden me from using my metabands until she returns, presumably with a better plan than the current one, which is to just "wait." She also told me to stay put in the apartment. Unbeknownst to me, the apartment that Derrick and I have been living in for the past few months is a veritable fortress. It's one of the reasons Derrick has been attracted to it all along. The windows are bullet and blast proof. Reinforced support columns are hidden behind drywall, essentially providing a separate foundation for our penthouse apartment. While it would be difficult to build an apartment *immune* to a direct meta attack with any kind of discretion, our apartment was advertised as meta-*resistant*. I guess I owe a thank you card to the eccentric millionaire who lived here before us ... whoever he was.

Derrick hadn't told me about any of these features because he thought doing so would feel like he was undermining me and my abilities. Deciding to live in a fortress in the sky isn't a very hardy endorsement of confidence in the idea that I could protect the place myself. I didn't take it personally, though. If anything, I was more pissed off that he hadn't told me sooner. It isn't foolproof by any stretch, but it would have given me some piece of mind, since I would never be able to protect Derrick twenty-four hours a day anyway.

This made Michelle and him feel more comfortable leaving me here by myself, but it doesn't make me feel any better. That's why tonight I'm planning to escape.

Well, not really "escape." I plan to come back after all. I plan to come back later tonight even. But I just can't stay cooped up in this fishbowl any more, not when I don't know if the people I care about are alive.

To get into our apartment, you need an elevator key. This is because the elevator goes straight into our apartment. I know, fancy. If it weren't for the key, anyone would be able to just hit the "P" button and walk right into our living room. The easy solution for making sure I wouldn't leave the apartment would be to just take away my key, which Derrick tried to do. I successfully argued with him that not only was that unsafe if there was an actual emergency and I needed to evacuate the building, but that it was also treating me like a baby. After some back and forth, Derrick relented and said he would give me the key because he trusted me.

Idiot.

He isn't actually that dumb, though. The elevator is Internet connected. Derrick can access it from anywhere he can get a connection and not only shut it down if he wanted to, but also watch via the security camera. He can even set up an alert to let him know if the elevator moved when he wasn't home, and knowing the nerd that he is, I'm sure he did just that. But, being the nerd that he is, he probably didn't consider the other way to get in and out of the apartment: the stairs. Granted, walking down forty-seven flights of stairs isn't a very attractive alternative, but for now, I'm telling myself it won't be as bad as climbing them later.

The fire escape door swings open and a blast of cool air floods into the stairwell. Autumn is quickly becoming winter, and I'm glad I thought to bring a coat, even if I considered just leaving it in the stairwell around the twentieth floor because it was too hot.

It's starting to get dark earlier, but even still, it's too early in the evening for the streets to be so quiet in the middle of what is usually a bustling area of the city. It's one thing to see the empty streets from the top floor or on TV, but it's entirely different to see them with my own two eyes. There's no one. Even most of the cars that are usually parked along the side of the street are gone.

Right about now is when I start to realize that I didn't really have a plan beyond just getting out of the apartment. I succeeded in doing that much, and I'm pretty sure I even did it without Derrick or anyone else finding out.

Now what?

TWO

It's after a few minutes of walking that I find I'm somewhat instinctively walking toward Sarah's house. It's not intentional at first, but after I realize it, it seems like the only logical place to go. I'm nearly positive that she's out of the city. She'd have to be. Her father works for The Agency and it's hard to imagine that any of them would feel safe staying in Bay View City after the breakout. Even The Agency doesn't have enough people working for it or the kind of resources necessary to mount anything like a retaliation here. If they went looking for a fight, all they'll get is a massacre.

Still, it's possible Sarah and Halpern could have gone to their house before they left the city, unlikely but possible. And without any other way to contact her, it's my best bet.

I still feel enormous guilt over listening to Michelle's orders to keep my metabands powered down and to not go looking for Sarah. If something has happened to her, I'll never be able to tell myself that I couldn't have stopped it. There's no use in that kind of negative thinking, though. Michelle told me being with The Agency was one of the safest places Sarah could be. A meta like me striking out on his own to find her would be a million times more likely to attract attention from Alpha Team than actually doing anything useful.

The walk takes longer than I remember, and by the time I arrive at Sarah's house, it's late. Most of the houses on the street are dark and empty-looking inside. I can't tell if it's just because the people who live in them are all asleep or if they've left town. It's been happening in droves. People are fed up with the violence and chaos and have been leaving Bay View City by the thousands. Most have no idea where they're going next, just as long as they're far away from here. A lot have relocated across the bay to Skyville. Some hope to just wait this out, see what Alpha Team does, and hopefully move back once everything is somewhat back to normal. Others think "normal" isn't something that we'll see in this city again and have started planning to put down permanent roots somewhere else.

The last mile or so on the walk to Sarah's house I don't see a single soul, meta or otherwise. I find myself glancing toward the sky over and over again, thinking that I see someone streaking past out of the corner of my eye, but when I look up, I see the same empty sky that was the norm for a decade before all of this started up again.

Sarah's house is dark and quiet, just like all the others on her block. I still approach it carefully, aware that while all these houses look empty, for all I know there could be entire families huddled together in their darkened living rooms, watching me through the gaps in their curtains.

When I reach the door, I'm not quite sure what to do. It's so quiet here that even knocking feels like it'll echo through the entire neighborhood, but a breaking and entering charge wouldn't be easy to explain to Michelle and Derrick, especially since I already promised Derrick that my days of being brought home in cop cars were behind me.

From the sidewalk, the door looks like it's closed, but upon closer inspection, I see that it's actually open slightly, barely even an inch between the door and its frame, like someone didn't pull it closed all the way on their way out, or as though someone set up a trap for me to walk into. Midnight's paranoia is still hard at work somewhere deep in the back of my mind. It's a strange coincidence, and I go back and forth with myself over whether or not I should go in. I'd like to think that I decide to go in because I'm brave and that I don't need to rely on my metabands to get me out of any trouble I might find, but really I know that it's just that I walked all this way, and I'm not about to turn back now for no other reason than sheer stubbornness.

I push the door itself without having to even turn the doorknob, and it swings open. It's almost pitch black inside, with the exception of a few rays of light streaming in from the full moon hanging above the city tonight. Still, it's enough light for me to recognize the space from my ill-fated, first dinner with Sarah and her dad. Walking down the hallway toward the dining room, I see the same photos on the wall of Sarah and her dad during happier times, presumably before all of *this* started again over the summer, and I can't help but feel somewhat responsible for all of it. What if it was my activating the metabands in the first place that brought all of the others crashing down to Earth? What if I had just kept them off and dealt with that monster in the woods with my own two hands? Would things have turned out differently, I wonder? It's an exercise in futility since there's nothing I can do to change it, though.

The living room also looks the same as when I was last here just a few short weeks ago. Nothing looks out of place, but then again, it's not like I took an inventory the last time I was here. It's also not likely that if Sarah and her dad came back here and left in a hurry that they would have remembered to take their favorite living room lamps before they left. If I'm going to find any sign of whether or not Sarah and Halpern have been back here since Silver Island was destroyed, I'll find it in their respective bedrooms. If there is anything they came back to grab, that's where they would have taken it from.

It still feels creepy to be skulking through their house without permission, especially when I make the decision to head upstairs toward Sarah's bedroom at the end of the hallway. Despite having the best intentions here, there's no way you can tiptoe into your ex-girlfriend's dark bedroom in the middle of the night without feeling like a real creep.

Before I'm able to reach the door, a noise stops me in my tracks. It's not especially loud, but it came from Sarah's bedroom. I stand completely still and wait to see if I can hear it again or if my mind is just playing tricks on me. A second later, I have my answer when I hear it again. This time I recognize it as a creaking floorboard and my heart starts racing. Someone else is in the house, and whoever it is, it seems like they don't want anyone to know they're here either.

It could very well be Sarah or her dad, but if one of them were here, it doesn't make sense that they'd have all the lights off, does it? The idea that they're both here and just asleep in their beds crosses my mind and my face immediately becomes flush with embarrassment just at the thought of having to explain to either of them what the hell I'm doing creeping around their house in the middle of the night.

Another thought soon takes over, not nearly as embarrassing but far more dangerous. It occurs to me that someone with bad intentions could have found out who Sarah and Halpern really are, and that someone could be taking advantage of everyone's focus and attention being elsewhere to sneak in here.

I stand waiting in the darkness of the hallway for what feels like an eternity, weighing my options. There really aren't that many. I can either keep going and see for sure who or what, if anything, is in Sarah's room, or I can turn around and leave the way I came. If there is something bad in Sarah's room, I don't really like the idea of turning my back on it, though. If I turn around and leave, I know that I'll just be back here again tomorrow night. My curiosity is so strong, it's just too much for me to ignore what might be behind that door. And if it turns out that something happened to Sarah or Halpern, I'll never be able to forgive myself for not investigating when I could've tonight, just because I was afraid.

Metabands aren't an option if I want to abide by Michelle's rule, so whatever is in that room, I'm going to have to face it without any help. I slowly make my way toward Sarah's room at the end of the hallway, careful to walk gently to avoid squeaking any of the floorboards and alerting whoever might be waiting in her room. The door leading to her room is already open for the most part, which makes it less likely that I'll find a surprise by the time I get to it.

From a few feet away, the room looks empty, but because of the angle, I won't know for sure until I'm actually inside. I push the door gently, just enough so that I can squeeze through. The blinds on her window are pulled mostly shut, limiting the light in the room, but luckily, my eyes have mostly adjusted to the darkness by this point. While I can't see everything, I feel confident enough that I'll be able to make out the shape of a person if there's one in here.

Inside Sarah's room, I find her carefully made bed. The drawers to her dresser are all closed. I run my fingers over the top of it and feel a layer of dust. There aren't any signs that Sarah, or anyone else, has been here in a while. Whatever I heard before must have been nothing. Normal, small sounds like a house settling become much more ominous when there are no other natural sounds to mask them.

Satisfied that the bedroom is clear, I head back downstairs. I remember briefly seeing a chalkboard with a grocery list the last time I was here. Below that chalkboard, mounted to the wall, I remember seeing a set of car keys hanging on a hook. It was a small thing, but it stuck out in my mind at the time because of the keychain. Halpern owns the same brand of car that my parents had and the logo on the keychain reminded me of them that night. If that keychain is gone, that would mean there is a good chance that maybe Sarah and Halpern came back after all to take the car. Of course, that's assuming Halpern didn't already have the car with him at Silver Island that day, which is very likely. I know that the keychain is likely gone either way, but still, it feels like maybe I'll get some reassurance if I see that it's missing. Maybe I know deep down it'll be missing either way, and I'm just ignoring that for some glimmer of the kind of hope that's been missing in this city for the past week.

I push past the free-swinging door that separates the

dining room from the kitchen, no longer as concerned with minimizing the noise I make. The keychain is missing, and for an instant, I feel a sense of relief, even if I know it doesn't really mean anything. Behind me I hear another quiet creak and that sense of relief disappears in an instant.

There's barely any time to process the idea that there's definitely someone in the house before I hear the swinging door behind me being opened. Instinct takes over completely and before I know what I'm doing, my arms are out at my sides, summoning my metabands from whatever alternate dimension they go to when I'm not using them. Before they've even fully materialized, my wrists are heading straight for each other.

There's a loud clang as the metal makes contact before Omni's suit ricochets out of the bands and envelopes my body. Before the swinging door has even hit the wall, I'm fully powered up and ready. If Alpha Team knows about this house, if they know who Sarah and Halpern really are, then they would have come here. If they're here, there's very little I can do to protect myself, but I'm not about to go down without a fight.

"Omni?" the voice behind me asks.

Without thinking about it first, I spin around. Not always the best thing to do when someone has just snuck up on you, but I couldn't help it. There, standing in the doorway to the kitchen, is my ex-girlfriend, Sarah Miller, and she's holding a gun pointed right at my head.

"Whoa, relax," I say, putting my hands up to show I don't mean her any harm in the hopes that she'll lower the weapon. Even if a bullet won't do anything to me, it's still not fun to get shot at, to say nothing of what the neighbors will think.

"Oh my gosh, sorry!" Sarah says, embarrassed, as she lowers the gun to her side. "It's empty. There aren't any bullets in it. I just ... I just heard a noise and didn't expect to see you standing here."

It's been so long since I've seen her that for a moment, I almost forget that she has no idea Connor and Omni are one and the same.

"I'm sorry," I say. "I just wanted to check up on you ... make sure you were okay."

"How did you know where I live?"

She's got me there. There's no reason Omni should know this. The personal and professional lives of employees who work for The Agency are kept strictly separate. Even Sarah's co-workers probably have very little knowledge of who she is outside of her work, so metahumans like me are kept even further in the dark. Before I can think of an answer to give her, I'm saved by her tendency to answer her own questions before the person she's asked even has a chance.

"What am I doing asking you how you know where I live? Of course you'd be able to find out where I live. You're buddies with Sherlock Holmes."

"Who?"

"Not the actual Sherlock Holmes, of course. He's fictional. I meant Midnight. That's what I call him: Sherlock Holmes. I don't think he appreciates it very much, even though it was meant as a compliment."

"Wait, you know Midnight? How do you know Midnight? Have you seen him? Is he okay?" I ask.

"I was just about to ask you the same question. I haven't seen him since he saved me."

"He saved you? I don't get it. You're the one who saved me at Silver Island."

"And you're welcome for that, by the way," she says before I have a chance to thank her properly. I know she's kidding, but I'm still mad at myself for rudely failing to thank my ex-girlfriend for saving my life from who I now know is the daughter of the man who killed my parents. A thank you is the least I should have been able to come up with for her.

"After I last saw you on Silver Island, I tried to escape through the tunnel back to the mainland. I almost made it, but in the confusion, no one realized that I hadn't come out yet. The tunnel was blown before I reached the end. I was buried in an avalanche of rubble," Sarah explains.

"What? How did you make it out then?" I ask.

"Midnight. He saved me. He found me in the rubble. I'm not sure how, but he did. No one else was even looking for me because they didn't know I was even missing. My dad was told I was in one of the other escape vehicles. He didn't realize I wasn't until later when they met at the rendezvous point and he couldn't find me. Even if someone other than Midnight had found me, I probably wouldn't be standing here today.

"I'd lost a lot of blood. Too much blood. I don't remember any of that, though. The first thing I remember is waking up in one of Midnight's ... places. Lairs? Is that what you would call them? Anyway, I woke up there, hooked up to who knows how many machines, and slowly made my way back to the land of the living."

"And what about your dad?" I ask.

"He's fine," Sarah tells me. "He's been better, obviously, but aside from a fractured elbow, he's okay. There's something else though ... he doesn't know about what happened with Midnight."

"Why didn't you tell him?"

"Because if he knew what actually happened, he'd never let me go back to work for The Agency. The only reason he's even letting me come back, I think, is because he doesn't know what else to do with me, and he's too busy to think about anything else. It's really a mess out there right now."

"Yeah, I've noticed that," I say before hearing a sound toward the front of the house. It's the doorknob on the front door being slowly turned. My powers aren't back to what they were before all of this, so I didn't hear anyone walking up to the house.

"Expecting company?" I ask Sarah, readying myself for whatever is on the other side of the door. If it's Alpha Team,

I can't imagine they'd use the front door.

The door swings open suddenly and reveals Halpern standing in the doorway, his hand on his unclipped gun holster. He sees me and smiles before putting the clip back in place to secure his weapon.

"Losing your edge, huh? You're not someone I ever expected to be able to sneak up on," Halpern says to me with a smile on his face.

"Well it's been awhile since I've suited up, in case you haven't noticed."

"Oh no, believe me, I've noticed. The Bay View City wing of The Agency might be shattered into splinters currently, but I don't think there's a person in this city that doesn't know what Alpha Team has been doing to the metas they find," Halpern says.

"I only turned these on for protection," I say.

"From Sarah?" Halpern asks with a chuckle. "Sorry, honey, no offense." The look on Sarah's face says she doesn't appreciate the apology. "As nice as it's been catching up, we really don't have time for chitchat, unfortunately. We're just here to grab a few things, and then we're gone."

"You can't leave here. This city is your home, both of you," I say.

"This city isn't *home* to anyone other than Alpha Team. There's no way to stop them right now, and I'm not waiting around here to find out what else they're capable of."

"So you're just giving up?"

"Just giving up? No, kid. But you've got to realize that there are some battles you just can't win. This is one of them for The Agency. We'll find a way to deal with this eventually, I promise you that, but right now there's not much any of us can do waiting around Bay View City to see what they've got planned next."

"So where are you going then?"

"I'm afraid I can't tell you that, but we're both going to places where we can continue to fight the good fight. There's still a lot of good The Agency can do, and this little war is far from over if we have anything to say about it."

"You said you're both going to *places*, as in plural."

"Very perceptive, kid. That old guy you hang around with must be rubbing off on you. Don't think that's going to mean you get any more clues from me, though. You know as well as either of us that the less you know the better it's likely going to be for everyone involved."

"Well that old guy I've been hanging around with hasn't been seen since Silver Island, so you don't have to worry about that anymore," I say to Halpern, knowing that it's not entirely true, since I just found out that Sarah has actually seen him since then.

"I'm sorry to hear that, but he's been through worse before. I'm sure he's fine. It'll take more than four or five of the most powerful metas the world's ever seen to put him down," Halpern says, waiting for a reaction before continuing. "That was supposed to be a joke. Guess it wasn't a very funny one.

"In all seriousness, though, kid, I'm sure the old guy's fine. He's probably just laying low for a little bit, just like most of us are. It's a dangerous place out there for anyone who hasn't picked these Alpha maniacs as the side they're going to throw down with if push comes to shove."

"And what about you? Who are you going to side with if it comes to that?" I ask.

"Me? I'm going to stay on the side I've always been on: neither. There're good metas, there're bad metas, just like any other group of people. You try to help the good ones while trying to stop the bad ones from hurting anyone along the way. That's all anyone can do. These things aren't going away any time soon. When they disappeared ten years ago, a lot of people thought that was it and stopped preparing for the day they might come back, and look how that turned out."

Outside I hear footsteps approaching the house. They're

faint. Whoever is making them is going out of their way not to be heard. If it weren't for my guard being up so high after Halpern was able to sneak up on me, even I wouldn't have noticed them.

"We've got company outside the house. Expecting more guests?" I ask Halpern and Sarah. Both look back at me as though they have no idea what I'm talking about.

"It's the Blanks," Halpern says suddenly. "It's got to be. They're the only ones who could walk around the neighborhood without getting bothered at this time of night. If they find a meta in here, we're all done. You've got to teleport out of here."

"Okay," I say, and then think of home with the intention of teleporting there. But, I don't. Nothing happens. My body stays exactly where it is.

"Come on, you've got to go," Halpern says.

"I'm trying. I just can't. It's not working. I don't know why it's not working," I say, the panic in my voice starting to show itself.

"Then power them down," Halpern says calmly and seriously.

"No," I say. I can't just power down. If I power down and reveal who I really am to Halpern and Sarah, along with potentially whoever is on their way inside, not only could we all be in trouble, but Derrick and Michelle will be too. Too many peoples' safety relies on my identity staying a secret.

"There has to be another way," I say.

"The wine cellar," Sarah says suddenly as she moves toward a carpet lying on the kitchen floor. She takes the carpet in both hands and pulls, revealing a trap door in the hardwood floor below.

"How did you know about my wine cellar?" Halpern asks her.

"Don't worry about it. Omni, get down in there."

"Is this really going to work?" I ask.

"Do we have another choice?" she replies.

She's got a point. I pull open the trap door and quickly descend down the three steps into a very small area lined with wine bottles. There isn't much room, and before I have a chance to adjust my position, Sarah slams the trap door over me, hitting my head and pushing me farther down. It's a good thing I'm nearly invulnerable or else that would have really hurt. I can hear the carpet being replaced over the trap door seconds before there is a hard knock on the front door and the sound of Halpern's footsteps heading toward it.

The door squeaks open down the hallway, and I can hear footsteps from multiple people coming through the doorway and into the house. I stare up toward the sound and concentrate, trying to see through the floorboards to the room above, but all I see staring back at me is darkness. My ability to see through solid objects is gone. What is happening to my powers? Not being able to teleport before worried me, but the past few days have been the longest I've gone without using my metabands, so I tried not to freak out when I wasn't able to do it. I thought maybe this is just something that happens when I'm not used to using them everyday for a little while. Maybe they're *not* like riding a bike? But now, not being able to see through anything? That's causing me to start worrying and making me think that the problem is with the metabands, not me.

"Who's in here with you?" a muffled voice barks from the kitchen above me.

"It's just me and my daughter here," Halpern replies.

"We received a call from one of your neighbors that they saw a known metahuman through your living room window."

Dammit.

"A metahuman? I don't think so. Which metahuman do they think they saw?" Halpern asks back, lying.

"Why don't *you* tell me which metahuman they would have seen strolling around your house, buddy?" the voice asks back.

Michelle was right. It was stupid to use my metabands.

Now Halpern and Sarah are getting grilled because I didn't listen.

"I'm really not sure what you're talking about, sir, but if it would make you feel better, you're welcome to look around. Actually, I'd feel safer knowing that you did if someone thought they saw a metahuman in here."

"You, check upstairs," the voice commands an unseen companion. "You, check the kitchen. You, come with me to check the bedrooms."

Footsteps spread out through the house, banging up a flight of stairs and down another hallway. Another pair are coming toward the kitchen. Whoever they're sending in here, I'm hoping that they're not the thorough type. Above me I can hear cabinet doors being opened and closed, curtains being moved, a pantry door creaking.

"Who exactly are you expecting to find in the refrigerator?" I hear Sarah ask. She's standing directly above me, on top of the carpet lying over the trap door. I'm guessing her choice of location wasn't an accident, and I feel a slight sense of relief that maybe I won't be found after all.

"You can never be too thorough, Sarah," replies the person rummaging through her kitchen.

There's a few seconds of silence before I hear Sarah's reply.

"How do you know my name is Sarah?" she asks.

"Uh, you said it, didn't you?" the voice replies back quickly, still opening and closing every conceivable hiding space.

"No, I didn't."

"Oh, well they probably said it on the call on the way over. Sometimes they give us the names of the people in the house before we check 'em so we can make sure everyone who is supposed to be there is there."

"I don't believe you," Sarah replies. It's quiet above me. The cabinets are no longer being checked. There's a reluctant sigh followed quickly by a gasp from Sarah.

"Jim?" she asks, seemingly unable to believe what she's seeing.

"Sorry," a voice I now recognize as Jim's, no longer being muffled by a mask, replies back.

"What are you doing? Why are you working with the Blanks?"

"Because we're doing the right thing. We're trying to save this city from what it's started to become: a playground for metas or those rich enough to buy them off."

"You can't be serious. A meta saved your life before. You wouldn't be here if it weren't for Omni. You're just going to ignore all of that now?"

"I'm not ignoring that. A meta did save my life, but from another meta. It wouldn't have needed saving if they didn't exist in the first place. We all got along just fine for thousands of years without them. Now people have to worry about whether or not an idiot with superpowers is going to drop a car on their heads while they're just trying to go about their lives. You call that progress? These are the people we're supposed to look up to as heroes, and why? Because they can do things we can't? That doesn't make them above the law, and that doesn't make them welcome in Bay View city anymore as far as we're concerned."

"And who is 'we,' Jim?" Sarah asks.

"He's in the kitchen," a voice from down the hall says, preceding a pair of footsteps, which grow louder as they approach. I hear some brief shuffling above me and realize that it must be Jim replacing his mirrored mask in anticipation of whoever is coming through the kitchen door.

"Well I'm glad that you can see there's obviously no metahumans here, sir," Halpern says to what I presume is one of the Blanks walking alongside him.

"You, why does it seem like you're anxious for us to leave? Do you have somewhere more important to be?" one of the Blanks asks Sarah.

"I already told you-" Halpern starts.

"Quiet. I didn't ask you. I asked her. I already heard your answer. Now I want to see if she gives me the same one."

"We're going to stay with family," Sarah says confidently. This isn't her or Halpern's first lying rodeo, and it's going to take a lot tougher questions than that to trip up either of them.

There's a loud crash that sounds like it came from outside the house, followed by commotion in the hallway leading to the front door. A new pair of heavy footsteps enters the house and marches into the kitchen to join Halpern, Sarah, a masked Jim, and at least one other Blank. Footsteps come from elsewhere throughout the house, the rest of the Blanks reconvening.

"Have you found anything?" a voice asks above me, and I recognize it immediately as belonging to Charlie. Of course. It all makes sense now, and I feel like an idiot for not realizing it sooner. Alpha Team is working with the Blanks. "Working with" is probably too strong of a term. Alpha Team doesn't seem like they're taking orders anymore. Now they've got the Blanks taking orders from them.

"No, sir, the house seems to be secure," Jim replies to Charlie, his voice now distorted behind a mask.

"So you called me out here for nothing?" Charlie asks back.

Um ... no, sir. We received word that a meta was at this location. We wouldn't have called you for backup if we hadn't."

"Backup? You think that I'm backup for you? You work for me, not the other way around. What good are you if a team of five can't even take out one metahuman, let alone if you can't even see if one is actually here before you come crying to daddy to help?"

"You're right, sir. I apologize, sir," Jim says.

"Are you in charge here?" Charlie asks.

"No, sir. He is in charge here."

The floorboards creak as Charlie walks across the room

toward the person Jim has indicated. It's quiet for a brief moment; then there's a loud snap and a heavy thud against the floorboards above me.

"A man who doesn't speak up and take responsibility for his own mistakes isn't a leader. Congratulations, young man, you just got yourself a promotion. Now, if we're done here, I imagine you all have places you can be of more use than a kitchen. I suggest you find those places," Charlie says. There's a popping noise, which I recognize as the sound of air being displaced by someone moving incredibly fast. It's followed by the hurried footsteps of the Blanks as they exit the house. Outside, faintly, I can hear a truck's engine start up, followed by tires squealing as they drive away.

I continue to wait, though. Without my enhanced vision, there's no way of knowing that they're all gone for sure, so I leave that decision up to Halpern and Sarah. A few seconds after the truck is out of earshot, the trap door is opened and the light from the kitchen illuminates the tiny space I'm huddled in.

"You need to get out of here now," Halpern says, offering a hand to help bring me out of the converted crawlspace. I take it and pull myself back out into the kitchen. Turning around, I see the body of a Blank lying on the floor, his head turned completely around in the wrong direction.

"I'm sorry," I say.

"Don't be. It's not your fault that man's dead. You were here because you were trying to do the right thing, and in the end, doing the right thing always saves more lives than it costs. Don't forget that, Omni. We're still the good guys."

I look over at Sarah, and while she's putting on a stoic face, it's obvious she's upset.

"I'm sorry. I know I shouldn't be upset. It's not very professional of me," Sarah says, directed more toward me than Halpern, but her words seem to be intended for both of us.

"It's not a sign of weakness to have that upset you. They

stormed your home and killed one of their own right in front of you. It's easier to pretend things like that are just the new normal now, but that doesn't mean that we have to accept it," I say.

"I don't think I could have said it better myself," Halpern says as he puts his arm around Sarah's shoulders. "Come on, kiddo. Grab whatever you need from here and let's get the hell out of here. There's not much more good we can do inside the city anymore."

Halpern nods at me. I'm not sure if it's in thanks or just a reminder that I have to get out of here too. If it is a reminder, I take the hint. The front door is still wide open. I turn toward it, dig my feet in, and start running. I'm grateful to find that my speed's still here, even if some of my other abilities have apparently decided to call in sick today. Within seconds, I've sped through the entire city, moving fast enough that anyone would be hard pressed to even see a blur. There's no one on the street to see me anyway.

I slow down just enough to make sure I don't blow out the windows of my building and head for the stairwell, making short work of the forty-seven flights. I flip the light switch on my way through the front door and have my metabands powered down before the electricity has even reached the bulbs overhead in the living room. In retrospect, it would have been a better idea to have powered down *before* I breezed in the front door, but I don't realize that until I see Derrick and Michelle sitting on the couch, waiting for me with their arms crossed like parents who just caught their kid sneaking in late after being grounded, which I realize isn't that far off as metaphors go.

"Oops."

THREE

"Do you have any idea the kind of trouble you could have gotten yourself into by powering up those bands tonight?" Michelle asks me. I look in Derrick's direction, but I'm not really sure why. I think part of me hopes that he'll step in and back me up, even though he probably has no idea where I went tonight either. Instead, he shares a look that tells me I'm on my own with this one.

"I'm sorry. I didn't mean to-" I begin before Michelle interrupts me.

"Connor, we don't have the option of diverting from the plan whenever we feel it's inconvenient. You're not the only one involved here, and you're not the only one who'll suffer the consequences if something goes wrong."

"I know. I'm sorry."

"It doesn't matter if you're sorry or not."

"It won't happen again. This was a one-time thing. I promise."

"You're right. It was a one-time thing because we're leaving Bay View City. All of us. Tonight."

"What? What are you talking about? I'm not leaving Bay View City. This is my home."

"You've lived here for six months."

"That doesn't matter. This is my home now, and I'm going to do whatever it takes to protect it. I'm not just going to pick up and run at the first sign of trouble."

"Connor," Derrick says, "this isn't the first sign of trouble anymore. No one is saying we're running away. We're just regrouping."

"More than regrouping. We're gearing up," Michelle says.

"Have you even seen the news yet tonight, Connor?" Derrick asks me.

I shake my head no. Derrick reaches toward the coffee table and picks up a remote control, which he uses to turn on

25

the television. The screen comes on, and it's immediately filled with an image of Charlie speaking into the camera.

"This just happens to be what's on at the very second you turn on the TV? I thought that only happens in movies," I say.

"It's DVRed, smartass. Just watch," Derrick says.

"Citizens of Bay View City. Thank you for offering me the chance to explain my actions as well as the actions of my colleagues. As most of you know by now, a number of days ago, we were summoned to the Silver Island Metahuman Detention Facility to assist in stopping a breakout ..."

"What? That's not true! They were the reason the breakout happened in the first place. If they hadn't shown up, none of this would be happening!" I burst out.

"I know that, Connor. We all know that. Just watch the video. It'll be much easier if I don't have to pause it every time you argue with the screen," Derrick says.

"... unfortunately that breakout has resulted in the deaths of dozens of civilians, people like yourselves who were simply going about their day-to-day business, regular, hardworking Americans. And sadly, some who were not even old enough to fully grasp the new world we're dealing with today.

"These deaths were all unnecessary. They did not need to happen. They happened only as a result of a policy that not only excuses metas from the consequences of their crimes, but dangerously gathers them together into facilities like Silver Island, facilities that taxpayers spend millions of dollars on to ensure that these metahumans are cared for and babysat, even when they refuse to remove and surrender their metabands.

"To that I say enough. The rumors you may have heard are true, but in case you haven't heard them, then let me be perfectly clear. Starting today, the people of this city will no longer have to lie awake at night wondering if or when a metahuman attack might take the lives of their loved ones. That's because as of midnight tonight, we are hereby giving notice that all metahumans within the Bay View City limits must surrender their metabands to us for destruction or vacate the city limits immediately. This is a decision that has not been made hastily, and unfortunately, we have learned over the past few days as we have worked around the clock to round up the remaining escaped prisoners from Silver Island that it is not a choice that could go any other way.

"Up until now, people who wish to live in a normal, metahuman-free society simply had no choice as of a few months ago when the metabands returned. Even if a city was completely devoid of metahumans, it simply would become a target for those who wished to cause harm, steal, or worse. This catch-22, as it were, made it impossible to have a city free of metahumans unless it wished to risk its own safety from outside attacks. Now, we can provide that safety and protection. As you witnessed a few short days ago, myself and my ... colleagues possess an ability many thought previously impossible: the ability to destroy metabands.

"Does this mean that no metahuman will ever try to cause harm to Bay View City again? I wish I could tell you it did, but of course it doesn't. That is why we will stand guard and protect this city from any outside threats it may face, foreign or domestic. It is our firm belief that knowing Alpha Team is watching over this city will mean anyone wishing to cause it harm will think good and hard before even trying. We will not distinguish between so-called good metahumans and bad metahumans, as if such a distinction could indeed ever even be made.

"Instead, we will simply stand behind our warning: If you are a metahuman, you are no longer welcome in Bay View City. We care about this city, and we care about its people. We will no longer risk the deaths of many for the privilege of the lucky few. This will be the only warning. We will not hesitate, and we will not take prisoners. There is no longer anything waiting in Bay View City for metahumans except death."

The video pauses and it feels like all the air has been sucked out of the apartment. Michelle and Derrick are both quiet, waiting for my reaction.

"Is he serious?" I finally ask.

"I'm afraid so. There've already been reports of metahumans forfeiting their metabands in droves downtown. So far it seems mostly to be the ones with weaker powers. We suspect the more powerful ones are weighing their options before they decide to give them up or vacate the city," Michelle says.

"Is it true that they can really destroy metabands?" I ask.

"We don't have any firm evidence of that, everything so far is anecdotal, but yes, we think that they can, at least in certain circumstances."

"Didn't they try to destroy yours, Connor?"

I look down at the still present, yet powered-down metabands on my wrists, specifically at the hairline cracks that have developed in both.

"They did, but Midnight stopped them before they could. Or before they could completely, that is. They were still able to damage them."

"Have you suffered any ill effects from the damage?" Michelle asks.

"Wait. That must be it. Tonight, when I used my metabands. It was the first time since Silver Island and my powers ... they were different."

"Different how?"

"Maybe not different, just some of them weren't there. It's like I just couldn't access them anymore."

"Which powers?" Derrick asks.

"Teleportation. That's the big one. My senses seemed to be dulled too. I couldn't see through objects any more."

"Hmm," Michelle says, "that's not good. Any others missing?"

"Not that I know of, but I didn't get a chance to test them all out yet."

"What do you mean, 'yet'?" Derrick asks. "There's no 'yet' here, Connor. Did you not hear what Charlie said on TV just now? I'm sorry, but they almost killed you the last time. You're not making me an only child."

Before I have the chance to say anything in return, Michelle interrupts.

"Surrendering your metabands isn't the only option here. There's another. Connor, it wasn't an accident that I sought you out. You know that by now, don't you?"

"I know that you've said that to me, but outside of that, not really. You've been keeping whatever you're doing a secret from me and Derrick ever since you told us who you really are. I'm not sure how you expect me to just keep waiting here with my bands powered down, trusting that you have some big solution to everything when you won't even tell either of us what exactly it is that you're planning."

"That's not exactly one hundred percent true anymore, Connor," Derrick says.

"What do you mean?"

"Michelle has explained to me what her mission was, and what her goal is in being here."

"Great. That's just great. Everyone knows what the plan is except for the guy who actually, you know, *has* the superpowers."

"Connor, you're not being fair. It's not like you've been exactly forthcoming about everything lately. I know things are crazy right now, but you have to know that I still trust you. Trusting you wasn't the problem. The truth is, I didn't trust Michelle, not completely," Derrick says.

I look to Michelle, expecting to see something resembling surprise on her face, but it's not there. I'm guessing, hoping, that they've had this conversation already. Otherwise, even I know that Derrick's getting himself into a world of trouble saying these things. I may only have a couple of months of girlfriend experience under my belt, but one thing I picked up on was: don't say you don't trust your girlfriend while your girlfriend is standing right next to you, even if you have plenty of probable cause. You know, like she lied about her name and her job and pretty much everything else because she was actually an undercover spy the whole time you were dating her.

"I needed to know I could trust Michelle for myself before she talked to you about all of this," Derrick continues. "I know you're a metahuman and you could throw me across the state if you wanted to, but you're still my little brother and technically my legal ward."

"Don't call me your ward. You know I hate that."

"Well regardless of what you think about it, it's the truth. I'd trust Michelle with my life, but I needed to see what she was talking about with my own eyes before I could trust her with yours."

"Okay. So now that all of that melodrama is over with, are either of you actually going to tell me what's finally going on?" I ask.

"Yes. Please, Connor, have a seat," Michelle begins. I consider telling her that I'd rather stand, but decide that it's immature, and I'd be doing it just for the sake of trying to show that she's not the boss of me. The truth is that I'm out of options and ideas. I'm hoping whatever she has to say is a better alternative to what I've been doing so far.

"The solution is moving to Skyville," Michelle says.

"What? That's it? We're just going to move? This is the genius plan that your secret little organization has come up with? You've got to be kidding me. If I just wanted to save my own skin, yeah, of course we could just move. You're not telling me anything new."

"Are you done?" Derrick asks.

"What?"

"I said, are you done? Because Michelle isn't done talking, and if you kept your trap shut for a minute, you'd be able to hear the entire plan."

"Honestly, I don't really care what the plan is if it means

just running away to hide."

"I'm sorry. He gets like this sometimes. I apologize for my *ward*," Derrick says to Michelle, trying to get a rise out of me. It almost works, but I decide to shut up and let her finish so this will all be over with and I can tell them I'm not leaving this city.

"Connor," Michelle begins, "Skyville wasn't chosen randomly out of a hat."

"I figured it wasn't. It's right across the bay and half the city's already moved there to get out of Alpha Team's way," I say.

"Half the city is an exaggeration, but the fact that many of Bay View City's residents have decided to move to Skyville is certainly something that is in our favor. It will attract less attention to move there," Michelle says. I scowl at her for the certainty in her language. "*If* you move there," she corrects herself.

"Do you know about Skyville Preparatory Academy?" Michelle asks.

"Sorry, I've been kinda too caught up lately to work on my college applications, so no, I don't."

"Well I think you would have a very hard time getting in," Michelle says.

"Thanks," I reply sarcastically.

"That's not what I meant. What I mean is that you'd have a very hard time getting in because the school itself never actually opened. It was nearly completed almost a decade ago, until The Battle happened. After that, pretty much all new construction around the country was stopped. Countless tons of equipment, cement, steel, and tens of thousands of construction workers were all moved to Empire City to help rebuild."

"Yeah, I remember that," I say.

"By the time work could be reconsidered on the academy, much of the interest had moved on. We were still in a deep recession caused by the fallout from The Battle and every metaband around the world deactivating overnight. No one wanted to spend millions and millions of dollars to finish building a school that was already over budget and that many people couldn't afford in the first place."

"I don't see what any of this has to do with anything."

"The economy and waning interest weren't the real reasons that construction was stopped. The real reason that Skyville Prep Academy was never finished was because there was no reason to continue pouring money into it if there weren't metahumans any more."

"I don't get it."

"Connor, Skyville Prep was just a front. Sure, it was a real school. You could enroll, take classes, get a degree, all of those things. For it to work it was essential that no one suspect what the school actually was."

"And what was that?"

"A training center for metahumans."

"Okay. And how exactly were you planning on keeping that a secret? Real school or not, I think once people saw metas flying in and out of their dorm windows, the jig would've been up pretty quickly."

"Very, very few of the students enrolled would have been metas. The rest would have been normal, everyday run-of-the-mill students. The students, faculty, staff, all of them, would have had no idea about the training facility since the training facility itself was built nearly a mile underground. Not even someone like you could have caused enough trouble down there for anyone on the surface to notice.

"Plans were drawn up for facilities around the country. The government had identified the importance of metahumans in the twenty-first century. They knew that nothing would ever be the same, and that if a group of metas decided to overthrow the government, there would be chaos, even if they didn't succeed. It was for that reason they wanted to at least try to have some kind of influence over as many metas as they could.

"They thought that by appealing to the patriotic nature of some, they'd be able to have them in their back pockets if push ever came to shove."

"How would a training facility have done that?"

"Many people underestimate the human need for feeling as though they're part of something. Skyville Academy would have given metas that opportunity, to feel that they weren't just people with extraordinary abilities and little else to offer. The facility would have given those who felt confused or alone the opportunity to learn about their powers, hone them, and better control them.

"In the years since metabands were first discovered, more people have been killed as the result of collateral damage than anything else. Someone like Jones? Yes, obviously he was very, very dangerous. He killed more people than any other meta, but the average person was still a hundred times more likely to be killed by a gargoyle falling from a building because one meta just threw another one into it than they were of getting their head twisted off by Jones."

"Yeah, but people knew that," I say.

"People *think* they knew that. Everyone knows that you're more likely to die in a car accident than a plane crash, but you're still a lot more likely to find someone praying before takeoff than you are every time they stick the key in the ignition. Same thing. It wasn't given as much media attention, but the government wanted it to stop. They knew that it was just a matter of time before an event like The Battle. They feared that an event like that would cause an escalation in metahuman violence that could ultimately lead to all-out war. If they couldn't confiscate every metaband out there and destroy them, then trying to help the good ones beat the bad ones while minimizing collateral damage was the next best thing.

"They knew that the general population wouldn't go for it, nor would most metas if it meant revealing their identities, hence the need for a secret facility. Adolescents and young adults were often those with the rawest abilities, and the most impressionable. No offense. If Skyville Academy worked, then the plan was to expand into other facilities. Plans had already been developed for other types of places, office buildings, factories that would have acted as fronts for underground training facilities."

"Okay, so there are training facilities underneath this old school that they never finished building. I'm still not sure how this helps me," I say.

"Tomorrow, the governor is going to announce that the school will be opened to accommodate the influx of Bay View City refugees. The plan is to offer curriculums for kindergarten through high school to any new resident of the city."

"That's going to be chaos, though. That has to be thousands and thousands of students."

"Exactly. The alternative is either trying to integrate all the new students into existing schools, which are already overcrowded, or simply doing nothing and ignoring the educational needs of all of these people. By offering this as a solution, the governor looks like he's being proactive. He's taking a beating in the polls for his response to Alpha Team's coup and with his eyes on running for president in a few years, he needs to do something big. Setting up an empty campus as a makeshift school for displaced voters' families will cost him next to nothing and make him look like a hero, and he doesn't lose anything.

"It also means that the training facilities located under the campus can be activated without any flags being raised. There will suddenly be thousands of confused students crawling all over the place, so the comings and goings of a few metas won't raise a single eyebrow, as long as we do it right."

"So if I agree to go along with this, and that's still a big if, when would we be moving?" I ask.

Michelle and Derrick exchange glances again, a sure sign

that there's something I'm missing or that they're not telling me and neither wants to be the one to do it.

"Um, there's no we, Connor. You'd be moving there on your own," Derrick says.

"Seriously?"

"It would lower suspicions. Derrick is in charge of one of the biggest meta news sites in the world. His deciding to suddenly move out of the city where the most important meta-related story is happening would look strange, to say the least," Michelle says.

"And what about you?" I ask her.

"My cover already implies a lot of travel. It would make sense for me to leave Bay View City since I only spend less than half of my time here as it is. Remember, we want to keep all of this as quiet as possible. No one should be doing anything out of the norm unless there is a significant upside."

"So nothing out of the norm like, um, I don't know, moving to another city randomly, like you want me to do?"

"Is it really so random, Connor? Your school was destroyed. Fellow students of yours were injured and killed. Meanwhile, you're also the younger brother of a prominent journalist who can easily afford to send you wherever he'd like. Would it really be so strange that you would be leaving a city in chaos to go to a different school? One of the dorm buildings that is actually finished on campus will be opened for refugee students in need of housing. I've seen to it that your housing will be provided by the school as well as the housing of the other metas who will be training alongside you."

"Let me get this straight then: you two are staying in Bay View City, but I'm moving to Skyville, where I'll have a place to live, on my own?" I ask, barely able to hide the smile starting to creep across my face.

"Yeah, but don't start getting any ideas about being able to lead some kind of swinging bachelor-slash-superhero lifestyle. You'll be taking a full class load so you can actually graduate on time next year, along with metahuman training at night and in the mornings before classes," Derrick explains.

"Who uses the term 'swinging bachelor' anymore, Derrick?" I ask.

"I think that means he'll go," Derrick says to Michelle.

FOUR

Even with the city nearly empty, it's still not very safe to be out this late at night. Under normal circumstances, Derrick would never allow it, especially since he just caught me sneaking out against his wishes literally about an hour ago. These aren't normal circumstances, though. Derrick and Michelle are shipping me off to Skyville tomorrow morning, first thing.

At first, he wouldn't budge on letting me go back out tonight. Then I reminded him that in twenty-four hours I'd be living in a different city, away from him, and that he wouldn't be able to keep an eye on me all the time anymore. If he was going to start trusting my judgment, now would be a good time, since he's basically going to be forced to starting tomorrow.

Growing up, you would think that I would have had more freedom than most kids my age. Aside from the grim reality of what not having parents actually means, most kids would think it was a dream come true. There isn't an American kid alive today who didn't at one time wish their parents would disappear, leaving them to their own devices. On paper, having a legal guardian in his twenties sounds great, nothing but video games and pizza every night. Well, that last part is actually true. Derrick couldn't cook his way out of a paper bag, which means I've probably eaten my bodyweight in pizza a hundred times over.

But there are parts of growing up with my brother as my legal guardian that a lot of people never think about, or realize. When our mom and dad died, Derrick barely had time or space to grieve. It just wasn't possible for him to be sad and take care of me at the same time. There wasn't any family to help. The city itself was in ruins, so outside help wasn't available either. As bad as we had it, there were others who had it much worse. Many looked at the two of us and thought we were lucky to at least have each other. They weren't wrong.

Derrick had no idea how to raise a kid. By the time he got stuck with me, he'd just spent the previous four years away at college. I'm sure he probably felt like he hardly knew this six-year-old kid who was basically still a baby when he'd first left for school.

Since he didn't really know what he was doing, Derrick made up for it by rarely ever letting me out of his sight when I was young. He didn't always know the right thing to say or do, but if he kept a constant eye on me, I think he figured that he could at least make sure I didn't stick my finger in an electrical socket or fall down a well. It might have made me seem cool to be the kid on a field trip who had his big brother there instead of a parent, but the reality is he only did it because he didn't want to let me out of his sight. The only difference between him and a helicopter soccer mom was that at least the helicopter soccer mom knew what the hell she was doing.

Luckily for Derrick, I turned out perfect despite his attempts to raise me to the contrary.

I got him to agree to let me go out on my own tonight partially because I promised that I wouldn't be gone long. I also had to leave my metabands at home, something that I normally would be safer *with* than without, but that was before Alpha Team started hunting down metas for sport. Promising not to power them up wasn't enough. Derrick had insisted that I leave them behind if I wanted to leave the apartment tonight.

There's really only one thing I want to accomplish during my last night in Bay View City. Well, technically, there are two, except I know that only one of them has any chance of happening, and that's finding Jim and saying goodbye to him. It's been a while since we've talked, and even longer since I've seen him without both of us having our respective masks on. He still has no idea that I'm Omni, and considering that he's taken sides with the Blanks, I can't imagine that he'd take the news too well if he ever found out.

It was only a few hours ago that I heard him at Sarah's house. Of course, he didn't know I was hiding under the floorboards at the time, and I don't think he would have appreciated the surprise. It's a long shot that he'd be back home already, but I really don't have any other idea where I could find him. I especially don't have any ideas that seem safe enough to try without a pair of metabands wrapped around my wrists.

His house is close to the old one that Derrick and I lived in, but that's pretty far from where I live now. Derrick offered to let me borrow his car, which was a huge relief considering the amount of walking I've had to do tonight. You don't realize just how tiring walking can be until you get used to flying everywhere and then get quarantined to your home for days. Part of me worries that this training in Skyville is going to involve preparing for situations like this, the non-meta kind, and I'm already dreading it.

Derrick would have never, ever let me borrow his car under normal circumstances, which means he must have really wanted me to be safe tonight. This car is his baby. Even I've only seen him drive it a few times. I actually suspect he goes down to the garage underneath our apartment complex late at night just to sit and admire it while it's there in its parking space. It's not a Lamborghini or anything, but it is a very nice luxury car. Black exterior and light brown leather interior that I'm constantly told I'm not allowed to eat inside of, even if this is only the third time I've actually been in the car. It was one of Derrick's first purchases once his blog really started taking off, which is part of why it's so important to him. Besides the superficial nature of having a nice car, to him it's proof that he was right all along to keep going down the path he was on, even when pretty much everyone else told him he was crazy and that no one was interested in metahumans anymore.

Fifteen minutes after pulling out of the garage, I'm back in my old neighborhood, scanning street signs to find Jim's block. It's amazing that in a few short months I've already forgotten little things like which streets Jim's house is between. It's been a while since I've been to this part of town, and I'm surprised at just how dead it is. Sure, it's late at night, but it's eerily quiet here. On the way, I occasionally see a lone stranger or two standing on a corner. Their eyes watch me suspiciously as I drive past. It doesn't take too long to figure out that anyone in this neighborhood who is out on the street this late at night is probably not up to anything good.

There's a light on inside Jim's room. It's faint since curtains cover the window, but it's still bright enough for me to see it from the road. I pull out my phone to text Jim and see if he's inside, but find that there's no signal at all. I shouldn't be surprised; there have been reports on the news of cell phone towers still being down all over the city from the Silver Island fallout. I'm not the least bit shocked that this area of town isn't at the top of the repairs list. I'll have to do this the old-fashioned way I guess and just hope that Jim doesn't freak out.

I walk up to the window quietly, careful not to wake whoever else might be in the house. Jim's family's house is ranch-style, just one floor, with a brick exterior. It's by no means rundown, but not exactly luxurious either. Utilitarian would probably be the most accurate way to put it. The neighbors' houses are situated very close, practically on top of one another. I carefully creep in between Jim's house and the neighbor's to knock on his window. At first I tap so quietly that even I can't hear it. After a few seconds, I tap again. Still nothing. Finally, I decide to just knock. Almost instantly the curtains are thrown open, and I'm practically face to face with Jim. The look on his face when he opens the curtains, before he can see my face, isn't one of fear, though. It's one of anger. It's a look I don't know if I've seen on his face before.

The look changes shape once Jim recognizes me through the reflection on the window, and now he just looks confused. I motion for him to stay quiet while waving for him to come outside. He holds up a finger to indicate to me to wait for a minute, before he closes the curtains.

A minute later, I can hear the screen door opening on the front porch. I slowly start walking in that direction to meet Jim halfway. He rounds the corner of the house and approaches with his hands tucked deep into a beige jacket. His shoulders are up in an effort to keep himself warm in the cool fall evening air.

"What are you doing here?" Jim asks.

"I'm heading out of the city for a while. I wanted to come by before I left."

"Giving up on this city like all the others, huh?"

"No, I'm not giving up."

"Then why are you leaving?"

"It's ... complicated."

"I'm sure it is. Things always get complicated once money starts getting involved."

"What's that supposed to mean?"

"Nothing. It's good, I guess. It's fine. Things have just changed with you ever since Derrick became a billionaire and you guys moved to that penthouse."

"Derrick's not a billionaire."

"It's a figure of speech. But I'm sure I'm not off by too many zeroes. It's fine. I'm glad someone's life improved once the metas started coming back at least."

"That's not really being too fair, Jim."

"It's not? All I know is that last school year Connor Connelly wasn't exactly likely to get voted prom king. Now you're loaded, you get a girlfriend, move into a million-dollar apartment, and that's pretty much the last I see or hear of you. I'm surprised you actually came to this side of the tracks. Am I safe to assume your chauffeur is waiting down the street?"

"Where is all this coming from?"

"It's been there, man. You just haven't been around for me to say any of it."

"First off, me and Sarah aren't even dating anymore. And second, Derrick doing well has nothing to with why I haven't been around as much."

"No? What does then?"

It was stupid of me to lead the line of questioning toward this. I know that I've been a crap friend lately. It's part of the whole reason I came down here tonight to say goodbye in the first place. The guilt from not being around, along with keeping huge secrets from him, has been eating me up inside.

In the beginning, I told myself that Jim couldn't know my secret because it would put him in danger. That's all out the window now because everyone is in danger. Jim knowing my secret would put me in danger, not the other way around. I know how he's been spending his nights, and I can venture a guess as to how he feels lately about metahumans. Telling him that I'm one of them would sever our friendship forever, and I'd be lucky if that was the only fallout.

"It's personal stuff, Jim. I don't really want to talk about it. I'm sorry I haven't been around, but you have to trust me that it has nothing to do with any of the things you think it does."

There's silence, which I think is about as close as I'm going to get to Jim agreeing with me and offering a truce. I'll take it.

"So, how are things with you?" I ask Jim, realizing the second after the words have come out of my mouth that there might have been a more delicate way to ask.

"Oh, you know, kinda terrible."

"Yeah, I heard a little bit. I'm sorry about your dad."

"Don't be. He'll bounce back from this," Jim says. "Now that the Alphas are kicking all of the metas out of Bay View City, he should be back at work in no time. He's expecting to get a call next week from his old job since the meta they hired turned tail and ran off, but he's not gonna take it. He's gonna tell them where they can stick his old job."

I don't ask, but I have a few ideas about where he might be talking about.

"Do you really think that this is such a good thing? All of the metas leaving the city?"

"Are you serious? I can't believe that you of all people are asking me that question. *Is it a good thing that God-like people who have the ability to kill us, destroy our homes, and ruin our lives are being told that they aren't welcome here anymore?* Of course it is. We'll all be better off without them. Well, I guess you won't since you're leaving town, but we will. The ones who stay."

"But what happens when some meta decides to try to take advantage of the fact that all the metas of Bay View City are gone and comes here to cause trouble?"

"That's what the Alphas are there for. Any metahuman stupid enough to risk losing their bands forever isn't going to pose much of a threat to them."

"And who watches the Alphas? What about that? How is anyone supposed to keep them in check when they're the only metahumans left?"

"Actions speak louder than words, Connor. We've already seen what the Alphas' true intentions are. They just want to cut through all the bull and face facts. Metahumans are dangerous and have caused more harm than good. Sooner or later they all fail, and they all fall. The Alphas aren't concerned with trying to be heroes or villains. They just want things to go back to what they were like before, when you could walk down the street and not worry about a metahuman turning you into a pancake because they felt like taking a joyride.

"They're not above the law, but all of them act like it. I'd rather have four metas keeping all the others out than a city full of them doing whatever they feel like, whenever they feel like it."

"I just think-" I begin to say, but before I can finish my

thought, I notice something strange next to Jim.

We're both standing on the patch of land between Jim's house and the neighbors', where the grass hasn't been mowed in a while. The taller blades sway slightly in the breeze. It's this breeze that catches my attention.

It's almost subconscious. My eyes notice it before my brain does, holding my gaze there almost as if to say, "Pay attention over here, dummy. Something isn't right." Something most definitely isn't right. Five feet behind Jim, over his right shoulder, there's a tiny bit of tall grass that didn't move when an especially strong gust of wind came through. It seems almost as though something was blocking the wind from reaching these particular blades of grass. In front of those blades, the grass is strange too. At first I thought it was a bare spot where no grass had grown. There are plenty of those around us, but this isn't one of them.

Now that I focus on it, I can see that it's not bare at all; the blades of grass have instead just been pushed down flat against the ground. I notice other small areas very slowly flattening out now too. The areas are moving backward toward the street.

"Hello? Connor?" Jim asks while waving a hand in front of my eyes, noticing that I appear to have completely zoned out.

"Jim," I say.

"Yeah?"

"Move."

He's confused at first, but before he even has time to fully process what I've just said, let alone understand why I've said it, the depressed areas of grass begin appearing more quickly.

It's an Invisible. I don't know who it is, or how long he's been standing there, but I know that there's one sure-fire way to find out, and that's catching him.

Jim still isn't sure what is going on when I push him out of the way and start running after a ghost. The invisible footsteps in the grass are becoming faster and heading for the paved road in front of me. Once its feet hit that pavement, trying to find them is going to be next to impossible. This is my one chance, so I take it and dive into the air, aiming for the footsteps and hoping for the best.

To my amazement, it works! Even when you know there's someone there, it's still a very bizarre feeling to feel yourself collide with what looks like open space. I'm not sure what part of their body I've hit exactly, but it's solid, not just an arm or a foot; these are legs or a torso. I wrap my arms around whatever it is and hang on as hard as I can.

The ground is coming up in front of me fast, but inches before I hit it face first, my fall stops, cushioned by muscle and bone. Someone else's muscle and bone, that is, which feels a lot better hitting the ground than when it's yours. I'm frantically grasping at whatever I can get a hold of on this person. After I've got a good grip on what feels like nylon fabric, I look up and see a trickle of blood on the sidewalk in front of us. Part of this person made it to the pavement after all.

"There's no use hiding anymore. I've got you, and I'm not letting go, so you might as well turn that off," I say to the invisible body I'm holding on to as it continues trying to squirm out from under my grip.

It's now that I remember that I don't have my metabands. Lunging at this person was pure instinct and not the good kind. Confidence is great; cockiness is not. The only reason I'm not completely freaking out is the thought that if they were powered or invulnerable, then I wouldn't still be on top of them. I was lucky, and I need to remember that.

"He said power down!" Jim screams from behind me. Before I have a chance to turn around and look at him, I see a sneaker coming toward my face. I wince and close my eyes, but it doesn't hit me. Instead, it makes a heavy thud as it hits what I presume to be the face of the invisible meta I've currently got pinned. "Power down!" Jim screams again as he winds up for another kick.

"Stop it!" I yell back, trying to use my right hand to block Jim's blow before it can reach the Invisible. Jim's foot hits my forearm hard and hurts so badly that I think he's broken it for a second. In the confusion and pain of what's happening, I momentarily lose my grip on the meta. A second later, I can feel invisible hands on me, pushing me off far enough to get his feet out from underneath me and use them to kick me off completely.

Jim lunges forward when he realizes what's happening. He makes contact with the metahuman, but his hands slip. His arms are flailing wildly, desperately trying to find something to hold on to in the thin air, but there's nothing there anymore, only the sound of footsteps running away down the road into the night.

Jim begins running too, following the sound of the footsteps, but after a few feet he must realize it'd be next to impossible to find the Invisible now, and he stops.

I'm laid out on my back in the street at this point, holding my right arm close to my chest. It's not broken, thankfully, but it still hurts like hell. I tuck it in close and use my free hand to prop myself up into a sitting position on the ground. Jim's walking back toward me, sporting a minor injury of his own in the form of ripped jeans and a bloody knee from where he landed in the street.

"What the hell was that?" Jim yells at me.

"I'm not sure. Must have been a metahuman."

"I know it was a damn metahuman! I mean what the hell was that with you letting him go?"

"I tried to hang on to him but he was just too strong and got loose."

"Why did you try to stop me?"

"Because you were going to kill him, Jim. He wasn't invulnerable or else I wouldn't have been able to tackle him. You were going to kick him right in the face."

Jim turns around and walks back into the street, looking off in the distance to see if there's any clue of where the meta might have gone. There's none, and Jim looks angry.

"Whoever that was, they were spying on us and they were breaking the law. 'No metas' means 'no metas', especially metas using their powers to try to spy on two citizens minding their own business."

"But that doesn't mean you can just take it on yourself to kill one of them."

"He could have powered down like we told him to and I would have stopped. He chose not to listen."

I can't believe what I'm hearing and struggle to make my way onto my feet.

"So you would have kicked that guy to death, just because you felt like it was your right to?"

"I would have done what needed to be done to get him to comply with the law. The Alphas pushed their message out everywhere. There's no excuse. He knew that he shouldn't be using his metabands in this city anymore, but he didn't care. Are we just supposed to have the rules apply to some people, but then allow others to skate by just because we don't want to deal with the consequences? That's the kind of thinking that ..." he trails off.

"That's the kind of thinking that what?" I ask him.

He looks down at the ground before raising his head and looking me dead in the eye.

"That's the kind of thinking that led to your parents getting killed," Jim says.

The words feel like a punch to the gut, and I struggle to rein in a sudden flood of emotions. Part of me is full of rage and wants to tackle him right there into the street. Another part of me is fighting back tears, but I'm not sure if it's thinking about them, or thinking about Jim being so far gone that he could ever say something like that to someone who's supposed to be his best friend. I wait a few seconds in silence to let the feelings pass and get myself back under control.

"I'll see you, Jim. Take care of yourself," I say before turning and walking back to the car.

I hope for Jim to say something as I'm walking away, to apologize. If he does, I don't hear it before the door closes behind me.

FIVE

"Is this everything?" Derrick asks as he walks from the front door of our building to his car. I'm standing with the trunk open, playing some version of Tetris with a bunch of bags and boxes that don't seem to want to fit right no matter how I rearrange them. You'd think I would have gotten better at moving by now.

"Yeah, I think that's the last one," I say to him.

"Don't worry about it," Derrick says as he balances on one foot while bringing up the other knee to help regain his grip on the box. "Your poor feeble old brother's got it."

"Good, you could use the exercise," I shoot back as I snatch the box from him and cram it into the trunk with the others.

"Go easy. I still have a few payments left on this beauty."

"If your car's going to get damaged by a few cardboard boxes, then I don't think it's worth what you paid for it," I say as I slam down the trunk door, then slam it a couple more times before the latch catches and it stays firmly closed. Derrick winces each time I press down.

"Where's Michelle?" I ask.

"She left for Skyville about an hour ago."

"Oh, I thought she was just going to get coffee or something."

"No, she said she wanted to get a head start on the drive. She still has a few things that needed taking care of apparently."

"It's not that long of a drive."

"Hey, I'm just the messenger."

"So, do you have any idea what all this is going to be like?"

"Aw, are you scared for your first day of school?" Derrick asks.

"You should know better than anyone that at this point I've had too many first days of school to get nervous anymore."

"Yeah, but you've never had a first day of school with other metas."

After our parents died, Derrick and I moved around for a bit. The first move was out of necessity. Empire City, where we'd lived and grown up, was practically condemned. So many buildings had been destroyed that there wouldn't have been any safe place left to live, even if we'd wanted to stay.

At first Derrick didn't know where to go. He'd just finished college and didn't even have a job yet, but now he was faced with two dead parents and the prospect of raising a little brother on his own. There was insurance money and government assistance, but both were slow to arrive. Initially we stayed at a shelter set up on the other side of the river at a decommissioned baseball stadium. I don't remember much about it, except that there were more people there than I'd ever seen before in my life. It was crowded and noisy, people crying and screaming all day and night because of the people they had lost or just from their own injuries.

Rumors started sweeping the stadium that Jones was on his way back to finish the job, or that other metas were on their way to the city to pick through what was left, even though there were plenty of conflicting reports saying that metabands all over the world had stopped working. People were scared, and scared people can be dangerous. Derrick was desperate to get us out of there as soon as he could.

Our dad didn't have any extended family left, or at least any that we knew about or could find. Our mom did, though, and the first place we moved to was Chicago, where she had a cousin named Maria we had never met before who offered to take us in. That place seemed fine enough at first. Maria was nice and accommodating. I didn't know it at the time, but Derrick later told me that Maria started asking more and more about the insurance money from our parents' policy. Eventually she started telling Derrick that she wouldn't be able to afford certain things unless he was able to sign over part of the inheritance to her. The final straw came when Derrick grilled her about our mother and found out that she had never even met her. From there it was pretty easy to figure out that the woman wasn't a real relative, just an opportunistic con artist. We were gone the next morning.

From there we spent a lot of time moving from town to town, city to city. Derrick had no idea how to raise a kid, and the world had changed. Everywhere we went people looked at us with the same pity. Derrick may not have known much about raising me, but he knew that he didn't want me to grow up feeling pity from other people. He said that a lot of people had lost their loved ones in The Battle, and that countless others lost people they cared about everyday to things like car accidents, cancer, diseases. Derrick told me that these peoples' grief was no different than ours and that we shouldn't allow ourselves to get lost in letting the world feel bad for us.

Bay View City was the first place we moved to that really felt like home. Even more than Empire City, especially since I was really too young to even remember what that was like before such horrible memories were associated with it.

We hadn't been in Bay View City that long, but it was long for us. It was the first place where we both started to put down any kind of roots. It was the first place where both of us started caring about other people, rather than just relying on each other.

The drive to Skyville takes a lot longer than we expect, but that's because neither of us thought about how many other people would have the same idea. There's only one bridge over the bay that separates the two cities from each other, and it's clogged with probably more cars than it's ever seen before. It takes hours of moving inch by inch before we even get close to the on-ramp. Derrick gets a text from Michelle fairly early in our trip to let him know that she's made it there already, apparently having beat most of the traffic we wound up stuck in.

It's late afternoon by the time we finally reach the Skyville limits. I desperately need to go to the bathroom, but Derrick tells me it's my own fault for getting such a huge coffee before we left and makes me hold it until we get to the campus.

When we finally pull up to the gates, the school isn't anything like how I'd imagined it. I hadn't really thought about what a school that had tons of money pumped into it over a decade ago would look like when that money dried up before completion. It's obvious that whoever initially started building this place thought it would look very, very modern, but ten years down the line, it looks ridiculous, just like most things made to look futuristic do once time has passed.

The buildings all look very monolithic, with lots of metal and glass, but also with strange splashes of bright colors throughout, like someone got a good deal on highlighter fluid and decided to use it as paint. Garish greens, blue, yellows and pinks accent what would otherwise be impressive-looking large concrete buildings. All over campus there are workers scurrying around, mowing lawns and power washing years of grime off of buildings. They're hampered by the huge crush of students and families trying to get settled in before the first official day of classes on Monday.

"So, what do you think?" Derrick asks me as he tries to find a parking spot somewhere, anywhere, on campus.

"Looks kinda dated," I reply.

"Well yeah, that happens when no one uses a place for as long as this place has been sitting in mothballs."

"Do you know where we're going?"

"Yeah. Sure. Kinda. I mean, I have a general idea."

This is not the kind of answer you want when you have to use a bathroom as badly as I do right now.

"I guess it doesn't really matter what I think of all of this," I say, gesturing out the window at some of the buildings we pass. "I'm going to be spending most of my time a mile down from here anyway."

"That's not necessarily true. There'll be a lot of

precautions in place to make sure that there isn't any suspicion raised about you or the other metas here, so you'll still be taking a full course load. Who knows, maybe you'll even graduate high school if you aren't careful."

Derrick sees a car pulling out of a spot ahead of him and springs into action, quickly pulling into it a split second before another car with the same intentions rounds the corner.

"Ha ha! Sorry sucker!" Derrick says, not realizing his window is open. The driver of the other car, a middle-aged woman dropping her son off, scowls at him. "Oh, sorry. Just kidding," he says with a nervous laugh.

I roll my eyes and unbuckle my seatbelt before opening the passenger side door. This is exactly what I'm talking about when I say people overestimate how cool my brother is. I step out of the car and stretch my legs, which feels great after being cramped in there for so long, but I'm also instantly reminded of just how badly I have to pee.

"I'm gonna go find a bathroom," I shout to Derrick as I cross the street and head toward the nearest building. Derrick isn't even out of the car yet, and I can hear him yelling for me to wait, but too bad because there is absolutely no way I can hold this any longer. I feel like I've got a time bomb ticking in my pants.

Six

Wow. I feel much, much better. It's like I've got a new lease on life. I leave the bathroom practically whistling and take a look around the building I'm in. I didn't notice much on my way in; I kinda had blinders on for anything that even vaguely resembled a restroom sign.

The building is surprisingly quiet, but it is a classroom building, and it is the weekend after all. Somewhere off in the distance, out of sight, I can hear a machine polishing floors somewhere upstairs. I'm standing in a large lobby, which has a strange feeling I can't quite place. I walk over toward a glass case that looks like it's meant for displaying awards or art, but it's completely empty except for a thick layer of dust lying on the shelves.

I realize what feels off. This building is old, but it lacks any kind of history. It's just been sitting here empty for a decade. It was built to accommodate thousands of students everyday, but not even one has walked through the doors practically since it was built.

After gazing at the empty cases and walls for more time than is necessary, I find my way back to the front door. As I cross the street, I see Derrick again struggling with an armload of boxes.

"Did you fall in?" he asks.

"Funny," I say as I jog across the street toward him.

"Here, give me a hand," Derrick says. I stop and clap for him briefly, giving him a taste of his own "bad dad joke" medicine. He doesn't take it well and deliberately drops the box he was holding on the ground.

"Whoops," he says flatly.

"Thanks. What if that was my nice stuff?"

"You don't have any nice stuff," he deadpans.

* * *

"This is it?" I ask after opening the door to my new dorm

room. The door hits the corner of one of the two casket-sized beds inside a room that is maybe the size of a nice walk-in closet. Derrick laughs. He must realize that it's way too small for two people to live in too.

"Yeah, of course it is. What were you expecting?" he asks.

Dammit. He's laughing at me, not the room. I push harder against the door, pushing the bed slightly across the floor. Once the bed is out of the way, I'm able to fully open the door and take in the space. "Taking it in" only takes about a second or two. I sigh and throw my duffel bag down on the closest bed.

"You know, when I was your age-" Derrick begins.

"Really, Derrick? You're going to actually pull the 'when I was your age' thing? You're twenty-nine, not ninety. I don't want to hear it."

This just makes Derrick laugh even harder. I'm starting to wonder if there's really a meta training facility here at all or if Derrick just thought this would be a funny way to get rid of me for the weekend.

"Man, I had no idea you had gotten so spoiled already. We've only been in the new apartment a few months and already your standards are all out of whack."

"I'm just saying, if I'm still supposed to keep you-know-what a secret," I say, flicking my wrists to materialize my metabands just in case Derrick isn't clear before flicking them again to make the metabands disappear, "then it might be a little hard if I've got someone sleeping six inches from my head every night."

"Relax," Derrick says as he rips the tape off of one of the cardboard boxes full of my books. "These people know what they're doing. I'd be pretty surprised if they roomed you with a regular person, considering the need for privacy. You should be glad. When I went to college they stuck four of us in a three-person room that was probably smaller than this one. I would have killed to have had to share my room with only one other person."

"But I'm not *in* college. I'm still in high school, just now I've got an extracurricular activity that takes up all of my time. What time does that go until every day?"

Derrick says something quietly and coughs at the same time purposefully so I can't hear him before he gives me the answer.

"Nine forty-five," he says. I honestly don't know how to react at first. I just look at him, waiting for him to say he's just kidding, but he never does. He just continues unpacking the box he brought up until it's empty of books.

"So I have a grand total of about fifteen minutes to myself every day if I want to get any sleep?"

"Hey, with great power, something something. I'm going back to the car to get another box. Start setting this stuff up. I've got to get going back to Bay View City pretty soon, especially if the traffic is still this bad."

"I'm pretty sure the traffic was *leaving* the city that's been taken over by megalomaniacal super-powered dictators, not going into it."

"Oh yeah, you're probably right. I don't drive enough to think about these things, I guess." Derrick exits the room and walks down the hallway, back toward the staircase we took up to my new room.

"You know, you can keep the car here if you're not going to use it," I yell out the door and down the hallway. Derrick laughs even harder at this than he did to my reaction to the size of the room.

I take another look around, hoping that it'll feel a little bit better now that there're half as many human beings inside of it. Nope, still looks ridiculously tiny. Maybe I am spoiled, but one of the upsides of having a brother who's so much older than me is that I've never had a share a room before.

"That's my bed, bro," a voice behind me announces.

I turn around just as the owner of the voice squeezes past me and into the narrow cinder block room. He's bigger than me by a fair amount, and I mean that in terms of both height and width. While he's not exactly in great shape, he's not what you would call fat either. If I had to guess, I'd say he spends a good chunk of his day at the gym, though. He's wearing a pair of mesh lacrosse shorts, a plain red t-shirt, and a sweat-stained baseball hat that he's turned backward and is resting on top of a nest of curly brown hair.

He doesn't offer his name or what he's doing here, so I'm left on my own to guess that he's my roommate. Great.

"So, are you my roommate?" I ask, trying to start something resembling a conversation.

"Yeah," he grunts back, not looking up from his phone to greet me. He's standing in the corner of the room, leaning up against one of the two bare desks. After a few seconds, I realize that he's serious about the bed my stuff is currently on being his.

"Uh, if you want this bed, that's cool. I didn't know someone was in here yet, so I just threw my stuff down on the first-" I begin to say as I pick up my bag. Before I can finish, though, I'm interrupted by my new roommate almost kicking me in the face as he plops down hard on the bed I just vacated. During the entire movement, his eyes never strayed from his phone. Guess he was really serious about wanting this bed.

"Tyler, honey, where do you want us to put your things?"

I look up and see a middle-aged woman struggling with a box that's almost the size of her. Instinctively, I rush over to help her with the box right before it looks like it's about to topple onto the floor. My new roomie doesn't even bother looking up from his phone.

"Thank you so much," the woman says. "You must be Tyler's roommate. How exciting!" She puts her hand out for me to shake it.

"Yeah, that's me it looks like. I'm Connor Connelly. It's very nice to meet you, Mrs. ..."

"Gordon, and it's Miss, but that makes me feel old, so please, just call me Stephanie."

"Okay, Stephanie," I say, feeling awkward calling a grown-up by their first name, which is weird because I hadn't felt awkward about calling a grown-up "Midnight" for the past few months.

"Give it a rest, Mom," Tyler says from what is now officially his bed before he heaves himself up. "Are you going to get the rest of my stuff or what?"

Stephanie Gordon gives me a 'what are you gonna do, kids will be kids' sort of look and turns around only to walk right into Derrick, who is carrying a box that is blocking his view almost entirely. He stumbles and drops the box, spilling my underwear out onto the floor. This makes Tyler laugh maniacally. He's definitely laughing way harder than how funny the situation actually is, which even I'll admit is kinda funny if for no other reason than Derrick is more embarrassed about it than I am.

"Oh my goodness. I am so sorry about that," Stephanie says to Derrick as she begins picking up my underwear and stuffing it back into the box. Okay, I take it back. Now I'm pretty sure I'm more embarrassed than Derrick.

"No, no, that's okay. It was my fault. I should've been more careful about where I was going," Derrick says.

It's obvious that he's not going to touch my underwear and pick it up off the floor, which is fine since I'm already trying to grab as much as I can before Ms. Gordon does. She realizes what she's picking up, why her son is laughing, and how red my face is, so she places the few clothing items in her hands into the box and allows me to pick up the rest. It's only now that she lifts her head up and looks Derrick in the eyes for the first time.

"Oh my," she says, blushing slightly and fluttering her eyelashes. "Now how on earth can a man this young and handsome have a teenage son?" Now Derrick is the one blushing.

"I'm Connor's brother, Derrick," he says, offering his hand for her to shake.

"Derrick, this is Ms. Gordon," I offer since it seems like she's too busy looking dreamily into his eyes to remember to do it herself.

"Colin, I told you to call me Stephanie," she says, still holding her gaze at Derrick.

"It's Connor, actually," I say.

"And it's Miss Gordon, not Ms. We wouldn't want anyone assuming the possibility that I'm actually still married," she says, still holding on to Derrick's hand. Now she's the one laughing maniacally, and I see where her son gets it. This might be the most uncomfortable I've ever seen Derrick.

"Give it a rest, Mom. None of the other parents are acting like this," Tyler says.

"Oh now, Tyler, I'm just being friendly. This is how adults talk to each other. He's always getting so embarrassed by me," Miss Gordon says to Derrick. "I'm sure your brother feels the same way about your parents, Derrick."

"Actually, no. Both our parents are dead," I blurt out, hoping that the shock of just coming right out with this will cause enough embarrassment on Miss Gordon's part that she'll stop flirting with Derrick. Although it's fun to watch, we actually do need to get moving. Though it would be fun to just walk out the door and finish unpacking myself, leaving Derrick here to fend for himself. My plan doesn't work.

"Oh my goodness. That is just the most awful thing I've ever heard," Miss Gordon says, covering her mouth with one hand and placing the other on Derrick's arm. When I said before that I've never seen Derrick so uncomfortable in my life, that's no longer true. *This* is now the most uncomfortable I've ever seen him in my life. "And you took care of your little brother here?"

"Yeah, I'm his guardian," Derrick manages to get out with volume barely above a whisper.

"That is just the most heartbreaking and brave thing I've ever heard. You're a hero, Derrick. I mean that. You don't see a lot of men who are so selfless like that nowadays," Miss

Gordon says, her voice trailing off toward the end.

"I'm going to get food," Tyler announces as he jumps up from his bed and stands, waiting for his mother and Derrick to move from the doorway so he can pass.

"I'll come with you, sweetie," Miss Gordon says. "Not to eat, of course. The only thing I eat is salad," she says to Derrick, trying to impress him.

"Are you sure you don't want to just stay here and continue embarrassing yourself?" Tyler asks. Neither of us knows where to look.

"Oh, stop! Now you're just being ridiculous. Your mother is allowed to talk to a stranger once in a while too, you know. Not that you're a stranger, Derrick. Not now anyways," she says, looking into his eyes again.

Tyler pushes past the pair and heads down the hallway, intent on not waiting any longer.

"I'd better go catch him. It was really a pleasure meeting you, Derrick."

"You too," I say before Derrick has the chance.

"And you too, of course, Connor," she says, barely turning around to look at me.

"You too. I'm sure we'll see each other around," Derrick says to her.

"I certainly hope so."

Seven

The rest of the move goes smoothly, thanks mostly to the fact that I really didn't bring much stuff. A lot of my things are still in boxes from the last time Derrick and I moved, so my rule was if I hadn't taken it out of the box and used it by now, it probably wasn't all that important in the first place. I'm feeling pretty smart about that decision, which means I'm sure to find out that I forgot something super important at the worst possible time in the very near future.

Derrick gets a phone call from his office and has to leave in a hurry. He doesn't tell me what the call is about, and I don't ask. Nowadays it could be a breaking story or it could be that the water cooler needs to be refilled. There doesn't seem to be any problem too small to bother Derrick about lately.

This is fine by me since it's not like there's a whole lot of room to hang out in my dorm room. Even if there were, I don't think I could take the awkwardness of watching Derrick getting hit on by a woman twice his age again.

I was hoping to get a chance to walk around the campus and get a better look at everything, maybe even meet some people. I probably wouldn't have actually gone up and talked to anyone, you know, the thing that is required if you actually want to meet new people, but it's still nice to have dreams. My pretend mingling will have to wait until later, though. On his way out the door, Derrick told me he'd heard back from Michelle and that she wanted me to come meet with her now. Hopefully this means I won't be getting my messages from her through Derrick anymore. Otherwise, this is going to start getting really tedious.

The place she asks me to meet her at is way, way on the other side of campus, which I'm actually thankful for. It's a nice fall day, and the walk gives me a chance to take a look around. Classes have already started for a lot of the people here. Since there's a steady flow of new students all the time, new classes are starting up every week. Maybe the only good thing that will come out of having state-mandated learning for the years prior to this is that everyone technically should be on the same page as far as lessons go, which should make it easy for students to come to this new school and pick up right where they left off ... at least in theory.

On paper, that all sounds great, but in reality I have to imagine people are still all over the map with what they've already learned and what still needs to be taught. Not everyone learns at the same speed, which is what the smaller classrooms are mostly used for, according to Derrick. Those rooms are perfect for after school tutoring and catch-up lessons. I was already warned to make sure I pay attention during class, because I won't have time for either of those.

The campus is full of people coming and going all over the place—the chaos of families dropping off their children. There seems to be thousands and thousands of students, a lot of them even younger than I am.

After walking what feels like the entire campus, I find the building where Michelle has asked me to meet her. The building looks out of place, but not for the reasons you'd expect. It looks out of place because it just looks ... ordinary. On a campus full of ugly, faux-futuristic buildings, this is the one old-brick building that wouldn't actually look out of place on a traditional college campus. The building is large with three floors, but still smaller than many of the others I've seen. From the outside, the building looks to be made entirely out of brick with a handful of windows in every classroom. The windows look like they haven't been washed in a decade, which is probably true.

There isn't an obvious entrance to the building, or at least there isn't one that looks like the big entrances I've seen on all of the other buildings on campus. After wandering around the outside of the building for a few minutes, I decide to start trying the windowless doors that look like they're emergency exits. The third one I try opens without a problem.

Rays of sunlight pour in from the outside, illuminating the absolutely insane amount of dust coating the floors and lockers. Looks like the cleanup crew either hasn't gotten to this building yet or they forgot it exists.

I walk down the hallway, checking the door numbers to find room 143, where Michelle is apparently waiting for me. At the end of a very long hallway, I find the room. There's a window in the door, and through it I can see an empty classroom. The walls are bare, but the desks are all neatly aligned and facing the front of the classroom. There's something else different: the room is clean, or at least much, much cleaner than any of the other classrooms I've looked into in this building so far.

I momentarily wonder if I should just wait in the hallway for Michelle since I don't see her inside the classroom. Maybe she'll be right back. Or maybe she got tired of waiting for me and left. Ultimately I decide that hanging out in the hallway here might not be a great idea. Even though this end of campus seems deserted, it might look suspicious for me to be standing around in the hallway of an abandoned building. The windows on the opposite side of the hallway face the campus, and anyone walking by would be able to see me plain as day.

Carefully, I check the doorknob of the classroom to see if it's unlocked. The knob turns with little effort, so I push the door open and immediately almost jump out of my skin. Michelle is standing right in front of me, waiting just inside the door.

"What the...?" I ask no one in particular.

Michelle is stifling a laugh at my reaction to her scaring the crap out of me. I pull the door closed and look through the window again: nothing, just an empty classroom. Swinging the door back open, there's Michelle, still standing there.

"Come inside; I'll explain," Michelle says with a smile as she takes my hand and leads me into the classroom. With her other hand, she closes the door. "Take a seat."

I choose the desk closest to the door in the front row since it's the nearest, and I actually feel a little bit dizzy after experiencing whatever the hell the trick was with that door.

"It's not a window. It's a very, very high-resolution 3D monitor panel. That's why you couldn't see me standing inside the room, because you weren't actually looking inside the room," Michelle explains.

"So it was a video feed?"

"Something like that. It's actually a little bit more complicated, but all you need to understand is that prying eyes won't find anything in this classroom if they come looking."

"Why go through all of that trouble just to conceal a classroom, though? There's nothing in here that looks like it's worth keeping a secret."

"Oh, Connor, you really think that this is just a regular classroom? You're disappointing me."

Michelle walks over to the desk at the front of the classroom and sits behind it. She fishes a set of keys out of her pocket and uses them to open one of the desk's drawers. I can't see what's inside the drawer from where I'm sitting, but I can see a faint blue glow emanating from it. A series of blue lights in the shape of a grid appears over Michelle's face, and I realize this must be some type of security system. Right on cue, I feel the ground beneath me moving.

It's subtle, making no noise at all. In fact, the way I notice it's even happening is that once again, I feel slightly sick to my stomach. While I'm not consciously noticing that the room is moving, my body can sense it. I look over toward the windows, and my suspicions are confirmed. Slowly, almost unnoticeably, I can see the outside view through the windows changing as the room descends and the bottom of the windowsill darkens.

"The initial descent is slow to avoid any disruption that might be noticeable from the outside. Once we clear the building's foundation, you'll notice that it'll start to pick up a bit."

The windows are completely dark, the outside world no longer viewable through them. I'm just going to assume that whatever electronic witchcraft powers the window in the doorway also does the same for the exterior windows.

All of a sudden, a huge pit grows in my stomach. I can feel that the room is dropping at a much, much faster rate. In fact, it almost feels like we're in a complete free fall. Out of instinct, I grab on tightly to the desk in front of me, like that would actually do anything if the room suddenly bottomed out.

"Sorry about the drop. It'll be over momentarily," Michelle says, looking so calm that you wouldn't think she even noticed it. And then, out of nowhere, the sensation just stops, like we've been caught. There's no jerk or anything. We just come to a smooth, but complete stop.

"Here we are. I told you it wouldn't be that bad," Michelle says.

"Actually you didn't tell me anything before you hit the basement button in your magic desk over there," I reply.

"Sorry about that. I thought it would be a waste of time to explain it to you when you were about to see it for yourself anyway."

"Still, a heads-up would have been nice. It might have helped me keep my breakfast down."

"You'll get used to it over time. Right now let's take a look around, shall we?" Michelle walks across the room and takes the doorknob in her hand. She waits for me to stand before pulling the door open and revealing what has replaced the dusty old hallways.

EIGHT

Outside the classroom door, there's now a hallway that's so long I feel like I can barely even see the end of it. Everything is gleaming and metallic, and LED lighting fixtures are spaced out evenly along the bare walls.

"We've still got a little ways to walk. Security is of the utmost importance here, so the main facility was built underneath a nearby lake. It's technically off campus, but still owned by the academy. The water helps shield any kind of radioactive activity that might happen down here and keep it undetectable to the rest of the world above," Michelle says.

I'm following her quick pace as we both walk toward the end of the long hallway.

"Radioactive activity?" I ask a little nervously.

"It's nothing to worry about. We don't expect to see any, but just in case. Like I said, you can never be too careful. Now is probably a good time to explain to you how the elevator that you were just in works. Moving large numbers of students down here without raising suspicion is important."

"Obviously."

"Every weekday afternoon, you'll be reporting to the classroom we met at today. The cover you'll be using, if ever asked, is that the classroom is used for after-school meetings for a student group called the Circle that helps the less fortunate in the community by providing assistance with daily tasks such as reading, accounting help, etc."

"Okay, so then what happens when a non-meta shows up at the classroom someday, looking for something to put on their college applications?"

"We have safeguards in place for that type of incident."

"Like what?"

"The student is informed that we don't have additional

room at this time, but we would still happily give them the recommendation for their application since it's our fault that more space isn't available. Based on what we know, ninety-nine times out of a hundred this will suffice, and we'll never hear from that student again."

"And what about the one in a hundred kid who shows up because they actually want to help and don't care about the credit for college?"

Michelle turns to me and smiles. "In those cases, we recruit."

"Really? You give them metabands?"

"No, unfortunately we don't have extras lying around, but there are plenty of non-meta operational roles that need to be filled. These require a lot of trust on our part since we must maintain complete secrecy around the project. We find that the type of student who's interested in helping out just for the sake of helping has the moral character we desire for our operational roles in most cases. In other words, they're the types of students who can keep a secret."

"And how do you make sure the metahumans that are here can keep a secret?" I ask.

"We don't."

"What do you mean you don't? I'm sure you have something in your back pocket to keep everyone in line. Some kind of failsafe or something if anyone ever spills the beans," I say.

Michelle stops walking and turns to face me fully.

"No, we don't. Everyone who's been invited to this school has been vetted, thoroughly. It's how we knew who you were before you knew who we were. We don't take any chances when we're choosing who to bring here, and we don't recruit anyone who would need to be threatened in order to keep our secret safe. That's the kind of thinking that got the world into the mess it's in. Not every secret can be safeguarded with the threat of violence. Sometimes you actually have to put in the legwork to find out what kind of person someone is, and if you're going to expect them to trust you, you sure as hell better trust them back."

I nod in agreement, and Michelle turns to continue walking while I'm still trying to process exactly what she said to me. It seems crazy that there're no safeguards against this place's secret being blown wide open, other than the word of the people here. It's a huge leap of faith on their part and a giant step forward if metahumans are going to find any kind of useful place in the world.

"This is our first stop," Michelle says as we approach a solid steel door. I stand aside and wait for Michelle to activate whatever retinal scanner or handprint reader is surely hidden in the wall. Instead, she just gives me a kinda confused look and reaches to grab the handle to the door. She twists it and it turns.

"Ah, fingerprint scanner in the doorknob? I guess that makes sense. Might as well make it one less step. Pretty cool stuff," I say.

"Fingerprint scanner? No. It's just a doorknob. Connor, I think you'll understand soon that this isn't The Agency. We're not all about secrets. If someone has earned our trust and is invited down here, we don't see the point in locking down every single door. We're not government funded, remember? So we're actually accountable for all the money we spend." She smiles as she swings open the door. "After you," she offers.

I'm not sure if I've ever seen such a large room in my entire life. It seems to stretch on forever, even farther than the hallway we were just in. If we were on the surface, I think the room would stretch beyond the horizon line. The ceiling isn't necessarily low, but it seems that way compared to the other dimensions of the room. Overhead, the same kind of LED lights from the hallway are spaced out as far as my eyes can see. Other than the lights, the room appears completely empty. There's a strange humming sound, but it seems likely that it's just the sound of the lights or a nearby generator.

"What do you think?" Michelle asks.

"Um, it's big?" I offer back.

"Do you have any idea what it's used for?"

"Not a clue," I answer honestly.

"I'll give you a clue then," Michelle says. She then places two of her fingers in her mouth and blows. Out comes a whistle so loud and so sharp that I glance at her wrists to make sure she's not secretly a meta herself.

Before the whistle comes to a stop, five people suddenly appear right in front of us. Four of them, a female and three males, are completely out of breath and drenched in sweat. They're doubled over or holding their hands on their head with their back arched, gasping for air. The fifth has a healthy sweat built up but is breathing in a much more controlled manner. She's Asian and has a slightly asymmetrical haircut; the dark hair on the right side of her face reaches down to her chin, but the left side is buzzed short. She's holding two fingertips to her neck while looking at the watch on her other wrist, timing her heartbeat.

I realize what this room is; it's a track. It must have only appeared empty because these metas were running around it so quickly that I couldn't even see them. The hum I heard was the sound of thousands of footsteps a second as they barely even touched the ground.

"Still wiping the floor with them?" Michelle asks the one runner who is barely winded.

She smiles politely in response.

"Connor Connelly, I'd like you to meet Susan Lee."

"You can just call me Sue; everyone else does," the girl says as she extends her hand to shake mine.

"Sue here is one of the fastest metas we've ever been able to verify," Michelle says. "I'd introduce you to everyone else, but, well, I don't think any of them are in the mood to speak right now, even if they could."

"You know, I'm pretty fast when I want to be too," I say.

"Sue's faster," Michelle says plainly.

"I'd be happy to show you if you're not satisfied with just asking these guys for yourself," Sue says, pointing to the exhausted metas, one of whom is dry heaving.

"I'm sure Connor would love to have you run circles around him, but we're on a bit of a schedule today. Next time," Michelle says as she turns to guide me back into the hallway.

"It might have looked like Sue was just showing off, but it's more than that. We don't know where the limits to many meta abilities lie. Pushing those limits is important, not only for the benefit of those involved, but also to learn what is possible for others," Michelle tells me as we head out the door and continue walking down the long corridor.

"Know your enemies and all of that?" I ask.

"Something like that. Here's the next room I wanted to show you."

Michelle opens the door and we walk into yet another enormous room. This one is complete with a high ceiling. It feels like we're inside an airplane hangar. Part of the reason for that is the gigantic airplane in front of me. Cars, trucks, trains and various other large objects are strewn throughout it.

"This is colloquially referred to as the weight room, for obvious reasons, but it's actually a lot more than that," Michelle says.

On the far end of the room, I can see that we're not alone. About a dozen other teenagers are using various pieces of workout equipment and weight machines. If it weren't for the airplane and other vehicles, the room would look just like any other gym, albeit a gigantic one. Michelle leads me over toward the machines.

"Why are they using regular workout equipment? I'm not trying to brag, but if my metabands were lit up and I tried using any of this stuff, I'd break it in half."

"Take a closer look," Michelle replies.

At first I'm not sure what she's talking about or what she

wants me to take a closer look at, but I walk over to one of the machines closest to me, making sure not to bother the rather large man who's pulling down a chain attached to a series of weights on the other end. The machine looks normal to me, though. It's not like I've used a lot of these things, but nothing looks out of the ordinary from what I can tell. I look back at Michelle and shrug my shoulders, hoping for a little help.

"Look at the weights," she says.

"I did look at the weights."

"Look at the markings on the weights."

I lean over slightly to take a closer look at the black slabs being lifted by the chain the man is pulling. Each is labeled "DWT" where normally you would see 'LBS'.

"What does DWT stand for?"

"Dead Weight Ton."

"Are you telling me that each of these weighs-"

"A thousand kilograms. About 2,240 pounds."

My jaw drops, and I unconsciously back up a couple of steps. Getting a few tons of weights dropped on your foot isn't something you spring back from, I imagine.

"But, how?" I ask.

"Extremely dense metal alloys. We have a meta on staff who's able to help us make them. They take up a lot less space than the old ones, that's for sure."

"Then why have all of this stuff around still?" I ask, gesturing to the plane, trains, and automobiles.

"The machines are for strength training. Even metahumans can always improve. Those are for practice."

"What sort of practice?"

One of the metas walking past us with a towel draped around his neck overhears our conversation on his way to what I assume is the locker room. He decides to give a demonstration and picks up the nearest car with one hand, launching it straight up into the air. I turn my head toward the ceiling and watch as the car sails up toward the rafters separating this room from the mile of rock over our heads. The car reaches its peak and is hurtling back down toward Earth. Well, I guess not Earth-Earth, since we're actually underneath it, but you get the idea. I get the idea too and start slowly shuffling backward, away from where it looks like this thing is going to land.

Michelle is watching too but must see my apprehension out of the corner of her eye. Without taking her eyes off the car hurtling toward us, she reaches out her arm and stops me from backing up farther. Before I have a chance to protest this though, the car lands safely in the outstretched palm of the man who threw it in the first place.

"Lifting is one thing; catching an object that was never designed to be airborne is another. You'd be surprised how often these things are used as projectiles by enhanced maniacs."

"Actually, I wouldn't," I say while thinking that I've used a car or two as a projectile myself when times were tough. Always empty, of course. I didn't realize that it was still considered a "bad guy" thing to do though, so I guess I'll have to stop.

"Follow me. I want to show you some of the rooms we use for one on one training," Michelle says as she leads me back into the hallway. We're now walking through an area that is devoid of doors completely.

"How did you build all of this?" I ask.

"It didn't happen overnight. The structure itself was actually built during the first wave of metahumans. Since the second wave began, our organization has reactivated and worked twenty-four hours a day to get this facility updated and finished. There's still a lot of work to do, but the basics are almost complete. The most important elements we needed, open space and cover from the general population, are in place now. That's how we've been able to start bringing students in."

"I get that, but how on earth did you build a bunker a mile

underground that's this huge without anyone noticing in the first place? How did you get the equipment down here? I mean, how did you get a jet down here?"

"Those things were easy for the most part. You'd be amazed how quickly you can get something accomplished when you've got contractors who can move objects with their minds and workers who can teleport."

"So someone just teleported that plane in here? You can't be serious."

"No, not someone. A few someones. It was a concerted effort, but the Brutes training down here were adamant about having a plane to practice catching. It doesn't come up that often as a problem, but when it does, they're apparently very difficult to handle. The nose just crumples and the wings shear off very easily.

"Ah, here we are. This is the next room I wanted to show you." Michelle opens another door and leads me inside.

Inside, the room is extremely plain and unimpressive compared to the previous rooms. There's only one person in this room: a guy about my age with a dark complexion and a short Afro-style haircut. He's wearing a crisp, bright white button-down shirt and wireframe glasses. In front of him is a deck of playing cards next to a small machine of some kind, which is resting on an aluminum table. He's staring intently at the cards to the point where I'm not even sure if he notices that we've walked into the room. Michelle glances at me and raises a finger to her lips, indicating that I should be quiet.

As if coming out of a trance, the guy shakes his head gently and looks up at us. A wide smile crosses his face and he rises from his chair to greet us.

"Connor Connelly, I'd like to introduce you to Winston Cliffe. Winston, this is Connor Connelly, also know as Omni." Before my hand is even halfway out of my pocket, Winston has grabbed it and is shaking it enthusiastically.

"Wow, Omni! It's great to know who you are. I mean, it's great to meet you and find out that you're you, that you're

Omni I mean. Of course you're Omni; you know you're Omni. I mean that Connor Connelly is Omni, and it's great to meet Connor Connelly, you. It's great to meet you," he says. This is getting confusing really quickly, but I appreciate the enthusiasm and give him a smile right back. There's something about him that I like already.

"Things can get very confusing around here very quickly with real names and alter ego names, as I'm sure you can imagine. For the most part, we like to use real names whenever possible. It helps to keep everyone's feet on the ground, so to speak, and mitigates the chance that someone will use an alter ego name out in the real world during conversation," Michelle explains.

"But what about someone using a real name while someone's, you know, powered up or whatever?" I ask.

"It's less of a concern. If someone overheard another meta calling you 'Connor,' that doesn't give them much to go by as far as finding out who you really are. Someone calling you 'Omni' while out in the real world eating lunch? That's a different story. We also find that you're less likely to use an alter ego name for another meta out in the real world if you're in the habit of only calling them by their real name when they're out of costume. It really just comes down to habit, but that habit can be important," Michelle says.

"I read all about how you took down the Controller in Bay View City. Awesome stuff, man. Way to think on your feet," Winston says.

"Thanks. Most of that credit belongs to Midnight and Iris, though. I was just the human punching bag," I say.

"Well, whatever you were, it sounded like it was awesome," Winston says.

"Winston here has a very rare ability that we're still trying to find out more about," Michelle says, changing the subject.

"Yeah, when I first got these things I didn't think they even worked," Winston says, referring to the pair of gleaming metabands wrapped around his wrists.

"So what can you do?" I ask.

"Winston actually has quite a few unique abilities. The particular ability he's working on now is especially interesting. The closest analog we have for describing it is that he's able to exert control over otherwise seemingly random outcomes," Michelle answers for him.

"Uhh ..." I say, struggling to make sense of what she just told me.

"What Michelle means is that I can basically control luck," Winston says.

"Control luck? What does that mean? How can someone control luck?"

"Take that stack of cards on the table," Winston tells me, motioning to the cards. "Put them in the machine to get them nice and random but don't look at them yet."

I do as he says and cut the deck of cards in half, placing each half on the plastic trays connected to the top of the machine. Once the deck is placed, the machine whirrs into action, quickly shuffling the cards and placing them neatly into the tray at the bottom of the machine in one tight stack.

Winston focuses his attention on the cards then closes his eyes. It's quiet for an uncomfortably long time, and I start to wonder if Winston has fallen asleep. Just then, his eyes snap open.

"Okay. Pick up the cards and look at them," he says.

I pick up the cards, looking at him again before I turn them over and seeing that he's already got that same grin back on his face.

I flip the cards over and start fanning them out on the table. The first card is an ace of spades. The second is a two of spades. The third is a three of spades, and so on.

It's not until I get to the face cards that the pattern breaks, when a king comes before a queen in the deck.

"Dammit, I was close," Winston says, laughing.

"So you're telling me this machine didn't put those cards in order?" I ask, thinking I know the trick.

"Technically, the machine did put the cards in order," Michelle interjects. "But Winston was able to exert enough influence over the randomness of the machine to put the cards into the order *he* wanted them to be in. This might not seem like much more than a simple magic trick, but what you probably didn't notice was *when* Winston rearranged the cards. He didn't focus on them until *after* they were already shuffled by the machine."

"Huh, I get it," I say.

Michelle stares at me, seeing right through me.

"Okay, I don't get it. Can you explain?"

"I've been able to influence situations as they happen since I found these bands, but the real trick is influencing them seemingly after the event has already passed," Winston says.

"Yeah, that's right. How the hell did you rearrange them after the machine had already shuffled them?"

"That's the part that we're still trying to understand," Michelle says. "Winston's abilities don't seem to be strictly bound by the linear aspects of time."

My eyes go blank again. Winston notices this time and picks up in English where Michelle left off.

"What Michelle is saying is that I'm able to control certain situations that have already occurred as long as the outcome is not yet known. Once you picked up that deck of cards and looked at it, there would have been nothing I could do to change the order the machine placed them in, but as long as the outcome was still unknown and flexible, I could change it. Kinda like Schrödinger's cat."

"The one that plays the piano in Snoopy?" I ask.

"It's *Peanuts*, and no," Michelle corrects me. "Winston's ability is something we're still learning about. Right now he might not be able to do much more with it than what looks like some slight of hand, but we have literally no idea where it could go. Abilities like this are why we started this center and why we're helping metas understand and explore their powers. Who knows what Winston might be capable of with his abilities one day.

"Well, we've interrupted your study session long enough, Winston. Thank you for taking the time to show us what you're working on, though."

"No problem. I needed the break anyway. Don't want to risk working too hard here and painting the walls with my brains," Winston says.

I give a small laugh, but Michelle doesn't. I'm starting to realize that her lack of humor wasn't part of her cover after all.

"Nice to meet you," I say to Winston, who nods and waves before sitting back down at his table. I follow Michelle out of the room and close the door behind us to give Winston back his privacy.

Michelle glances down at her watch.

"Hmm. I didn't realize how late it's gotten. I think we have time to visit one more room today before I'm going to have to leave for a meeting."

"That's fine with me. I'm sure I can get myself into plenty of trouble exploring on my own."

"No, no, no, no, no. You're going to be heading back to the surface. We've already accelerated your onboarding process significantly. We'll pick back up tomorrow."

"Seriously? I was just kidding about getting into trouble. I'm not a little kid, you know. I won't do anything stupid," I say, almost having even myself fooled.

"It's not that, Connor. What you have to understand is that this facility, this entire endeavor, it's not just about heroics. It's not just about taking on as much as humanly possible, or metahumanly possible as the case may be. It's about making this, all of this, sustainable. You're still going to have to live your life as normally as possible for this to work."

"I've gone this long without needing any help keeping my identity a secret."

"It's not just about keeping your identity a secret, Connor. It's about keeping you tied to humanity. People who don't keep a foot in that world wind up like ..." She trails off, realizing she shouldn't finish her sentence.

"Like who? Just say it. Like Jones?" I ask.

"Like Midnight."

The statement catches me off guard. I'm well aware that Midnight hasn't always been the best role model to look up to as far as work-slash-life balance is concerned, but everything he's done has been for the greater good. I'm not sure if he's still out there or not, but if he is, I'd bet my life that that hasn't changed.

"Here we are," Michelle says, breaking the awkward silence and bringing me into the last room of the day.

This room is different from the previous ones, which makes me even more curious about what's waiting behind the other closed doors. This room looks more like an old pawnshop or garage than a state-of-the-art metahuman training facility. The walls are lined with shelves containing books, various machine parts, sparring dummies, and about a million other things that I can't even identify. There are random people throughout the room, moving things from shelf to shelf or working on a pile of spare parts at a workbench. It's total sensory overload. Someone could probably spend years in here going through all of this stuff.

"Hey there," says a voice from behind me that startles me out of my daydream.

I turn around to find someone who looks like they have actually spent years doing just that. It's a teenage boy, maybe fourteen, with thick, black-framed glasses that magnify his eyes. Under those eyes are a series of dark, baggy circles that don't look like they belong on the face of someone this young. He's wearing a pair of tight jeans with holes in both knees and a t-shirt that references some movie that I'm not clever enough to get.

"Hey, I'm Connor," I say.

"Oh, I know who you are, Omni. It's great to finally, actually meet you. I'm Trevor," he says. He doesn't actually extend his hand to shake mine, though, and instead just kind of stands awkwardly in front of me, seemingly waiting for me to pick up the loose thread of the conversation. I glance over to Michelle, hoping for her help in navigating this particular social minefield, but she's speaking in hushed tones on her cellphone. Her body language suggests that the call is important and that she's not to be disturbed. Great.

"I thought we weren't supposed to call each other by our alter ego names down here?" I ask, trying to make conversation.

"You're right. Just couldn't help myself this time. You're not going to tell on me, are you?"

Tell on him? Does he think this is a kindergarten?

"No, your secret is safe with me."

"Thanks."

And here's that awkward silence again. Trevor is just staring at me, looking me right in the eye and not breaking contact. I don't think he's even blinking. Michelle's still on the phone. Dammit.

"Soooo, what's all this stuff?" I ask.

"This stuff? It's just a bunch of random stuff."

This is even harder than I thought it would be. I'll take fighting another meta in the sky above a city over thirty more seconds of this conversation if it's going to be this hard.

"I can see that. I meant more like what is this room for?"

Trevor still just stares.

"Like, what do you do in this room?"

"Oh, you mean what are my abilities?" he asks.

"Sure, that's close enough."

"My meta name is Machine. When my bands are powered up, I can absorb and take on the capabilities of nearby machinery."

"Any machine?"

"I'm not entirely sure yet. That's why I'm down here. I'm going through a bunch of various makes and types of machines to find out where my weaknesses and vulnerabilities might lie."

"That's really interesting. Can you show me an example of what you're talking about?" I ask.

A wide smile instantly materializes across his face like he's been waiting for someone to ask him that his entire life.

"Sorry about that," Michelle says suddenly as she interrupts and inserts herself into the conversation. "The person I wanted you to meet is right around the corner here."

"Oh, Trevor here was just going to show me-"

"I'm sorry. We're on a very tight schedule. There will be plenty of time to meet everyone and learn all about them in the coming weeks, though, I'm sure."

Trevor is completely deflated.

"Next time?" I ask him.

His demeanor changes back, and he's all smiles again. I smile back and follow Michelle, who is already speed walking down an aisle of junk shelves. They seem to stretch on forever and are filled with just about everything you could imagine.

"This is our miscellaneous inventory room," Michelle says without turning back to look at me, assuming that I've caught back up with her. "Everything in here is free to use during off-hours and downtime, but it cannot be removed from the facility."

"Okay, but, um, what is it?" I ask.

"It's simply an inventory of, well, I guess just about everything. We've found a lot of newer metas who exhibit ... unusual powers and abilities. I'm sure Trevor explained a little bit about his ability?"

"Yeah. He was just about to show me when you came over."

"You owe me one then. He would have kept you there all day explaining how they work. The truth is, though, we still don't fully understand much about them. That's what this room is for: learning. For that reason, we have it stocked with just about everything you could imagine."

"I've noticed that. This place looks like a Wal-Mart had a baby with a mausoleum."

"Ah, here's who I wanted you to meet," Michelle says a half second before I round the corner.

The narrow shelves piled to the ceiling with crap give way to an expansive open space. The flooring is covered with blue padding like you would find in a gymnasium. The walls, or where I assume the walls would be if I could actually see them, are completely covered floor to ceiling with weapons: swords, maces, nunchucks, shields, knives, throwing stars, baseball bats, and a bunch of other stuff I don't even recognize but have pointy, sharp ends.

"Connor, this is Nathanial Brubeck. Nathanial, this is Connor Connelly," Michelle says.

I reach out my hand for him to shake. I'm starting to feel like I'm a politician or something today. Nathanial looks at it carefully for a second, almost like he isn't sure whether to trust it or not, before finally shaking my hand.

Nathanial is tall and muscular, looking much more like a "man" than a teenager, at least much more than anyone else I've met here so far. I'm guessing he's an early bloomer, but even still, he must be a year or two older than I am. His hair is dark and long, reaching down to the line of his jaw. His hair, as well as the rest of him, is covered in sweat, but he doesn't seem to be out of breath.

He does, however, seem to be very, very intense. I'm not sure if he's mad that we've interrupted ... whatever we just interrupted, or if this is just how he is.

"Nice to meet you," I offer.

He nods and turns back to the blue mat.

"He can be a little intimidating," Michelle whispers to me. "And he's not much of a people person."

"Yeah, I picked up on that," I whisper back. "So, what's his ability?"

"Just watch."

Nathaniel walks to the center of the gymnasium mat and stands still, closing his eyes. He waits.

Without warning, tennis balls come flying from some unseen holes in each of the walls. Just as quickly a pair of katana blades appear in his hands. He slices each of the balls before they can reach him. They each fall into two evenly split pieces on the ground.

A large medicine ball is ejected from the wall that his back is facing. He spins around on his heels and the sword in his right hand transforms into a full body-length shield, like one a Roman warrior would have used. In fact, it looks like it even has an old Roman symbol on it. The medicine ball collides with the shield and falls to the ground with a thud.

Another hole in the wall opens up and unleashes a flurry of basketballs. There must be dozens of them, each one bouncing at different heights and speeds. Nathanial doesn't miss a beat, jumping head first over the first one right before it can hit him.

In midair, the shield and katana both join together to form a Bo staff. Upon hitting the ground with both feet, Nathanial thrusts the Bo staff behind him, hitting the first bouncing basketball square in the middle, sending it flying into the opposite wall. The other balls are quickly dispatched as well. Some are swung at and others are bashed until there is just one lonely ball left, lazily bouncing toward him. He casually walks over to it and thrusts out his Bo staff one last time, spearing the basketball like a shish kabob. The air slowly hisses out of the deflating ball while I pick my jaw back up off the floor.

"Whoa. That was incredible," I say out loud to no one in particular. It just kinda comes out.

Nathanial glances over at me before he goes about picking up all the pieces of tennis balls and basketballs that are strewn throughout the gymnasium. When he's finished, he comes over to join Michelle and me.

"That was really very impressive," I say. "So your

metabands enable you to do all of that?"

"No, training enables me to do all of that," he replies.

"Nathanial's ability allows him to create almost any type of non-projectile weaponry you could ever imagine, but his fighting abilities are all natural," Michelle says for him.

"You're telling me that aside from the little sword morphing thing, you could have done that without metabands?"

Nathanial gives a small nod along with a small smirk.

"Thank you for the demonstration, Nathanial." Michelle turns and waves for me to follow her.

Once we're out of earshot from Nathanial, I start peppering her with questions about his abilities, but Michelle assures me that everything we've just witnessed, Nathanial was able to do before he even found his metabands. I push her for more information about him, but she tells me that he's very shy and that they respect the privacy of the students here. If there are parts of someone's past that they do not wish to share, that is their decision, not the decision of someone like Michelle.

She's truthful with me and tells me that there are some people here who were not always "good," but that if a person has been invited here that should be assurance enough for me that they have great potential for "good." While they try to remain as open as possible, in contrast to The Agency, there are still some areas where trust is required on both ends.

We reach the main hallway again, and without asking, I turn left to head back the way we came. Michelle grabs the back of my shirt and turns me back around.

"Isn't this the way back, though?" I ask.

"It is, but it's not the only way out of here," she says.

"What do you mean?"

"For a plethora of reasons there are multiple entrances and exits from the facility. Did you think we built a concrete and steel bunker a mile under the earth and only put in one exit door? That wouldn't be very safe or legal."

"Something tells me that the fire marshal hasn't been down to inspect this place."

"Follow me," Michelle says with a knowing smile.

We walk farther down the featureless hallway until we reach what, to me, seems like a random door.

"How do you remember what's behind all of these doors? They all look exactly the same," I say.

"There's a system to it. You'll get the hang of it. In the meantime, though, I'm afraid this is where I'm going to have to leave you."

"You're not coming back up to the surface with me?"

"No, there's still some work I have to take care of down here, but I trust that you'll be able to take care of yourself for the rest of the night."

"What am I supposed to do, though?"

"You're sixteen and I've just given you the night off to do anything you'd like and you're asking questions? Are you the type of kid who reminds his teacher when she forgets to assign homework too?"

"Point taken."

"It's been a stressful week for you, Connor, and I know that this is all very new to you, both upstairs and down here. Take tonight to settle in a little bit. Explore. Meet regular people. Talk to them."

"Wow, this seems weird coming from you."

"It's important that you retain some semblance of a social life. People will notice when you're not around, so being able to have social connections to fall back on will become important for establishing your day-to-day identity."

"Oh, so this is really more about making sure no one suspects me?"

"They aren't mutually exclusive, Connor. If you really want this life, you're going to have to start learning that quickly."

"So what's behind this door? Another classroom that's

secretly an elevator?"

"Something like that. After you," Michelle says as she opens the door and steps aside to let me in. The room is much, much smaller than the classroom-sized elevator we took down here.

"What do I do?" I ask.

"Don't worry about anything. The elevator will take care of it. Just remember to act natural when you reach the surface. I'll see you tomorrow," Michelle says, closing the door.

I can't manage to get out the word "wait" before she closes the door on me completely. As soon as the door clicks shut, I can feel that I'm already gently accelerating. The small room quickly reaches its top speed before gradually slowing down before we reach what I assume is the surface.

The ceiling above me silently slides open and I see white tile and a florescent light overhead. I'm still staring up at it when the ground clicks into place, and I look around to try to figure out where I am. It's seemingly another small room, just like the elevator itself, but then I turn around and see it.

A toilet.

A second later I hear the sound of another toilet flushing and then running water.

They have a secret toilet elevator, and of course that's the one Michelle would put me on to re-enter the real world.

NINE

My first semi-conscious thought for the day is that there is no way the alarm clock can be right. It definitely not only feels like I just set it, but that I hadn't even fallen asleep yet before it started blaring. The last thing I remember is entering my room, thinking how insanely tired I was, and the next thing I know, this stupid alarm is going off.

I roll over and find out pretty quickly that the alarm clock isn't faulty. The harsh sunlight hits me in the face before I even have a chance to turn the damn alarm off. Eventually the alarm falls to the floor, and in the process some button must have been hit because it finally stops. It might have stopped because it broke, but at this point I really don't care.

Every fiber of my being wants to go back to sleep right now. It would be so easy too. Just roll over, close my eyes, and let the rest take care of itself. It would certainly be a lot easier than what I know I have to do instead, which is get up and make sure that I'm not late for my first day of classes. I'm already behind on the year, so sleeping in on day one would probably earn me a swift butt kicking from Michelle or someone else.

One leg at a time, very slowly, I pull myself out of bed. Realizing that I'm not the only inhabitant of this tiny room, I do my best to keep noise to a minimum, but when I look over at the less-than-twin-size bed on the other side of the room, it's empty. It seems like my new roommate was up and out the door before me this morning, which offers me a nice little bit of privacy, something I feel is probably going to be in short supply in the coming weeks and months.

The communal showers in the restroom weren't one of the perks I was looking forward to in living here, and I'm even more disappointed when I find there's a line waiting for free stalls. That explains why Tyler was up so early. I see him a few people ahead of me, waiting in line, and give him a wave, which he doesn't return.

By the time I've showered, changed, and gotten myself all the way across campus for my first class, I'm at least five minutes late I figure.

"Ah, you must be Mister Connelly?" the older man with gray temples and a receding hairline standing at the front of the class room says. "Tell me, do you have a good excuse as to why you're fifteen minutes late for my class?"

I could have sworn it was only ten. Maybe his watch is fast.

"I'm sorry about that. There was a line for the showers this morning, and I didn't realize the classroom was all the way on the opposite side of the campus," I offer.

"Mister Connelly, you and the others lucky enough to be offered housing in the dormitories here have been offered this with the explicit understanding that this is meant to aid in your studies. Almost all the other students in this classroom drove, walked, or took public transit to campus today, yet you, a student who actually *lives* on the campus, was later to class than all of them. How do you explain that?"

Okay, I guess he's not letting it go. So much for taking it easy on my first day.

"It won't happen again," I say.

My words aren't acknowledged. Instead, the teacher turns his back to me and goes back to writing on the chalkboard. I take this to mean our conversation is over and quickly move to find the nearest desk I can so everyone will stop staring at me.

The rest of the day goes more or less like this in every classroom. I'm already behind on coursework and showing up late to most of them does little to win me any sympathy from the teachers. All of my classes are scheduled back to back, starting as early as possible so I can finish as early as possible and get to the training facility. This campus is gigantic, though, and whoever designed my schedule, my guess would be Michelle, gave very little thought about how much time it would take to get from class to class without using my metabands.

After getting out of English class at 2:00 p.m., I have just enough time to grab something for lunch from the dining hall before I'm expected to meet for my "after school activities" at the Blair Building. It's the closest thing I have to a break all day, and I start to feel like I'm getting a second wind as I trek up one of the many, many rolling hills toward the cafeteria.

I might be exhausted, but I'm still very curious and excited, honestly, for my meta training. I've had these metabands turned off more in the past week than any time since I found them. Blowing the dust off of them and stretching my legs a bit has quickly become the light at the end of the tunnel for my first day here on campus.

As I approach the dining hall, I see what looks like another light at the end of this crappy day.

"Sarah?" I ask.

The blond girl talking with a group of students near a piece of bronze art outside the hall turns around.

It is her.

She glances around at first, not quite sure who called her name. Then her eyes catch mine. At first she looks confused, no doubt as surprised to see me on campus as I am to see her.

"Connor?" she says as I get closer. She squints her eyes as if she isn't completely sure that it's me.

"Yeah, it's me," I say.

She turns to the group, which hasn't noticed me, and tells them that she'll be right back. She walks to meet me halfway, jogging a little at one point to save me a few extra steps. It's only been a couple of days since I've seen her, but she hasn't seen me, or me as Connor rather, since we broke up more or less.

"Oh my gosh, what are you doing here?" she asks.

"Going to school, duh. Why, what are you doing here?" I reply.

"Smart ass," she says as she punches me in the arm. Things feel like they haven't changed between us for a moment, but that couldn't be further from the truth, and I need to keep reminding myself of it. "When did you get here?" she asks.

"Derrick just brought me up yesterday. What about you? I didn't even realize you were here."

"Yeah, sorry about that. Me and my dad had to leave Bay View City pretty quickly. Something about the board at his company being nervous about operations being based there with everything that's going on, I think," she lies. "It all happened pretty quickly. I meant to text you once I got settled here."

"You seem like you're settling in pretty quickly," I say, motioning toward the group she just walked away from.

"Oh, them? They're in my physics class. We're meeting for a study group during lunch."

I'm not surprised to see Sarah making friends so quickly. It's one of the things I've always liked about her. The fact that she and her dad were almost killed a week ago is something you wouldn't believe, even if someone told you. That's just the kind of person she is. Resilient. Whatever is going on inside her head doesn't stop her from keeping up with the outside world. It's a skill that I've been envious of since even before I had to worry about juggling two different identities.

"And what about you? Are you fitting in here okay so far?" she asks.

"Me? Oh yeah, of course," I lie.

"Connor Connelly, you know that I know when you're not telling me the truth still, right?" she asks, completely oblivious, I hope, to just how wrong she is about that.

"I'm getting there. Just a little burned out after my first day."

"You'll be fine," she says.

"Hey, Sarah, come on. You're holding us up again," one of the guys in the circle of study buddies waiting for Sarah yells over to her. He's taller and looks older than me, and I'm immediately jealous.

"I better get going. I'd offer you to join us, but I wouldn't want you to try killing yourself with a spork while you listen to all of us going on and on about physics."

"Oh yeah, sure, of course. I have to get going anyway. I just stopped by to grab something quick before I headed off to my next class," I say, glancing down at the time on my phone to see that once again, I'm already late. "On second thought, it looks like I don't have time for that. I'd better take off before they suspend me for being late so many times on my first day. I'll see you around, though?" I ask.

"Yeah, I'm sure of it."

"See you later, Sarah."

"Later, Connor," she says before heading back to join the group of students who are beginning to enter the dining hall. A few look back at me, and I can see them asking her who I am. I can't hear her response, and I wonder what she told them. It doesn't matter now, though. We're not together. Both of us have secrets we're hiding from the rest of the world, and it's not like the world has been getting any less complicated lately.

Just worry about getting to training, I tell myself. Everything else takes a backseat to that.

"Who was the hottie?" a voice behind me that I don't recognize asks.

I turn around and see that it's Winston, the meta with the ability to control luck that I met yesterday.

"That hottie, as you put it, is my ex-girlfriend."

He winces in embarrassment at what he just asked.

"Sorry about that."

"It's no problem. You didn't know. Unless you did know. In that case, you're a real jerk," I joke.

Winston smiles and slaps me on the back, happy that I'm not mad at him.

"Well, look man, there's no need to cry over it, right? Plenty of fish in the sea and all of that. You don't want to be tied down when you're here with literally thousands of other potential future ex-girlfriends."

"That's easy for the guy who can control luck to say."

"Hey, I can tip luck in my favor, but not people. That's free will. I can't control what folks think."

"Sucks to be you."

"No way. Can you imagine what it would be like to be able to control someone's thoughts and actions? That's too much power, too much responsibility. How would you use that? How would you know when it was right and when it was wrong? Nope. Those aren't the kind of decisions I want to have to deal with, thanks. So what's your girlfriend doing here? Is she a meta too?"

"No. I thought she was for a little while, but she's not."

"That's lucky. It's best to keep this whole meta business and real life separate, I think."

"Well that wasn't the case either. She wasn't a meta, but she was involved."

"She knew you had powers?"

"No, it wasn't like that. It was ... complicated," I say, realizing that I have to watch my words. Sarah's secret isn't mine to share. Hell, Sarah doesn't even know that I even *know* her secret.

It feels strange to be able to talk to someone like this. Only a few people knew my secret before, and even they couldn't really put themselves in my shoes. You might find this hard to believe, but Midnight wasn't the best at listening when it came to my girl problems. This is different, though. Winston might not have the same powers as me or have gone through everything I have the exact same way I did, but we're more alike than we're different.

Who knows, maybe it'll be nice to talk to someone like this

who understands, as long as I'm careful to make sure that the only secrets I spill are my own.

"Yeah, I know complicated. Listen," Winston begins, "I've got an idea. Why don't you come hang out tonight. It's just a small group of us, but we can make it into an official welcome party for you."

"You don't have to go through that kind of trouble," I say.

"It's not trouble; it's a good excuse. Better than the current reason we're using to have it."

"And what is that?"

"That we're bored."

This makes me laugh.

"I'm serious," Winston says. "You don't even know yet. It sounds like a great idea, living on campus, not having grown-ups around and everything, but the reality is that when everyone else on campus goes home for the night, and after we're done with meta training, it is booooooring here. Plus, it'll help you keep your mind off of old what's her name."

"Sarah."

"See, I've forgotten all about her already. You will soon too. Trust me."

TEN

If I thought that the center was out of the way from the rest of campus, the place I'm heading to makes it seem like it's the center of the universe. I'm currently trudging through an undeveloped, heavily wooded part of campus that I actually needed Winston to show me on a map in order to find.

The reason this particular area is so far out of the way is that it was originally intended to be part of the meta training facilities, except it never got even close to finished. The underground tunnel was dug and cleared out, but nothing was ever built on top of it. Since it would look really suspicious for students to be walking out into the middle of the woods everyday and seemingly disappearing, the decision was made to abandon this part of the facility. There's talk of one day linking it to the rest of the training grounds, but for right now, there's really no need for it. There aren't enough metas here to fill even half the current training areas as it is.

As I continue my way through the woods, I check my phone again to see what time it is. It's already close to eleven, and I'm hoping that the rest are still actually here. Sure, ten isn't *that* late, but the hours here are brutal. Classes start at 7:00 a.m. and go until 3:00 p.m. Then from three until seven every day, we're expected to train. After that, we can eat dinner and spend our free time however we want, as long as we remain on campus.

Apparently I'll get used to the schedule, but I was dead on my feet by the time dinner rolled around tonight, and I wound up sleeping right through it. Tonight's gathering would have started hours ago, so considering everyone else has to get up early too, part of me expects to not find anybody. I'm kicking myself for sleeping through dinner and not tagging along with everyone else up here. Out of every school I've been to throughout my childhood up until now, this is the one that I'm the most desperate to fit into, because if I can't fit in with a bunch of other metas my age, I don't even know what else to try.

Finally, after what seems like an eternity of searching, I find it. I'd be lying if I said that the idea that this was all some kind of initiation prank hadn't run through my head a few times, but here it is. Since there's no building to disguise the entrance to the underground facility here, the powers that be decided to use the next best disguise they could think of: a gigantic boulder.

Keep in mind, of course, that the people who made this facility in the first place didn't count on the building above it never being built. But when it wasn't, they didn't want to just flood the tunnel with cement or collapse it with a controlled explosion, just in case they later changed their minds and decided the tunnel would be useful for something. After all, building massive underground tunnels isn't exactly easy, or cheap, even if you're using a meta labor to dig them. You still need engineers to make sure that the structure itself is viable, otherwise you'll find yourself trying to rescue people stranded a mile underground one day.

The nice thing about using a boulder to cover up the entrance is that it's really pretty easy for a metahuman with enhanced strength to get in, though. According to Winston, none of the faculty knows that any of the students know this place exists. Actually, according to him, most of the faculty doesn't even know it exists. The only way the students stumbled upon it in the first place was through echolocation. One of the metas here apparently *heard* this place from miles away and could tell there was something hollow far underground where it shouldn't be.

Winston warned me that if I was late I'd have to pick up the boulder by myself, which really wouldn't be an issue unless I didn't happen to have enhanced strength, but lucky for me, I do. I bring my hands out and flick my wrists to make my metabands appear back on my wrists before tapping them together to activate. I consciously decide not to activate my uniform since I don't want to be the guy that shows up to a party wearing his work clothes unless I'm sure everyone else is doing it.

I push my shoulder into the boulder and dig my feet into the damp earth underneath me. The boulder moves with little effort and rolls slowly over to one side, exposing a shaft plummeting straight down into the earth. It's so long that the end of it is represented by just a pinhole of light. There's a ladder, thankfully, for those who can't fly or just those who are invulnerable but don't feel like taking a mile-long free fall. On the underside of the rock, I can also see a simple, crude metal handle mounted to the rock itself. I take it that this is there to pull the rock over yourself when you descend down the ladder, which takes care of my question about how I'm supposed to get the rock back in place once I'm inside.

For a moment, I wonder again if I've already missed the party with my stupidly timed nap, but when I focus I can hear the faint sound of music wafting up from the tunnel below. It sounds like people are still here, so I swing my legs into the shaft and grab onto the boulder's handle to pull it back into place on my way down.

Geronimo.

ELEVEN

"Hey, Connor! You actually made it," Winston says as I approach.

I'm walking down a monstrously huge cavern toward a group of maybe about a dozen people. They're quite a ways away from the entrance but easy enough to find since there's really only one way to walk once you get down here.

Winston wasn't kidding when he said they never finished the facility down here. Aside from the ladder and the fact that the tunnel itself looks to be almost perfectly circular, you wouldn't know that it was manmade. Everything is exposed and dark. The ceiling is at least fifty feet above me. The ceiling, walls and floor beneath are all just exposed rock and dirt.

The group I'm heading toward looks like they only have a few items with them. From what I can see there's just a few folding chairs and a Bluetooth speaker playing music. They're lit from what looks like a fireball hovering overhead in midair. I guess there's no need to bring a flashlight when you've got enough metas around. Get more than a few together and odds are one of them will have some kind of power that will take care of it.

As I get closer, Winston walks over to meet me halfway and claps me on the back, handing me a cup.

"So glad you could join us. We were starting to get worried that you got lost or accidentally got yourself pinned underneath that boulder up there," he says.

"No, I figured it out eventually," I reply.

"Great. Let's get you introduced to some people here," Winston says as we approach the group.

Heads start turning toward me, and I begin to feel incredibly self-conscious all of a sudden.

"Everybody, this is Connor. Connor, this is everybody," he says.

The crowd responds by saying, "Hi, Connor!" in unison, making me feel like I'm at an Alcoholics Anonymous meeting before I reply back sheepishly, "Hi, everybody."

They then turn their backs again and go back to their own conversations.

"You're not going to introduce me?" I ask Winston quietly.

"I did introduce you," he says.

"But you didn't tell me any of their names."

"That's all on you, big guy. Say hi to people. Make small talk. No one's going to bite. Oh, except for Steve. That's one of his powers," Winston says.

"Really?" I ask.

"No, not really. Loosen up a bit, dude. We might be a little different, but we've all got one very big thing in common that most people don't have," Winston says, holding up both of his wrists to show me his metabands.

I smile and nod to him, silently agreeing to follow his lead and try to be as little of a social weirdo as I possibly can.

"Hey, you're from Bay View City, right?" a girl closest to me asks, apropos of nothing.

I guess that's just how conversations start? I realize that I recognize her and spend half a second trying to remember where from, before it comes to me that I saw her at the training facility yesterday. Duh. She was the one literally running laps around everyone at the track.

"Uh, yeah, I am," I say before the silence between us gets any more awkward than it already is.

"Did you leave once the Alphas kicked out all of the metas too?" she asks.

"Yeah, but not because of that," I say.

"Why then?"

"Well, yeah, I mean technically because of that, but I wasn't running away. Just had to regroup, you know. Think things through for a bit. Michelle suggested it'd be a good idea to come here."

"So what kind of powers do you have?" she asks. It feels

strange to be having a conversation like this out in the open. I've never spoken with anyone in a group setting like this about my abilities when I've been out of uniform. There are a dozen other kids here, all metas, and this passes for just normal, friendly chit-chat, I guess? I'm definitely going to have to get used to this.

"Um, let me think. Strength, flying, speed, invulnerability, vision stuff," I say.

"What kind of vision stuff?"

"Just ... like ... enhanced vision, I guess? I can see through a lot of different materials, like an x-ray almost."

"That's a lot of abilities. If you could teleport you'd have all the big ones locked down."

"I can teleport. Or at least, I used to be able to teleport."

"What do you mean, 'used to be able to'? How did you lose one power but still hang on to the others?" she asks.

"It's my metabands. They were damaged. Ever since I just haven't been able to do it."

"Your metabands were damaged? They're literally the strongest things known to man. How could they have gotten damaged?"

I hadn't noticed up until now, but there seems to be a decent-sized group eavesdropping on our conversation. With the revelation that my metabands are damaged, they are a little less shy with pretending that they haven't been listening. One by one, individuals have started turning their full attention to this conversation, inching closer so they can hear. No one seems concerned with pretending anymore. I wouldn't be either if I had just overheard someone saying that their metabands had been damaged.

"They were damaged in a fight ... with the Alphas," I finally say.

"Holy crap. You're Omni," a voice from the crowd says.

I nod.

"Weren't you the first to find one of the second wave metabands?" Susan asks.

"Yeah, supposedly," I reply. Suddenly I'm starting to feel even more self-conscious than I was before.

"Are we supposed to be impressed by you or something?" another guy from the crowd asks. He's taller than I am, with jet black hair and a vintage-looking t-shirt.

"What? No. I didn't mean to make it sound like-" I start.

"You think you're better than us or something?" the same guy says to me.

Somehow I've managed to almost start a fight just by answering what I thought were some simple small-talk questions. Now I remember why I hate small talk.

"Look, I don't think I'm better than anybody, and I'm not trying to impress you or anything. Susan was curious about who I was, and I told her. That's all. I'm not trying to cause any trouble," I say.

This seems to work for the time being, and individuals go back to their previous conversations, and the crowd around me thins out. Out of the corner of my eye, I spot a small cooler filled with drinks and excuse myself in an effort to go grab one.

Okay, so going over and grabbing a soda will take approximately twenty seconds or so if I include the time it takes to open it. Now I've just got to figure out what I'm going to do to fill the time after that.

Everyone else seems to be deep in their own conversations, and I feel like the odd man out. I hear laughing a little bit farther down the cavern and decide that following it is probably a good way to occupy myself. Better than standing around like the only weirdo without anyone to talk to at a party, at least. And besides, when has following the sound of laughter down a dark, mile-long underground cave ever gotten anyone into trouble, right?

On the edges of the light, I find a small group of six all laughing hysterically at the one in the middle. The one in the middle is frantically trying to find something, which is making all the others just laugh even harder. I start to feel concerned, but then I can see that the one in the middle is laughing a little bit too, even if his eyes are watering.

Finally, one of the members of the group relents. He puts his hand out into the air with his palm facing skyward. Tiny flecks of blue and white begin swirling in the air, forming a tiny tornado in his hand. The specks begin to stick to each other and multiply. Within a few seconds, he's holding a perfectly spherical ball of ice.

I don't think it's even fully formed before the kid in the middle lunges for it and shoves it into his mouth. His face is completely enveloped in steam as soon as the ball of ice hits his tongue. I'm still confused about what's happening, but everyone else is laughing even harder now and a look of relief passes over the kid's face.

"How long was that?" he asks once he seems to have caught his breath.

"Thirty-eight seconds," someone from the crowd tells him.

"All right, not bad, not bad," another says as everyone starts to mockingly applaud.

"Hey, what are you guys doing?" I ask the guy who just created the ice ball, showing the full extent of my party-mingling social skills.

"Do you want to try? Are you invulnerable?" a girl standing next to him asks me.

"Pretty much. But what am I agreeing to try?" I ask.

"You know the cinnamon challenge?" the ice maker asks me.

"Yeah. When you try to swallow a full tablespoon of cinnamon without coughing it out? Is that what you guys are doing?" I ask.

"The idea's the same, but we don't use cinnamon," he tells me.

"So what do you use then?" I ask.

Without saying a word, the girl next to him picks up a nearby rock the size of an acorn. She holds it out in her hand and concentrates. As she does, the pupils of her eyes begin to glow red as though they were lit from behind by fire. A second later the rock in her outstretched hand is glowing bright red.

She's using her abilities to heat it up to the point where it's almost lava.

"What do you say?" the ice ball maker begins. "Think you can keep one of my sister's fireballs on your tongue for longer than thirty-eight seconds?"

"Oh, I don't really think-" I begin before I'm interrupted.

"I knew it. This guy isn't invulnerable," Ice Guy says.

"I'm invulnerable. It's just that invulnerable or not, I don't really like the idea of putting something like that in my mouth."

"Aw, come on, new guy. It doesn't really hurt that badly. It's just a little bit of fun," the fire starter says. "We barely get anytime to ourselves, and when we do, there's not a whole hell of a lot to do around here. We've got to find some way to blow off a little steam."

"Is that supposed to be a pun?" I ask.

"It wasn't, but it was pretty good. I'll have to remember that one," she says as she puts her hand out toward me and begins to heat up another rock. It's nice to see that even at a fancy private school and with superpowers, kids still find new and inventive ways to peer pressure each other into doing stupid things that nobody really wants to do.

"Fine," I say, relenting to it. I haven't made many strides in the whole friend-making thing since I got here, so I'd better start somewhere, even if it is with putting molten rock into my mouth. I stick my hand out to grab the rock, hoping that maybe I can cheat a little bit and grab it before it's at its hottest.

Right before my fingers touch the rock, I can see her expression start to change, but it's too late. My pinky finger grazes the palm of her hand right as she tries to pull it away and out of my reach. Her mouth has already started to form the word "don't" when I feel it.

The pain. It's unbelievable. The heat is so intense that it actually feels like cold at first. For an instant, it feels like my pinky finger is going to fall off, and in that instant, I really, really wish it would if that means this pain would stop. Before the full pain has even hit, I've retracted my hand back into my chest, covering it with the other hand, and collapsed onto the floor into the fetal position. After the brief moment of worry has passed, the sound of laughter fills the cavern again, even louder than before.

"You're not supposed to touch it with your hands, dummy," the fire starter whispers into my ear just as I'm getting my feet back under me, working to stand up again. "The rock is hot, but when I'm using my power, my hands are the same temperature as the surface of the sun. Even when you're invulnerable, that's going to sting."

"Note taken," I say, shaking my hand violently in the air like that's actually going to do anything to rid the lingering pain.

"Here," the ice-maker brother says before slapping a big pile of fresh ice into my hand. "This will take a little bit of the sting out. It's supercooled to absolute zero, so it'll keep frozen for while. Just don't leave it on there too long or else you're going to have the opposite problem with frostbite, and trust me, that can be just as bad. My name's Calvin, by the way."

"Connor," I say, using my free hand to awkwardly do a lefty handshake with him.

"Sorry about all of that," he says.

"It's fine. I mean, it was pretty funny," I say, able to crack a hint of a smile now that the impulse to try to rip my own arm off just to stop the pain has faded.

"No, it wasn't funny. It was very, *very* funny," Calvin says.

"When did you get here?" another member of the group whose laughter has subsided to that of a chuckle asks me.

Wait, did this really work? Can you really just make an ass of yourself and people will just become friendlier? Why hasn't anyone told me about this sooner?

"Just this morning, actually," I reply.

"Wow, they're really just throwing you in the deep end, huh?"

"Yeah, I guess so. As you can see I'm still wearing my floaties."

This joke falls so flat on the floor that you would think it was another one of my superpowers.

"Are you new to being a meta?" the fire starter asks.

"No, I've had my bands for a little while now, actually."

"Wait a minute," a different girl says. "You're Omni, aren't you? I heard that they were going to try to recruit you for here."

"They already told you about me? So much for the whole secret identity thing."

"There's no such thing as secret identities here. Everyone's an open book ... within the group that is, at least. It's the only way they say we can stay sane."

"What does that mean?" I ask.

"They call it metahuman dissociative disorder. They say it's what happens when someone with metabands keeps them active too long and decides to just ignore or abandon their normal, pre-meta life. It's supposed to lead to all sorts of delusions of grandeur, lack of empathy, you name it. It's what they think happened to Jones that turned him so crazy, you know, in the end," Calvin says to me.

"Well it's not like talking about having metabands is something most regular people would understand," I say, finally starting to regain feeling in my hand.

"Exactly. That's part of the reason why this place exists. Hell, I still think that they know we come down here at night sometimes but just allow it because it helps us from feeling like we're under constant surveillance."

"Allow it? I say they built this place *so* we'd have a place to go. I still don't trust that there aren't cameras hidden here everywhere. I'm Clara, by the way," the girl who nearly burned my hand off says as she offers her own for me to shake. "Don't worry, I'm powered down."

I hesitantly stick my hand back out to shake hers. Right as I'm about to touch it, she grabs it and screams, causing me to yelp and jump. The entire crowd starts laughing again, and I realize that that was the point.

"Weren't you the one who let all of those detained metas escape from Silver Island?" a voice asks from the newly gathered crowd.

This momentarily stops all other side conversations, and suddenly the cavern is very quiet. The person who said it works his way through the crowd while many of those gathered move to get out of his way.

It's Nathanial, the weapons expert from yesterday. The one with a bad attitude who seemed like he especially didn't like me. I guess we can tally that up as a certainty now.

"I didn't let them escape," I say, trying not to start a fight but still standing up for myself. People I care about were hurt that day, and I can't just let someone say it was my fault without correcting them.

"But you didn't stop them from escaping either, did you?" Nathanial asks, now stepping out from the crowd completely.

This garners a gasp and a few scattered murmurs from the crowd. This was the one place where I thought I maybe had a chance at fitting in, but so far, this Nathanial guy seems to be going especially out of his way to let me know that that won't be the case.

"I did my best to stop the prisoners from escaping, but my primary concern that day was protecting the lives of the employees there," I tell him.

"But people still died, didn't they?"

"What's your point?" I ask, beginning to lose patience even though I don't want this to escalate further than it already has.

After everything that's happened, though, I just don't quite have the inner Zen required to let this roll off my shoulders.

"My point is that not only did innocent people die, not only did meta-powered prisoners escape, but you also created the exact kind of power vacuum that the Alphas needed. And look at what's happened. They have an entire city under siege and there's apparently nothing anyone can do about it. And it all happened because you thought you were different. You thought you were someone special."

"No, I didn't."

"Yes, you did," Nathanial says, raising his voice. "You thought because you were the first of the second wave that somehow the rules didn't apply to you. You thought that you could just go into any old situation, guns blazing, and come out smelling like roses. You never thought about the hard decisions that should have been made that day."

"And what decisions are those, since you seem to be such an expert?" I ask, kinda surprising myself even with how aggressive I'm being, but I'm mad, and I don't intend to back down from this anymore.

"Come on. You know what you should have done. Everyone here knows what you should have done. You should have killed those prisoners so it never would have come to that in the first place. They deserved whatever they had coming to them if they weren't willing to give up their bands after they did what they did. And you should have taken out your little girlfriend, Iris, too. It would've saved one of us the trouble down the road."

This is the straw that breaks the camel's back. I move to take a step forward, but before my foot can touch the ground, I feel a burning heat on my shoulder. I turn back to look at Clara, who is shaking her head at me.

"It's not worth it, Omni," she says.

"My name isn't Omni. It's Connor."

"What are you going to do, Mister First Meta?" Nathanial asks. "You know you weren't even the first meta in the second wave. There were plenty of other metas out there already. You were just the only one vain enough to step into the spotlight, and now we all have to deal with your consequences. We'd be up on the surface instead of a mile underground if your stupid stunts hadn't scared half the country to death."

"You can't fight him," Clara whispers to me.

"Yeah, I can. He barely even has powers," I say to her without ever breaking eye contact with Nathanial, letting him know I'm not afraid of him.

"No, I mean you can't fight him. The school has a zero tolerance policy for violence. You agreed to it the second you stepped on campus. That's the only way this place can remain safe, and more importantly, secret. Nathanial's been here for a while. He knows the rules, and that's why he's trying to bait you. He knows that once you throw a punch at him, that's it. You're gone."

Clara's words make complete sense, and I start to feel the rage leaving my body now that I can see what Nathaniel is trying to do.

"See? I knew you were too scared to fight. You're exactly the kind of coward I imagined you'd be," Nathanial says.

"I'm not scared. I'm just not stupid enough to get kicked out of here. If you feel differently, feel free to throw the first punch," I say.

Nathanial laughs in a way that feels like he's just trying to stall because he can't think of anything else to say. I've met enough bullies in my time at a dozen different schools that I actually do feel pretty stupid for letting him get under my skin so easily.

I guess that since I've gotten superpowers, I've been out of practice as far as being bullied goes.

"Actually, I have a better idea," Nathanial says. "How about a little game of chicken?"

"Are you kidding me? We all have some kind of superpower courtesy of aliens, or gods, or who knows what, and you want to get into cars and drive at each other as fast as we can to see who's the bigger man? You realize how ridiculous that sounds, don't you?" I ask.

"Not cars. I guess you've forgotten all about that dragon The Controller made you fight already?"

"See, I knew you were secretly a fan. Why don't we just end this, and I'll go ahead and autograph whatever you'd like," I say sarcastically. This gets a pretty good-sized laugh from the crowd, so I decide to see if I can push it further. I can practically see Nathanial's face turning red. "Or do you want a selfie? We can do a selfie together if that's what you really want instead. Or hey, why am I being so stingy to a fan? I can do both."

Nathanial smirks, catching on to the idea that if I can't fight him here, the next best thing for me is humiliating him. He's not new to bullying either.

"Actually, I had something a little more fun in mind. Carter," he commands, and a nebbish-looking white boy a little younger than I am steps out from behind the crowd, "are you up for a little elevator work?"

TWELVE

"I don't need this, you know. I can fly."

I'm standing next to Carter and Nathanial on a very small platform made of solid iron. I know it's made of solid iron because I watched it being made. One of the other metas here can suck iron molecules from pretty much anything: the air, trees, water, other human beings, you name it. From there it's a simple matter for him to rearrange those molecules into just about anything he wants. Right now he can only handle very basic shapes, like this thin, rectangular platform we're all standing on, but he's working to improve.

In front of us is everyone from the group that was previously spending their night a mile underground. We're above ground now, though, right by the entrance to the cavern. I should say that while we're all above ground, I'm actually *more* above ground than they are. The group is quickly shrinking as the platform I'm standing on rises up into the air.

Carter is, of course, key to the platform's ability to levitate. I certainly don't possess any type of ability that allows me to cause anything to fly other than myself, and Nathanial doesn't either, as far as I know. From the brief explanation I got before I jumped on this flying platform of death, it seems that Carter is able to control air pressure and temperature. He's apparently become quite good at this, as he's able to create an air thermal right underneath the iron platform that's strong enough to push it, as well as the three of us standing on top of it, straight into the air. Carter is along for the ride since, as with most abilities, he's able to have more exact control over it the closer he is.

"So it's going to go like this," Nathanial says as we clear the tree line of the surrounding forest. We have to be at least two hundred feet in the air now. With the group below us out of harm's way, Carter really starts to open up the throttle on his powers. Nathanial has to raise his voice to compensate for the increasingly loud howl of the air current pushing the platform higher and higher into the night sky. "We both have our metabands powered off, and they're going to stay powered off. Once Carter brings us as high as he can, me and you are gonna jump."

"Okay, and then what? I don't think I'm really into the idea of a suicide pact," I say.

"Without your metabands activated, you're going to fall," Nathanial says.

"Right. I think I figured out that part already."

"From there, it's just simple straight-ahead chicken. First one to activate their metabands loses. Whoever comes closest to the ground without splatting, wins," he says to me.

"Wins what?" I ask.

"What do you mean, wins what? You just win."

"Okay, but like what do I win? Because right now I'm not seeing the upside of risking my life to impress a bunch of people I just met."

"If you want to chicken out and head back down to the ground, I'm sure Carter here would be happy to oblige. Is that really what you want to do, though? It seems like you're having enough trouble here as it is making friends. I can't imagine everyone seeing you as a coward would help much."

"I'm not a coward."

"Great, then this will be the perfect way to prove it."

I look down at the ground a thousand feet below me. Growing up, I always had an irrational fear of heights. I think part of it came from knowing how my mom and dad died. When I was little, sometimes I would wake up screaming in the middle of the night. The nightmare was always the same. Mom and Dad are in the building, but they're trying to get to the roof before The Battle starts. I'm running up the stairs after them, but they don't see me or hear me yelling.

Everyone is running up the stairwell, pushing and shoving

each other to try to get to the roof. Some are on their way up there to try to get a better glimpse of the battle. They're the ones who don't know that the foundation to the building has already started crumbling. The others, the ones who know what's coming, are trying to reach the roof before the building collapses. They're hoping, against all odds, that some salvation is waiting for them on the roof: a helicopter or maybe another meta saving people from their fate.

Once everyone reaches the roof, there's nothing there, though. That's when the building starts to tilt. Everyone is sliding and clawing, desperately trying not to go over the edge, including me. The last thing I see before I wake up every time is my mom and dad right as they go over.

I thought my metabands had effectively cured me of my fear of heights. After all, it would be kind of hard to fly if it was still an issue. There's something different about this situation, though. I don't know if it's that my metabands aren't activated or if it's just the small detail of standing on a platform that shouldn't even *exist* let alone be floating a thousand feet in the air, but I can start to feel sweat beading up on the back of my neck. That familiar feeling from my nightmare is creeping in, and suddenly, I just want all of this to be over and for both of my feet to be back on the ground.

"You still with us there, Omni?" Nathanial asks me.

"Yeah, I'm here. Let's just get this over with."

"Second thoughts?"

"No, I'm just getting bored up here," I say.

Neither of them believes me.

"Okay, so here's how it works. We both take our metabands off and place them here on the platform-"

"Wait, no one said anything about taking metabands off," I interrupt.

"Relax, it's just for a few seconds. Have to make sure neither of us secretly has ours booted up, right? The only way to make sure is to have us both start from the same place, with both of our bands placed on the platform here.

That way we can be sure there are no shenanigans," Nathanial explains.

I'm liking all of this less and less by the second.

"Fine," I say, slipping my metabands off of my wrists after powering them down. My fear of heights is only growing now that my brain realizes I'm back to being a frail human, the smushy kind that doesn't do well with a thousand-foot fall.

"Okay, now place them on the platform in front of your feet, just like mine," Nathanial says.

I involuntarily hesitate for an instant, the fear welling up inside of me, but I push past it in the hope that this will all be over soon and place my metabands down at my feet.

"Good. Stand up straight and get ready. On the count of three, we both grab our bands and jump. If you hesitate, Carter here will see it and you'll lose. As long as that doesn't happen, then it's simple: last one to activate their bands wins. Ready?"

I decide against replying verbally out of concern that my voice will betray me and crack, revealing to Nathanial just how scared I really am. Instead, I simply nod, trying to keep my poker face as stone-like as possible.

"One ... two ..."

Nathanial never says three, though. Right after the count of two, as I'm staring intently at my metabands, barely able to wait to get them back on, I'm pushed. I never even saw the push coming because I could barely see Nathanial out of the corner of my eye, but I hear him laughing just as I go over the edge.

The platform above me is rapidly shrinking into the moonlit sky. I've fallen from this height before, higher even, but never without my metabands, metabands that are still sitting up on that platform, which is growing farther away from me by the second.

I'm used to time feeling as though it has slowed down in situations like this. Part of that is the abilities that the metabands give me when they're on, but another part is just the regular old human brain experiencing sensory overload and slowing down to try to interpret and compute it all. Without the bands on, though, it doesn't feel like there's enough time for my life to flash before my eyes before I smack into the ground.

I close my eyes and brace for the inevitable impact, but it doesn't come. Instead, it's replaced by laughter. Carefully, I pull one of my tightly shut eyes open to look around. I'm no longer feeling the sensation of falling, but I don't feel like I'm back on the ground either. I certainly don't feel like I *hit* the ground. That, I think I'd notice.

Above me, the platform, Carter, and Nathanial are all gone. Only the empty night sky remains. Below me is another story, though. Stretched out all around me from adjacent trees is what looks like a gigantic spider web. The only difference, besides this one being human-sized, is that it is also glowing in a bright red hue, like a grid of laser beams in a spy movie.

The net I'm caught in is slowly lowering back toward the ground at the speed of a fast elevator and the laughter is turning into applause. Beneath me, the group is cheering.

It was fake, some kind of prank that I'm the butt of. I momentarily consider trying to pretend to laugh along, like I was in on it the whole time too, but my body won't let my brain override the emotions running through it.

Once I reach the ground, the net vanishes and the applause begins to die off. A few offer me a hand to help get me back on my feet, but I don't accept any of them. I'm mad, and whether it'll do any good or not, I want everyone here to know it. This seems to make everyone laugh even more.

"Aw, come on. Don't be like that. It's just a little fun. We do it to all the new guys," Nathanial says.

Adrenaline is still coursing its way through my veins, and I'm so mad that I can't even speak. All I want to do now is find my metabands and go home. Not back to my crappy, tiny dorm room that I have to share with some entitled jerk. No, right now I just desperately want to go back to Bay View City. It doesn't even need to be the apartment. I'd settle for the old house Derrick and I had. If anything, I think I'd prefer that.

"Fine, okay. Mission accomplished. You hazed me. I've been initiated. I get it. Now please just give me my metabands back," I say, breathing in through my mouth and out through my nose to try to bring my heart rate back down and get my anger under control.

I look around, trying to spot where my metabands are, but I don't see them anywhere. The group that assembled to watch me almost crap my pants has started to splinter off. Some look like they're going home, and others are heading back toward the hole, eager to continue their night off now that the fun of watching me be humiliated is over.

"Seriously, guys, I need my metabands back," I say. There's barely any response. A few turn their heads toward me and offer a shrug of their shoulders, suggesting that they don't know where they are either.

I'm tired, and I've had enough tonight. Up ahead I can see Nathanial trailing behind the group, busy recounting what just happened to a small group of other guys who are laughing along with him. I call out his name. I can't tell if he doesn't hear me or is purposefully ignoring me, but in either case, he doesn't turn back.

I jog up to catch up with them, still calling out his name. I know that I'm close enough for him to hear me, but there's still no response. My blood is nearly boiling as I jog a few steps ahead of him and plant my two feet, standing directly in his path. There's no way he can ignore me anymore.

"Give them back," I say as calmly as possible.

"Give what back?" he asks in return, which gets more giggles from the idiots hanging around.

"Enough. Just give them back so I can go home," I say.

Behind me I can hear whispers and shuffling feet. The others have started heading back in our direction now that there's a chance of more drama.

"Tell you what. Why don't you just go home, and I'll take a look around for them first thing in the morning," Nathanial says.

"Now," I say. I can feel my face becoming flush red.

"Ohh, I didn't know you were a tough guy. That changes everything then, doesn't it? It's too bad you didn't have a pair like this back when you let half your city get destroyed."

THIRTEEN

They say that hindsight is 20/20. I've always taken that to mean that looking back at a situation and seeing things clearly is easy, but seeing things for what they are in the moment? That's what we have trouble with. While I know *intellectually* that that's true, in hindsight, I think I still would have punched Nathanial in the face. I mean, deep down, I knew in that moment it was a bad idea. I don't regret it, but I maybe wish I hadn't punched him *quite* so hard.

Most of the time nowadays I rarely regret hitting someone harder than I should have, but that's because nowadays, when I'm hitting someone, it's because they're a "bad guy," and I'm a "good guy." Before I got these metabands, the number of physical altercations I'd been in was very, very low. Single digits for sure. And I never, ever started them. Back in those days, I was a near master at avoiding fights. When you've moved around as much as I have as a kid, you either have to get good at fighting or *really* good at avoiding fights. Luckily for Derrick's health insurance, I picked the latter ninety-nine times out of a hundred.

The main problem with deciding to be the one who started a fight, for once, is that I was the guy *not* wearing metabands. And that's why I'm sitting here with approximately half of the bones in my hand broken, fractured, or just plain shattered.

I'll probably be blamed by the others for being the one who brought faculty attention to the cavern, but the truth is that there were already faculty members on their way out to the site before the punch even happened. Someone else on campus had posted on social media about seeing Nathanial, Carter, and myself up in the air. A team was dispatched into the woods within seconds to find out what was going on.

They were probably relieved that it was just students out there in the woods at first. I'm sure their worst fear was that someone else had stumbled on the cavern by accident, which could have led to others becoming curious about what else was hidden on campus. If they were relieved, that relief was short-lived and quickly replaced by anger.

All of this has led to me sitting here, back underground, waiting for X-rays of my hand. You might think it's a colossal waste of time and energy to take X-rays of my hand when putting my metabands back on would fix all the crushed bones in a second or two. Personally, I think it's a giant waste of time and energy. Michelle disagreed, though.

Nathanial gave up my metabands pretty quickly after the faculty threatened him with expulsion if he didn't, but the metabands were handed over to them, not me. It's not like you could really "hand" something to me in this condition anyway. Any section of my right hand that isn't broken is too purple and bruised to move. Michelle decided that this would be a good time to teach me a lesson.

So that leads us to the present, where I'm sitting on a metal hospital gurney deep within the underground facility, clutching my bandaged and broken right hand and wanting even more desperately than before to just go home.

"Hi there. You must be ... Connor?"

The question comes from an older man as he enters the doorway. He's balding, with salt and pepper gray hair, and a tightly manicured matching beard. He's wearing a white lab coat and flipping through pages on a tablet that he's looking at over the top of a pair of circular wire-frame glasses.

"Yeah, that's me."

"It's a pleasure to meet you. Although I will say that I had hoped it would be under slightly more accommodating circumstances."

"You don't like meeting people for the first time when they've broken part of their own body doing something stupid?" I ask.

"No, that part I don't mind. I've met plenty of people that way over the years. The part that I mind is getting dragged out of bed in the middle of the night to do it."

"Fair enough."

"I'd shake your hand, but, well, you know. In any case, I'm the physician."

"I kinda figured that part out, with the lab coat and all."

He pauses to look down at how he's dressed.

"No, no, that's not what I meant. Well, that is what I meant, but I meant you can call me The Physician."

"Okay. You don't have another name you like to be called by?"

"Well my real name is Doctor Phillips, but what's the point of agreeing to be the on-call physician for metahumans if you can't have a little fun?"

"So ... you want me to call you The Physician? Like, pretend it's your meta name or whatever?"

He glances back up from his tablet and smiles, which I take to be a confirmation.

"Okay, so, The Physician ..." I say.

"Yes?" he replies, beaming at the fact that I'm calling him by the name he's asked me to use.

"When can I get my metabands back so I can fix this hand up? Michelle did a great job bandaging it before she left, and I don't mean to make light of her work, but I just really think I could do a much better job once I have my bands back."

"Of that I have no doubt," he says, still not looking up from his tablet.

There's a long silence as I wait for him to continue, but instead he just keeps leafing through the pages on his screen while muttering to himself.

"It's just that the pain medication Michelle gave me isn't really doing the trick, you know?" I say, trying to push the subject.

"Ah, yes. Of course, sorry," he finally says.

He places the tablet on a nearby metal table, like the kind you'd expect to see a scalpel and other surgical tools resting on. With the tablet secure, he begins riffling through the pockets of his lab coat. Finally, he pulls out my metabands from deep within and hands them over to me.

I take the bands with my one good hand and place one in the crook of my left arm so I can hold it steady while I gently guide my bandaged right hand through it. The other is slightly easier to put on by holding it in my lap as I guide my left hand into the opening. With both bands in place, they instantly adjust and tighten around my wrists. The feeling of relief comes quickly, and I feel better already. Inside my right hand, I can hear tiny snaps and pops as the muscles move out of the way for the bones to snap back into place.

"Thank you, doctor," I say.

"Umm," he says, pointing to his name badge, which I hadn't noticed before now. It clearly says "The Physician" right on it.

"Sorry. Thank you, The Physician," I say, which makes him smile again.

"Connor," he begins, picking the tablet back up off the nearby table to reference, "I assume you know that we didn't withhold your metabands purely for the sake of punishment."

"I assumed you didn't do it just to punish me," I say as I start unwrapping the bandages off of my right hand now that I won't be needing them anymore.

"Well, no, punishment was definitely part of the reason we withheld them. It just wasn't the only reason," he says. He can see the look of surprise in my eyes and continues. "I had nothing to do with that decision of course. That, you will have to take up with Michelle. However, I was called since we rarely get the chance to inspect cases like these."

"Cases like what?"

"Cases where the owner of a pair of metabands has somewhat seriously injured themselves and doesn't have immediate access to their personal pair of metabands. We wanted to take a closer look at your hand and the healing process, to see what, if any, residual effect the metabands have on your physiology after they've been deactivated and removed from your person."

"And what did you find?"

"Nothing conclusive at this point, but some very interesting data to pour over in the coming weeks."

"Well, I'm glad I could be of help to someone tonight then. I don't mean to be rude, but am I able to go back to my room now? I'm going to go ahead and guess that you don't give out sick notes, and I've got a 7:30 a.m. math class that I was dreading getting up for even before my unexpectedly adventurous night," I say.

"Yes, yes, of course. We have all the samples we wanted so you're free to go."

"Thanks, doct— I mean, Physician," I say as I hop off the gurney and head toward the door.

"Actually," The Physician announces, "there was one thing that I wanted to ask you about, if you have the time."

"Sure," I reply reluctantly as I halt my march toward the door to turn and give The Physician my attention.

"Your metabands. While they were in my possession, I had them examined and run through a full spectroanalysis as well. There are some elements to them that are quite different from previous sets I've seen in my time as a researcher. I'm not quite sure what the differences mean at this point, or if they're of any importance or not, but there was one element to them that I am positively sure I've never seen before: the tiny cracks that are running throughout both."

"Yeah, I know the ones you're talking about," I reply.

"My apologies if you've already answered these questions for Michelle. I haven't had a chance to look through your entire file yet. Usually I'm brought in for a full medical exam for all incoming students, but your arrival was a little later than usual, and I was unavailable at the time. Can you tell me, were the cracks present when you first found the metabands, or have they only become visible since the metabands came into your possession?" he asks.

"No, they weren't there when I got them. It happened recently. During the fight over Silver Island."

"Hmm, I see. Is it safe to assume that this was the work of Iris then?" he asks.

"No, it was one of the Alphas, before Iris came after me."

"That's not very reassuring news to hear."

"Iris isn't bad, you know," I say.

"You mean the same Iris who freed a prison full of metahumans and left you for dead?" he asks.

"I know how it looks, but there was something ... different about her that day. I'm not sure what it was, but that wasn't her."

"You knew her well then?"

"Well, no. Not exactly."

"So your judgment that she was acting out of character is based on...?"

"It's hard to explain, but I could just sense it. There was something wrong."

"Well there are cases of metahumans gaining additional senses in some instances. Since these senses were not present at birth, it can take some time for the subject to adjust to them and learn how to interpret them. In your case, I would be careful to trust those types of instincts before you fully understand them."

I nod in agreement, mostly because it's so late and I'm too tired to argue.

"Have you noticed any changes in your abilities since these cracks first appeared on your metabands?" The Physician asks me.

"I have. There are some things that I used to be able to do that I can't anymore."

"Such as?"

"Teleportation."

"Really? That is fascinating. Absolutely fascinating. I have a lot more questions for you, but for right now, I believe it's time to call it a night, for the sake of both of our sanity. But I'll be seeing you tomorrow afternoon, and we can resume this conversation with the aid of a few scientific instruments."

"As long as I get to go to bed, I'll probably agree to just about anything," I say.

Fourteen

Last night I was worried that I was so tired the alarm might not wake me up on time this morning. It turns out there wasn't anything to worry about since my new roommate, Tyler, wakes me up with something way harder to ignore than an alarm clock: the stench of half a can of body spray that he seems to think is a good alternative to taking a shower. Pretty soon I'm up and out of bed, getting ready for my day as quickly as I can just so I can get out of this room and get some fresh air.

Outside, the weather feels especially crisp. Fall is in full swing and winter seems like it's not far behind. Last winter was especially mild in this part of the country, and I'm hoping for more of the same this year if I'm going to be spending half my day trudging across this sprawling campus. It sucks enough as it is already. I don't want to find out how much more it can suck when there's snow.

Math is the first class of the day, and it's kind of nice to use that part of my brain for a little bit. As far as I know, no one in this class is a metahuman, so I'm able to just be a normal student for a little while without having to deal with stares from people who know what happened last night. I'll have to deal with the consequences of all of that later today, but the further it can be pushed off into the future, the better. That's pretty much my philosophy on most things in life nowadays. I'm sure that will work out well for me and not backfire horrifically in the future. Yup.

Lunch is a solitary affair today too. I head toward the food court and look for whatever place has the shortest line. The line for Six Guys Burgers is, predictably, practically out the door. Jalapeno Burritos isn't much better either. Looks like I'm going to have to go with the old standby: pizza.

The generic, no-name pizza stand is barren of anyone, except the two employees behind the counter, which doesn't speak very highly of their food, but even bad pizza is still pizza, so I decide to give it a shot. As I approach, the employees continue their conversation, completely oblivious of me standing there. I'm starting to understand why nobody comes here.

"I'm serious, dude," says the employee stuck behind racks meant for holding pizzas after they come out of the oven.

"No way, didn't happen," says the long-haired employee tasked with manning the cash register. The guy who is completely ignoring me.

"I'm telling you, bro. I saw it with my own two eyes. Right out over the woods behind campus," the other says.

Uh oh.

"There aren't any metahumans in this area, dude. If there were, I would have seen them. Someone would have seen them. Skyville is a meta ghost town, no matter how badly you wish it weren't. Just admit that you're making it all up. Why would you have even been hanging out in the woods last night anyway, man?"

"I was just, uh, going for a walk, you know," he says.

"And did you happen to 'partake' in anything during your walk?"

"Are you guys open for lunch or should I just go wait in line at one of the other stands?" Clara asks. These guys might not have noticed me standing here, but I can't really blame them, considering I didn't notice Clara standing two feet away from me for who knows how long.

"Sorry about that. What can I get you two?" the cashier finally asks me.

* * *

I think this might be a new record. If it's not a new record, then it's certainly somewhere in the top three for sure, but I'm almost certain that this is by far the shortest amount of time I've had to eat lunch alone at a new school. Initially, I'm still pretty pissed off about what happened last night and whether Clara had a hand in it, but this seems like an olive branch, and I'm not really in the position of turning down new friends right now.

"So, you like pizza, huh?" Clara asks to break the silence after we find an empty table to sit at.

"I like pizza and hate lines, so that place seemed like the best move, today at least," I reply.

"The pizza tastes like cardboard that someone put spaghetti sauce and string cheese on, but there's never a line. I assume you've got a pretty packed schedule like the rest of us, so don't be surprised if you bump into others from our little after-school activity there."

"I'll keep that in mind."

"Listen, I'm sorry about last night," she says after an awkward silence.

"It's okay. It's not your fault."

"No, but I didn't do anything to stop it either. We started doing little initiation pranks a while back, but we haven't had any new recruits in a while, and I guess it just escalated quickly when someone new finally came in. Some people have had a little too much time to figure out new and humiliating ways to welcome newbies."

"So you don't roll out the red carpet like that for everyone?" I joke.

"Nope, only the ones everyone feels threatened by apparently."

"People feel threatened by me?" I ask, completely confused.

"Yeah. Not in the physical sense or anything. You seem like a nice enough guy and the faculty does a pretty good job of running background on everyone before they get here, so no one's *afraid* of you, at least not in that sense. They just think your abilities make them look weak in comparison. A lot of the people here can do one or two things well, but you've got the full smorgasbord of powers. Everyone who gets a taste of what it's like being one of us wants that."

"Well, that may have been the case before, but I might

have to permanently scratch a few of those powers off the back of my trading card soon."

"What do you mean?"

"Ever since Silver Island, there've been things that I used to be able to do that I can't anymore. I'm not sure if it's permanent or not. I actually have to do some tests today to hopefully find out more about what happened."

"And what happened?"

"It was the Alphas. One of them, Beta, hit me and Iris full on with a blast of energy. It caused my"—I look around quickly to make sure that no one is eavesdropping and decide to be a little ambiguous just in case—"*bracelets* to crack."

"Your metabands *cracked?*" Clara asks at a volume much higher than the one I'm currently using to speak to her.

"Yeah."

"I wouldn't tell anyone about that if I were you," she says, oblivious to her yelling.

"I kinda figured that, which was why I was whispering."

"Oh, right. Sorry."

"Anyway, since that happened, there are things that I used to be able to do that I can't anymore. I'm not sure if it can be fixed or not."

"That's gotta suck."

"It does, and I'm still getting used to it. But that day, honestly, I just felt lucky to get out of there with my life. Half-working metabands are just a bonus."

"Wow, yeah. I can imagine anything, or anyone, strong enough to crack those things is pretty dangerous. I'd heard rumors that they were able to destroy metabands, but I've never met someone who actually saw it close up," she says.

"Lucky me. So, enough about my abilities, or current lack-there-of. What's your story?"

"What do you mean 'what's my story?'"

"What's your story? Where are you from? How'd you get your ... you know."

"I'm from around here, actually. I was already going to

school here when I got my bands. Found them stuck up in a tree."

"Next to a cat?"

"No, not next to a cat. I was walking home one day, and I don't know why, but I had this sudden urge to look up, and there they were, dangling from a pair of branches about twenty feet in the air. I don't know how long they were up there before I found them, but I did. Before I knew it, they were changing my class schedule here and telling me about hidden entrances and stuff."

"That kinda stinks that they changed your schedule. I used to move around a lot before. I know how it can be to have your routine uprooted like that."

"It wasn't so bad. Most of the classes I was in I hated anyway, and I never really made that many friends here in the first place. The program feels like a much better fit for me."

"It's nice to hear that at least someone is getting something out of it."

"You'll come around. You haven't even been here for a week yet," she says to me, knowing that I don't believe it.

"So I know what you can do, but I still don't completely understand your brother's abilities."

"What don't you understand? I heard you already got a pretty close-up look at them."

"Yeah, but that doesn't mean it makes any sense to me," I say.

"Basically, he can control water."

"I figured that much out, but I still don't really understand it. So like he can control the temperature of it? Freezing and stuff?"

"No. That's a pretty common misconception. A lot of people think those guys are Elementals, but they're not. Not in my opinion, for whatever that's worth at least."

"So what can he do with water then?"

"It's hard to describe. Maybe the most accurate way to put

it is that he can control its movement, the way it flows and moves. He can also communicate through it, they think, but they're still learning more about that."

"What, you mean like he can talk to fish?"

"It only works one way. They can talk to him. Kinda."

"What do you mean? What kind of things does a fish have to say?"

"Not much, really. They're pretty much as stupid as you'd imagine them."

I try to contain my laughter, but it's no use.

"It's not funny, you know. It sucks. The first time he found out he had it was at one of those Chinese food restaurants with a fish tank. An hour of eating with our family while trying to ignore two-dozen fish yelling, "More fish flakes, more fish flakes!"

Now I'm not even trying to hide my laughter. Clara finally smiles too.

"In retrospect, it was kinda funny, I guess. That doesn't mean he's going to start eating fish again any time soon."

"Fair enough. No one likes their food talking back to them," I say. "So do you know anything about what they have in store for me today? The Physician just said that they'll be running more tests on me. He didn't really elaborate."

"That's fairly standard for noobs around here. They'll throw a whole bunch of tasks and tests at you, see which ones you can do, which ones you can't, how well you do them, etc. Then they'll rank you on the Matheson scale.

"Matheson scale?"

"It's what they use to rank how powerful you are based on a bunch of different criteria. Then they use that rank to decide what you can use more training on. Basically they're looking for any latent abilities you may have that they can further hone."

"But why go through all of this trouble?"

"Well, they say it's so they can figure out how we can help

when there's a need, but they'll also admit that a lot of it has to do with learning more about how the metabands work in the first place and maybe getting closer to figuring out where they came from."

"And have they gotten any closer?"

"I wouldn't hold my breath."

* * *

The rest of the school day is pretty standard. And by pretty standard, I mean me mostly being confused as the teachers go over a bunch of concepts and material that I missed during the time my school was leveled by two metas. For the most part, the teachers are understanding and eager to offer after-school tutoring. I thank each of them for their offers but politely decline, citing others subjects that I'm even further behind in and that I need to attend tutoring for after school. They all understand and accept the lies for excuses, but what they won't accept is me permanently trailing behind everyone else. That means there won't be a whole lot of free time for me in the upcoming weeks.

The final bell rings at 2:30 p.m. Most of the campus is smiling and in a great mood. Their day is over, after all, and they have the rest of the afternoon to themselves.

It's a different story for me and the handful of others that are making their way toward the far end of campus, heading to a fictional after-school activity, mindful that there's no one acting overly curious, seeing if they can tag along.

When I make my way to the classroom that Michelle showed me, room 143, the door is already locked. A locked door means that the elevator is currently in use. Standard protocol for this is to immediately walk away and avoid bringing any attention to it. Standard protocol also says that I'll either have to wait the four or five minutes it'll take for the elevator to come back up or make my way to the men's room and use one of the elevator stalls. It's a little more than slightly humiliating to have to travel via toilet after being used to flying wherever I wanted to go before.

FIFTEEN

Upon reaching the facility via toilet elevator, I quickly realize that I actually don't have any idea where I'm going. This place is massive, and Michelle didn't give me any instructions yesterday other than to just come here after classes were over.

Today is much busier than yesterday. The hall is full of metahumans finding their way to the various rooms where they'll train, learn, or be tested. Some are powered up already and in their full uniforms. The various colors, suit types, cowls, helmets, and domino masks make this place look like the weirdest Halloween party you've ever been to.

No one seems to notice me standing in the middle of the hallway, looking completely lost. I guess some things don't change. An older man, or at least too old to be a student, locks eyes with me and heads my way.

"Connor?" he asks.

"That's me."

"I'm John Foresight. Michelle asked me to come find you. I'm one of the instructors here, and I'll be walking you through your tests this afternoon."

"Sounds good."

I wait for him to say something else, like which way we should head or which room to go to, but he doesn't speak. Instead, he just stands there, staring at me, seemingly waiting for me to say something.

"You don't recognize me?" he asks finally.

"Um, I don't think so. Did I meet you yesterday when Michelle was showing me around? Sorry, I'm not great with faces."

"No, no, no. I suppose you might not recognize me out of uniform. I get that. The Blue Lightning costume *was* pretty iconic."

I just continue staring at him since I have absolutely no idea what he's talking about.

"Really? How old are you?" he asks.

"Sixteen."

"Hmm, that doesn't make sense. You're certainly old enough to remember."

"Oh, wait a minute. Were you the guy that got stuck up on the roof of the Imperial State Building when all the metabands stopped working during the first wave?"

The name Blue Lightning finally rings a bell with me.

"I wasn't stuck-"

"Yeah, I remember now! You were completely naked because you didn't have anything on underneath your suit, and once your metabands powered down, the suit disappeared and you were stuck."

"All right, first off, there are a lot of factual inaccuracies to the story that got passed around. I wasn't naked. I had my underwear on at the time. And I'd never used my metabands without clothing underneath before, contrary to what all the tabloids said. That was the first time, and I just happened to be the victim of some very bad timing.

"And second, I wasn't stuck. The door on the roof was unlocked, and I was able to get back to the ground level on my own. I just had to walk the 109 flights."

"In your underwear?"

"That part's not important. Listen, I'm here to run you through your tests today. We can discuss my exploits from my time as a metahuman later."

John turns to begin walking, waving for me to follow. We walk past a series of doors with mysterious labels on them: "Water Tank," "Vacuum," "Speed Track."

"Don't worry. You'll get the chance to get a closer look at all of those soon, Connor," he says, noticing that I'm not following as closely behind as he would like. "Here we are. After you."

John opens a door that is simply labeled "Strength" and steps aside to allow me to enter first. The first thing I'm struck by is just how quiet this room is. The instant the door clicks closed, it feels like someone hit the mute button on reality. All of the chatter and ambient noise from the hallway full of students are instantly silenced.

"It's a little strange at first, but you'll get used to it. The silence that is. Once you see a few of the other chambers, you'll understand why all of these rooms need to be soundproofed so extensively."

I look around the room for a place to put down my backpack and find a metal stool near the far wall. The room itself is small and mostly empty. The walls are made of the same brushed aluminum found lining the hallways outside. They're without any type of markings, the lone exception being what looks like a touch screen embedded into one of the walls.

In the center of the room are two handlebars. One is in the middle of the floor, attached to a small base. The other is hanging from a thin cord attached to the ceiling.

"So, first things first. This is the strength testing room."

"Michelle showed me a strength training room yesterday, but it didn't look anything like this."

"That's because it's not a strength training room. It's a strength *testing* room, Connor. There's a very big difference there."

I'm the only one in the room with him, but John is speaking like he's delivering the State of the Union address. It's like the room is full of thousands of people hanging on his every word, but I can't see them.

"Yeah, they didn't have anything like this back when I was out there slugging it out. Wish they had, to be honest. It would have been nice, you know, just to know exactly *how* strong I was. Sure, people may say I was one of the strongest metas that there has ever been, but you're always gonna get a couple of knucklehead naysayers who want to see the empirical proof."

John is rolling up his sleeves, revealing less than impressive forearms, and I'm not quite sure what he's doing.

"These machines here were built and designed, with some input from yours truly, to accurately gauge metahuman strength. Since we aren't entirely sure where the upper limit of that strength may be, a new way of measuring it had to be designed. You didn't think we just used plain old weights did you?"

"Actually, I never really-"

"Of course we didn't. They'd be too big! Way too big. And heavy, naturally. So we designed these babies. Bored holes way into the earth, even farther down than we are now. They rely on Earth's natural gravitational field and electromagnetism to provide resistance."

"So like a big magnet?" I ask.

This question seems to puzzle John, despite the fact that I'm pretty sure this was exactly what he was just talking about. Instead of answering my question, he plants his feet on either side of the floor-mounted handle, and I start to see where this is going.

"Do me a favor, Connor? Head over to that wall there and ratchet this bad boy up, will you?" He asks in a way that's not really asking while rubbing his hands together and stretching from side to side in preparation.

I walk over to the wall where the touchscreen is embedded and tap the screen to wake it up. A bunch of abbreviations and numbers appear. Dozens of them. This thing is obviously a lot more complicated than John has let on. I turn to ask him what I should press next.

John is hunched over the handlebar, both hands firmly gripped. At first I think he's just getting into position to lift it, but then I notice his face. Its color is changing shades from beet red to a deep, dark purple. His lips are pursed and his eyes are squinting almost shut. He's trying to lift the handlebar with literally all of his might. I'm not sure what to do or say, but a second later, it doesn't matter.

"Argh!" John yells as he exhales a huge breath. He lets go of the handlebar but remains doubled over, breathing in and out in ragged gasps as the natural color begins slowly filling his face back in.

"Ha! Well, that's what I get for thinking I'd still be able to lift the kinda weight I could back when I was a metahuman. Still, had to give it a try. I got it off the base there a little bit, but she just didn't want to give me anymore," he says to me.

He didn't move the handle off the base. It's lying exactly where it was when we first entered the room. "So, how much weight was on there?" he asks, gesturing toward the touchscreen.

"Oh, I'm not sure. I couldn't really figure out how to use it," I tell him.

"The whole thing's in metric because of the German guys who built it. Tap that button on the right side of the screen and it'll let you know how much weight was on there. Just give me the metric units, and I'll do the math for you."

I do as he instructs and then read out the numbers to him.

"Umm, it looks like it was set to fifty kilograms."

"That's impossible. You're probably looking at it wrong. You've probably still got it set to pounds."

"But pounds are even less than kilograms, right?"

"Never mind, it doesn't matter," John says in an attempt to save face that's about thirty seconds and fifty kilograms too late. "We're not here for you to watch me lift weights ..."

"Right, I mean ... you didn't really lift it."

"It moved a little bit. Besides, it's set for metahumans, so, you know, there's probably something like that to it. I'm not really one hundred percent sure how these things work."

"Didn't you say you helped design this?"

"Design it, yes. But design is different from engineering it. You can explain to someone how you want something to work until you're blue in the face—"

"—or purple."

"Right, or purple," he says, not getting the joke. "But at the end of the day, they're going to build it the way they want to build it, and there's not a whole hell of a lot you can do about it. In any case, come on over here. Let's get you saddled up."

John rotates his arm around his shoulder socket while massaging it with the other hand as he crosses the room and exchanges places with me.

"Okay, first we're going to need to get some baseline readings without your metabands activated," he says.

I bend over and pick up the handle, not expecting it to be as light as it is. While I was only intending on getting ready, I've actually pulled the weight up without really trying.

"No, you have to do it without your metabands active first," John says.

"They aren't."

He looks puzzled for a minute, as though he can't understand how I could lift more weight than he could, despite the fact that John looks like he hasn't lifted much more than a sandwich in the past ten years.

"All right, well, put the weight down then. I must have calibrated it when I pulled it just now and it reset itself for non-metahumans," he says, still trying to make ridiculous excuses for himself. "It doesn't matter. Let's see what we've got here now."

He taps on the screen while simultaneously pulling a pair of bifocals out of the front pocket of his salmon-colored polo shirt. With his glasses in place, he squints in front of the screen, trying to read it. Finally he seems to have found what he was looking for and begins tapping at the display, pushing up virtual levers and twisting virtual dials. After a few seconds of this, he pulls his hand back to look everything over and seems to be pleased with where it's all set.

"All right. We're all ready then. Do your thing," he says.

I'm not sure exactly what he means, but I assume he means to pull the handle again. I begin to lean over and place my hands on the holds.

"No, no, no. Do your thing first."

He sees that I'm still confused and elaborates.

"Activate your bands. The metabands. Turn on your metabands."

"Oh," I say, slightly embarrassed that I didn't understand.

With a thought, my metabands appear on my wrists, and I quickly strike them together for activation and then lean over again to grab the handles.

"Wait," John says, stopping me a second time. "That's it?"

I'm not quite sure what he means. I haven't even tried to lift the handlebar yet.

"That's all you do? Connor, Connor, Connor," he says, abandoning his post at the touchscreen and crossing back over toward me. "These," he begins, one hand on my shoulder, the other grabbing my right arm by the metaband, "are not toys. Nor are they just a simple tool.

"These, Connor Connelly, are the most amazing technological achievement that man has ever seen. These are what separates us from the rest of humanity," he says, strongly implying that he still considers himself a metahuman. "When you turn these on, it's not like turning on a toaster. It's like turning on life itself. It's like turning on millions of years of human achievement and understanding. It's like turning on the culmination of everything the human race stands for. You don't just click them together like you're unlocking the door to your car across a parking lot. You turn them on with some style, some panache. You've got to show the world just how amazing all of it really is."

"But isn't one of the first rules that you shouldn't let anyone else know you've got them when you're not disguised?"

"Yeah, yeah, of course. But that doesn't mean you should forgo any theatrics when you turn them on, even if it is just for an audience of one."

"What do you mean, theatrics?"

"Showmanship. Okay, let me see if I can explain it in simpler terms. What do you usually shout out when you activate your metabands? Pretend this isn't just training and you're in a real pickle. What do you yell out?"

"I'm not really sure I follow."

"Geez, you're really going to make me work for this, huh kid? Okay, so when I had my metabands, whenever I activated them, I would accompany the activation with the phrase—" He clears his throat before shouting in an extremely loud voice, "'All good and evil across the lands, beware the power of my metabands!'"

John looks at me with a smug smile as the words he's just screamed continue to echo throughout the room. I am at a complete loss for words.

"So you would yell that when you turned on your metabands?"

"Every time."

"But ... why?"

"Forget it, Connor. If I'm going to have to explain everything to you, we're never going to get through all of these tests today, and we're already behind as it is."

While this doesn't answer my question, I'm happy to drop the subject if it means hurrying this up past its current glacial pace. John taps a few buttons on the touchscreen and then turns back to me once he's ready.

"All right, Connor. I'm going to start you off at five thousand pounds. That might be a little overly ambitious, but we can always back it off. Whenever you're ready, just go ahead and give that-"

John stops talking because I've already lifted the handle up to my chest.

"Hmm, all right then. Looks like you're a little bit stronger than I thought. Go ahead and lower it back down there and let's try a little bit more weight."

I do as he says and wait while he readjusts the machine. On his mark, I bend over and pick up the handlebar again.

"Amazing. That's decuple the amount of weight," he says, more to himself than to me.

"Decuple?" I ask.

"Ten times. You're going to have to start picking up on this scientific lingo, Connor. I can't explain everything, you know."

I place the handlebar back on the floor and wait while he, again, adjusts the parameters on the screen.

"Okay, let's see what you've got," John says, motioning for me to try picking up the handlebar again.

I wipe my hands on my jeans to remove the sweat from my palms and lean over the bar. Wrapping my fingers around the handlebar, I can already feel that it is much more firmly seated in place than during my prior two attempts. I try pulling it upward just using the strength in my arms, but it won't budge.

"Ah, there it is. You had me worried for a second that there was something wrong with the equipment. I'll go ahead and readjust it back down a bit."

"No," I say as he turns to the display. "Just give me a second. My stance wasn't right."

Fully aware that now I've got to at least pull this stupid handlebar off the floor if I don't want to look like an ass, I readjust my feet and make my stance a little wider. I squat down, remembering that thing people always say about lifting with your legs and not your back. Or is it back and not your legs? I'm not completely sure, but I'm going to use everything I've got this time.

At first it feels like the handlebar just isn't going to budge. I start to feel bad for laughing to myself about John's attempt now that I'm sure my face is turning ten different shades of purple too. But then, I feel a slight give. The handlebar is no longer completely resting on the floor, and I can feel that I'm supporting the full weight. I dig down deep, hoping that if I pop my arm out of my shoulder the metabands will take care of fixing it later. I don't think I'd want John popping it back in.

Unleashing a weird grunting noise that I didn't know I had in me, I slowly pull the handlebar further, past my ankles, then my knees. By the time it's up to my waist, it starts to feel easier. Maybe it's just that the worst part is over, or maybe my metabands are just realizing I need a little more juice and helping to compensate.

Finally, almost ten full seconds later, I've pulled the handlebar all the way up to my chest. I look over to John for the first time and his jaw is practically on the ground. I can feel my arms trembling and the muscles beginning to burn.

"Can I drop it?" I ask through clenched teeth.

There's no response from John, who is still just staring at me.

"Can I drop it?" I ask, a little more urgently this time.

John snaps out of it long enough to give a nod, and I immediately release the handlebar. It snaps back into place on the ground instantly. The metallic clang of the bar hitting the floor with that kind of momentum rings throughout the training room. I'm bent over with my hands on my knees, wheezing to catch my breath.

"How much was that?" I ask through gasps.

John looks back at the screen, double-checking the weight to make sure before he tells me.

"That was centuple the original weight," he says.

"Centuple? What is that, twenty times?"

"No, it's a hundred times. You just lifted 500,000 pounds. That's almost what a 747 weighs."

"Great. That's good to know in case I ever need to pick one up."

* * *

The rest of the day follows more or less the same pattern. John sets up a test that he doesn't think I can do, and I blow it out of the water. We attempt to test my running speed on a specially built treadmill housed in a separate room, but it maxes out before I'm able to hit what I think is even close to my maximum speed. That means moving over to another room meant more for testing agility than speed.

This room, labeled "Endurance 2," contains a track over

ten miles in diameter. It's more of a circular tunnel than anything else. It makes me think of what a subway line would look like if they forgot to put down the tracks. Orange LED lights line the walls every hundred feet or so, and the walls themselves are baffled and built to withstand multiple sonic booms.

John waits in an alcove near the entrance and watches as I run. I have to enable my suit for this test, unless I want my pants to catch on fire from friction. There's a reason why a lot of metahumans don't wear corduroy.

Later he shows me the tape from my trials. In the beginning, I look like a blip that appears in front of the entrance every few seconds, but after I break through the sound barrier, the occasional blip turns into a streak, and then that streak turns into a solid wall of red.

* * *

The final test of the day involves flying, or more specifically, speed and agility while flying. They already know I can fly, obviously, but not necessarily how well. I've always assumed that every metahuman who could fly more or less did it the same way, but apparently that's not the case. While I just have to imagine myself moving through the air to do it, others rely on different methods. Some are able to "launch" themselves into the air, traveling great distances but ultimately succumbing to gravity sooner or later. Others can fly, but not at any kind of speed. This effectively makes them human blimps and not particularly effective crime fighters.

The test takes place in a gigantic warehouse-sized room. The ceiling must be at least twenty stories high and the room could easily fit a dozen football fields or more. It's not until I enter the room and look around at just how big it is that I realize it's been a while since I've really flown. Flying around Bay View City was a big no-no after Silver Island, and the same goes for above ground here on campus. All of a sudden I'm excited about being able to stretch my wings again. My figurative wings, that is. I don't have real ones. That would be weird, even weirder than being able to fly.

"Last test of the day, Connor. How are you feeling?" John asks me as he taps at his tablet.

I assume he's entering notes or results from the other tests today, but he could just as easily be playing a game for all I know. He seems pretty intent on not letting me peek at what he's doing, and judging from what I've learned after spending a day with him, I'd be surprised if he wasn't playing a game on there.

"I feel great. It's nice to finally get to exercise some of my abilities. I was starting to worry that I'd forgotten how to use some of them," I answer.

"They're like riding a bike, Connor. You never really forget. To this day I remember the feeling of flight. The wind in my hair. The earth beneath me. That feeling of complete and total freedom."

"You could fly when you were a metahuman? I didn't know that."

"When I was a metahuman? No. I'm talking about my Cessna. Yeah, I used to have one of my own back in my heyday. That was before the sponsorship money dried up and I had to sell it to get the creditors off my back. You'd think the bank would jump at the chance to have a metahuman as their official spokesman in exchange for forgiving a few late loan payments, but apparently not.

"Anyway, this is a test that will combine a few of your skills so we can accurately judge not only your individual abilities, but also how well you're able to integrate them with each other. It's not like walking and chewing gum at the same time, you know. Some abilities can be very difficult to use simultaneously.

"To start with, let's have you hover up there into the middle of the room, and I'll explain how this is all going to work."

I do as he says and lift myself effortlessly into the air, gliding to what looks to be about the center of the room before coming to a stop. When I turn back, I see that John has climbed a ladder along the side of one of the room's walls. At the top of the ladder is what looks almost like a tiny flight control tower. John finds a seat inside the small window-lined perch and moves a microphone into position in front of his mouth.

"All right, Connor," he says, his voice amplified through the microphone to fill the room.

"I have enhanced hearing, you know. You don't have to use the mic," I tell him, having to shout since I don't have a microphone myself.

"The test regulations require that the proctor uses a microphone, so that is what I will do, thank you," John says into the microphone, causing a massive amount of feedback that makes both him and me wince. "Okay, we'll start off nice and easy. I'm going to be releasing a drone into the room. It has a kill switch located underneath its belly. All you need to do is catch it and press that switch to deactivate it as quickly as possible. Got it?" John asks me.

"Got it," I reply, thinking to myself that this sounds like a piece of cake.

John presses a button in front of him, and on the far side of the room, I can see a tiny opening appear in the wall. A section of the wall has receded, and a machine about the size of a toaster emerges. The drone holds itself in the air with four rapidly spinning helicopter blades, emitting a soft, consistent hum. It remains a few feet from the wall, completely still, waiting in the air. I look over to John, not sure if I should go yet or if there's a problem with the drone. He looks back at me and simply gestures toward the drone, telling me to go deactivate it. I shrug my shoulders and glide forward.

Everything seems to be going fine until I am right in front of the drone and reach out to find its deactivation button. An instant before my fingers reach it, the drone's blades suddenly turn off, sending the whole thing plummeting toward the floor. I think there's a problem at first, except the drone powers its blades back up a foot from the ground, preventing what would have been a nasty collision with the ground.

I follow, lowering myself to the ground after the drone. Again, everything seems too easy until I reach out to grab the drone. All at once, the helicopter rotors spin into high gear, emitting a sharply pitched whine as the drone rockets back up toward the ceiling and out of my reach.

Glancing over at John, I see a smirk growing across his face, and I realize that this is part of the test. Of course the drone was never going to be easy to catch. I smile back at him, hoping to catch the drone off guard when I rocket myself back up to the ceiling.

A split second later, a very loud gong echoes through the room. It's the sound of my head colliding with the ceiling after the drone quickly moved out of the way and I missed it again. The room's speakers click on to broadcast the sound of John laughing and then click back off. He turned on the microphone just to laugh at me. On top of that, my head really hurts since I wasn't expecting it to hit anything and didn't have time to brace myself. Even with superpowers, I can still hurt myself through my own clumsiness. Another one of my unexplored powers.

The drone hovers back to the center of the room, where I began the test. It doesn't have a face since it's just a machine, but even still, I feel like it's taunting me. I launch head first toward it. This time I won't make the same mistake of assuming that it will stay in place long enough for me to reach it. Sure enough, it takes off sideways right before I reach it, but now I'm following it.

It darts back and forth across the room, covering an almost impossible amount of ground in an instant, zigzagging in every possible direction with seemingly no rhyme or reason. But I don't give up. I stay on its tail as it moves throughout the gigantic room, never straying more than a few feet but never close enough to grab it either.

My eyes are locked onto it like a homing missile, and I'm more determined than ever. I make myself as wide as possible with my arms and try to prevent it from doubling back on me. It's confined to just a corner of the hangar and its movements are even more erratic. It doesn't have the amount of space it needs to outmaneuver me, and finally, when it's completely cornered, I grab it. The drone struggles and twists to break free of my grip, but there's no way I'm letting go of it. With the button on its underbelly pressed, the light on top of the drone changes from red to green, and it gently returns back to the center of the room before lowering down to the ground.

"Not bad. Usually it takes a good twenty minutes before the test subject realizes they can't just chase the damn thing to catch it. Let's see how you do with a few more," John says over the loudspeaker while tapping away at the console in front of him.

A few seconds later, what seems like hundreds of new doors along the wall open all at once. From each, a single drone flies a few feet forward before locking into place as their lights change from green to red.

* * *

It takes nearly an hour for me to put down every last drone and another twenty minutes of having to listen to John tell me about how they didn't have tests like this back when he was a meta, and that he couldn't fly, but if he could he would have finished the test in five minutes, tops. I don't know if I could honestly tell you which was more exhausting: the drones or listening to John brag about something that he's never actually done.

There's nothing worse than thinking you're done with a test only to find out there are more questions printed on the back of the page. The equivalent to that for me today is forgetting that, even when I'm done with the tests John has put me through, I still have to head over to meet with The Physician for even *more* tests. These are tests that I'd have to undertake anyway, but the fact that my metabands are damaged has piqued his interest even more. Honestly, I'm just glad I don't have to spend any more time with John today.

Walking down the corridors, I wouldn't have realized it had gotten so late if it weren't for the relative emptiness. One of the many disadvantages of being a mile underground is it makes installing windows difficult, logistically speaking. The halls aren't as empty as they were last night, but certainly much more empty than they were earlier this afternoon. From what I can tell, the students that are still here are doing the equivalent of extra credit work, practicing abilities that aren't quite honed yet, or at least not honed to the point where they'd feel comfortable practicing them in front of an audience.

"Ah, Connor, there you are," The Physician says to me as he emerges from the exam room I'm walking toward. "I'm afraid we'll have to reschedule tonight. As much as I'd like to learn more about you, I have a more pressing matter that I must attend to this evening. I hope you understand."

The tired grin across my face must say it all to him. I couldn't be more relieved to be let out of an obligation than I am right now. I practically want to race him to the elevator.

Part of me definitely wonders what the doctor, and everyone else who isn't a student for that matter, works on during the day. Tonight that wondering will have to wait, though. I've got my mind on a hamburger and nothing on earth is going to stop me from getting it.

Sixteen

After I finish scarfing down a late dinner, I head back to my room since I've got not only nowhere else to be, but also nowhere else to go. I'm hoping that Tyler isn't waiting in the room we share, but I know that is probably hopelessly wishful thinking. From what I can tell, he barely even leaves it to go to class.

Before I even reach for my doorknob, I can tell that my wish isn't going to be granted tonight. There's laughter coming from my room. Not the kind of fun, carefree laughter you hear from people just having a nice time. It's the kind of almost yelling, aggressive laughter that sounds more like a way of claiming territory than anything else. Worse yet, from the sound of it, Tyler isn't alone in there either.

The second I put my key in the keyhole, the laughter is immediately silenced. I can hear rummaging and shushing noises coming from behind the door. When I turn the doorknob and open it, I find the room is packed full of people like a clown car. For the past couple of days, I've barely been able to fall asleep since I've felt so crowded having just one other person in this room; now there's inexplicably over a dozen. There's a stale stench of cheap beer hanging in the air too. Ugh. This is the last thing I wanted to come "home" to.

"It's my roommate everyone. It's cool," Tyler announces from somewhere in the depths of the tiny living quarters. Instantly, the room turns its collective back to me and conversations resume. Hidden red plastic cups reappear from every nook and cranny in the room.

This is maybe, literally, the last thing on earth that I want to deal with. What I want is to crawl into a little tiny ball and go to sleep for the next week. That's going to be really hard to do unless I don't mind sharing my bed with the dozen or so other kids currently using it as a couch. Oh, great. Even if they weren't sitting on it, it looks like my pillow is drenched in a mixture of beer and I don't want to know what else.

I shuffle along the wall of my room, apologizing as I inevitably bump into people who are technically only guests of one half of this dorm room.

"Shut the door!" Tyler yells unnecessarily loudly from across the room.

I sigh and turn around, apologizing to these strangers for a second time as I move back along the wall and toward the door. Once I'm close enough to touch the handle, it occurs to me that I don't want to stay here, even if it is my room too. I walk back out into the hallway and close the door behind me.

As I walk through the otherwise quiet hallway, wondering what I did in a past life to deserve getting the only jackass on the floor as my roommate, I hear something. It's the fuzzy click of a walkie-talkie, followed by voices around the corner. Loud voices. Authoritative voices. Adult voices. It's the police, and my guess is that I know exactly why they're here and where they're going.

I quickly spin on my heels and head back to my room. Even if this isn't why cops are here, they're sure to hear the noise coming from the room and decide it's worth a closer look. I don't waste time knocking and instead quickly fling open the door. All eyes in the room are on me, but I can't seem to find Tyler's face in the crowd to warn him. That's when he steps out from around the corner of the entryway, near the closets. He's inches from my face.

"All right, bro. Enough's enough. I tried to be nice, but apparently you don't take a hint well," he says.

"Tyler, listen, you gotta hide all this stuff and get everyone out of here," I quickly babble out before I'm cut off.

"Are you stupid or something? The only one getting out of here is you," he says.

And with that, he shoves me. We're standing so close to each other that the shove catches me off balance, and I fall backward through the door, landing on my butt and sliding across the waxed linoleum floor into the door opposite ours in the hallway. A chorus of laughter sweeps through the room so loudly that it makes the impromptu party's previous volume seem like a tea party.

The door slams shut, but I can still hear the laughter. It isn't until I'm back up on my feet that I realize my metabands have already materialized around my wrists. Did I do that? Did I summon my metabands subconsciously, or did they just appear on their own because they somehow sensed I was in danger? Both thoughts are equally concerning, but my more immediate problem is that I can't focus hard enough to make them disappear again. With no way to get rid of them and the threat of being seen with them growing, I turn and walk briskly down the hallway in the opposite direction of where I heard the radio noises coming from.

I don't dare look back, even when I can hear the door being pounded on and the police announcing themselves. Oh well, I tried to warn them, I think to myself, and I'd be lying if I said I didn't think the dose of instant karma was pretty funny.

Seventeen

It's 10:00 p.m. on a Thursday night, and I've really got nowhere to go. That's not to say that I'm not extremely grateful for avoiding what I'm sure is a mess with the police. As frustrating as Tyler throwing a party in my room without even telling me is, I can't even imagine how ticked off I'd be right now if I was being interrogated for underage drinking.

The thought of heading down to the facility crosses my mind since technically it's open to us twenty-four hours a day, but after spending most of my day underground and knowing that I'll be back there tomorrow, it's just not that appealing. Private time to myself is few and far between currently. I should really enjoy it while I've got it. Fresh air, the sky, all of that stuff.

After about fifteen seconds of fresh air, I'm bored with it and take out my phone to see if there's something there that can distract me. I'm walking with little direction, just kinda wandering toward the main library and water fountain as I go through what seems like an endless list of spam and status updates in my feeds. After a few minutes of this, I decide to declare social media bankruptcy. There's just no way I can get through this much junk after being basically offline for a week.

I'm desperate to find out what's happening back in Bay View City, but any news I can find is frustratingly vague or off topic. I reach the campus's water fountain and find myself a place to sit along its wall. As if on cue, the screen of my phone changes to indicate an incoming video call from Derrick. I tap answer.

"Well, well, well. So I guess you're still alive after all, huh?" Derrick asks once the call begins.

"Yup, I am."

"All right, just wanted to check. See you later," Derrick says as he pretends to end the call.

"Sorry I haven't been able to talk much lately."

"Much lately? I haven't seen or heard from you since I dropped you off."

"Yeah, sorry about that. I've been really ... busy," I say, trailing off as I realize it might not be the best idea to have this conversation on a phone in case the call is being tapped by any of the seemingly endless number of enemies I seem to be accruing lately.

"Don't worry. This is a secure line. It'd take all the computers in the world working together for about ten thousand years to break the encryption, and as much as I might miss having you around to bother me lately, I actually don't have that much time to talk right now anyway."

"Thanks," I say as I glance over my shoulder to check that someone isn't listening in on our call the old-fashioned way by just sneaking up behind me. The fountain sits in the middle of campus and offers sight lines for hundreds of yards in every direction. If someone tried sneaking up on me, I'd see them coming from a mile away.

"So, tell me all about your first day at school," Derrick asks in a mocking tone, like he's asking me how my first day of kindergarten was.

"Good. Well, I mean, not all good, but not bad."

"Yeah, Michelle's been keeping me updated."

"How does Michelle know what's been going on with me? She's barely even been here all week."

"You think that no one on the faculty there talks to each other? She's your recruiter. She gets confidential daily updates about your progress, and then she shares those confidential updates with me of course."

"That's adorable. I'm glad you've found such beautiful domestic bliss together. You're not at all concerned about how she lied to you about everything, even her name, for most of the time you've known her?"

"Eh, I get why she did it. She had to. Nothing is black or white nowadays. Not anymore."

"Speaking of which, how is everything going back at home?"

"How much do you know already?"

"Not much, really. They've done a pretty good job of keeping us literally underground all day. By the time I'm done with regular classes, and then metahuman training, I barely have enough energy to do my homework and eat."

"Things here are quiet."

"That's good then, right?"

"No, it's not good. The Alphas have taken up residence in the old Keane Tower. They've run almost every metahuman out of the city. The handful that have been foolish enough to try to fight them haven't done very well."

"Why is it foolish? I think it's brave to try to stand up for your city against them. I'm still ashamed of myself for not staying to fight."

"Don't say things like that, Connor. It's not that cut and dry. You can't just dive head first into conflicts without a plan and expect to make it out alive every time. Sooner or later the odds will catch up with you. Look at Midnight," Derrick says, immediately aware after the words have left his mouth that he probably shouldn't have said them.

"Midnight is alive, Derrick. I told you what Sarah told me. He saved her life. And he doesn't dive in head first without a plan. He always has a plan."

"He used his suit to save her, but that doesn't mean he was able to save himself. I'm sorry, Connor. I know he was your friend, but you're going to have to face the reality eventually. If Midnight is still alive, then where is he? No one has seen him since Silver Island. Trust me. I've got my ear to the ground, and if there were even so much as a rumor of someone seeing him recently, I would've heard about it."

I don't respond to Derrick since I'm not really sure what to say. It's useless to argue about this since neither of us has definitive proof that Midnight either is or isn't alive. I'd rather change the subject than think about the possible reality that Derrick is proposing.

"What about the people of the city, the non-metahumans? How are they reacting to having the entire city quarantined?" I ask.

"The city doesn't see it like that. A lot of people left, you know that, but the people that stayed are adapting. They're just regular, normal folks who want to be able to go to work without worrying about their train getting picked up and used as a weapon by a random person with God-like powers. I get it. You were too young to really understand what it was like during the first wave. People were scared. They didn't understand what was happening or why. Even before The Battle, there were lots of regular citizens that lived their lives in fear of being the random victim of a meta-related action."

"But what about all the good that metas have done? There were countless times they acted and saved people from disasters and accidents that had absolutely nothing to do with the metas that were around. Car accidents, plane crashes, natural disasters. There were always metas there willing to lend a hand and help in ways no one else could. People knew that not all metas were bad," I say.

"True, some people knew that deep down, but that wasn't what they saw on the news. Cameras didn't show up every time someone in a leotard saved a cat from a tree. It doesn't matter what the odds were or how many good metas were out there compared to bad ones. At the end of the day, people fear randomness more than anything else. You can take precautions against a natural disaster. You can't take precautions against a meta throwing another one through your office window."

Derrick is right. I know that. I understand why people are scared, and I know Derrick doesn't agree with it. He's just trying to explain it to me. Don't shoot the messenger, Connor.

"I just don't get why people would be willing to trust the Alphas. It seems insanely hypocritical."

"Better to trust the devil you know. And in this case, people would rather put their trust into four metahumans who have vowed to rid the city of all the rest. They're seeing the immediate results. The Alphas protect the city from outside metahumans. That's the only time they've used their powers."

"And what happens one day when all the other metas decide to give up on Bay View City once and for all? The Alphas will keep their place on top of that tower and everyone will just trust them to keep their word? What happens when they get bored and decide they want more than just Bay View City?"

"You're preaching to the choir, Connor. I'm not saying it's right. I'm just trying to help you understand what the atmosphere is like here. It's quiet, too quiet. Crime is almost non-existent. The skies are empty, meta-free. It's only a matter of time before the other shoe drops."

"Are you okay? I mean you, personally? Couldn't you be a target for them considering you report about metahumans?"

"Yeah, I'm fine. I've been in this game for a long time, and there's no place I'd rather be than right here as far as reporting goes. The Alphas don't have a reason to do anything to me. We've been fair in our reporting of what they've done. If anything, we've brought people into the city to replace the ones who have left. People from all over the country who are tired of metas are coming here in droves. They think it's some kind of metahuman-free oasis."

"I'm glad to hear you're okay at least," I say.

There's no response for a few seconds, and I can see Derrick looking off screen at something else that has grabbed his attention.

"Sorry, I'm just- Are you seeing this?" he asks as he turns his phone's camera toward the television in our living room.

On the screen is what looks like a breaking news report. The camera is working to focus on the scene. Near the top of the screen is the word "LIVE." At the bottom is a graphic that reads, "Metahuman Captured By Blanks Within Bay View City Limits."

There's a mob of people and confusion in what looks like somewhere near downtown. The streets are lined with nice stores and fancy restaurants. On the streets are at least two-dozen Blanks in the middle of a larger, angrier group of maybe a hundred or more.

The Blanks are struggling, almost causing a pileup of people, as they strain to hang on to another, unseen person buried somewhere in the middle of the crowd. The unmasked people along the outer edge of the crowd are all screaming and hurling garbage or whatever they can find at the middle of the huddle.

Suddenly the camera tilts up, seemingly at an empty sky, before it finds the subject it's searching for. There, hanging silently in the sky, slowly descending toward the scene of chaos, is Charlie.

He looks different than when I last saw him. Behind him is a flowing black cape that hangs all the way down his body and past his feet. His identity is no longer obscured either. His face is older than I would have expected considering how quick he was even before finding his own pair of metabands. Across his cheek is a large scar, one that I would have to assume was inflicted prior to him becoming a meta. His hair is gray, as well as his eyes, both of which add intensity to his already steely glare.

Someone in the crowd yells to look up. One by one, this spreads throughout the assembled masses until they're all looking up at Charlie and shuffling aside, clearing a space for him to land. It's only now that the camera can see what is in the center of the mass: a lone metahuman.

His uniform is yellow with purple accents running throughout his torso, culminating in an entirely purple cowl. His face is bloodied and the uniform is in tatters as he struggles to stand on his own now that the crowd has backed away from him. He's in bad shape and the faint blue pulse on his metabands indicates they're on extremely low power. By the look of the shape he's in, any reserve power is likely being used for life support systems at this point.

Charlie lands gently and takes his time surveying the crowd before turning his attention to the beaten metahuman.

"Who found this man?" Charlie asks the crowd.

A lone Blank steps forward.

"I did, sir. He was captured during a reconnaissance operation," the Blank says.

"Reconnaissance operation? You faked a mugging and waited for one of us to respond. It wasn't reconnaissance; it was entrapment," the bloodied meta yells.

"You'll have your turn to speak," Charlie says to the yellow metahuman without averting his glance from the Blank.

His tone is calm and slow. He's not afraid of this metahuman or any others. His patience sends a chill down my spine.

"His name's Utilitarian. We've been tracking him since yesterday, waiting for him to show off those shiny new metabands he's got. When he did, we pounced. I'd guess he's only a level two or three. It didn't take much to overwhelm him," the Blank says.

Charlie doesn't respond. Instead, he turns his attention to Utilitarian, sizing him up and down as though he's trying to figure out exactly what to do with him.

"Were you not aware that Bay View City is a metahuman-free district?" he finally asks.

"I knew, but I couldn't just turn my head when I saw a man being attacked. I wasn't going to use my metabands again, but I had to do something. I couldn't just walk away and do nothing," Utilitarian says.

"And if you knew metahumans were no longer permitted in this city, why, may I ask, are you still here?" Charlie says.

"Because this is my home. I was born here, and I intend to die here. Who decided you were in charge and got to choose who is allowed to have metabands and who isn't?"

"The people decided. They decided they'd had enough of false gods destroying their homes and killing their loved ones. It gives me no pleasure to use these ... instruments," Charlie says, looking down at the gleaming metabands wrapped around each of his wrists. "If it were possible to destroy them tomorrow and still keep the scourge that is metahumans out of this city, I would do so in a heartbeat. However, until that day comes, I will reluctantly use the same instrument as those who wish to harm Bay View City to keep them away."

There's a long silence among the crowd as everyone waits. No one knows what will happen next in this stalemate. One side will inevitably have to back down, and it's pretty clear who that's going to be.

Utilitarian holds his rib cage, wincing in pain, staring at Charlie through a swollen black eye. His expression changes as he seems to admit to himself that he's been defeated. Like a rubber band snapping, his uniform recedes back into his metabands. He then removes them, letting each drop to the ground. They both land with a thud you would associate with a much heavier object. Neither bounces or rolls, but stay exactly where they first hit the ground.

Utilitarian stands in front of Charlie, now as a regular man. His injuries are even more pronounced now that the metabands are off and he stumbles onto the ground. The person underneath the uniform looks like he's about Derrick's age, with dark red hair that's been shaved down into a buzz cut. Even without his powers, he's still physically intimidating.

Charlie takes a couple of steps forward toward the man who is now on his knees and places his hand on the man's shoulder.

"Thank you, I appreciate the gesture. However, the rules have been set in place. All metas were told to forfeit their abilities or leave Bay View City. You chose to do neither. To me, that implies that you think yourself above all the others, that rules are simply for other people and do not apply to you. Unfortunately, that is the type of attitude that has put this planet into the predicament it faces currently. It gives me no pleasure, but a society where individuals do not face repercussions for their actions is a society continually on the brink of anarchy."

"I understand. I'll do my time at Silver Island."

"Silver Island? No, I'm afraid that isn't an option any longer, but at least you'll get your wish about dying in Bay View City after all."

The man looks up in confusion as he puts together the meaning behind Charlie's words. Before he has time to form a response, there is a red glow from Charlie's eyes that transforms into a pair of parallel beams of light.

An instant later, it's over, and the man's lifeless body slumps onto the street.

Charlie takes a moment of silent observation directed toward the man he's just murdered. The crowd does not speak. Whether that's out of respect or fear isn't clear.

"I'm sorry you had to witness that. I'm sorry, but not regretful. If witnessing the punishment of one man who thought he was above the law means another watching tonight decides to lay down their arms, then it was worth it. This one death might mean the prevention of countless others in the future, and no price can be put on that."

Charlie turns his back on the corpse lying in the street and faces the Blank standing apart from the crowd who claimed to have brought Utilitarian here in the first place.

"Step forward," he commands the Blank.

The Blank freezes, uncertain that he should follow Charlie's wish. The Blanks rely on their anonymity. It's what gives them power in a world full of super men and women. After a reassuring nod from Charlie, the Blank slowly walks forward. Charlie reaches out toward him, offering his hand.

Part of me knew it before I even saw it, but I didn't want to give it weight by admitting to myself that it might be true. The clothes, the way he carries himself, the way he spoke. I knew who it was from the second he stepped forward and put out his hand. I knew even before I recognized the watch around his wrist—the watch his father gave him for his birthday.

How could you have done this, Jim?

EIGHTEEN

For what seems like an eternity, Derrick and I just stare at each other through the tiny front-facing cameras on our phones, neither of us sure what to say about what we've both just seen.

"I need to come back home," I announce to Derrick, breaking the silence.

"No," he replies immediately.

"My best friend basically just brought a man to his own execution. I need to know if he knew that was what was waiting for him."

"What does it matter?"

"It matters because I need to know if my best friend is still inside that person or if he's just completely lost. This is my fault. I relied on him for everything. He wasn't just my best friend. He was my only friend from the day I met him until I found these bands. And once I found them, I abandoned him. He needed me, but I wasn't there for him. He would have never done any of these things if I'd been there for him instead of trying to help everyone else."

"That's not going to bring Utilitarian back. And Jim didn't kill him. Charlie did. Even if Jim knew that was a possibility, he's not the person who pulled the trigger."

"Does it even matter?"

"Yes, it does. Jim can still be saved, but not by you. Not right now."

"Then when? After it's already too late? Or after he gets himself killed when Charlie decides Jim's broken some rule too?"

"Connor, all I know is that if you come back to Bay View City now, it's a death sentence."

"I'm stronger than Utilitarian."

"I know you are, but that doesn't matter. All it means is you'll put up a little bit longer of a fight before they ultimately kill you."

He's right. I know he's right. I can feel it in my gut, but that doesn't change the other feelings I have. It doesn't change that I want to be there, trying to help, trying to make Jim see that what he's doing is wrong. And it won't change what's already happened.

"Look, Connor, my inbox is exploding. I'm going to have to go and deal with all of this. Are you okay for tonight, though?"

I consider giving him the silent treatment, but that would just be immature at this point. Derrick doesn't have all the answers, and neither do I. He's got enough to worry about without me needlessly worrying him about me doing something stupid tonight.

"You're not going to do anything stupid tonight, are you?" he asks, reading my mind.

"No, I'm not."

"Promise?"

"Yeah."

"Good. I know that all of this looks bad right now, but this isn't the end. You just keep your head down and do what you're there for, and I know eventually your time to make things right will come."

"Okay."

"I'll talk to you tomorrow. Try to get some rest."

The screen goes blank as Derrick disconnects before returning to the home screen. Getting some rest would be nice right about now, but even if I was able to put everything that's happening in Bay View City out of my mind, it's unlikely that I have a place to sleep tonight yet. My guess is that it'll take a while to issue tickets to everyone from Tyler's little soirée. Plus, it might not be a great idea to return to the scene of the crime since I'm sure Tyler suspects me of ratting him out.

I lock the screen of my phone and shove it back into my pocket before standing up and heading back toward my dorm. Even if I shouldn't go back to my bed yet, it's still probably a good idea to head in that vicinity. It's quiet tonight, but a nearly full moon means that it's exceptionally bright considering it's almost midnight. Hours earlier, this area was a sea of thousands of students, but now, as far as I can tell, I'm the only one. That is until I notice a shadowy figure rounding the corner of the dining hall.

This time I don't ignore my instincts, and I can tell who it is right away by her walk: Sarah. First I have to watch my former best friend serve someone up for execution on live television. Now I'm running into my ex in the middle of the night in the campus equivalent of a dark alley. Great.

"I thought that was you," Sarah says once she's close enough to not have to shout.

"Who else would be wandering around the campus alone in the middle of the night?" I ask jokingly.

It's maybe the first time I've spoken to Sarah like a real person since we broke up. I don't know, maybe it's the seriousness of everything else that's going on in the world. It feels like there's little left to lose, and the problems between her and me are infinitesimally small compared to everything else.

"Well, if I had known that, I would have come looking for you here sooner," she says with a smile. Great, now that we're not together anymore we're back to me having to try to figure out what's flirting and what's not again. "So what brings you all the way out here on this lovely autumn evening?"

"Just felt like taking a walk. Hadn't talked to Derrick really in a while, and since my room is currently filled with police officers anyway, it seemed like a good idea to take the call somewhere else."

"Police officers?"

"Don't worry. I threw them off my trail. Actually, they're just busting my roommate for a party. I'm giving him his space until they're all done. What about you? Any particular reason you're out here this late?"

"Just heading home. I was over at a friend's for a little bit but ... I decided it was time to go home," she says.

There's hesitation in her voice, and I'm not sure if she decided to be vague mid-sentence for my sake or for hers.

"Well, I can walk with you if you'd like," I offer.

"I couldn't ask you to do that. I'm all the way on the other side of campus."

"It's really no trouble. My room was packed like a clown car full of bros, so I think it's going to take a little while for the cops to get through them all and clear out my room anyway."

"Okay then, that'd be nice. Thanks."

"No problem," I say and we begin walking across the campus's mall in the direction of Sarah's dorm.

"So how do you like this place so far?" Sarah asks me.

"Aside from having a jerk for a roommate, missing home, and being swamped with classwork, you mean? It's pretty good. How about you?"

"I like it, I guess. I miss Bay View too, though."

"Did your dad move out here?"

"No. He's traveling for work." I don't know if that's true or not, but it's not worth pressing the issue since even if she knows, she can't say. "That's another thing that I miss: the internship he got me at his company. All of that kinda went on the back burner when everything got crazy back home."

"Yeah, I can imagine."

"Derrick's still holed up in Bay View?"

"Yeah. I don't feel great about him running a meta-news site in the middle of the only city in the world where metahumans are banned, but he's stubborn. Says that he needs to be there to do his job *the right way*."

"Ha, yeah. He sounds like my dad," Sarah says before seeming to catch herself having said something that might have hinted at what her dad actually does more than she's comfortable with.

I can tell she's wracking her brain to think of a subject to change to, but she doesn't have to.

"Sarah!" someone yells from behind us.

We both turn to see a guy who looks a year or two older than us. He's wearing a canary-yellow polo shirt and khakis. His hair is frozen in place by what looks like an entire container of hair gel, and judging by the way he's walking, it looks like he's drunk. He jogs to catch up with us.

"I thought you said you were gonna tell me when you wanted to leave so I could walk you home?"

"Oh, yeah. I just got really tired all of a sudden so I ducked out early. My friend Connor here is walking me home, though, so I'm all set. Thanks," she says and turns her back, continuing her path back home. "Just keep walking," she says to me under her breath.

"Hey," Canary Yellow says to our backs. He yells, "Hey," again, but Sarah gives me a look that implies she wants me to ignore it and just keep walking, so I follow her lead. Suddenly I hear him yell, "Hey," a third time, but he's much closer now.

Then a hand violently grabs Sarah by the shoulder and spins her around.

"Whoa," I yell, putting myself between Sarah and this idiot so quickly that I don't even realize what I'm doing until I've already done it.

I immediately have to focus my mental energy on making sure my metabands don't materialize right now. I can feel my heart rate rising and adrenaline pumping.

"This doesn't concern you," he says to me as I stand my ground. "Look, I'm the one who told Sarah about this party tonight, and I'm the one who got her in, which wasn't easy, so she should be going home with me tonight."

He's trying to reason with me like Sarah isn't standing there, or like she's an inanimate object instead of a person.

"I'm not *going home* with him, and even if I was, that's absolutely none of your business," Sarah says to the guy.

"Come on, Connor."

She turns and continues walking. I've barely turned my back on this lunkhead standing in front of me when there's a quick flash of light and everything goes dark. Before I realize what's happened, I'm laid out on the ground.

This waste of space just sucker punched me!

I haven't even regained my bearings before I hear, "You son of a-" followed by the sound of something hard hitting flesh. There's a crunch, and then I'm no longer the only one lying on the ground.

Canary Yellow is right next to me, holding his nose as blood gushes out of it and runs down between his fingers.

"Come on," Sarah says, extending her hand out to me to help me off the ground. I take it as I try to shake away the stars floating around my head. She's still holding my hand, using it to hurry me along with her as we leave.

"You might want to get that checked out. I think it's broken, by the way," she yells over her shoulder.

* * *

"Thanks for standing up for me back there," Sarah says as we near her door.

"I should be the one thanking you. Where did you learn how to do that?" I ask.

Right after the words come out of my mouth, I realize that the place she most likely learned how to do that was The Agency. But that doesn't make sense. She was a computer tech there for the most part. It doesn't make much sense to train someone with that kinda job how to fight, especially when all the fighting skills in the world aren't going to do much in the face of a pissed-off metahuman who's being locked up.

"My mom," she says while she fumbles with her keys to open her dorm room. "She made me take karate classes when I was a kid. Said I needed to learn how to protect myself. That was before she took off herself, of course."

"Well, whatever the reason was, I'm glad you were there to

kick that guy's ass for me," I say.

Sarah gives me the kind of smile that reminds me of how much I miss her everyday.

"Anytime," she says before leaning over and giving me a kiss on the cheek. "Don't be such a stranger, okay?"

"I'll try," I reply.

"Goodnight, Connor."

"Goodnight, Sarah."

Nineteen

Class the next day, or rather "regular" class the next day feels like a blur. I'm barely able to keep my head off the desk all morning. When I got home last night the party was over, luckily, but the place was more or less trashed. Tyler was passed out on his bed, sleeping on top of the covers with his sneakers still on, but at least I didn't have to deal with him awake. That didn't make pulling the vomit-stained comforter off my bed and sleeping on a bare mattress any more enjoyable, though. At least I made sure he was still alive when I left for class this morning. He should owe me for that one.

The only thing getting me through today is knowing that my tests should finally be over and done with at the facility. That means my training, the actual reason I'm here in the first place, should finally begin. I expect it to be hard. It wouldn't be very valuable training if it wasn't. Even though I'm exhausted, my curiosity about what exactly I'll be doing later today is helping me forget how severely sleep deprived I am.

It takes a lot of restraint not to flat out run to the Blair Building when the final bell rings. Everything about the building is supposed to be about discretion, though. No one runs to after-school study circles, so that means I shouldn't either.

* * *

"Hello there, Mr. Connelly," Michelle says when the elevator door opens at the basement level of the facility.

"Hi, Michelle. I was starting to think I'd never actually see you here again," I say.

"You're not that lucky."

"What are you talking about?" I ask.

"I know you're not especially fond of me."

"Why do you think that?"

"You mean besides lying to you and your brother about who I am for months and then bringing you to this new place where you don't know anyone and we run you ragged?"

"Oh yeah, all that stuff. It's fine. Water under the bridge. Honestly, it's just good to see a familiar face."

"I'm glad to hear that. It's good to see you again too."

Michelle waves for me to follow her down the hallway.

"Why were you back in Bay View City? Aren't pretty much all the metas run out of there by now?"

"I was following up on a few potential recruits. Also, Derrick *is* still my boyfriend, and despite your opinion of me as a cold-hearted liar, I do still have feelings."

"So you missed him?"

"Yes."

We keep walking in awkward silence. I'm not quite sure why it's so hard for Michelle to admit that she *likes* her boyfriend, but I'm guessing it has something to do with her being undercover so much. It's got to be hard to let people in when your entire life is otherwise full of lies and misdirection. I'm just glad to hear the truth about her feelings for Derrick, even if she's pretty terrible at articulating them. If he hadn't found Michelle when he did, I was worried that I'd have to start trawling the old folks' homes for him.

"We're going to be in here today," Michelle says as she places her hand on a palm plate to open the door next to it.

Beyond the door is a large room, but I'm used to that by now. What's different about this room is what it's full of: dummies.

There must be a hundred human-sized dummies, standing upright, arranged throughout the room. Another difference with this room is that there's a large glass window overlooking it. Behind the window I can see an array of computer equipment and chairs. There're already a few people seated in those chairs, typing away so diligently that they hardly even notice Michelle and me as we step into the room.

"This is our Collateral Damage Reduction Simulator. We call it 'CoDRS' for short around here," Michelle says.

"Of course you do. Who doesn't love acronyms?" I ask rhetorically.

"Within this room, we're able to simulate a wide spectrum of disaster scenarios, the purpose of which is to train the metahuman subject in tactics applicable to saving human lives in such situations."

"So I have to save the dummies?"

"More or less, yes."

"Seems straightforward enough."

"It may seem that way, but often it's not. Tell me, what's the biggest distinction between a metahuman like yourself and a metahuman that the general public would consider a menace?"

"I'm not a bad guy?" I ask, not quite sure what she's getting at exactly.

"No, the biggest difference is that you, and as a whole, *we*, are sensitive to human causalities above all else. It's what separates a metahuman with just good intentions and a hero. It's making the right decisions in the moment, when those choices aren't black and white, but the outcome may potentially affect thousands of lives."

In front of us, a door on the far wall opens. From behind it, Nathanial and Calvin walk out.

"Ah, I didn't know you boys were here already," Michelle says. "Connor, you've already met Nathanial and Calvin."

The pair enter the room, both activating their metabands and corresponding uniforms. Calvin's is deep blue with metallic silver accents running throughout. Nathanial's is entirely black with only his eyes visible, not unlike a ninja outfit.

"Yeah, we all know each other. So what, we're all training together now?"

"In a way. Nathanial and Calvin will be assisting today, but they will be fighting against you rather than with you. As you know, Calvin is an Elemental with the ability to control water. Nathanial has the ability to create almost any type of weapon imaginable. Their only goal during this exercise will be to escape this room to fight another day."

I materialize my metabands and activate them. Since the other guys are in uniform, there's no reason why I shouldn't be too. So with a thought, the deep-red Omni uniform seeps out from my metabands and wraps around my body. Calvin smirks. I'm not sure if it's because he's excited to see me as Omni or if he's just excited for the fight that's coming.

"All right, boys, before we get too excited here, let's go ahead and take a minute to lower our power output. We don't want anyone getting hurt during training, nor do we want anyone putting a hole through the walls again," Michelle says, directing the last part at Calvin.

"I'm still sorry about that if it helps," he says.

All three of us do as instructed and dampen our powers by dragging a finger across one of our metabands, deactivating a series of blue lights.

"So what's my goal then?" I ask Michelle as I feel my power slowly ratcheting down.

"Your goal, Omni, is very simple. You are to retrieve the item inside this box."

Right on cue, a box about the size of a microwave oven rises up from a previously obscured opening in the floor. I'm starting to think that every surface in this place is hiding something behind it.

"What's inside the box?" I ask.

"It could be stolen valuables, or a weapon, a bomb, or a pair of inactivated metabands. It could be anything, really. Today, it doesn't matter; the box is simply a stand-in for an item in Calvin and Nathanial's possession that you must attempt to retrieve while they do everything they can to stop you. In this particular scenario, they will not be trying to harm civilians unnecessarily, but they are also not required to put any effort into avoiding harming them either, so keep that in mind."

Nathanial cracks his knuckles and Calvin bends his head side to side, loosening his neck.

"Okay then. Are there any final questions before I retire to the observation level so one of you doesn't accidentally splatter me along with these dummies?" Michelle asks.

We all shake our heads. We're ready.

"Good. Then I'll leave you to it. Wait for the countdown before you begin."

Michelle walks through the doorway that Calvin and Nathanial used to enter the room, and it closes behind her. A few seconds later, she appears in the window to the observation deck above the room, and she takes a seat and begins fiddling with some of the controls on the computer in front of her.

"Beginning CoDRS training sequence," a computerized voice booms through unseen speakers hidden somewhere in the walls, "in three, two-"

Before the disembodied voice can say 'one,' some kind of small throwing knife appears in Nathanial's hand. He sees me notice it and, in an instant, flicks it toward me. The knife cuts through the air so quickly that I know immediately I have no hope of dodging it. I might not have had a chance even if my powers were at a hundred percent. The knife tumbles through the air end over end as it flies straight for my head, but right as I flinch to prepare for the impact, something strange happens: it misses.

"Civilian casualty," the computerized voice declares. I turn to look behind me and see that the knife found its true target; it's wedged right between the eyes of one of the dummies. I turn back to face my sparring partners, and even though the bottom half of his face is obscured by his uniform, I can tell by his eyes that Nathanial is smiling.

"It's going to be like that, huh? All right then," I say right before launching myself head first in Nathanial's direction.

My right shoulder slams into his rib cage, and I wrap both arms around his torso tightly, taking him along for the trip. I slam right into the spot where there had been a door only seconds before. The wall holds under the impact, and I can feel something crack inside Nathanial right before I'm thrown in the opposite direction.

I'm starting to choke, my lungs filling up with water. I can't see or hear anything over the sound of thousands of gallons of water hitting me at high pressure. I don't need to be able to see or hear to know that it's Calvin attacking me. Without looking, I fly straight up into the air. The torrent of water follows me, but not quickly enough to stop me from getting a good look at the current situation. Nathanial is slowly working his way back up to his feet as Calvin stands in the center of the room, focusing his efforts on trying to keep me grounded.

I have to think. Nathanial and Calvin both must have weaknesses that I can exploit. Calvin is the more immediate threat, or at the very least, annoyance. I can't concentrate on how to open up that box when I've got water being blasted in my face. The pressure and speed of the water is so high that it's almost solid. That's when it occurs to me what Calvin's weakness might be.

It's been a while since I've had to use the ability, which will make it a little harder to control. I block the hurricane of water with my hands to try concentrating for a second. With my eyes closed I can hear the first tiny crackling noise from inside the jet stream of liquid.

It's working.

I double down on concentrating, focusing all of my energy at the water. There's a sudden loud pop, and when I open my eyes, I can see it worked.

I froze it all, starting with the water that had been hitting me and then all the way down the line until it reached the end. Calvin's arms are almost completely encased in solid ice, all the way up to his shoulders.

Nathanial's turn. He's already running toward Calvin to break him out. I use the opportunity to fly at the box set up in the middle of the room, hoping that the impact will be enough to break it open.

Instead, I find myself sprawled out on the ground, my head throbbing with pain from where it smashed into the stationary box. I look up and see that the box is still there, completely intact. Smashing it probably wasn't a good idea in the first place since I don't know what's in it or if it's volatile, but I wasn't thinking about it in the moment. In the moment I saw an opportunity and took it with my now very sore head.

I look over toward Calvin, half expecting to see him laughing at me, but his attention is on Nathanial. Nathanial is standing in front of him, conjuring a large broadsword in his hands. As soon as the sword materializes, he brings it down with all his strength, right into the ice currently restricting Calvin's arms. The ice shatters like it were made of glass, and Calvin is free again. The two turn their attention back toward me, which is exactly what I want.

Calvin is first. Having learned his lesson about getting too close to me, he hangs back and uses his ability to create something made from water that he doesn't have to be in physical contact with to control: a water cyclone. The cyclone is small, maybe only ten feet high, but it is spinning with an intensity you would never see in nature. Once it ramps up to a speed where it no longer looks like water as much as just a white blur, he pushes it forward. There's no use blocking it. Before it even reaches me, I can feel myself being pulled toward it.

I'm leaning on the back of my heels, digging in and trying to resist the pull, but my feet are slipping and the cyclone is only getting closer. Soon it's over and I'm sucked inside.

Everything is a wet blur as I spin around and around, quickly losing my bearings. Beyond the mist of the turning water, I briefly see a glimpse of what I'm waiting for. The overhead florescent light glints off the steel blade of Nathanial's sword as it rushes toward me. I can only assume that Nathanial is on the other end of it since I can't actually see him.

I estimate the speed he's running at based on the split second glimpse I get of the blade, and right when I think Nathanial is only feet away, I launch straight up into the air as hard as I can. I know that with the cyclone pulling at me, I'll have to give it my all if I have any hope of escaping before Nathanial's blade finds my neck.

At first it feels like I'm not even moving at all; then suddenly the cyclone loses its grip on me and I'm moving fast. There's not enough room or time to stop, and once again I find the top of my head acting as an impact brake, this time using the ceiling to stop. There's a loud thud from the two nearly invulnerable objects, the ceiling and my head, colliding into each other. The violent clash nearly knocks me out cold, and I collapse straight back down to the floor. The cyclone is disappearing. Water is everywhere, the result of Nathanial's blade slicing through the funnel, disrupting the natural vacuum and causing the cyclone to collapse.

I land with a splash and try to pull myself back onto my feet, but I can't even get my hands to cooperate with me, let alone entire limbs.

It's one of the biggest reliefs in my life when I hear the computerized voice say, "Training Sequence Complete." Was there an emergency shutoff?

"Dammit!" Nathaniel yells in frustration.

Calvin is on his back, panting to catch his breath, no doubt drained of a lot of his energy after the cyclone was destroyed. And behind me on the ground, just as I'd hoped, is the top of the box, cleanly severed from the base.

"Well done, Mr. Connelly," Michelle says into a microphone in the observation booth. "Very clever move to use your adversaries' own attacks to gain the outcome you desired. I have every faith that you will pass this training scenario with flying colors one day."

"One day?" I say in between gasps. "I just opened your box. I finished the task."

"Indeed you did, Connor, and that is no small feat. However, you forgot about the most important part of the exercise, and the one you were told was given priority over everything else."

Michelle clicks off the microphone and gestures for me to turn my attention to the back of the room. There I see what she's referring to: the dummy with the knife stuck into its head.

"But that's not fair. He threw that knife before you even gave the command to start."

"And you think your enemies are going to play by the rules? Maybe you can tell the next grieving family member you're very sorry their loved one is dead, but the bad guy didn't play fair, so it's not your fault. I'm sure they'll understand," Nathaniel says.

I really wish that I had tried to take Nathanial down first now. It wouldn't have helped me finish the exercise successfully, but it sure would have felt good.

"Unfortunately, he's right, Connor. Don't worry, though. We'll have plenty of chances to run the simulation again," Michelle says.

* * *

"So I take it you're mad about the way the exercise went?" Michelle asks.

I'm up in the observation room with her. She's asked me to come up here to discuss my performance and any questions I might have.

"No, I'm not mad. I'm frustrated. You told me there were rules here, so I tried to follow them."

"Like how you followed the rules the other night and used your powers on campus?"

I don't respond.

"If you're going to break the rules around here, don't be

surprised if we do it right back at you, Connor. We're trying to prepare you for the real world out there, whether it's fair or not."

"But I've already been out in the real world. I've already had to fight people who don't fight fair. If you had just told me the gloves were off in the first place, I would have known."

"That's just it, though, Connor. The gloves can't be off for you. You have to be better than that. You have to set an example that might seem impossible for others to live up to, but that comes to you as second nature."

"Even if that means innocent people get hurt? Because that's what would have happened today if this had been the real world and I'd played by the rules."

"That's why you're here. That's why you're training. No one ever said that you couldn't handle yourself out there already, but that's not what we're asking of you. We're asking you to hit a higher mark that no one else has so far, and we're only asking you to do it because we believe that you can."

I'm still not sure what to say, so Michelle takes the cue to keep talking if she wants this conversation to continue.

"Did I ever tell you how this place came to be?"

"Yeah, Derrick already told me about how they started building it during the first wave of metahumans."

"That's part of it, but do you know where the funding came from for this place?"

"No. I guess I just always assumed it came from the government or something."

"Ha, I wish. But you already know that the government has nothing to do with this place. They've already got their solution for how they think metahumans should be dealt with, or at least they thought they did until Silver Island was ripped apart," Michelle says.

She starts collecting a few papers from the desk in front of her and packing them into her bag.

"So where did the money to build all of this come from

then?" I ask.

"From my mother. She wanted to build a place where metahumans like her could train and learn. A place where the good guys learned how to win."

"Your mom is a metahuman? You never told me that."

"My mom *was* a metahuman. She passed away during the first wave, unfortunately."

"Oh, I had no idea. I'm sorry to hear that," I say to her.

"Thanks. You had no idea because I don't talk about it with a lot of people. Derrick knows. Some of the faculty here know, but that's about it. Why don't you follow me to my office and I'll tell you about it."

TWENTY

Michelle's office is located in a hallway that I haven't been down before. This hallway is much less sterile looking than the ones that house the various training rooms. For starters, this one has a carpet; that alone is a massive upgrade in the "not feeling like a hospital" department. It reminds me of a mix between the interiors of the actual school buildings above us and a nice hotel. Michelle leads the way to her office and swipes a badge, followed by a retinal *and* palm scan before the door's lock clicks open and allows us in.

"That's an awful lot of security," I say, meaning it more as a question than a statement.

"Can't be too careful. The security system knows that I'm not alone and requires additional checks to verify that you're a welcome guest and not someone with a gun to my head. If I hadn't used all three forms of identification, or if I had used them in a different order, the security system would still let us in, but it also would trip a silent alarm. I figured you probably would want to take a pass on having a rifle pointed at your head this afternoon."

"Good guess."

The office itself is nothing special, but if I had to guess, out of all the offices here which one was Michelle's, I would have guessed this one. It's clean and everything has its place. On top of the plain, brushed aluminum desk is nothing but a computer monitor, keyboard, and trackpad, not a single scrap of paper, no mementos from the outside world, no photographs of family on the desk. The walls are similarly bare with the exception of a TV monitor. There aren't any diplomas on the wall like you'd expect to see in a faculty office, but then again, Michelle's not the typical faculty member.

"Have a seat and take a break for a few minutes before I shove you back out the door to go to law class."

"Um, it's after hours. I don't have any more classes today," I tell her, wondering if being down here so long might be starting to mess with her perception of day and night.

"Not upstairs. Down here. You didn't think this training was all just physical stuff, did you? You're going to be taking a few more traditional, sit-down type classes here too," she says.

I take the only swiveling office chair across from her desk. She opens up a mini-refrigerator underneath her desk and takes out a few ice cubes, which she then places into a large glass that also mysteriously appears from under the desk.

Is she making herself a drink? Wow. Just when you think you know a person.

"I don't know about you, but I need a drink after today. Can I offer you anything to drink, Connor?" she asks me.

"Umm, I'm underage," I tell her.

She looks at me quizzically before looking down at her glass and laughing.

"You think I'm drinking alcohol in my own office, in the middle of the afternoon?" she asks, laughing again before I can answer her.

She reaches beneath her desk again and pulls out a pitcher from the unseen fridge. Whatever it's full of, it looks disgusting. It's dark green and the consistency seems to be somewhere between slime and chunky soup.

"This is kale, beet juice, spinach, garlic, and carrots," she tells me as she pours the concoction into the glass sitting on her desk. "I take it you're not interested?"

"No, I think I'm going to pass. Thanks, though."

"Well if you change your mind, don't be shy. It's not as bad as it looks. I find that it really helps to re-energize me after a long day."

Michelle kicks her shoes off under her desk and leans back to put her feet up, swirling her green health juice around in her glass with the ice. She takes a sip, which she seems to genuinely enjoy. I guess everyone's got their vices; sometimes they're just not actual vices.

"So, where was I?" she asks.

"You told me that your mom built this place," I say.

"Ah, right. Well, that's not actually a hundred percent true. A lot of the structure had actually been in place prior. The bunkers were built during the height of the Cold War as a fallout shelter. When the Soviet Union collapsed, they stopped work on it only to resume not too long after when some of the higher-ups in the US government became concerned that a place would be needed to house government officials in the event that there was ever a metahuman attack that wound up destroying large portions of the country."

"So it is a government facility? I thought you said it was autonomous."

"A few of the tunnels were once built by the government, but they've long been private property. After The Battle, the government updated its priorities. Instead of worrying about how to protect itself from seemingly nonexistent metahumans, it changed gears and began working on ways to reverse engineer metabands."

"Derrick's mentioned a little of this to me."

"I'd imagine. Derrick knows more about some of this stuff than I do even, which is saying something. Anyway, the tunnels were sold off to a private corporation years ago. Since then, they've changed hands multiple times until we acquired them and finished building out the facility here. The original project to build them was completely off the books, not much use having a secret bunker if others know where it is, so we're confident that it's been completely forgotten about by now. It was little more than some bare caves when we acquired it. Nothing like it is now."

"How did your mom earn enough money to do all of this? Most of the metas during the first wave didn't really focus on using their powers to get rich."

"Not the ones you hear about, unless they happened to kill

someone while they were doing it. Then they became a 'villain' in the eyes of the media, and then you were sure to hear about them. Not my mom, though. She made sure she didn't rock the boat when she earned her fortune."

"And how was that, if no one knew about her? It seems like if you're not going to steal, the only other surefire way is some kind of endorsement deal."

"Nope, she didn't do either. Mom was a little more enterprising than that when it came to getting rich."

"How do you mean?"

"She found a unique way to acquire valuable minerals without stealing them from someone else. She mined asteroids."

I have trouble comprehending what Michelle's telling me because it seems too farfetched.

"She mined asteroids? Like she took minerals out of asteroids and brought them back to Earth?"

"Yup."

"But how? It's not like asteroids are just hanging around out there. She would have to travel into somewhat deep space, or at least deeper than astronauts have ever gone. And deeper than any metahuman who's returned to talk about it. I would have heard about a metahuman who could survive that. It would have been huge news."

"And that's why she never talked about it. Her buyers preferred not to ask questions about where she acquired the minerals. When someone shows up at a meeting offering to sell you hundreds of pounds of gold or diamonds, you just assume they didn't get it legally. And if that doesn't bother you, you usually don't ask either. The less you know, the better."

"But why would she keep it a secret that she could travel into space? That's a pretty unique ability."

"She kept it a secret because she always felt guilty on some level about what she was doing. Here we were in a world full of metahumans, super heroes, really, people who could do things we never imagined. The entire world was fascinated by them. Even the ones who were terrified were still completely enthralled by them.

"This was a time of a lot of suspicion, though, even jealousy. If you were a metahuman and weren't using your powers to help people or save them, then everyone started asking what you were using the powers for. It usually didn't take too much digging to unearth embarrassing or damaging stories about anyone who wasn't pulling kitties out of trees. Once that narrative was set, it usually wasn't too far of a leap to brand someone as a villain.

"Mom just didn't want to deal with any of that. She wasn't interested in being a hero. She just wanted to provide for us, for her family."

"So why fund a school for metahumans then?"

Michelle takes a deep swig of her green juice and wipes her mouth before placing the glass back on a coaster on her desk in front of her.

"Because she realized late in life just how selfish it was to keep powers and abilities like hers all to herself. Unfortunately, she learned this all too late."

There's a silence hanging in the room, but I'm intensely curious about what exactly happened. I weigh the consequences of asking for a few seconds before Michelle speaks up.

"You want to know what happened, don't you?" she asks before I can decide if it's a good idea or not.

"How did you know that's what I was thinking?"

"I know a lot about you, Connor. Your natural inquisitiveness is one of the reasons we brought you here in the first place. It's okay to ask. I reserved telling you out of concern for the memories it might stir for you, rather than my own reluctance to recount the story again.

"My mom died during The Battle. She changed her mind about how she was spending her life before that day, though. That happened when my sister died."

"I had no idea. I'm sorry to hear that."

"Mom was out somewhere toward the end of the galaxy, looking for a big asteroid she'd read about in a scientific journal. There was speculation that the rock might have been composed almost entirely of diamond. It was going to be her one last big score. Enough money to make sure even her great-great-great-great grandkids would be very wealthy men and women.

She'd been gone for over a week. I was barely an adult myself at the time, but she trusted me to watch my sister, Lily. Lily was around the same age you are now, maybe a little bit older. She was killed during a metahuman battle in the middle of the city. One of the metahumans threw a car at another and missed. I wound up in a coma for six months. Lily didn't make it.

"When mom came back, she was devastated. She had never found the asteroid she was looking for, but it didn't matter to her any more anyway. She didn't even want the money she had, said it reminded her of the fact that she hadn't been there for the two of us. From that day on she used the money to start building this place. She wanted a place where metahumans who were on the fence about how they should use their powers could come and learn how to use them for good, learn how to use them to help people.

"She put the money into a trust in my name. Obviously she couldn't include in the trust that I was only to use the money for all of this," Michelle says as she gestures toward the facility around us, "but she made me promise. That was only a few days before The Battle."

"I never heard about her being involved in The Battle."

"You wouldn't have. She never wore a costume or anything like that. And she didn't fight. She hadn't had much of a chance to really learn since she spent so much time in space. On the day of The Battle, the most valuable ability she had was her invulnerability. It wasn't enough to save her life when the buildings started coming down, but it was enough to help her get some people clear before they fell.

"In her mind, as long as there were people out there with metabands doing harm, then it was the duty of others with the same abilities to do what they could to stop them."

"So would she agree with the Alphas that we'd all be better off had metabands never existed?" I ask.

"She probably would agree with that. She wouldn't have agreed that in order to enforce that idea there should be four metahumans who are given the reins. That doesn't solve anything. All it does is concentrate power.

"If we could put the genie back in the bottle and make metabands magically go away forever, then we could have a debate about the merits of that. We could argue whether it would be worth the sacrifice to ensure no more innocent people died, and whether we would be willing to risk that who or what created these things wouldn't come back for them.

"But we can't do that. We have to play the hand we're dealt. That's what my mom understood in the end, and what we're hoping everyone here understands too. And with that said, you'd better get hustling if you're going to make it to your law class on time. Doctor Hawk hates it when people are late."

TWENTY-ONE

So it turns out that Doctor Hawk is just an old guy named Leonard Hawk who has a Ph.D. in Law. He's not, as I imagined in my mind, a seven-foot-tall half-man, half-bird metahuman. This is maybe the most crippling disappointment I've experienced since I got here.

The classroom looks similar to the "real" ones upstairs, with the notable exception that this one looks like it was designed this century. There's no chalk or white board. Instead, a high-definition touchscreen display covers the entire wall at the front of the classroom.

In the classroom, I see a lot of familiar faces from the few days I've been here already. According to Michelle, this is one of the mandatory classes that all metahumans here have to take. There's not enough room for everyone to take it at once, since apparently the class lends itself to *lots* of questions that take up a big chunk of the classroom time, but by the time everyone graduates, they'll have come through at least once.

Just because the faces are familiar doesn't mean they're all friendly. Just about everyone who was out in the woods the other night was caught and punished, and of course, rather than blame Nathaniel or themselves for being out there in the first place, they blame me. In fairness, they had been hanging out in the caverns for weeks without anyone on the faculty having any idea, so I'll concede that *technically* it was me who got them all caught.

The display wall is showing multiple television channels from all over the world, as well as half a dozen lines of scrolling text with different news items. I'm amazed anyone can concentrate on their own pre-class conversations with the information overload happening in front of us. Represented on the screen, I can see all of the major meta news channels, as well as some overseas channels that I'm not familiar with.

The channels are a mix of talking heads and shaky camera phone footage of metahumans flying, running into burning buildings and fighting each other. My eyes scan over all of the screens, half expecting to see Derrick's big head on one of them, giving his insights about everything that's been happening in Bay View City live via satellite to a host. I don't find him, but my eyes do get caught on something.

It's previously recorded footage of the prison break at Silver Island, footage that I've seen countless times. When Derrick and Michelle had me under virtual house arrest, it was pretty much all that was on TV all day, every day. Even if it hadn't been on TV constantly, I would have still seen it hundreds of times on my tablet. After the breakout, I was obsessed with it and with trying to find some detail that everyone else was missing, some clue that gave any kind of idea about what the Alphas' weaknesses might be, or just a clue about what happened to Midnight, especially before Sarah told me that he was still alive.

The same question that I asked myself every time I watched this footage was now literally written across the screen: What Happened to Desmond Keane?

I would add to that what happened to Iris too. The general public doesn't know much about her role in the events that day. No footage of her was found, nor was she well known enough to become a focal point of the media narrative. That all belonged to Desmond Keane. In the time since Silver Island, the Alphas have placed the blame for everything that happened squarely on him and the media has been all too happy to play along. Now he's the boogeyman. No one knows where he is or if he's even still alive, but the public is reminded daily that he can come back when everyone least expects it, and God help you if you're not a metahuman when he does.

Leonard Hawk suddenly stands from his desk and instructs the few students milling around talking to each other in the aisles to find their seats. The classroom itself seems to sense that Dr. Hawk is ready and the display wall changes to an all-white surface with the words "Citizen's Arrests" appearing at the top.

"Take your seats, everyone, take your seats," Dr. Hawk says as he moves to the lectern in the front of the room and opens his briefcase, shuffling papers and pulling a few out for later reference.

Despite not actually being half-man, half-bird like I had hoped, Dr. Hawk does *kinda* look like a bird. His frame is thin and his suit seems to hang off of him. He looks like he's in his fifties or sixties, and his hair is an unnaturally dark black, likely the result of being dyed to try to make him look younger than he is. It doesn't. He has a small, almost invisibly thin pair of spectacles perched on top of what is a truly humongous, crooked nose. For his sake, I hope the nose came later in life, because I can't even imagine the amount of teasing that happens to a boy with the last name Hawk and a nose that looks like that.

He picks up a remote control on the lectern and lowers his glasses to try to identify the labels on it before he glances up at the screen and realizes that the presentation has already started on its own.

"Sorry about that. I hadn't realized the show had already started. They must have shown me how to use this damn thing a thousand times, but I still don't get it. Can't teach an old dog new tricks, I suppose. Anyway," he says as he picks up a cylindrical object off the desk and keeps it in his hand, "today we'll be talking about Citizen's Arrest."

He uses the object in his hand to draw a digital line underneath the words on the screen. Seems like he's got the hang of the virtual marker at least.

"Now, unless I've been derelict in reviewing your personal files, no one currently seated in this classroom is a member of law enforcement, the courts, or the military. Why is that important? Because that means you are, by definition, citizens. That means the rules, regulations, and laws surrounding any detainments you make fall under a different set of guidelines than those working for a branch of the government."

"Dr. Hawk?" a student sitting in the front row asks as she raises her hand.

Dr. Hawk sighs before he acknowledges her, and I remember what Michelle said about there being a lot of question askers in this class.

"Why does it really matter? I mean, when one of us catches a bad guy, it's not like the police, or whoever, is going to ask how we caught them," she says, not realizing that's not really a question as much as it's just a statement.

"Nine times out of ten, you'd be right, Miss Quinn," Dr. Hawk begins, "but what about when it might not be so clear-cut? What about if you apprehend a metahuman committing a crime of which there are no other witnesses? Or what about if you apprehend a metahuman *before* they actually commit the crime that you suspect they are planning?"

"If you've got a good relationship with the public and the police, it doesn't really matter, though. They'll take your word for it and take the guy into custody," another student chimes in. "It's not like they're just going to say, 'Sorry, we don't believe you,' and just let the guy go."

"No, in many situations, the authorities will take your word for it and take the suspect into custody without many questions. The problem we're addressing today isn't one that occurs at the time of arrest. It's one that can occur later, when the suspect has their day in court and argues that you did not have evidence of their supposed crimes. Now rather than a lawful arrest, one that a police officer can perform based simply on reasonable suspicion, you have just unlawfully imprisoned a person. This means not only may you be in danger of being arrested yourself, but also that the case against the suspected criminal will be dropped as the result of a mistrial."

"That's why I don't bring my bad guys to the cops. Just bring 'em to The Agency. They don't ask a whole lot of questions," the same student says, eliciting some knowing chuckles from others in the room.

"Well that is an option, and we all saw how well they did with detaining the suspects at Silver Island after all," Dr. Hawk replies.

The class is filled with a mixture of laughter and surprised gasps. I feel eyes on me, and suddenly I'm acutely aware of just how many people at this school see me as part of the failure at Silver Island. It bothers me more than it should, because on some level, I agree with them. On some level I know that I'm to blame.

"The purpose of this class, and certainly this entire school, is to change the way we, or rather you, think of your place in society. As we're continuing to see in Bay View City, there are many in this world who wish metahumans did not exist.

"If there is to be a place for metahumans in our society, it will involve working alongside the already established laws. When one thinks that because of their powers or abilities the laws no longer apply to them the same way, they're on a very, very slippery slope, one that often ends with a scenario similar to the one we're seeing in Bay View City, I believe.

"Returning to the idea of citizen's arrest, the biggest difference between an arrest you make and one a law enforcement officer might is that you are not protected by what is known as Mistake of Fact. This means if a mistake outside of the officer's control or knowledge has been made without their awareness, they cannot be held responsible for the false arrest. For example, if a police officer arrests a private citizen because they believe they have a gun on them, they are protected, in most cases, if the suspect does not actually have a firearm, as long as he or she can present probable cause.

"If one of you believe a suspect has a gun on their person

and you detain them, and it turns out you were wrong, you have opened yourself up for possible litigation. At the very least, the arrest, and any other evidence obtained as a result, will become null and void. At worst, you may find yourself being served with a lawsuit."

I'm not exactly sure why, but this makes some in the class laugh.

"I know that for many of you the idea of being forced to appear in court to protect yourself in a lawsuit is laughable, but it is a very real risk. Failure to appear in court can result in a warrant for your arrest, which on the whole can make your part-time careers as vigilantes and freedom fighters hard, if not impossible.

"You may all think that you're invincible because you're young and because some of you actually *are* invincible, but that doesn't mean the law can't make your lives very difficult, and it doesn't sound like the metahuman circus is going to be hiring again any time soon," Dr. Hawk says in what seems to be uncharacteristically frank terms.

He doesn't sound angry, but he does sound serious, and the effect is felt by the rest of the class, which quickly stops laughing.

"I'd like to show you all an example from a court case during the first wave. You'll probably find it difficult to concentrate on the actual proceedings thanks to the clothes being worn at the time, but you're just going to have to ignore that. Let's just say that the first wave of metahumans might have done more damage to America's idea of what was considered fashionable at the time more than anything else."

This gets a laugh from the classroom, but this time it's one that Dr. Hawk was seeking, of course. He again removes his glasses to more closely examine the buttons on the remote control.

"This all used to be a lot easier when you could just roll a TV set into the classroom, but I suppose that's probably before most of your times, even before you came to this suped-up *classroom of the future*," he says, likely parroting how the classroom technology was pitched to him.

"Do you need help, Dr. Hawk?" a student from the second row asks.

He waves her off.

"No, no. I've got to learn how to operate this myself sometime or else it's going to be a very long winter for all of us, I'm afraid. Hmm, here we go."

The teacher points the remote at the wall of the classroom and hits a button that he seems confident will perform the task he's trying to accomplish. It half does. The screen blinks and changes from displaying the fake white board back to the multichannel interface that was on when I first came into the classroom. There are a few scattered snickers throughout the room as Dr. Hawk mumbles some intelligible curse word under his breath and continues examining the remote.

One by one, students in the class seem to realize that this may take a while. There's scattered chatter throughout the room as they turn to talk with each other. Some pull their phones out to get a quick game in. My phone's currently dead, the result of forgetting to find out what the Wi-Fi password is down here and instead just leaving my phone searching in vain for a cell signal a mile underground for the past few hours. Luckily, I've got about thirty different TV channels on right in front of me.

A lot are on commercial breaks, but as my eyes wander from screen to screen, one channel grabs my attention. I squint my eyes to try to see it more clearly from my seat in the back row of the classroom. At first it's like my brain can't fully process what I'm seeing, but without even thinking, I'm on my feet, walking closer to the screen to see.

A few students glance up at me as I walk past them, my eyes locked on the screen, but most turn back to their conversations or phones quickly. Dr. Hawk is still cursing the remote control as I inch toward him and the screen.

The sound is a faint mix of all the channels. They're almost completely indistinguishable from one another. All I can make out are one- or two-word snippets, completely out of context. But there's no doubt about the words I'm reading on the screen splashed across Meta News 1: "Reports of Suspected Silver Island Terrorist 'Iris' Spotted in Colbytown."

"Quiet," I say almost under my breath at first. There's no response from the rest of the classroom, so I quickly find myself suddenly yelling it instead. This works, although I can still hear a few quietly laughing at me, the crazy new kid who just yelled at a class of peers to be quiet.

"Mister Connolly, can I help you?" Dr. Hawk asks in a way that's meant to snap me out of whatever it is I think I'm doing.

It doesn't work since I still can't hear what they're saying on the channel. Without a second thought, and barely moving my attention from the screen, I yank the remote control out of Dr. Hawk's hand and quickly find the button to bring this channel up front while muting all of the others.

"... reports are flooding in over social media that the fugitive metahuman known as Iris has been spotted in Colbytown and is currently making her way toward the downtown area. Iris is wanted in connection to the recent prison escape at Silver Island, which resulted in the escape of many of America's most dangerous metahumans, almost all of which are still unaccounted for. Federal law enforcement has instructed all residents of Colbytown to remain in their homes until further notice and not to attempt engaging or in any way interacting with this dangerous individual. We have the Meta News 1 quadcopter en route to the scene and hope to be able to bring you live pictures as the drama unfolds."

"How do I get to Colbytown?" I ask Dr. Hawk. He's still in slight shock from me grabbing his remote and ignoring his instructions.

"Wait ..." the blond newscaster says as she puts her hand

to her ear, indicating that she's receiving more news via her earphone. "This just in: we've received word that the metahuman known as Enforcer is currently en route to Colbytown from Empire City and is planning to neutralize the situation. At this time, we, again, remind residents to stay in their homes. We also caution all other metahumans in the area to not interfere with what we assume may become a standoff in the downtown area of Colbytown. Federal officials have extended temporary emergency law enforcement privileges to Enforcer, meaning he is the only metahuman permitted to engage with Iris at this time. The governor's office has issued a statement reiterating this warning and explaining that they wish to keep collateral damage to an absolute minimum. Any other metahumans on the scene will only exacerbate what is already an incredibly dangerous situation."

"How do I get Colbytown?" I ask, now practically screaming the question.

There are gasps from the classroom.

"Are you deaf, Mr. Connolly? Did you not just hear the statement that was issued?" Dr. Hawk asks rhetorically.

"Fine, I'll figure it out on my own. How do I get out of here at least?" I ask, remembering how long the elevators take, since during classes, they are usually set back to wait at their default positions above ground.

Dr. Hawk is still not answering me. I take a step closer to him. I seem angry, but it's really just panic. I ask him again.

"Mr. Connolly, I'm well aware that I cannot stop you from doing what you please, but if you intentionally break the law, I'm afraid there's nothing the school can do to protect you from the consequences, and that's not even mentioning how dangerous Enforcer is and how likely it is that you will get yourself killed if you decide to disobey and travel to Colbytown."

"I know how dangerous he is. That's why I need to go. He'll kill her. He won't ask any questions or take her into custody. He'll murder her and he'll get away with it. I can't let that happen. How do I get out of here?" I ask one final time.

Dr. Hawk sighs with the recognition that if he doesn't tell me, it may just make the situation worse at this point.

"There are emergency tunnels every five hundred meters in the main hall. They're hidden behind the overhead lights. The ones that are blue have a false ceiling above them. Behind those false ceilings are escape tunnels. They're not ideally discrete and are only supposed to be used in cases of extreme emergency."

"Good. That's what this is. Thanks, doc," I say, happy that if I'm going to die, I at least got to say, "Thanks, doc," in an appropriate context once in my life. Probably won't be too many chances to cross any more items off the bucket list before I get to Colbytown. I rush out of the classroom, but not before embarrassing myself in what will likely be the last time these people see me by mistaking a pull door for a push.

I run toward the main hallway, trying to remember in my mind's eye if I ever noticed that some of the overhead lights were a different color before. It doesn't matter now, though. I've just got to get to one, and when I see it, I'll know.

Reaching the main hall, I turn left and then right quickly, trying to see which direction might have the closest emergency escape. From here I can't tell, so in a moment of panic, I just choose right and start running. Light after light passes above me, but they're all the same bright white. Could Dr. Hawk have lied to me? Are there actually no emergency escapes down here after all? Maybe he just told me this to get the dangerous-seeming kid out of the classroom long enough for security to have a chance to respond.

But then I see it, way down the hall, off in the distance, one light that stands out amongst all the others. The hue of blue is subtle, but noticeable when compared to the others if you're looking for it.

Five hundred meters. I'm panting from running full out, but I can make it without slowing down, I think. I'm not sure what's wrong with Iris, but I know that somewhere deep down, this isn't her. It can't be. This isn't the person who I met above the clouds on the night I found out I wasn't alone in this world as the sole metahuman any more.

I'm so busy thinking about how I can't fail protecting her that it hasn't even occurred to me that I don't need to be running. It took a lot of work to get out of the habit of producing my metabands without a second's thought and now I've gotten so good at it that I forgot to even turn them on.

My pace slows ever so slightly as I thrust out both of my arms. The metabands appear instantly, and I'm glad to see that my self-control hasn't disappeared. I bring them together in front of my chest and the Omni suit explodes out of each to wrap my body. My feet are no longer touching the ground as I begin to levitate and then fly down the hallway. I'm not sure how "fake" the fake ceiling is, but when in doubt, it's probably best to fly at full speed. If Dr. Hawk was lying and there's just more bunker and earth hiding above this light fixture, I'm going to have a hell of a headache tomorrow.

The florescent light explodes into a thousand glass shards, followed by a layer of steel, concrete, and wood. Dr. Hawk was lying; there isn't an escape hatch, or at least, this isn't it, but then suddenly there's no resistance. I continue to fly up, faster and faster. It's dark, but I reach out my hand ever so slightly, and I can feel the wall of the tunnel I'm in. He wasn't lying after all.

Even though there's no resistance, I bear down and push myself to fly faster. A mile underground might seem like a long way, but it's not when you're flying as fast as I am, and if the exit of this thing is anything like the entrance, then I'm going to need some speed to break through it cleanly.

There's a pop, followed by a split second of silence, and then light. Not much, but the moon's providing enough to see what it was below me that caused the silence: a marble fountain in the middle of campus. There's a trail of water falling back to the earth below me and thankfully not a soul in sight. I might have succeeded in keeping both my and the facility's secret safe, even if that won't be enough for them to ever allow me back here again.

TWENTY-TWO

Any fear that I have of being able to find Colbytown quickly disappears once I'm able to get high enough into the air. It's a clear night, which is extremely lucky, because I don't think I'd be able to find the downtown area of Colbytown if it wasn't. Miles in the distance, I can see part of the town where the buildings are taller and brighter. That has to be it.

Just before I take off in the direction of Iris's last sighting, I hear a strange noise in the distance, almost like a soft rumbling. It grows louder and louder until, without warning, I'm tumbling end over end in mid-air. I regain my balance and tilt myself upright again, turning back toward the city to see what the hell just happened.

In the air above the city, I see it, or rather, him. It's a bright yellow streak across the otherwise empty night sky, the same shade of yellow as Enforcer's suit. If he's already here, then I don't have much time.

I'm a streak of color across the night sky too, heading straight for Downtown Colbytown. As I approach, the buildings become clearer, and I can see massive traffic jams backing up cars for miles as everyone tries to flee the area and avoid whatever's coming next. Behind one of the taller buildings, I see the debris from an explosion flying into the air. Looks like I've found my destination.

I fly over the building, hoping to gain some idea of what I'm heading into before I'm neck deep in it. Perching on top of the building's antenna, I see her below, standing in the middle of an intersection: Iris. There's something off about her, besides the fact that she's using an electrical pole as a baseball bat, sending parked cars and sparks sailing all around her. The area seems to be clear of any pedestrians, which must mean that she's been here for a while, long enough for anyone nearby to flee.

Her eyes look vacant and distant, and she's moving in a

way that looks strange. She's moving slowly, but not necessarily deliberately. I may very well be looking at a shape shifter who is simply mimicking Iris. Why someone would bring that kind of attention to themselves seems very odd to me, but there are plenty of metahumans who have done weirder things. And if someone wanted to be on TV, looking like one of the country's most wanted metahumans while wreaking terror across a city is a pretty good way to do it.

The notion that this isn't the real Iris and instead merely a fake brings up another question that I don't want to think about: If this isn't Iris, then where is she? It's a question I've been asking myself constantly these past couple of weeks, but for all the horror I felt when I heard this newscast, there was a huge part of me that was relieved she was still alive, at least for now anyway.

Out of the corner of my eye, something new catches my attention. It's a yellow blur, Enforcer, streaking down the road Iris is standing on. Cars are being thrown left and right out of his path, bouncing off of buildings and overpasses as he gains speed. Without having come up with a plan yet, I push off of the antenna, diving at a forty-five degree angle toward the street.

The part of my impromptu plan that involves putting myself in between Enforcer and Iris works. Unfortunately, the remaining tenth of a second that I have to figure out my next move proves to not be enough time. Enforcer barrels into me at almost full speed. The world becomes a blur as we both tumble down the street, out of control. The small glimpse I catch of his face tells me that he's been caught off guard and wasn't expecting something or someone to appear in the road in front of him. A streetlight overhead catches something shiny, and now I remember who Enforcer is.

Besides strength and speed, Enforcer has the fairly unique ability to control the composition of the molecules that make up his arms. He can't transform them into very complex objects, but that doesn't really matter when you can turn them into razor-shaped blades. Those must be what I'm hearing. His blades are scratching and scrapping the asphalt as he tries to find a hold somewhere in the road to slow down his tumble.

Beneath my feet, I feel the ground for an instant and react immediately, pushing myself into the air. I turn back as my momentum finally slows, and I'm hovering ten feet above the street. There's dust and debris in the air from our collision. Through it I can see the silhouette of Enforcer as he marches toward me.

"You've got to be freakin' kidding me," he announces in my direction. "I came here thinking I was just taking the girl in, but now I've got her little boyfriend too? That's gotta be worth some kind of bonus on top of her bounty."

"Sorry, I don't think anyone's put up a bounty for me," I respond.

"No? You don't think they'll want to see what the little turd who's aiding and abetting a wanted metahuman has to say for himself? Because I'm guessing if the United States government isn't interested in you, which I sincerely doubt, then at least the Alphas would be willing to toss a few coins my way for your head."

Coming from anyone else that would be a figure of speech, but coming from a guy with three-foot long daggers for arms, I take it a little more literally.

"Look," I say, trying to reason with him, "I know what it looks like, but there's more to it than this."

"Indulge me then. What more to it is there? She helped bust a bunch of criminals out of jail, and now she's trying to destroy a city. Seems pretty cut and dried to me."

"Well, I mean, when you put it that way, yeah, it does sound kinda bad. But this isn't her. There's something wrong. I know that's hard to believe. I wouldn't believe it myself, but I know her. Just give me two minutes to talk to her. Maybe I can figure this out, and we can end this in a calmer way."

Enforcer doesn't wear a mask. I'm not sure if it's because

he's able to change his facial features to make himself unrecognizable when his metabands are on, or if he just doesn't care about people finding out who he is. Regardless of the reason, his entire face is exposed. For a second, I see a look that might indicate a chink in his armor, and for that second, I think maybe he's considering my offer. Maybe he's thinking about giving me a few minutes to talk to Iris and solve this without any further violence. This thought only happens for a second, though, because in the next one, a bus flying through the air smashes into the back of my head.

When I stand back up, a full block away from where I was standing before I was hit, my first concern is making sure the bus isn't full of passengers. A wave of relief washes over me when I see the sign in front is set to "Not In Service." It'd be a lot harder to argue that Iris isn't a killer if she'd just thrown a busload of people at my head.

I turn my attention back down the street, scanning for any kind of movement. The street is empty, aside from the settling concrete dust all around. There's an explosive sound three blocks to my right, and I'm off running in that direction. I round the corner and spot Enforcer embedded into the side of a building but still breathing. Iris is on the other side of the street, her arm still outstretched, and her hand balled up into the fist that just sent Enforcer through a foot of concrete.

"Iris!" I yell toward her.

Her head slowly turns in my direction. She looks the same as she did the last time I saw her, which is the same as the first: purple and black uniform; blond, almost white hair; and glowing, pupil-less white eyes. It's difficult to put my finger on exactly what's "not right" with Iris when her eyes are pretty expressionless to begin with. She doesn't speak or respond to her name.

"Please, you've got to stop this. I don't know what's going on with you, or why you're doing this, but I know this isn't you," I plead.

"What do you know about me?" she asks in an otherworldly, flat monotone that throws me off for a minute and only reaffirms my suspicion that something outside of her control is seriously wrong with her.

"I know you. I know where you come from. Midnight told me everything. I know how you must feel, but it doesn't have to come to this. There's still a chance to get help."

Iris stares at me for what feels like an eternity, and I stare back, keeping my ground, hoping that there's something in her that will listen and take my offer. I'm so focused on her that I don't even hear the sound of concrete crumbling behind me before it's too late and I'm laid out on the other side of the block.

I guess Enforcer just woke back up.

"That was a warning, Omni. Your first and last. I don't want to kill you, but I will if you get in my way. Turn around and leave here if you want to keep your life," he yells down the street at me as he wills his hands back into flat, sharp edges. He then turns his gaze back to his primary target.

She's already taken advantage of his divided attention and punches him in the back so hard that I actually have to duck as he flies past before skidding to a stop farther down the desolate street.

I look down the street toward Iris, and she seems confused about where she is and what she's doing. It's another opportunity to try to get through to her, and it might be my last. When Enforcer regains his senses, I don't think he'll be playing with the gloves on any more. There's a serious danger to the city with her on the loose like this, and he's not going to risk any of that with a fight between the three of us. He'll be looking to take both of us out of the fight as quickly as possible, no matter what that means.

"Iris!" I yell down the street as I stumble toward her.

Through the glowing whites of her eyes there's something that looks a lot like a hint of recognition.

"Omni?" she says in an unsure whisper.

"Yes, it's me. It's Omni. You need to stop this, Iris. You need to surrender. If you don't, he's going to kill both of us. I can't protect you."

The look of recognition fades back out of her face and is replaced by a steely mask again. Enforcer won't stop until she's down, and I can't fight him while being attacked by her at the same time, not on my own at least.

Iris comes at me swinging, and I duck to avoid her punch from making contact. There's a temporary hesitation where I think I can see her coming to her senses again, but before I can say anything, she's hit with a huge piece of concrete debris. I turn to meet a charging Enforcer head-on, only to find myself slammed in the back by Iris's feet. I fall to my knees and Enforcer hurtles over me to attack Iris. She catches him and then throws him into a nearby building, his body smashing through layer after layer of concrete and glass.

Iris turns back to me when she suddenly stumbles and falls. There's a look of panic back in her eyes.

"Omni, help me," she says to me.

I run to her and try to help her back onto her feet, but she's weak and barely able to stand.

"What's happening to you?" I ask her.

"It's him. He's doing this to me," she says.

"Who? Who's doing this to you?"

Suddenly, there's an explosive pop to my right. Hurtling through the air is a sewer cap, which lands in the road, swiveling in a circle until it settles. A shadowy figure slowly emerges from the open sewer grate.

"Keane did this to her," the figure says before stepping into a pool of light created by one of the streetlights.

It's Midnight. And being dragged behind him is a bloodied, unconscious Keane.

"You're alive!" I exclaim, not realizing until that moment that part of me had actually wondered if it were true. I never should have doubted it.

"There isn't time. I have to get Iris out of here before

Enforcer comes back for round two. Omni, you need to transport Keane to a secure detention facility quickly before he regains consciousness. The closest one is in Albuquerque. If you leave now and fly close to your top speed, you should make it there before he wakes up. We've only got one shot at this."

"But-" I begin.

"Now!" Midnight shouts at me.

I take Keane's limp body under my right arm and take one last look back. Midnight is helping Iris move down the street as the sound of Enforcer beginning to stir in the building above echoes through the empty streets.

"I can handle him, just go!"

* * *

The night air is cool. It makes it much easier to fly when the air is like this, especially when I've got to tow along a passenger and worry about making sure he doesn't get hit in the face by a goose or something.

I can't help but look at Keane's unconscious face and wonder what kind of monster could do what he's done. He must have had Iris under his control for weeks, forcing her to do what he wanted. At least that's what I have to assume for now until I get the entire story, if I ever get the entire story. It's possible that Midnight will just return to wherever he's been lying low this entire time and bring Iris with him. There are plenty of people who want Iris dead for what they think she's done, and I'm not sure they're going to listen if someone like Midnight tries to explain that it wasn't her fault.

I think I feel a twitch from Keane, and my heart skips a beat. If he was able to take control over Iris, then he would have no problem doing the same to me. In the distance, I can see the facility: a nondescript building out in the middle of the New Mexico desert. There aren't fences or barbed wire surrounding it like you see with a regular prison. No need for that kinda stuff when half the people you're keeping locked up can fly. I get close, and suddenly, a blindingly bright spotlight is in my face.

"Attention! You are approaching a secure metahuman detention center. State your name and purpose or we will open fire," an amplified voice announces in a message that I'm going to have to assume is targeted at me. I'm flying so fast and the spotlight comes so unexpectedly that I nearly drop Keane from the surprise.

"I'm Omni. I have Keane with me," I say into the light, using the hand that isn't keeping Keane from falling to his death to try to shield my eyes.

There's silence in return. They're not expecting me, and they certainly aren't expecting Keane. It's a risk to let me in when all of this could be some kind of trap if I'm not who I say I am. It wouldn't take a shape shifter to look like me, just put on a red uniform and show up with an unconscious guy saying he's Keane.

"I don't mean to seem rude, but I don't know how much longer this guy's going to stay out," I say, worrying that Keane is going to wake up any second and instantly take control over me.

"Come in through the south entrance," a different voice finally says.

I fly over the top of the facility to the south side, but all I see is a featureless wall—no windows and certainly no doors. There's a click as the PA system comes back on again.

"No, your other south," the voice says flatly.

If I wasn't so scared of Keane waking up, I'd be embarrassed.

I travel back to the other side of the building where I see multiple armed guards waiting with their guns drawn. Looks like this is the place.

I land and place Keane on the ground. The guards immediately swarm both of us, demanding that I keep my hands in the air. One of the guards takes a small electronic device out from his pocket and uses a needle attached to the top of it to pierce Keane's skin. A small droplet of blood is sucked into the needle as the guard stares at the device's screen, waiting. The other guards don't move their position or lower their guns.

"It's him," the guard says after a confirmation beep is emitted from the device.

The others move quickly to secure Keane onto a gurney and roll him into the facility.

"You're welcome," I say in response to a thank you that was never given as the guards all abandon me to rush back into the facility.

"We do honestly appreciate it, Omni." Halpern emerges from behind the open doors and walks over to me. He offers his hand for me to shake, and I take it.

"So this is where they moved you out to," I say to him.

"Yup. It's no Bay View City. Hell, it's not even Duluth. It's the freakin' desert. But at least it's not being held hostage by a bunch of lunatics right now either."

"Always looking on the bright side."

"We've been looking for Keane day and night since Silver Island, never finding even a sliver of a lead on him, so thank you. I heard your friend Midnight had a hand in this, so thank him for me too. Of course, if you'd brought Iris in, we'd really be throwing a party for you."

"She had nothing to do with this. Keane was controlling her against her will."

"I believe that, I truly do, but that doesn't mean we don't have to speak with her and get her side of the story. She's still a wanted criminal. Why don't you come inside and we'll catch up?"

Twenty-Three

As I walk through the halls with Halpern, I'm in awe of the size of this new detention center. The Agency was already deep into the process of building it when the escape happened at Silver Island. Once that center was destroyed, additional funds were immediately freed up in order to upgrade this new prison and open it as soon as possible. It's incredible how quickly something can happen when you have the money to hire metahumans to build it for you.

It's not done yet, as evidenced by the exposed scaffolding at the far end of the main building, but it's in good enough shape to start holding metahumans. Each cell has been built as it's own self-contained unit. This makes escape more difficult since the cells are physically independent from one another. It also allows the various electronic systems to run independently of each other. In the case of a hacker breach, the person doing the breaching would need to work on each cell individually to open them. Of course, they don't expect anyone to get through the safeguards they have in place, but it helps make a worst-case scenario slightly less worse.

The separate self-contained units also mean that transportation doesn't require the prisoner to even leave their cell. The cell simply goes with the inmate to whatever off-the-books black ops site The Agency has hidden somewhere even more secretive than this place.

"We can even bring a containment unit right to an ally in the field now. There's no need to transport a suspect on your own out in the open. Just radio ahead to us and we bring the containment unit to you," Halpern tells me.

"It's a pretty long flight from Albuquerque to Skyville. I think I'll stick to bringing them in the old-fashioned way," I say.

"You're thinking small time, Omni. We don't fly the containment units out from here. We have containment units

217

in storage in every major city in the United States. We can deploy almost anywhere in the country within thirty minutes, usually faster if it's going to a populated area where we likely have a containment unit closer."

"And then what happens to them?"

"Come, I'll show you."

Halpern leads me to his office. Compared to the rest of the facility, his office feels surprisingly homey. There's wood paneling covering the walls, carpeting, even a nice leather lounge chair. All that's missing is a fireplace, although if I mentioned that, he'd probably reach under his desk and press a button to make one spin out from behind a wall somewhere.

On his desk there's a framed photograph of himself and Sarah, which he catches me looking at.

"Don't worry. Sarah's fine. She's taking the rest of the semester off from her internship after our little incident on Silver Island. We both decided it would be better for her to focus on her education right now. She's up at a private school far from Bay View City. She seems to like it. I think she might even have herself a new boyfriend."

I wasn't expecting to hear that, and it takes an extra second or two to process. I would have rather gotten clocked in the head by a bus again than think about Sarah with someone else. There's too much going on to worry about silly things like my personal life, the little bit of it that's left. Iris is alive, Midnight is alive, and I'm probably going to have to find a new place to live now that I've directly violated one of the most important rules of the school: no outside metahuman action without approval.

"Have a seat," Halpern says to me, gesturing to the empty chair opposite his large wooden desk.

I sit and think about how I always feel slightly ridiculous doing something normal like sitting in an office while I'm wearing this uniform. It definitely cuts a more striking visual image when I'm flying over a city than sitting at a desk.

Halpern taps a few keys on the laptop sitting on his desk and the painting of sailboats behind his chair changes to a three-by-three grid of security monitors.

The monitor in the center of the display shows the inside of a small, empty cell. The others show various angles of what appears to be the main lockup area. There are maybe two hundred cells, although less than a quarter of them seem to be occupied at the moment.

The front of the cell displayed in the center monitor is frosted glass, which turns transparent right before it retracts into the wall. A group of five security guards enter once the cell is open. Four of them are each holding one of Keane's limbs as they carry him into the cell. He's still unconscious. The fifth guard holds an assault rifle trained on Keane's head. Keane is placed face down on the floor, and the men retreat from the cell. The instant the last is out, the frosted glass door closes in front of them.

Halpern and I watch as Keane slowly regains consciousness and starts looking around at his environment to try to piece together where he is.

"Welcome back, Mr. Keane," Halpern says while holding down a key on his keyboard.

His voice echoes through speakers that seem to be piped directly into Keane's cell. Keane looks directly at the camera and remains silent.

"I think you'll find that this facility is a little cozier than the previous one. However, you're a wealthy man, Mr. Keane. If you were willing to surrender your metabands, I'm sure you would have no problem finding legal representation that could get you transferred to one of those nice country club prisons. I hear there's one in Empire City that has bocce ball now."

There's still no response from Keane other than his dead-eyed stare into the camera in the upper corner of his tiny cell.

"I'm taking that as a no from you, then?" Halpern asks.

Keane slowly closes his eyes. It looks as though he's concentrating on something, and a second later, we learn what it is.

Simultaneously, every prisoner in the facility begins pounding on the walls of their cell in unison. Keane's using his powers to control all of them at the same time. I'm not sure if Keane's powers have grown stronger or if he was just bluffing about how strong he really was all along. He continues to stare into the camera as the rhythm of the pounding prisoners intensifies, becoming louder and faster.

It's a show of power, a small demonstration that while the walls of this cell might be able to contain him for now, they can't ever fully contain his powers.

"I really wish you had reconsidered doing that, Mr. Keane," Halpern says before pressing another button on his laptop.

From the perspective of the camera in his cell, I can see some type of gas being released into the room. Keane stands his ground, even as the gas begins affecting him and his legs begin to wobble.

"What are you doing? You can't just execute him!" I yell at Halpern.

"No, we're not executing him. The gas is simply to incapacitate him. If he wants to show off his powers, we can show ours off too."

The pounding begins to lose its rhythm before it stops altogether, and Keane slumps to the floor of his cell, passed out cold. Halpern taps another key, and the valve releasing the gas closes.

"The outer walls of the containment floor are lead-lined. He can't use his abilities outside of his cell. If it were up to me, we'd line all the containment units with it too, but apparently it's a 'health hazard' to live in such close proximity to it. Plus, it wreaks havoc with our own wireless systems, so it's what we have to settle for. He doesn't realize it, but we're studying his abilities remotely even as he sleeps. If he's not going to take those bracelets off, then we'll figure out how to break him psychologically. Eventually he'll be begging us to take his metabands from him."

"Is that the right thing to do?" I ask.

"It's the safe thing to do. We'll keep him sedated most of the time, occasionally reviving him to offer the chance to forfeit the metabands. If he refuses, back to La-La Land he goes. The amount of time we'll keep him under will increase over time until it becomes obvious to him that he can either give up or spend the rest of his life asleep."

"Doesn't that seem kind of cruel?"

"It's all in his hands. We'll stop the second he asks us to by giving up his metabands. I wouldn't lose any sleep worrying about him. That's not why I asked you to join me here, though."

"No?"

"I wanted to talk to you about Bay View City."

"Oh. What about it? Do you have a plan for taking it back?"

"No, we don't. What I wanted to tell you about Bay View City is this: stay away from it."

"I don't understand."

"I know it's your home. It was my home too, and I'd give almost anything to be back there with my family. But the simple truth is that it's too dangerous for you to return there. Not just for you, for everyone. The Alphas blame you for what happened at Silver Island. If you go back there, they'll make sure you don't make it back out alive, and they won't care about what happens to anyone who's in their way."

"So that's it? We just give them the city? It's just theirs because they said so?"

"Omni, it's not that simple. We need to take into account the lives of everyone in that city. I don't like the idea of a city under a dictatorship, but you can't argue with the results. Homicides are down to virtually zero. Property values are rising. The people of Bay View City feel safe. People around the country are moving there *because* there aren't any metas."

"Except there aren't 'no metas.' There are four, four extremely powerful metahumans that everyone in that city is just trusting to make all their decisions for them."

"It's what they want, though. Even if it's not right, you can't force an entire population to change what they've become accustomed to just because you don't agree with it."

"You're right, I don't agree with it, and I'm not making any kind of promise about staying out of there," I say as I rise to my feet, preparing to make my exit.

"Omni," Halpern says to my back as I head toward the door, "if you're not going to play ball, then I'm afraid this is going to have to be the last visit you're going to make to one of our facilities. You've been a powerful ally and a good friend even. But I can't put the lives of everyone who works for The Agency at risk by continuing to work with someone who has a target on his back."

"A target that was put there by a bunch of egomaniacs who want to rule the entire country one day like kings."

Halpern looks at me for what seems like a long time, considering what to say. Finally he settles on the simplest option.

"Goodbye, Omni."

My anger doesn't allow me to respond, and instead I walk out without saying another word.

TWENTY-FOUR

I take the long way home, except there's really not a "long way" when you can fly as fast as I can, and I'm also not going home. I've just been told by one of the last people I know from home that I can't go back there. I've spent most of my life feeling like I didn't have a home. For the first year I lived there, Bay View City felt the same way: just another city in the seemingly endless list.

We had left Empire City all those years ago because everyone did. There was hardly anything left by the time Governor and Jones were done. Even though that was the day the first wave of metas ended, no one knew that yet at the time. It took about a week before the city was able to breathe again, after having previously lived in terror that the Governor and Jones were going to come crashing back down to Earth any minute, leaving a crater where the city once stood.

Derrick hadn't traveled much before and had no idea what to look for in a home, so we just kept moving, never really feeling comfortable anywhere. At the time, Derrick told me we had to move to find work or to save money, but looking back, I know he felt the same thing I did: no place felt like home anymore.

Bay View City was different, even before the second wave started. Derrick was working from home and starting to actually make money blogging about metas. Not a lot of money, not at all actually, but it was enough to supplement the government paycheck that was supposed to make up for our parents not being here anymore. We never really talked about it, maybe because we both felt like if we did, it would jinx it or something, but Bay View City had begun to feel like home.

When I found that first pair of metabands, that clinched it for me. I'd never felt more like a part of something than when I was flying over that city. Even now, when I'm supposed to feel more like I'm part of a group than ever at the academy, I still feel alone. It's not going to help that I'm almost certainly not going to be allowed back in after I directly ignored direct orders. On top of all the other rules at the academy, the rule about following the rules seems to be the one that they're the strictest about. For all of these reasons, I'm not in a rush to get back at the moment, but even when I take my time, I'm still back more quickly than I'd like.

It hasn't really occurred to me before I arrived that I'm not sure how I should re-enter the campus. There are very strict rules about wearing active metabands above ground when you're on campus, especially when, like me, you're hundreds of feet above campus.

For a moment I consider powering down off campus and trying to catch a bus or cab to avoid breaking any more rules. Ultimately, though, I decide that I've already broken more than enough rules to get myself expelled ten times over, so why delay the inevitable? At this point I just hope whatever cover story they give me to explain why Connor Connolly was expelled from the academy isn't too embarrassing. I've already heard a rumor that the last metahuman who was expelled was given "public nudity" as the official reason he was kicked out.

I'm hoping that's just something they tell new kids to scare them into following the rules. Hopefully they just tell me something nice and ordinary to say, like insubordination, if my roommate asks why I'm leaving tonight.

* * *

Before I arrive at the campus, I briefly consider the idea of just pretending none of this happened tonight and just heading back to my room. Even with my asshat of a roommate there all the time, it'd still be nice to at least get some sleep and deal with all of this in the morning. That's wishful thinking, though. They'll know that I'm back on campus. They'll know that I'm back in my room. I'm not sure if it's surveillance or if they've just got something on my door that tracks whether I'm there or not, but I know that they'll know. I might as well just deal with the inevitable.

When I arrive at the derelict building that contains the elevators to the underground facility and find that all the doors are locked, I think they might have already revoked all of my security clearances. The entrance to the building uses a series of elaborate but invisible security measures.

There's a hidden palm scanner built into the door handle, since having it as a plate up on the wall of the building might be a little bit too conspicuous. There's also a series of infrared cameras monitoring the building's exterior. These cameras are specifically looking for movement and eyeballs. The same physics that cause redeye in photographs are being used here to make sure there aren't any prying eyeballs looking in the direction of the building before it lets one of us in after hours. They don't want too many people noticing groups of certain students coming here night after night when the rest of the building looks more or less empty.

I take in my surroundings, hoping to find a couple taking a midnight stroll or a student heading back from a late night, something that indicates to me that the building is locking me out because someone's watching, not because my access has been revoked. There's no one nearby that I can see, though, and my prospects aren't looking good.

As a last ditch effort, I tell myself I'll try the library entrance before I give up for the night to wake up early and pack my bags in the morning instead. The library entrance is one I haven't used yet myself. Michelle told me about it on my third day here, but it was only to be used if there were no other options. None of these secret entrances are worth much if they don't stay secret, after all. It was part of the original facility, and due to its relatively public location, there hasn't been an opportunity to update many of the security features. On the plus side, that means if any entrance is still going to work for me, it's going to be that one.

The library is close by and open twenty-four hours a day, which is why it was originally suitable for an after-hours entrance. I enter the building through the main entrance and notice that it's very quiet in here, even for a library. Glancing down at the time, I see that it's past midnight and I no longer wonder why it's so empty in here. There's a student manning the librarian's desk, busily reading a textbook and taking notes.

The overnight shifts are likely to be staffed by students. I'd imagine that's because I can't think of few more thankless jobs than "overnight librarian." She doesn't even glance up from her textbook as I walk by, too engrossed in her own thoughts as I head for the stairs. The elevator would be easier, of course, but the elevators have security cameras. Specifically, these elevators have security cameras that the facility has no control over, so it's better to stay off them. There probably isn't someone watching the feed live who would notice someone who enters the library but never leaves, but it's better to be safe than sorry.

During the initial wave, one of the first big metahumans to have their civilian identity publicly outed was the victim of an accident. A man had been robbed at gunpoint at an ATM. When the security footage was reviewed later, they found footage from just a few minutes earlier when a metahuman had used the same ATM vestibule as what they thought would be a good place to activate their metabands in secret.

The security guard sold the closed-circuit videotape to a celebrity gossip show and cashed out big time. Ever since then, people have been anxious to try to catch a metahuman activating their bands on video, even though the tabloids don't pay nearly as much for that type of video anymore thanks to all the potential legal trouble as well as the lack of mainstream public interest these days.

The entrance I'm looking for is on the sixth floor, in the

periodicals section. Even before the Internet, when the only way to look up old newspapers and magazines was to use these weird rolls of microfilm, I have to imagine this area was still deserted pretty frequently. There's nothing to "browse" here, just shelves full of rolls and rolls of film labeled with just the newspaper name, month, and year. If you're looking for something, you'd already know where it was before you ever came to this corner of the library. As I hoped, I find the locked door I'm looking for in the corner past the last shelf.

I almost forget as I approach that there isn't a hand scanner here, just a regular old-fashioned key. Michelle made me put the key on my keychain in front of her so she'd know I'd always have it on me. I carefully glance around to make sure I'm not being watched, even though I haven't seen a single person in here other than the girl watching the first desk, and put the key into the keyhole.

The door opens and reveals ... nothing. Just a small, closet-sized space that looks like it hasn't been dusted in a very long time. I step inside and close the door behind me. I never thought I was claustrophobic, but being inside the pitch-black closet that I'm essentially locked inside changes things a little. A pair of red emergency lights click on, and the ground beneath me starts moving. The elevator is slow, part of the reason being that it needs to remain completely silent until it's past the six floors of the library. Even subtle noise could arouse the suspicion of library employees over time. The other reason it's slow is because it's so damn old.

* * *

After what feels like a two-hour ride, the elevator slowly comes to a stop. The elevator door slides open, and I step out. A series of motion-activated lights flicker on, and I realize that I'm in a portion of the facility that I've never seen before.

The walls and floors are different, older looking. This must be where the original facility was built, before Michelle's expansions. I don't know why I didn't realize it earlier, since the library elevator is quite a long distance from the Blair Building. It's going to be a long walk, and at this point, I just want to get this all over with so I can go to bed.

When I reach the intersection of the hallway where old meets new, I'm not surprised to find Michelle waiting for me with her arms crossed. She has the bored expression of someone who's been waiting for a long time.

"Well that took you long enough. Did you walk here from New Mexico?" she asks.

"How did you know that's where I took him?" I respond.

"Connor. After all of this time, you still have to ask how I know these things? We don't like to intrude on personal lives-"

"You mean like the time you started dating my older brother just to get close to me so you could find out who I was?" I shoot back before I have much chance to stop myself.

I guess that had been boiling just under the surface for a while.

"You know that's not true," she says, her voice filled with disappointment that I could even make that type of accusation still.

"I'm sorry. I didn't mean that. It's just been a long night, and I don't want to delay this anymore. If you're going to kick me out, just do it so at least I can get back to my regular life."

"You can't go back to your regular life. None of us can. Our regular lives disappeared forever the night you woke up with those bracelets around your wrists, Connor. You still don't seem to understand that."

"Well, you won't have to worry about what I do and don't understand anymore after tonight," I say.

"You really don't understand how we work at all, do you?"

"You told me that if I did what I did tonight, then I wouldn't be allowed back here. It's pretty cut and dried to me. I don't know why you're drawing this out more than you have to."

"You're missing the point. Do you really think you would have been granted access to that elevator if we were kicking you out tonight? You think we would have let you just come in here and wander the hallways alone? You're really not giving us the credit I thought you would have by now."

"So I'm not kicked out?"

"Follow me," Michelle says as she turns to walk down the hallway, back in the direction of her office.

"Connor, I've been thinking a lot about what you said to me. I'll admit that I've been overly concerned with the secrecy of this place. That's still crucially important, but it shouldn't be the be all and end all when it comes to our policies. The world is no more ready for metahumans today than it was when they first started showing up all those years ago. They may never be ready for you. But the one thing that may help is offering the idea that at least some of you are beacons. You may not always be able to save the day or rescue the hostage, but you can still be the idealized versions of yourself that many of us never can. It won't be enough for everyone, but nothing ever will."

"You can't please all of the people, all of the time? Is that essentially what you're saying?"

Michelle stops talking to think for a moment.

"Yeah, I guess it is. My point, Connor, is that what you did tonight was brave. It was the harder of two choices."

"It wasn't harder for me."

"I understand that now, and I understand that that's what makes you different, and it's ultimately why I wanted someone like you here in the first place. I thought our rules and guidelines would make it easier for all of you to deal with the situations you're faced with. Despite the fact that most people think they would love being a metahuman, I'm not so naive as to think that it doesn't take its toll.

"You have the ability to help almost anyone in almost any situation, but even you can't be everywhere all the time. How do you deal with that type of pressure and that type of guilt?

We'd hoped that by imposing the kinds of rules we do that it would help alleviate some of that pressure. We'd hoped that when there were people you couldn't help that at least you could place that burden on us, rather than on yourself. But I underestimated you. And if I underestimated you, I can be pretty sure that there are others here that I've underestimated as well."

We arrive at the door to Michelle's office and stop. She glances at me before pressing her palm up against the security scanner and twisting the doorknob.

I almost don't notice him at first when Michelle opens the door. I'm not expecting anyone to be in her office, and even when he's not trying, he's still pretty good at not being seen.

"Midnight?"

He turns toward me and away from the wall of Michelle's books that he's been looking through. His cowl is off and his face is covered in bruises and abrasions, but they all look as though they've been tended to.

"Hello, Connor," Midnight responds.

"I ... I don't understand ..."

"It's okay," Michelle says. "I know that before tonight you weren't even sure if Midnight was alive or not."

"That's because he didn't reach out to tell me, even though he easily could have any time," I say, throwing a mean glance in Midnight's direction.

"Connor, acting like this isn't going to help," Midnight says, his eyes piercing right through me.

I'm not sure if he knows just how much saying something like that pisses me off at this exact moment, and that's what makes it even more infuriating.

"I thought the idea behind this place was no more secrets between each other? That once I was in, things wouldn't be kept from me anymore?" I ask the pair.

"It is, Connor. That's why you're here. Neither of us wants to keep you in the dark, and despite whether you want to believe me or not, this hasn't been some big conspiracy to keep you from knowing anything. This is the first time I've actually met Midnight face to face," Michelle tells me.

"I brought Iris here," Midnight says. "I've been in communication with Michelle as of a few days ago. I had my theories about what was happening to Iris, but very little proof. All I knew for sure was that once she was out in the open again, it would only be a matter of time before Alpha Team came after her. I can't keep her safe, not on my own. This facility is the right place for her, at least right now."

"Iris is here too? Am I getting pranked or something? All of this is an awfully big three-sixty from what I was told about this place when I came," I say.

"One-eighty," Midnight says, almost under his breath.

"Excuse me?" I ask.

"One eighty. Three sixty would mean you were back where you started."

This is exactly what I need: a math lesson from a guy wearing tactical armor.

"Iris is here, and she's safe. We intend to keep it that way. She's resting, but The Physician has already been to see her. As you know, her powers are different from yours and the others here. They're somehow innate, not being tied to metabands of any kind. We're keeping her under observation for the time being, but The Physician is confident that she'll be able to power down of her own accord soon," Michelle tells me.

She flicks a button on the laptop resting on her desk and one of the wall monitors lights up. On the screen is Iris, curled up on what looks like a hospital bed inside a small room. Watching her like this feels strangely invasive, and I don't like it.

"So you're keeping her in solitary confinement? The cells on Silver Island were bigger than that," I say.

"Not solitary confinement. We're protecting her," Midnight says.

"From who?"

"From herself. The hooks that Keane had into her mind ran deep. The physical distance between them is allowing her brain to begin healing itself. Control is returning back over to her, but she's still dangerous. Iris hasn't been herself in a while, and the transition can be jarring," Midnight tells me.

"How long had he been controlling her?" I ask, running through my memory, trying to think of all the things I've ever said to her, wondering what Keane knows.

"We're not entirely sure. He's only had the type of control he demonstrated at Silver Island for a short period of time, we imagine," Michelle begins, "possibly only an hour or two, but taking over her mind wasn't done overnight. It took weeks of effort to slowly break through her mind's safeguards, especially without alerting her to the fact that someone was literally trying to hack her brain."

"So now what?" I ask.

"We're going to be keeping her under observation tonight. We'll see how she's doing in the morning and figure it out from there."

TWENTY-FIVE

The next morning I wake up early when I hear a text message come in on my phone. I could sleep through my alarm clock for an hour straight with no problem, but the little *ding* of a new text message wakes me up immediately for some reason.

The message is from Michelle. She's asking me to meet her outside the Blair Building, not inside, which is already strange. What's even stranger is that she texted me like a normal person. She didn't use a messenger or an encrypted message or anything like that.

* * *

Michelle told me before I even got here that she'd have a place for me to go during the fall break. It feels like cheating to have a long weekend off after barely even being here a week, but I'm not complaining. The reason Michelle told me she'd find me a place to stay is two-fold. The first reason is that I can't stay on campus. The dorms are closed down and everyone is kicked out essentially. There are places to stay in the underground facility, of course, but staying there would mean basically having to lock myself in. No coming and going as I please when the campus is supposed to be completely empty.

The second reason she told me she'd have a place for me to stay is she doesn't want me going back to Bay View City. It's become a very dangerous place for metahumans, and just by being there, I'd be taking a lot of risks, according to her.

I'm not entirely sure how, maybe I've got some mind control powers myself hidden somewhere, but I actually manage to convince Michelle that going to visit Derrick in Bay View City would be the best course of action. Along with that had to come a promise that I wouldn't use my metabands under any circumstance. I agreed and even offered to leave my metabands at the academy if that would make her feel better about the whole thing. She refused, though, saying that even though the academy facility is about as secure as anything can be, it's still not perfect. There's not much someone could do with my metabands if they got a hold of them, but the one thing they could do without even trying is prevent me from using them.

The safest place for my metabands is on me. Well, not actually *on me*, more like phased slightly out of sync with our dimension, but still the same idea. Still, the gesture of offering to leave the metabands behind seems to have been what pushed her over the edge into letting me go. It also helps that if I was going home, she'd be able to give me a ride and see Derrick herself. I'm not above using my brother as a carrot to get what I want.

Michelle insists on not telling Derrick that we're coming, citing some presumably nonexistent paranoid idea that doing so would somehow jeopardize the entire operation. What I really think is that she just wants to surprise him and doesn't want to admit it.

Despite them being useless at the academy, I haven't gotten out of the habit of carrying my apartment keys with me everywhere I go still. Maybe it's just the nice reminder that somewhere else in the world I have a place to sleep that isn't two feet away from one of the worst people I've ever met, or maybe it's just habit. In either case, Michelle is excited to find out that I have them on me since that means we can head straight upstairs without Derrick knowing we're here. This does little to convince me that she doesn't just want to surprise him and, for some reason, feels like she has to use the security excuse to justify it.

We both remain completely quiet during the elevator ride up. It's one of the few times I've seen a genuine smile on Michelle's face. She's actually having fun, as hard as that is to believe. I put a finger to my lips as the elevator slows and we reach the top floor.

If we weren't sure if we would catch Derrick by surprise

or not, we're pretty damn sure now. The apartment looks like the rest of the residents of the building have started using it for garbage storage. There are pizza and Chinese takeout boxes piled high in the sink, empty beer cans, dirty clothes, leftover food. It's so disgusting that it takes a few seconds for me to notice the grossest thing in the room: Derrick sitting on the couch in his underwear, looking like he hasn't showered or shaved in a week, headphones in and completely unaware that we're in the room. I smirk as I realize that this is the perfect situation to sneak up and scare the crap out of him, but before I have the chance, Michelle steals my thunder.

"What the hell happened here?" she yells.

Derrick jumps so high that he almost looks like he can levitate. He rips the headphones off and turns to us. His eye contact bounces back and forth between the two of us before finally settling on Michelle, the one of the two of us who isn't laughing hysterically.

"What are you doing here?" Derrick asks, suddenly aware that he's barely wearing any clothes, as he tries to cover himself with some couch pillows.

"I didn't know you wore tighty-whities! Didn't you grow out of them when you were like eight?" I ask.

"They're not the same ones!" Derrick yells back at me, totally picking the wrong question to address first.

"What happened?" Michelle asks again, even louder this time.

"I wasn't expecting anyone," Derrick says as he runs to his bedroom, presumably, and hopefully, to get some pants.

"You weren't expecting anyone? That's your excuse for this? Were you not expecting anyone literally ever again? Because that's about the only reason all of this makes sense," Michelle says.

Derrick reemerges from his bedroom wearing a pair of shorts and a ratty old t-shirt. For some reason, these strike me as probably being the cleanest items of clothing Derrick has access to.

"Sorry, I just ... you know ... thought I'd relax a little bit," Derrick says.

"Relax?"

"Yeah. Well, that and I've been working a lot," Derrick says, surveying the room for himself. "I guess it has gotten a little bit out of control now that you mention it."

"Yeah, just a little bit. You're not keeping your fingernail clippings in a glass jar somewhere now too, are you?" I ask.

Derrick apparently doesn't deem the question worth answering.

"I just ... I've never been on my own for this long. I guess it just kinda got out of hand. I'll clean it up. It's just stuff."

"Really, really gross stuff," Michelle says as she lifts up the lid to a nearby pizza box before snapping it closed in disgust after seeing what's inside.

"Wait, what are you two doing here?" Derrick asks.

"Fall break!" I shout as I walk over to the armchair where I have to sweep a pile of junk mail and catalogs onto the floor before I can make room for myself to sit.

"Fall break? That's a thing?" Derrick asks.

"Hey, it's not my place to question these kinda things. I just do what they tell me," I say.

Now Michelle is giving me the same look Derrick did when I asked about the fingernail jar.

"The campus had to be cleared out so neither of us could stay. It seemed like a good opportunity to come visit," Michelle says.

I detect in her voice that she's slightly disappointed Derrick doesn't seem happier to see her. He must hear it too, because he comes over and gives her a hug and kiss finally.

"I'm sorry. I didn't mean for it to sound like that. I'm thrilled you guys are here, both of you. A heads-up phone call about an hour ago wouldn't have diminished the surprise, though, and it would have given me the chance to clean a little-"

"And put pants on ..."

"But I'm still really glad that both of you are here. Don't take this the wrong way, but is it safe for him to be here?" Derrick asks Michelle.

"I can hear you, you know," I say without looking up from the electronics catalog I found buried under all the junk.

"He's promised not to use his metabands while he's in Bay View City," Michelle says.

"Still here. Still can hear you. Maybe this would be a good time for me to go take a walk. I'm sure you two have lots of catching up to do, or at least cleaning up. That, I want no part of."

"Where are you going to go?" Michelle asks.

"I dunno, around. This used to be my city, remember?"

"Yeah, I do remember. I remember the time you almost bled to death in the woods, the time you put a crater in Smith Street, the time you-" Derrick says before I interrupt him.

"I get it. I get it. I'm not going to get into any trouble. I just want to stretch my legs for a bit, visit the old neighborhood, see how things have changed since I left."

"You've been gone for a week," Derrick says.

"I know, but this is a very up-and-coming neighborhood. I'm sure there's a new gelato place or something like that that's opened up in that time."

"There actually is a new gelato place around the corner. How did you know that?" Derrick asks.

"Really? I was just kidding. I don't think I even really know what gelato is to be honest with you. It's just one of those things that starts popping up all the time when rich people start moving in."

"Says the sixteen-year-old living in a penthouse apartment."

"Hey, you earned that money fair and square, Derrick. Don't let anyone take that away from you."

"Let him go, Derrick. He'll be careful," Michelle offers

while giving me a look that tells me I'd better not make a liar out of her.

Derrick's sigh before he says anything tells me that he's already decided to relent and give up trying to keep me cooped up in this apartment the whole weekend.

"Just don't-" he starts.

"I know. I know."

"What do you know?"

"Don't use my metabands, don't get into trouble, don't do anything stupid. I know. I've got it. Do you worry about me this much when I'm at the academy?"

"I don't have to; that's Michelle's job," he says, giving Michelle a smile, and she smiles back.

"I'll be back later," I say. "And Derrick? Try to clean this place up a little bit. It's embarrassing."

"What do you care? You don't live here anymore."

"I didn't say it was embarrassing for *me*."

Michelle catches my meaning quicker than Derrick and does her best to stifle a laugh.

"All right. Get out of here."

TWENTY-SIX

It isn't until my feet hit the street that I realize just how much I've missed this place. I fell asleep on the drive in and really didn't see much of the city or if it had changed. I'm not sure what kind of change I expected to see so quickly, but so far the only difference is that the sky is strangely free of anyone flying around in it. What used to be the craziest sight you could imagine became the norm very fast. Now it seems strange to see it empty again.

Almost instinctively, I find myself wandering toward where I always used to go when I had no place else to be: the nearest Squarebills. Technically, it's not the nearest since there are two others on the same block, but this one always has the fastest Wi-Fi and cleanest bathrooms, so it's the default for me.

The city is busy, and I have to remind myself that while I might be off from school, everyone else has work today. Suckers.

I decide to take the long way since I'm not exactly in a hurry and should probably wait until after the lunchtime rush anyway if I want to snag a good table.

The park is full of commuters enjoying, or at least tolerating, their lunches on benches and fountain walls. A volunteer tries his best to block my path and hit me up for a donation, but as I get closer, he must realize I'm younger than he thought. He decides to save his energy for the artsy-looking guy a few steps behind me.

There's something else different about the city, something that I can't quite put my finger on. The people seem ... relaxed.

I approach the Squarebills counter and order my usual gigantic iced coffee. It's always the usual, even in the winter. As I ease into one of the booths out of the way from the main entrance, I look around at the people sitting here.

There's a couple on what looks like a lunch date, a few businessmen working on presentations, and several aspiring writers working on their screenplays. These people didn't stop existing when the second wave started, but it isn't until just now that I notice I haven't seen normal people just doing normal things like this in a while.

People didn't stop going to places like Squarebills a few months ago, of course, but they would avoid ones like this in the middle of the city. Or if they came in, they'd take their coffee to go. It wasn't something that anyone talked about or that the news covered, but there's something different now. Most people weren't afraid to be out in the middle of the city before, but the energy was different. There was a nervous excitement about it. It could be dangerous if you were caught in the crossfire, but it could also be something extraordinary. You could be out for a coffee break and look up into the sky to see people doing the impossible.

You might think that would make most people feel like their own lives were boring and humdrum in comparison, but the opposite was true, I think. It made people, some people at least, feel like they were alive during an extraordinary time filled with extraordinary possibilities. I have to imagine that it was like this when we first landed on the moon. Sure, everyone was terrified that Russia was going to launch their nukes at us at any given second, but seeing images of someone playing golf on the surface of the moon might have made it feel like it was all worth it on some level. There are a lot of different opinions about what it's like to be alive right now when all this is happening, but the one thing no one could ever call this time is "boring."

I'm so lost in my own thoughts that my brain almost doesn't even register when Jim walks in. He sees me right away and a broad smile crosses his face. He decides to skip the coffee counter and just come straight my way.

"What are you doing here?" I ask.

"What am I doing here? What the heck are *you* doing

here? You didn't get kicked out of that fancy-pants academy already, did you? I hope Derrick can still get his deposit back," Jim says.

I stand up to greet him and surprise both of us when I decide to hug him instead of just slapping hands with him.

"Wow. You haven't been gone *that* long."

I break off the hug and immediately feel foolish. I didn't even think about how that kind of display of affection would look to Jim. He doesn't know that I know about his involvement with the Blanks. "Involvement" is my way of trying to distance Jim's actions further away than he actually is. He isn't just "involved;" he's one of them. He's part of a group that hates metahumans like me. I have no idea how he would react if he ever found out the truth, so I still intend to keep it to myself.

"Sorry, new school just kinda sucks. It seems like it's been a really long time since I've seen a real-life friend," I offer as an excuse for my behavior.

"It's no problem. I miss having you around too, but you're telling me that after all of this time, changing schools every year or so, you still don't know how to make friends?" Jim asks.

"You can lead a horse to water, but that doesn't mean you can make him drink it."

"I'm not sure if that saying applies to this situation."

"I don't think it does either, but it sounded like it could."

"No, it didn't."

"You're right; it didn't. And yeah, I still suck at making friends."

"You're lucky that when you were at Bay View I decided to take mercy on such a loser."

"Oh, like you're Mr. Popular now?" I ask.

"You haven't been around. I've had to broaden my horizons. Try out some things outside of my comfort zone. Spread my wings a bit."

It hadn't occurred to me that my virtual disappearance

from Bay View City would affect someone like Jim. Maybe he's just being sarcastic, but then I can tell there's a grain of truth behind his words. If my new life as Omni drove Jim toward the Blanks when I wasn't around, then my moving away has to be making it worse.

It seems like classic cult mentality: find the ones in the crowd who feel alone and disenfranchised. They're always the easiest to force your own opinions and beliefs on in exchange for something as simple as friendship, somewhere to be, something to do. The destruction of our old school couldn't have helped either.

In that moment, I suddenly and desperately want to tell Jim my secret. I want to tell him why I was distant and why I had to leave. Maybe it's the relative calm that the city is under, but the Jim sitting across the table from me feels like the Jim I used to call my best and only friend. He feels like the one that I could tell anything to without judgment and vice versa.

"Jim, listen. There's something I've got to tell you about," I say.

"Is it about the new guy Sarah's dating? I've already heard about that. Sorry."

"Wait, what?"

"Oops. I guess that wasn't it. Forget I said that."

The idea of telling Jim my secret is violently thrust out of my brain by this new information, which pushes everything else out of the way too. I'm not sure why this feels like such a punch to the gut. I mean, I suspected it after all, but hearing it from someone else now still just sucks.

"Crap. I really wish I hadn't said that," Jim says. "You're back in town for two minutes and the first thing I do is rip your heart out of your chest."

"No one ripped my heart out of my chest. We're not together anymore. It's not like she needs my permission to see someone else now," I say, meaning every word, of course, but still not being thrilled about the idea of it.

"Well if it makes you feel any better, I hear the guy's a real ass."

"Why would that make me feel better?"

"Would you rather hear that he's awesome and better than you in every possible way?"

"No, but I'd kinda rather not hear anything to be honest with you."

"Right. You're absolutely right. Forget I said anything. Let's change the subject. What was it that you were actually going to tell me?"

My mind blanks when I try to remember at first, but then it comes back to me that I was just about to spill my guts to Jim about my metabands for pretty much no reason other than I was just glad to see him and didn't want him to hate me. It's probably good that he dropped the Sarah bomb to bring me back down to earth a little bit. I might trust Jim, but I have to assume he's still a Blank, and that means I wouldn't be just trusting him with my life, but also with the lives of everyone around me if he knew the truth.

"Oh, um, I forgot. Sorry," I lie.

Jim rolls his eyes at me, either to make fun of me for forgetting something so quickly or because he doesn't believe my lie. I'm not quite sure which.

"So how's the new school, besides the fact that you haven't made a bunch of new rich friends yet?" Jim asks, trying to change the conversation himself.

"It's ... weird."

"How so?"

I spend half my day a mile underground with a bunch of other super-powered freaks that have no idea how to use their powers or what to do with them, I think.

"Just really small classes. Makes it harder to goof off without it being really noticeable," I say instead.

"I hear that. Can't be smaller than the current classes at Bay View High, which consist of exactly zero students, though."

"They haven't set up anything temporary yet?" I ask.

"They have, but it means taking the bus like two hours each way, so a lot of us just opted for homeschooling."

"Who homeschools you?"

"Technically, I do."

"Does that actually mean anything?"

"Well I'm sitting in a Squarebills in the middle of the afternoon on a weekday, so I'll let you figure that out."

"But what about college applications and stuff like that? Aren't they going to ask a lot of questions about that?"

"They would. I wouldn't know, though, since that would require actually planning on going to college."

"You're not going to go to college?"

"No way. Why would I? Do you know how many CEOs and millionaires are high school dropouts?"

"Yeah, but that's all anecdotal."

"Whos-a-whatal? Sounds like someone got themselves a thesaurus at that fancy new school."

"It just means that they're one-offs. There are cases where people have dropped out and gone on to be successful, but they're the exceptions."

"Technically, I didn't drop out of school, so I've already got a leg up on those guys."

"What are you going to do instead?" I ask.

"I dunno. I'll figure it out, though. I mean, I've got a whole eighteen months. Anything could happen in that time."

"Well, not really *anything*."

"Look at how different your life is from eighteen months ago."

If you only knew the half of it, I think to myself.

"I just think you should probably reconsider. It's already really tough out there. It's gonna be even worse without a college diploma."

"So you think because you started going to some private *academy* that all of a sudden you're some scholar doling out advice everyone should listen to?"

"No, of course not. I'd be saying this no matter what."

"Well, whatever. You don't have to worry about me."

"It's not worrying, Jim. It's just that I hope you're thinking everything through."

Jim is about to respond when the words are stolen out of his mouth by the horrifying sounds of metal screeching against pavement. Everyone in the Squarebills turns their head to the big plate-glass window at the front of the store just as the sound is accompanied by a huge crash followed by a pop.

People are on their feet, hurrying to the window with looks of dread that I recognize from when this city wasn't metahuman free. It's that mix of morbid curiosity combined with the hope that you don't see anything truly horrible because you know that you won't be able to look away if you do.

From my seat, I can see clearly what's happened, or the aftermath at least. There's a small, dark blue hatchback pinned against an oak tree at the edge of the park. The pinning is being done by a van that is at least three times its size. Jim reacts first, jumping out of his seat and running for the door. He glances back, and without a word, I follow his lead.

Jim is sprinting across traffic as it slows to a standstill of rubberneckers. I struggle to keep up with Jim as he pushes past a small crowd of onlookers keeping their distance. He reaches the hatchback and climbs in through the backseat window without hesitation.

Before I'm able to reach the car myself, I feel a heavy hand grab me by the bicep.

"Stay back," the hand's owner says to me, more of a warning than a suggestion.

He's a Blank, his voice heavily distorted to protect his anonymity. More Blanks are emerging from different corners of the park. They may have been dispatched to try to help with this emergency, but they may have been around the entire time, only donning their masks when there was a need to act.

I look back at the car and can see Jim struggling to free himself from the wreckage he jumped into without a second thought. There's an arm wrapped around his shoulder. It's the driver of the car, a father holding a crying toddler in his other arm as he braces against Jim to steady himself. His face is bloody, but all things considered, he looks okay. Jim brings him over to a group of three Blanks who guide him to a waiting sport utility truck, explaining that they're going to take him to the hospital.

Once Jim hands the pair over, he turns back to the wreckage. Just then, there's a small explosion. Fire and thick black smoke begin pouring out of the other vehicle, a white cargo van. A weak cry for help comes from somewhere unseen in the wreckage. Jim runs toward the sound but is headed off by a Blank who walks out from around the other side of the accident scene.

"Don't," the Blank says to Jim.

"What do you mean, don't?" Jim asks back.

The Blank holding me is watching this scene as well, and I take advantage of his temporary distraction to wiggle free of his grip. I run toward Jim, with the Blank chasing after me. Jim hears me coming toward him and turns. He waves off the Blank behind me without a word.

"The other driver's drunk. I could smell the booze on him from five feet away. The back of the van is full of fertilizer bags. This whole thing is about to go up. We've got to get these people back," the Blank explains to Jim, ignoring me.

"But what about the driver?" I ask.

"Screw him. He's lucky he didn't kill anyone. Let him burn," the Blank says before pushing me aside to start yelling at the crowd to back up immediately, explaining that the van is close to exploding.

The crowd begins to panic and scatters in all directions. Jim stands silently frozen. He doesn't know what to do.

"Jim, we've got to get that guy out of there," I say to him.

"We can't. You heard the Blank. He's getting what he deserves," Jim says, his eyes unfocused and staring into space.

"You don't really believe that. He doesn't deserve to die," I say, trying to get into Jim's line of sight and hopefully snap him out of this.

The crowd of people is almost a full block away, and it's quiet. The only sounds are the crackling of the spreading flames and the distant moans of the man trapped in his vehicle.

I give up trying to talk sense into Jim. Time is not on this guy's side. I run around the wreck and find a bloodied man hanging halfway out of the driver's side window of the overturned van.

"Are you okay?" I ask.

There's no response, but the rise and fall of his chest tells me that he's still alive, just unconscious. I reach into the car to see if I can pull him out. Just then, another pair of hands reach in too. Jim's by my side.

"Screw it. I don't care what he did. I'm not just going to let someone die," he says.

We're both fumbling, trying to reach inside the smashed car to detach the man's seatbelt, but it won't budge. I remember something about not moving accident victims if you can help it since they may have spinal or internal injuries that you can't see, but this guy is dead either way unless we get him free.

"Just go, get out of here before this whole thing goes up," Jim says, still trying desperately to pull the man through the smashed window.

"I'm not leaving," I reply, not wasting even the second it would take to look at him when I say it.

"Well then all three of us are going to die."

"You leave then."

"I can't. I need to try."

The fire hits some of the spilled fuel spread across the

pavement and starts burning even more intensely. I nervously look toward the back of the van where the explosive fertilizer is. This isn't working, and I'm not going to let this man die either. If I had my powers I'd be able to open this van up like a tin can and have this guy clear of the explosion in half a second.

It's time to break my promise to Michelle.

"Jim, get the hell out of here," I yell, trying to startle him into listening to me, not only to get him clear from danger, but also hopefully clear from seeing me activate my metabands.

"I'm sorry, Connor," Jim says, coughing from the smoke

There's defeat in his voice. Not just because he's not going to be able to save this man, but because he knows that I'm not going to listen to him and clear the area like he wants me to. The flames are more intense than ever, and I can barely even see Jim or the man through the thick black smoke.

"Screw it," I say as my metabands materialize around my wrists, which I then bring together to activate.

I raise my red-covered hand to the roof of the van and peel it back like a banana. With my right arm, I grab the man and with the left I grab Jim. I pivot on the ball of my left foot and push off just as I hear the high-pitched squeal of pressure building up in the back of the van, the pressure of an explosion.

Even moving as fast as I can, there isn't time to completely outrun the fireball at my back if I want to also make sure I don't injure this man any further. I'm only a few steps away before I throw myself over them, shielding the pair from the blast. Smoke and rubble fall over my back like a shower, and then it's over.

Before the smoke clears, I can hear both Jim and the man coughing, and I know that they're okay. I pull myself off of them and step back, looking around to make sure that no one else is nearby. Mostly I'm looking to check for any casualties, but I'm also trying to ensure that no one saw me activate my metabands.

The coast is clear.

Jim slowly works his way back onto his feet. He turns and faces me, taking in the crimson suit before locking his eyes with mine. I should say something to him. I should apologize for lying to him. I should explain why I've done the things I've done. I should say something, anything, but the words just don't come.

"Get out of here," Jim says flatly.

There's no sense of anger or urgency in his voice, just pain. I start to open my mouth, reflexively thinking that he wants me gone because I've lied to him all this time, but then I remember where I am and what activating my powers could mean right now: The Alphas.

So I say nothing and instead take one last glance down the block where I see the crowd starting to come back in this direction. They see me, a metahuman in a city where metahumans are banned. I'm not sure if they're happy or mad, but I don't intend to wait around long enough to find out.

I turn my head toward the sky and, in an instant, I'm gone.

TWENTY-SEVEN

I don't even think about flying directly back home. When this city was crawling with metahumans, it was easy enough to duck into a building from the roof, where I could reasonably sure no one would see me. Even that might have been a stupid risk.

I take a last look over my shoulder. The skyline is clear. There's a jet way off in the distance and a helicopter heading toward the scene of the accident, but nothing else. Time might be running out, so I look for a place to land. It needs to be close, and it needs to be as unpopulated as possible. Landing in a busy intersection isn't going to help with this disappearing act. Below me, I see something that looks like it could work and I swoop down into a dive.

I'm plunging back toward earth head first, as fast as possible without causing a shockwave or any other kind of disturbance that will bring unwanted attention to me. At the speed I'm traveling at, few people would notice me as more than just a strange object out of the corner of their eye. Before they gave it their full attention, I'd already be gone from the sky.

Fighting the instinct to slow down and prepare for a landing, I keep my head firmly in place and keep plummeting, all the way down and right into a huge pile of trash. It was the best place I could find to land on short notice without having to worry about anyone seeing me. My powers might be able to protect me from a lot of things, but they can't do anything to protect me from the smell.

I wait silently, deep in the massive pile of trash, focusing on the sounds around me, listening for the distinctive boom of another meta flying through the sky, but it doesn't come. All I can hear is the sound of dozens, if not hundreds, of rats scampering out of the garbage pile.

The Bay View City Municipal Landfill isn't the kind of

place that gets many lunchtime visitors. That's why I flew into a pile of garbage at high speed. "Pile of garbage" might be a little bit of an understatement. This is a mountain of garbage and evil. The smell is overwhelming, and there's at least thirty feet of it between my head and the rest of the world above me.

When the threat of being ripped apart by an Alpha becomes more welcoming than spending another second breathing through old diapers and discarded cans of dog food, I start to swim for the surface. I fight every instinct I have to not just fly out at super speed, telling myself that someone may still be waiting for me out there.

After a grueling five minutes, I'm finally out of the pile and back breathing fresh air on the surface. Well, not really fresh air. I'm still in a landfill, after all, but compared to where I was, this smells like heaven.

To my relief, there's no one around. I need to get this suit off as soon as possible. Anyone, even a garbage man, seeing me like this and I'm right back to the situation I started from. I raise my wrists and stop right before I click them together, looking at the banana peel clinging to my forearm. Clenching my teeth, I make my body vibrate at supersonic speed. Dirt and slime fly off of me in every direction. Once I'm somewhat satisfied that there's nothing left clinging to me, I power down.

It wouldn't have been as safe, but it sure would have been easier to keep my powers on while I trek through all of this trash on my way toward what I hope is an exit. My balance was never great to begin with, but trying to keep my equilibrium on top of all this shifting, rotting garbage while also holding my breath is really testing my limits.

When I make it back onto solid ground, I take off running for the exit, still looking overhead every few seconds, waiting for an attack that thankfully never comes. I emerge from the entrance to the landfill, running past a driver who does a double take from the cab of his garbage truck. I can see the top of my apartment building from here. It's easily still at least a couple of miles away, though, so I'd better start walking.

* * *

I contact Derrick on the way back to tell him everything's okay. Well, not really *okay*, but my head is still attached to my neck, so it's something. I'm out in the open here, though, which means I can't actually call him and have to use text instead. Derrick thinks that the Alphas are just too powerful to trust phone calls anymore. While he trusts that the encryption he's using is unbreakable, he worries that one of the Alphas might be close enough to zero in on my voice out here in the open and listen in on our conversation.

It's paranoia beyond belief, even for Derrick, but part of me thinks he might actually be right. I decide it's better to be safe than sorry and don't push the issue any further. He tells me to go home and wait. He would go there himself too, but he's worried about today's actions leading to someone getting closer to figuring out who I really am. If that's the case, then him leaving work in the middle of the day and during a big breaking story would only add fuel to that kind of speculation.

After I walk through the front door of the apartment, all I want to do is take a shower. I might have waited until I was out of the trash heap to power down my metabands, but I still had to walk through quite a bit of grossness before I was completely out of there. The long walk home, most of which was uphill, didn't exactly help with the smell either. As nice as a shower sounds, the first thing I do once I calmly close the door and all of the blinds is run over to the TV remote. Derrick would kill me if he knew I was sitting on his nice, new leather couch after taking a swim through the city's waste, but what he doesn't know won't hurt him.

I flip over to one of the meta news networks, sure that they'll have some kind of live report while I also scroll through the different websites on my laptop that cover this type of thing. I checked all of them on my phone during my walk, but I couldn't find anything at all about any metahuman sightings in Bay View City. Did Jim not tell them what happened? Was it possible that no one saw me? I suppose anything's possible, but it seems extremely unlikely.

As I wonder aloud what the hell's going on, a breaking news graphic splashes across the screen, and the video cuts to an anchor sitting at her desk, reading from a stack of papers that have just been handed to her.

"We apologize for interrupting your previously scheduled programming to bring you some breaking news. We've received word that earlier this morning Bay View City witnessed its first confirmed metahuman sighting in nearly two weeks at Regis Park in the downtown area. Witnesses on the ground confirm to MNN that the suspect bore a strong resemblance to the metahuman known as Omni, who has not been seen since his involvement in the unauthorized release of dozens of inmates from the Silver Island Metahuman Containment Facility. When asked if this metahuman may have been responsible for the nearly fatal two-car accident that occurred in the area at the time, officials said that all possibilities are being investigated."

They think I'm responsible? If it wasn't for me, the *almost* fatal car crash would have definitely been fatal.

"At this time, we've been told to advise citizens to remain in their homes until the metahuman in question is found or confirmed to have left the city. He's to be considered extremely dangerous. Sources also tell us that the Alphas may already have a suspect in custody at this time, although that has yet to be confirmed."

It's then that I remember Jim. I didn't call him after I landed for the same reason I didn't call Derrick: all eyes were on Omni and anyone who could be found to be connected to him would be in danger. I figured that they would question Jim and ask him what I said and what I knew. If someone was close enough to have seen me and recognized me as

Omni, then that means they were probably close enough to have noticed the two of us talking. Could they really think Jim was Omni, or were they just trying to get information out of him?

I feel sick to my stomach, suddenly realizing how strongly the situation pointed to Jim as the metahuman they were looking for. He was the only person that the other Blanks would have recognized that stayed close to the accident when everyone else had run.

Anyone there who heard about a metahuman saving the second victim would have assumed that was Jim. Add to that the Blanks' paranoia and constant backstabbing and it's easy to see Jim being turned in. From what I've heard, turning in a suspected traitor is a one-way ticket to an easy promotion among their ranks, even if you're wrong.

That means that the Alphas probably have Jim, and if they do, they won't take "it wasn't me" for an answer. I don't know what they'll do to him. Even if all they get out of him is the truth, that means everyone I know is in trouble.

TWENTY-EIGHT

Out of all of the stupid things I've done, what I'm doing right now might be the stupidest yet. I'm not sure how stupid it can be considered when I have no other choice, though. If I do nothing, my secret will be revealed and Jim will be killed or, most likely, both.

This is what I have to keep reminding myself as I fly through the air, heading toward Keane Tower.

The tower's exterior hasn't changed since I was last here, but its ownership has. After Keane was found guilty of using his telepathic abilities to coerce his business associates into agreeing to unfair and worthless deals, his assets were seized and his business declared bankruptcy. After Silver Island was destroyed, the Alphas moved into the tower and claimed it as their own. There wasn't anyone around who could dispute their claim, so that's where they've remained, and that's where I'm assuming I'll find them.

As I approach the building, I pull back on my speed and raise my hands into the air.

"It's Omni. I'm not here looking for a fight. I think you might be holding the wrong person in there, and I just want to talk. Once that happens, I'll leave Bay View City and never come back. I promise you," I say.

I wonder if they'll be able to hear the slight increase in my heartbeat, which is a surefire indicator that my promise to never return might be a lie. But if it means getting Jim back in one piece, I'll keep to my word.

Far below me, I can see hundreds of people gathering in the streets with their heads tilted skyward. They're watching my every move and listening to my every word. This is what I counted on, maybe the only thing I could actually count on: drawing a crowd. The Alphas may rule Bay View City through intimidation and fear, but I'm hoping that they'll see starting a war in the sky right now is exactly what they claim to be trying to prevent. No one in that crowd below could say that I came here to fight, so if it happens, that's all on Alpha team.

I hover in the air above the city for minutes, waiting. I used some of my power to project my voice loudly enough so that I'm sure it can be heard. Despite the temptation, I stop short of trying to use any kind of enhanced vision to see through the walls and into the building. It's not like that ability has been working well lately, not since Charlie crushed my metabands anyway.

After seven minutes, there's movement. A mirrored window on the eighty-third floor swings open. It's an invitation to come inside.

* * *

Much of the furniture and equipment from the last time I was here, when this was still Keane's building, has been removed. Where there was once a sprawling cubicle farm, now there's nothing but open space. I walk through the space and toward the door of the office that used to belong to Keane, keeping my head on a swivel the entire time. A nagging voice in the back of my mind keeps telling me that this feels like a trap. How could it not feel like a trap? I've been invited into the home of a group whose publicly stated goal is to rid Bay View City of metahumans for good, and here I am, the first metahuman Bay View City has seen in weeks just strolling in for a visit.

As I approach the glass walls of Keane's office, I see him: Charlie. He's sitting with his feet up on Keane's huge wooden slab of a desk. He seems to be making a point of disrespecting Keane's possessions. Charlie's wearing black fatigues and boots, and his face is uncovered. He's not quite old enough to look like a general or anything like that, but he looks like a military man who's nearing the end of his better days. After the scar on his cheek, the most noticeable aspect of his face is that it is tanned and weathered, the look of a man who's spent years, decades even, in warmer climates.

His hair is cut close. Not quite a buzz cut, but not too far off, sprinkled with more gray than dark brown, but still thick and full.

He's speaking to someone just out of my field of vision who is obscured by a pillar. Alpha Team looks at ease in this castle in the sky. If he noticed me coming in, then he's purposefully making an effort to seem like he hasn't. Suddenly he throws his head back in uproarious laughter, which I can see but can't hear through the thick glass walls. As his laughter dies down, his eye catches sight of me, but his expression doesn't change. He waves me into his office with the trace of a smile still on his face, like I'm an old friend he's been expecting to come by for a while.

My heart feels like it's about to beat right through my suit when I reach for the stainless steel handle of the office door and pull it open.

"Come in, come in," Charlie says, standing to greet me and offering a seat in one of the chairs opposite his desk. "I assume you've already met James."

Jim turns his head to see me but doesn't stand. His expression is hard to read and the calm all around me is making this feel even more like a trap. Jim doesn't necessarily seem comfortable, but he also doesn't look like he's being held against his will. Has he told them my secret? Have I so betrayed his trust that his loyalties lie with this man now?

"Can I get you anything? Water, juice, coffee?" Charlie asks, his gaze directed over my shoulder at a younger man wearing an expensive suit who I didn't see when I came in.

I shake my head, and Charlie waves the man off without a word.

"Please, sit," Charlie asks me again.

"I'd rather stand, thanks," I reply.

"Suit yourself, but if this were a trap, you know that being seated or standing wouldn't really matter. You've already put yourself into a potentially very dangerous situation. Taking a load off your feet wouldn't make a whole hell of a lot of difference.

"I've been speaking with young James about your heroics earlier this afternoon. Very impressive stuff if I do say, Mister...?"

"Omni."

He smiles.

"Of course. I didn't think getting your true identity out of you would be that easy. To be honest with you, Omni," he says in a tone that tells me he thinks calling me by my alias is ridiculous, "I really have no interest in who you actually are."

This is the first real indication I have that Jim hasn't told him anything, or at least hasn't told him the truth. Charlie could be lying to me, but I choose to hold onto the small chance that he's not.

"Tell me," Charlie says as he wanders over to Keane's old drink cart and pulls out a bottle of whiskey amongst the dozens of fancier-looking bottles. He pulls the cork out of it and splashes some into a rocks glass before capping the bottle and putting it away. No fancy cocktails for this guy. "What do you truly know about those things?" he asks as he motions to the metabands on my wrists.

"I know enough," I say, trying my best to sound tough.

Charlie throws his head back and lets out a boisterous laugh that's so loud it makes me involuntarily flinch. I'm not sure if he saw it, but if he did, the tough-guy act I just tried has been completely negated.

"Omni, if this conversation is going to be all monosyllabic on your end, then it's going to be a lot longer than it has to be. I thought your old buddy Midnight did enough brooding for both of you?" he asks rhetorically with a smirk. "Now there's a guy I actually would like to know more about. Very interesting character, that one. How he's been able to hold his own in a world filled with metahumans for this long is certainly something to be respected, even if he's often on the wrong side of things. I've had a lot of training in my time in the service. A lot of training. Usually with a guy like that, I could tell you ten different things about him just by how he fights. I could look at how someone like that throws a punch and tell you where he learned it, who he learned it from, how long ago, the list goes on. But his methods are almost completely alien to me. It's not as though there's a lot of footage of him to go by, but still. Fascinating stuff. I won't lie. I'd be very interested to learn who it is under *that* cowl. But under yours? It really doesn't matter to me."

He finishes pacing back and forth in front of his desk and walks around to the other side to take a seat. Once he's seated, he takes a long sip from his whiskey.

"Wow, that is good stuff. I don't think I've had whiskey this expensive since the time we raided King Abdullah's castle back during the Krykstan skirmish. Very good stuff," he says as he places the glass on the desk in front of him.

Jim sits quietly with his head facing forward, ignoring me.

"Why did you tell everyone that I'm dangerous?" I ask.

"Because you are dangerous, Omni. You're very dangerous. All of us are."

"You told them that I caused that car accident."

"I did nothing of the sort. Unfortunately, despite the appearance that we completely run this city and all the media within it, that simply isn't the case. The news reports what the news wants to report."

"And that just happens to usually be anti-meta rhetoric?"

"Well what do you expect from a world that has been ravaged by people like us?"

"Don't group me in with you. We're nothing alike."

"I'm sure you believe that, but sadly it's simply not the case, because at the end of the day, we're both the same. We're humans. And humans have weaknesses. Flaws. Vulnerabilities that no metabands can overcome. The sooner other metahumans realize and accept that, the better off all of us will be. There's a reason why the news reports stories the way that they do. It's because they fit in with the narrative that normal citizens expect and want to hear. Do you know how many people left Bay View City after we imposed a ban on metahumans here? Five percent. That's it. Only five percent of people who called Bay View City home felt that our new law was so terrible that they had to leave."

"But you're only counting people who have the ability to leave. Lots people in this city have lived here their entire lives and so have their families. Just because they didn't leave, doesn't mean they agree with what you're doing."

Charlie shrugs and looks into his whiskey glass.

"I'm sure you're not entirely wrong, but you're missing the point."

"Which is?"

"You see yourself as a hero. A savior."

"I just see myself as someone who does what they can to help."

"That's bullshit!" Charlie exclaims in a burst of rage as he slams his whiskey down on the desk, spilling half of it onto the floor before straightening himself in his seat and clearing his throat. "I apologize for that. It's just that I've heard that excuse before. I've heard false humility. I've heard good intentions. But power corrupts. And the world has seen what this type of power has led to in the past."

He's talking about The Battle. Jim has barely looked at me since I walked in, but now I can tell he's trying even harder not to.

"So your solution is to get rid of all the metahumans except for you and your buddies? How does consolidating power into the hands of the few fix the problem you're talking about?"

"I never said that was what I was talking about, which brings me back to my original question, which you so flippantly tossed aside with a smart-ass remark: How much do you know about how those things on your wrists actually work?"

I remain silent, partially because I don't know a lot about how they really work and partially because the little I may know is the last thing I would tell him if he doesn't know already.

"You're guarded about this. I can see that. I can understand that, even. You don't know me, and I don't know you. Why would you tell me something that I might be able to use against you? I'll start then by telling you something about my metabands that I haven't heard about any others.

"I can feel when other metahumans are close. It's hard to describe, and it only works if the bands are active, but it's uncanny. When you showed up at that accident today, an accident which I fully believe you had nothing to do with, incidentally, I hadn't learned about it from television. I learned about it from these," he says, holding up his wrists to show me his own metabands.

"I could feel your power nearby. That's how I knew you were here. It's how we were sure, prior to your arrival today, that we were a city completely free of metahumans."

This isn't something I've ever experienced before, and it makes me wonder how else Charlie's metabands are different from my own.

"Do you know why I could feel your power, Omni? I'll tell you. It's because we're connected."

"Oh no, is this going to be one of those 'Luke, I am your father' type speeches?" I ask.

There's a brief pause, and it seems like I've just infuriated him. I can feel my muscles beginning to tense up and my adrenaline surging as I wonder if this is going to be it, if this is finally when we're going to have it out. But it doesn't happen. Instead, Charlie throws his head back and laughs again, even harder than last time. He's laughing so hard that tears are rolling down his face, and he's having trouble catching his breath.

"I heard that you were witty like that. It's a defense mechanism, I'm sure. Something you do when you're not sure what else to say, but still, I have to admit, that was very funny. I should have been clearer. It's not just you and I that are connected, Omni. It's all of us. And I don't mean that in the tree-hugger sense of the word. I mean literally. There is some unknown force that ties all of these bands to one another.

"Has it ever occurred to you why it was that shortly after you found your metabands that the rest literally started raining from the sky?" he asks.

I let my guard down slightly. I know that there's something more happening here, something else going on that I just don't quite have a grasp on yet, but the truth is that I have wondered. My head has been full of questions about the pieces of metal wrapped around my wrists since they first appeared, and my curiosity is getting the better of me.

"What do you know about my metabands that I don't?" I ask.

"Not a lot. And I'm certain that there are things you know about yours that I don't. They're very personal items, after all, adapting to their owner's physiology so closely that they refuse to work for anyone else, granting abilities unique to each owner. They become a part of you, as we've found out ourselves as well, obviously.

"No, there isn't much more that I know about your metabands than you do, save one thing. If they are indeed all connected in some way, yours are the linchpin."

"I'm not sure what you mean by that."

"Do you remember The Battle of Empire City?" he asks.

If it weren't for the suit I'm wearing, I'm positive I would have started breaking out in a sweat. Of course I remember The Battle. Everyone remembers The Battle. Is he asking me because he knows who I am and that my parents died there?

"Of course," I answer, trying to make sure no emotion seeps through into my words.

"It was a silly question. Everyone remembers The Battle, of course. It's what changed our opinions about metahumans forever. After two of them destroyed half of a city, they were no longer something to be admired; they were something to be feared. That was the day we learned that even with the best intentions, they can cause more death and destruction than we could ever imagine.

"A lot of people forgot that feeling. They forgot the feeling of inadequacy, of powerlessness that the entire world shared that day. I was well into my military career by that time and was deployed to Empire City in the aftermath. The things I saw there dwarfed anything else I'd ever seen before or since in my time fighting for this country.

"That was when we all decided to put our foot down. That was when the government started planning for how to deal with this type of problem."

"And what happened?"

"Nothing. The Governor and Jones never came back. The other metahumans lost their powers. Some disappeared, some tried to turn their former status into pathetic reality television careers. Most importantly, though, people forgot. They forgot how they felt on that day when we saw two gods go head to head and take half a city with them. Funding dried up. The public lost interest in trying to find ways to fight a war against an enemy it had become convinced was never coming back.

"What very few thought about was what it meant that the deaths of The Governor and Jones were what brought all the other metahumans to their knees. No one put the pieces together and realized that it was the destruction of their metabands that muted all of the others. That is, until you arrived.

"You were the first, just like The Governor. And just like him, your arrival heralded the coming of all the rest."

I can feel a knot forming in my stomach as I begin to realize what he's saying and what it means. The Governor sacrificing his life ended up disabling all the other metabands because his were the first. His metabands were tied to all of the others, and when they ceased to exist, destroyed in the twenty-seven million degree inferno of the Sun, so did all of the other metabands.

"So if you think killing me would accomplish your goal of ridding the planet of metahumans, why spend all of this time explaining it to me? Isn't explaining how and why you're going to kill the good guy something they teach you not to do in like Supervillains 101?" I ask.

"Is that how you see yourself, as the good guy?" Charlie asks.

"I don't like to classify the world into little boxes like that."

"I'm glad to hear that. I agree completely."

"But you've tried to separate the world as metahumans and humans, as if we're less than humanity because of our abilities, abilities that you have yourself."

"I'm fully aware of the contradictions. Many see my group as the villains while many more see us as the heroes. Real life isn't always as black and white as people would like. I think that's something you're well aware of yourself. You've killed before after all, haven't you?"

"Only to save the life of an innocent victim, and that was an accident that happened before I learned how to control my powers."

"Ah, yes, of course. An accident. And how many accidents are the general public supposed to accept from metahumans every year? Just a few? Dozens? Hundreds? Where is the line there? Where do we start to calculate how many lives we're comfortable destroying in the name of allowing others to have this type of power?"

"If you've made up your mind already, then why are we still talking?" I say, my hands at my sides still, but slowly clenching into fists in anticipation of an attack.

"You still don't get it, do you?" Charlie says as he rises and walks back over to the rolling bar to prepare another drink. "How could I stand here and talk about how I want to stop the type of destruction caused during the first wave only to turn around and do the exact same thing myself? I haven't invited you here for a fight. That would accomplish nothing and only serve to contradict my goals. I haven't invited you here to kill you. I've invited you here to ask you to forfeit your metabands of your own volition."

"You want me to just hand my metabands over to you?"

"I don't want you to hand them over. I want you to join us in destroying them. You've seen the power our metabands possess, and you no doubt know by now that we have the ability to destroy them. But, by destroying the first pair, we'll effectively destroy every pair out there, including our own."

"And why would you want to do that?"

"To save the world. To stop another family from being ripped apart by a car being thrown into the sky and landing on a child twenty blocks away. It's not too late. We can go back to the way things were. Metahumans can be something that future generations only read about in history books, a strange blip on the timeline of humanity, but one that didn't threaten the entire future of our species as it does today.

"I understand that this is a lot for you to take in, and in the spirit of peace I'm going to ask you to take your time thinking about what I've just proposed to you. I think that if you do, you'll realize that you have the opportunity to change the entire world for the better with your decision. You might have power now, but doing this? Doing this would be true power. And true courage. Something a pair of metabands could never give you or anyone else.

"Think about it. I'll be waiting for you when you make your final decision," he says as he sits back down at his desk, putting his feet up again as he takes a gulp from his rocks glass.

I turn and begin walking out of his office and toward the window I came in through.

"Oh, and Omni?" Charlie calls to me as I open the door leading to the rest of the office building. "If you ever come back to Bay View City, it had better be to destroy your metabands. You don't want to see what happens if you decline our offer and think you can return. Consider this your only warning."

TWENTY-NINE

I've made the argument repeatedly to Michelle and anyone else who will listen that it's redundant for me to have to take a history class on metahumans. I'm already spending half my day training as a metahuman. Why do I need to sit through a class about it in regular school too? It's strange. I never imagined that I'd be wishing for something like a math class, but here we are.

Michelle's argument is twofold. The first reason being that I'm the brother and legal ward of one of the most well-known metahuman reporters in the world. It would be at best weird and at worst suspicious if I seemed to have absolutely no interest in metahumans. The class isn't especially easy to get into since so many want to take it, and turning down a seat in the class would raise more attention than Michelle feels comfortable with.

Her other reason is she thinks my knowledge of metahuman history isn't as good as I think it is. Of course I scoff at this, which leads her to giving me a pop quiz.

"Who was the fourth metahuman to become unmasked during the first wave?"

Uhhh ...

"Which professional sports league was the first to issue a ban on metahumans?"

Hmm ...

"Which first-wave metahuman held the world land speed record, and what was that record in miles per hour?"

Okay. So I haven't necessarily paid attention as closely as I should have all the times Derrick droned on and on about this stuff when I was ten years old. So what? That stuff isn't important when you've got your own pair of metabands. What use is knowing about some dumb world record from when I was a little kid when I know that I can personally break it myself any time I want?

The only consolation is that the class has a few other secret metahumans in it, people that I think I'm actually starting to be able to call my friends. There's a certain camaraderie, if you can call it that, between all of us. This is only intensified when we all have to sit through classes like this one, making faces at each other while Ms. Drew recites half incorrect facts about metahumans from a textbook that's close to being as old as I am.

After class, I'm heading for the door when Winston cuts me off at the pass.

"Learn anything new about these overrated false gods today?" he asks while giving me a knowing wink.

I laugh in return to be polite, but I'm still looking over my shoulder to make sure no one overheard him and somehow figured out through his sarcasm that we're both secretly metahumans. Midnight's paranoia is creeping into my own thoughts, yet again.

"Are you coming to my party tonight?" he asks.

"Umm, what party tonight?" I reply.

"Maybe you didn't hear me the first time. I'll try again. I know you can be kind of slow. Hey, Connor. Are you coming to *my* party tonight? Does that answer your question about 'what' party tonight?"

"Yes, it's *your* party."

"And they say you can't learn any new tricks," Winston says with a punch to my arm. Not a hard punch, though, a joke punch, the kind of punch a friend gives another friend, which is different from the punches I'm used to, which were previously from bullies and more recently from super-powered maniacs.

"Yeah, sure," I say while trying to figure out in my head if this is the first time I've actually been personally invited to a party by the person throwing the party.

"Cool. Eight o'clock. See you there," he says as he turns to leave for the next class.

"Wait, where do you live?"

"Off-campus apartments."

"You don't live on campus? Why? I thought we all had to live on campus?" I ask.

I don't even notice that a straggler has unintentionally crept up behind me on her way out the door. I'm not sure if she heard me and it looks like Winston isn't either. He gives her a tight-lipped smile as she squeezes past the two of us.

"You've got to be more careful. Luckily, you're weird to begin with so she probably just thinks you're dumb."

"Well that's a relief."

"Steve will give you a ride there. He's got a car here, as long as you don't mind walking home. It's not far."

THIRTY

When Winston said he lived in an off-campus apartment, he failed to mention that, while that's technically true, he actually has the entire building all to himself. His family is in the real estate business, and they own the place. Michelle prefers to have all of us live on campus, but Winston managed to talk his way into being able to stay at his own place. He successfully argued that it'd look strange for him to live in a cramped dorm room when he could be living here, practically across the street from campus. Of course, that's total bull, but Winston's no dummy. He used Michelle and the academy's own paranoia about secrecy to help him skirt one of their own rules. Genius.

There's a bunch of reasons why they want all of us staying on campus, but one of the biggest ones is so they can keep an eye on us and make sure we don't do things exactly like what Winston is doing right now. I'm not sure how they expect us to act like "normal" teenagers, though, if they don't want us to find ways to break the rules without them knowing now and then. Of course, I also half expect that they're fully aware of Winston's little plan and still have eyes on us somehow. Maybe they understand that letting us do stupid things like this keeps us from doing even stupider things down the line when it matters more.

While I figured this would be bigger than a "small get together," I wasn't expecting the type of party I find in front of me as Steve and I walk up to the building. There are people *everywhere*: people hanging out on the front lawn, people packing the multiple balconies lining the front of the building, people flowing into the backyard and pool.

"Connor! You aren't actually physically limited to leaving the campus after all," Winston says as he breaks off from a group he's talking to and gives me a hard clap on the back.

"Do people really think that?" I stupidly ask.

"No, not really. Not all of them, at least. I wasn't sure if you were going to show up tonight, though. You're the last person I would expect to make fashionably late entrances."

"Steve's car battery died before he came to pick me up, so any fashionable lateness can be chalked up to him."

"Ha! I'd tell him that, but it looks like he already found where the pool is."

I look over my shoulder and see Steve kicking his sneakers off before running toward the pool and yanking his shirt off with one hand right before he leaps into the air for a cannonball. Those already in the pool, and therefore already wet, cheer for him. Those standing alongside the pool's edge, all of whom were dry up until a second ago, are not as impressed.

"Here, I just grabbed this for myself, but it's all yours. I'll get another," Winston says as he pushes a red plastic cup into my hands.

"Oh, I don't really drink," I say.

"You're not driving tonight, and you've actually managed to make it off campus. One drink isn't going to kill you."

I hesitantly sniff the red liquid sloshing around in the cup.

"It's not poisoned. Trust me," Winston says.

What the hell, I think to myself before I take a swig.

"Ugh, this is terrible," I say. "What is it?"

"Oh, come on! There's hardly even anything in it. It's mostly just fruit punch."

"That's what I'm talking about. It tastes like old candy mixed with pure sugar."

"Relax, it'll grow on you."

* * *

Winston wasn't kidding when he said I'd get used to the taste. After my third cup, I don't even notice it anymore. All of a sudden I'm either finally having a good time, kinda drunk, or both. Probably both. Winston cuts me off after that, whispering into my ear something about loose lips sinking ships. I have to ask him to repeat it three times before he finally just explains that I have to be careful about keeping my secrets secret.

It turns out that I turn into a real Chatty Cathy when I'm buzzed. I can't help it, though. All of a sudden my social anxieties are gone, and I'm having conversations with my classmates like it's completely normal or something. This is with my *real* classmates for the most part too, not just the other metas. I'd been so worried about my secrets that I'd barely spoken to most of them before tonight out of concern that I wouldn't be able to keep track of all the lies I have to keep. Now I realize that I do a better job keeping my secrets when I'm not thinking about them constantly. Who knew?

There's about a dozen of us in a circle all talking and laughing about the way Mr. Yancy pronounces the word "fusion" in chemistry class. The way he says the word rhymes with "onion" for some reason. I'm not doing much of the talking, but I'm still there.

A new person I don't recognize joins the circle and is introduced by a friend of hers as Ashley. She faces the circle and pivots around slightly on the balls of her feet, giving each of us a small wave as a means of introduction. Most of us give her a small wave back to say hi, including me. That's when I notice her wrist and feel my heart skip a beat. She notices me staring and the conversation slowly quiets down.

"Everything okay with you?" she asks me.

"You ... you're wearing metabands," I stammer out, feeling my face beginning to become flush.

"I am, so you'd better watch out," she yells at me as she assumes a mock fighting stance. Everyone else in the circle laughs, except me. They all notice that I'm not laughing, which seems to make them all laugh even harder.

"They're not real, Connor," Claire from chemistry class says to me. Ashley notices that I must still look very confused and steps forward to show them to me more closely and explain.

"They're fakes, obviously. If I were a metahuman, I

wouldn't be hanging out with these losers," she jokes, drawing more laughs and a handful of mock protests. "I got them online. They're supposed to be super accurate looks-wise, obviously. I won't be picking up any cars with these on unfortunately."

She takes one off and places it in my hand.

"Wow, it really does feel like a real one," I say. She looks at me puzzled. Crap. I just did the thing that Winston was afraid of me doing. "I mean, from what I've read."

"Oh, for a minute there I thought you were going to tell me that you've actually held one in real life."

"Ha, no, no, of course not."

"I was going to say. From what I've heard, most metas aren't too eager to let someone else try their metabands on, even if they know they won't do anything, especially after that little trick that Iris girl pulled on that nerd who tore up Bay View City."

"Trick?"

"When she teleported away with them. I heard she put them on the moon."

"Mars, actually."

Ashley is giving me the same "how did you know that?" look as before.

"That's what I heard, anyway."

There's a familiar clap on my back again and Winston's voice.

"Connor here has a brother who's big in the metahuman news industry. Isn't that right?" he asks.

"Um, yeah," I say as he gives me a suddenly deadly serious look that tells me that I've got to be more careful about what I'm saying.

"Really? Who does he work for?" she asks.

"Um, connollyreport.com," I reply.

"Oh my God! You're kidding. That is, like, my favorite site. I'm not even kidding you. I have it set as my homepage."

"Connor here is being modest. His brother doesn't *just*

work for them, does he, Mr. Connolly?" Winston says with a smile.

Ashley's eyes widen as the realization hits her.

"Wait, your brother is Derrick Connolly? Get out of here."

"Yeah, he is."

Ashley suddenly ignores everyone else standing in the circle and cuts through them to stand closer to me.

"And you're Connor Connolly? Like, the real Connor Connolly?"

"Umm, yeah," I say with a nervous laugh.

"I remember reading all about your story. How Omni saved you and that little girl in the woods that night. That was the first metahuman sighting in years and years, and you were actually there!"

"Yeah, I was."

"Can I ask you a question?"

"Sure."

"What was he like?"

I catch Winston out of the corner of my eye as he moves from our small group onto another, playing the host, but not before he gives me a look that seems to say, "Remember, don't be an idiot."

"He was ... I don't know. Red?"

"Wow. I can't believe you actually met Omni."

"Well I didn't really *meet him* meet him. It was more like I just kinda saw him, you know?"

"Still. That must have been incredible."

"Yeah, I mean he was kinda incredible, now that you mention it."

I hear a throat being cleared behind me and see that it's Winston again as he walks past, another reminder not to lay it on too thick. I can't help it, though. It's nice to have someone asking questions and showing interest in me, even if they don't realize that it's me.

"I'm sorry if I'm like totally fangirling out. I'm just a big meta geek, as you've probably picked up on by now."

"I'm the last person to call anyone else a metahuman geek after living with Derrick my whole life. That guy is like a pocket protector with legs when it comes to geeking out about this stuff."

"Oh, right. I forgot that you and he were orphaned. That's why you live together, right?"

And just like that this conversation has gone from fun and flattering to awkward and weird. Usually I'm the one who does that, so it's actually kinda nice for someone else to step up to the plate for once.

"Sorry, I shouldn't have said that. I forget that these kinds of things happen to real people sometimes, you know?"

"I know what you mean. It's okay. Don't worry about it."

"So, do you know if Derrick is hiring any interns for the winter break?"

"Sorry, I have literally no idea."

"Hmm, well do you think you can ask him for me?"

"Um, yeah. Sure."

"Great!"

She stands staring at me with a goofy grin on her face. I can feel the awkwardness increasing as the length of time where neither of us is saying anything grows longer.

"Do you think you can ask him now?" she asks me.

Is she serious? I look at her eyes and can see that yes, she is absolutely serious.

"Oh, I'm not really sure if he's busy right now, you know?"

"Totally. I totally know ... but there's really only one way to find out."

She's totally, totally serious. What do I do? I don't want to be mean, but I also don't like being put on the spot like this. Should I just call Derrick and ask him? What would I even say? "Hey, Derrick, I snuck off of campus even though your girlfriend specifically told me not to, and now I'm at a party where I'm a little bit drunk and some weird girl won't stop asking me to ask you to let her work for you, so what do you think?"

I'm beginning to realize that Ashley's idea of awkwardness is out of step with the rest of the world's as she just stands there like a statue, waiting, with no sign of letting me off the hook. My hand reaches for my pocket to grab my phone. Am I really going to call Derrick right now? Maybe I can just pretend like I'm dialing his number and then say that there was no answer?

Just as I pull my phone out of the pocket of my jeans, I feel it buzzing. I look at the screen and see that it's displaying "Caller Unknown." I used to see things like that and just assume it was some telemarketer, but I know better nowadays.

"Can you excuse me for just one minute?" I ask.

Ashley's expression barely changes as she waits. She doesn't take the cue to step back a little bit and offer me some privacy, so I turn to make some for myself.

"Hello?" I say into the receiver.

"Where are you?" Midnight asks on the other end.

Ah, saved by the masked vigilante.

"Um," I say as I consider lying for a moment before I realize how futile that usually is with him. "I'm at a party."

"Get to the rooftop of the parking garage a block south from your current position."

I should have known that, of course, he knows where I am already. He was asking more about *why* I am where I am. He's not mad at me for having snuck off campus, even though it's super against the rules. The fact that he's passing up an opportunity to yell at me means whatever is going on is serious. And when it's serious, he's not going to tell me anymore than what is absolutely necessary, especially over the phone. And from the sound of it, all that's absolutely necessary for me to know is that I get to that rooftop.

I hit the end call button without saying goodbye, remembering that he never says it anyway and feeling slightly proud that I got to end the call for a change.

It's definitely less than ideal to leave this party when I'm actually having a good time, but I'd be lying to myself if I didn't admit that I'm kinda excited to jump back into action. I have no idea what Midnight is up to, but these types of nights have been few and far between lately. Training is fine and all, and it's nice to be somewhere relatively safe during the day where I don't have to constantly look over my shoulder, waiting for some random attack, but neither is a replacement for a night of cracking bad guy skulls.

Before I slip my phone into my pocket, I feel it buzz again, and I look down to see a new text message, also from an unknown number.

Tell no one. You have 3 minutes.

Pretty safe to assume that one's from Midnight too. I hadn't planned on announcing to the entire party that I was leaving early to go meet up with my vigilante friend for some undisclosed mission, but I didn't think it would be a big problem to mention it to some of the other metas here. When I think about it, I realize that the only reason I feel that way is because I know it would make a few of them jealous. It's not malicious. It just feels good to be enviable once in awhile. It feels good, but maybe it's not *actually* good for me. That's the type of attitude that gets people in trouble, sooner or later.

It's also probably a bad idea since there are at least one or two people here who would want to tag along. They'd flat out insist. I know they would, and even if I said "no," they'd try to follow anyway. I can't even imagine what the look on Midnight's face would be if I showed up at the agreed upon rendezvous point and just happened to have a couple of friends looking to come along with us.

I'm still a few feet away from the group I was hanging out with, but none of them are looking in my direction. If I'm going to make it in time, I'd better beat feet. There's no time for goodbyes, especially when they'd just bring questions that I wouldn't be quick enough to come up with answers for. A few will wonder where I've disappeared to, maybe even worry a little bit, but it'll be fine. I'll text Winston after I'm with Midnight. Keep the details vague, but let him know that I'm fine.

Working my way through the crowded backyard and through the sliding glass door leading into the house, I can see that the party has started growing exponentially in just the short time since I've arrived. There are tons of people I don't recognize. I'm not even sure anymore if most of the people here go to the academy.

As I move through the crowd, I'm feeling grateful that there are so many new people here and so many eyes that don't recognize me. It's fewer people to think about where I've gone. If the other metas here don't know where I went, then they won't have to lie when anyone else asks them. *If* anyone else asks them, of course. I think I'm probably overestimating just how missed I'm going to be at a party this big.

Right before I make it to the door, a second before my hand reaches out for the knob, I'm recognized.

"Connor?" Sarah asks from my right.

I hadn't seen her standing there. I didn't even know that she was at this party, but of course she's at this party. Everyone's at this party. And of course she would see me now, when I'm trying to sneak out the door.

"I thought that was you," she says as she makes her way toward me.

She reaches out and gives me a hug, a friendly hug. No different than any of the others she's given me in the past on the surface, but there's something different about it. I can just feel it.

"You're not leaving, are you?" she asks.

"Yeah, unfortunately."

"You've got to be joking. I feel like this party just got started."

She's been drinking. Not a lot, but enough to be feeling good right about now, the same way I was feeling before

Midnight called me away. Now I just feel kinda dizzy and uncoordinated. "I was kinda hoping when I saw you that we'd maybe have a chance to catch up ..."

"With me?"

"Yes, with you, dummy," she says in a tone that reminds me of how things used to be. "It's silly that we're both here in Skyville and barely even hang out. I know things didn't exactly end ideally, but things were also kinda crazy at the time."

That may be the biggest understatement anyone has ever made in the history of humanity. Even if I wasn't a metahuman and she wasn't working at The Agency, it would have been an insane time. It was an insane time for everyone in Bay View City. Throw in both of our secrets, me knowing hers, her being in the dark about mine, and you have maybe the most complicated situation a new relationship could ever run up against.

"I've just been thinking about everything a lot lately."

"And?" I ask hopefully.

No. I can't ask any questions right now. A crowded party where we're both a little drunk, isn't the place to have this type of conversation under normal circumstances, let alone when I've got an angry vigilante waiting for me on a roof somewhere, scowling at his watch, I'm sure. Well, not his watch. He doesn't wear a watch, but I assume he's got a little clock in that cowl somewhere, considering everything else it's stuffed with.

"And ... I don't know. I guess that's probably why I wanted to talk in the first place. Try to figure a few things out. Maybe I'm just being stupid ..."

"No, you're not being stupid. It's just ..." I say.

Dammit. Think. I've got to come up with an excuse. Say my stomach isn't feeling well? Then she's gonna think that I'm leaving just so I can go poop. That's never a good idea, especially when it's a conversation with your ex-girlfriend that you kinda never really got over.

Don't start thinking about how you're not over her.

Just say something, anything, so this stops being so weird and awkward.

"I'm meeting up with a friend," I finally blurt out.

Not a lie at all really, but I'm certainly leaving out some of the more interesting details.

For a second, she looks a little confused. If I wasn't preoccupied or drunk, I'd make a joke here like, "Y*es, I actually have a friend. Don't look so surprised.*"Before I have the chance to think of anything more clever, her eyes widen and her expression changes to something resembling disappointment.

"Oh, I see. *That* kind of friend," she says.

"What?" I ask, genuinely confused.

I hear my own voice rise an octave and realize it's because I think she somehow knows about Midnight, that she somehow knows who I really am and that she somehow knows where I'm heading.

"It's fine, Connor. We broke up. You're allowed to see other people."

"Huh? No! No, that's not ... no," I stammer out.

She thinks I'm already seeing someone else when nothing could be further from the truth. Suddenly I realize that, as bad of an idea as having a conversation about us and what happened between us might be tonight, having her think I've already moved on is even worse.

But what else can I tell her? I start trying to convince myself that flat out denying it is the best idea since there's a chance that if she thinks I'm seeing someone, she might try to follow me to see who it is. But I know that she's not going to do that. That's just me trying to justify it to myself. She's not going to follow me. She's not like that.

"Seriously, Connor. It's fine. You don't have to explain anything to me. You don't owe me anything," she says. I can tell that she doesn't fully mean it, but she feels embarrassed now and isn't sure what else to say.

"It's not like that," I say as I take a quick glance at my watch. Damn, I'm already late. Midnight is not going to be happy. "I'm sorry, but I actually really have to run."

Sarah gives a tight-lipped smile and nods to me.

"We'll talk, though?" I say, meaning for it to sound like an invitation but having it come out sounding more like a plea.

"Sure."

I smile back at her, forcing it myself somewhat too, and turn to head out the door and out of this situation. The front porch of the house is filled with even more people, most of whom are sitting on the tall steps leading to the front door. I curse them under my breath as I contort my feet to fit into the tiny slivers of open space as I descend the stairs.

Suddenly I'm angry at everything. I'm angry at how all of these circumstances have colluded to ruin what started off as such a great night. My initial eagerness to use my powers again has given way to feelings of anger and disappointment. The one thing that makes me stand out from everyone else in a good way is now compromising my regular life.

The crowd continues along the stairs and into the front yard with even more people spilling into the street. I stop for a moment to get my bearings and figure out the direction I need to head toward to meet Midnight. It's so loud out here that I can barely hear myself think. Cars are pulled up along the curb with their doors open as their stereo systems compete with each other, forming a loud, mangled mass of noise. If Winston isn't careful and doesn't ask some of these people to leave, he's going to have the cops show up.

Right as I'm thinking this, the cops show up.

They've obviously been lying in wait nearby until they had enough backup. A dozen cop cars come screeching from around every corner on the block. If you're going to try to wrangle this many people, you'd better come prepared, and that's exactly what they did.

I breathe a sigh of relief when I see this, because I'm already across the street and clear of the party. If I'd left a few seconds later, I would be stuck in that house with no way out in time. I start to pull my phone out of my pocket to check the time again, jogging to make up the lost seconds, but before I have a chance to hit the home button on my phone, I hear someone yelling in my direction.

"Hey! You! Freeze!"

At first I'm sure they aren't talking to me. They must be yelling at someone else, someone trying to make a run for it from the party.

"Are you deaf? I said freeze!"

The second shout is louder and closer. There's no one else near me that he could be talking to. Instinctively, I turn in the direction of the yelling. I lock eyes with a police officer for an instant before I'm blinded by his flashlight.

Any doubt about whether or not he was talking to me is instantly removed.

"On the ground, now!"

There's only two choices I can make. I can do as he says, stop my jog, and get on the ground. If I'm lucky, I'll be able to explain to him that I was leaving the party already, and I wasn't trying to run from him.

The other option is to turn this jog into a sprint and hope I can outrun him. My reaction time is slower right now, and I'm taking way too long to figure out what I should do. That's when I remember the drinks I had. He'll smell them on me. I'm sure of it. And even if he didn't, he'd still make me do that test where you have to say the alphabet backwards or something. One way or another, he's not going to let me go just because I tell him I was already leaving.

In the distance something in the sky catches my eye. At first I assume it must be a metahuman, but as I focus my attention on it, I can see it isn't a metahuman at all. It's a reflection in an otherwise dark night sky. The reflection changes, catching moonlight as it turns. For just a fraction of a second, when the moon hits it just right, I can see its entire outline and tell what it is: a jet.

There are only a few people in the world who would have their own jet with some kind of advanced cloaking technology, and only one that I know personally.

It's Midnight, and he's leaving without me. No choice now, I think, as my jog becomes a full-on sprint. Behind me I can hear the jangling of handcuffs on the police officer's belt as he chases after me. It hasn't even occurred to me what I would do if I were caught, which is why I can't get caught.

The footsteps behind me are growing closer. I underestimated how quick the cop could run, and I realize that the chances of me putting more distance between him and myself are slim. It's time to pull the emergency cord.

With a thought, my metabands appear around my wrists again. I chance one last glance over my shoulder to see where the cop is, hoping that he's far enough away still to have not had the chance to get a good look at my face. In the second that I take my eyes off the road in front of me, my right foot catches a crack in the road. I'm airborne, but not in the way I'm used to.

Instinctively, I put my hands out in front of me, not even thinking about the metabands I'm wearing. Luckily for me, once they're active, they don't require much more thought to turn on. The metabands just barely graze each other as I put my hands up in front of me just inches before I'm about to slam into the ground. Not exactly the most graceful powering up sequence, but it still counts.

Time around me slows. The metabands sense the imminent danger I'm in and adjust to give me time to get myself out of it. As the suit leaks out of the bands and wraps itself around me, I pull up, and my nose just barely kisses the asphalt as I swoop into the air.

I take another look over my shoulder now that I don't have to worry about falling and breaking my face. The cop chasing me slows his running to a halt. He's doubled over, trying to catch his breath.

I made it. Now I just have to catch Midnight.

*　*　*

Scanning the cloudy nighttime horizon, it's difficult to spot him at first, but within a few seconds I'm able to make out the heat trail coming from the jet's engine about a mile in front of me. Head down, I push myself hard to catch up with him. Within seconds, I reach the jet and realize I have another problem I didn't anticipate: getting inside. The jet is all black and appears completely seamless. I can't even find where the door would be on this thing, so I move around to approach the cockpit, or at least what I assume is the cockpit. The reason I can't tell for sure is that the windows, if you can even call them that, are completely tinted over.

I hang in front of the jet for a few seconds, figuring Midnight has to see me inside. I consider knocking politely on the window, but ultimately decide against it, knowing that Midnight's likely already mad at me for being late. After a few seconds, I hear the sound of hissing pistons and moving mechanical parts coming from the rear of the plane.

A previously hidden cargo bay door reveals itself, and I waste no time finding my way to it and enter the plane. Once inside, the door snaps shut, and I can feel the area re-pressurizing before a door at the front of the bay area slides open.

"You're late," Midnight says from beyond the door.

I head toward his voice, through the sliding door, and into the cockpit area. It's a tight squeeze and there's only one seat, which Midnight is currently occupying as he stares ahead at the starless night sky in front of him. The tinted cockpit window is not only crystal clear from this side, but also filled with information overlays showing a three-dimensional, textured map of the ground beneath us hidden below the clouds.

"Sorry about that. Ran into a little trouble with the local law enforcement," I say. He turns his head to give me a stern look. "Don't worry. They didn't get a look at my face."

I consider suggesting to Midnight that he should have had

me fly him wherever it is that we're going. Even with dragging him along behind me, I can easily fly at least twice as fast as this jet. Then I remember the last time I suggested flying the both of us somewhere. It didn't end well. Apparently Midnight doesn't like people picking him up.

"So, where are we off to in such a hurry?" I ask.

Without a word or taking his eyes off the night sky in front of him, Midnight hits a couple of buttons, and a screen behind him blinks on. Displayed on it is a large white man whose face looks pulled and distorted. His mouth is three times larger than it should be.

"The street name he goes by is Chomp. He was one of the escapees from Silver Island that hasn't been caught yet," Midnight says. "In case you haven't guessed it already by his name, his metahuman abilities give him a nearly indestructible jawbone and teeth. He can bite through any material known to man. He's used his talent to break into stores, homes, bank vaults, you name it. He wasn't a high priority recapture until this was found last night on the streets of Seattle."

Midnight hits another button, and the screen changes to show something that looks like a steel birdcage crossed with a bike lock.

"What is that?" I ask.

"That was his muzzle. While Chomp could bite through nearly anything, that was the limit of his abilities. In order to keep him from simply eating his way out of Silver Island, this headgear was designed to keep anything larger than a plastic straw away from his mouth."

"Why the size of a plastic straw?"

"That's what they fed him through. Shortly after the headpiece was found, a local liquor store was burglarized. The bite marks on the cash register match Chomp's."

"So how do we find him? There must be a reason he went to Seattle. Does he have family there, former business associates?"

"No. He did once, but Chomp owes a lot of bad people a lot of money. Going to any of them for help wouldn't get him more than a bullet between the eyes."

"So then why go back there at all? Seems a lot riskier than just finding a new city and starting over."

"He went back to Seattle because it's the only city with these."

The screen changes again to show the interior of a fast-food restaurant. The angle and quality of the footage tells me that it's from a security camera. Before I have a chance to ask what exactly I'm looking at, I see a tall, bulky man wearing a scarf around his face enter.

"That's him. Did he rob this place too?"

"No. He bought a dozen hamburgers."

"Okay. So what's illegal about that? Ignoring of course that he most likely paid for those hamburgers with money he stole."

"That's not what we're concerned with. The name of this place is Hammy Hamburgers and it's Chomp's favorite. He needs a tremendous amount of calories every day for him to do what he does, and my guess is that he'll be back there tonight. There's a reason why he didn't just rob the place after hours: he wants them to stay in business so he can keep eating there. If my hunch is correct, he'll be back."

* * *

The plan is relatively simple, at least as far as Midnight's plans usually go. Although he's always quick to criticize me for underestimating enemies, the speed with which he has to react to Chomp's reappearance leaves very little time for his usual elaborate traps.

Soon after they took over Bay View City, Alpha Team made it their publicly stated goal to recapture and execute every escaped prisoner from Silver Island who hasn't surrendered. Even the few who have surrendered haven't been seen or heard from since. Alpha Team insists that they're being kept in a secure, off-site facility far from any populated areas. They also claim that giving any more information about where this place is would jeopardize the security of it. At the end of the day, though, the simple truth of the matter is that most people just don't care. They see these criminals as less than human. Whether they live or die isn't something that concerns most. In their minds, they aren't privy to the same basic human rights the rest of us enjoy.

Alpha Team has placed bounties on each of the escaped prisoners' heads. Most of the escapees can't be caught by traditional means, though. Most can only be caught by another metahuman, and given Alpha Team's general attitude toward metas, few expect that they will actually keep their end of the bargain.

So here I am, sitting alone in a Hammy Hamburgers, slowly nursing a soda and waiting. My metabands are powered down, but still active around my wrists and hidden under the sleeves of a sweatshirt.

I'm here as a lookout, and it is *boring*.

Really, really boring.

I'm seriously kicking myself for having left the one party I've ever had fun at to come sit in a fast-food place all night by myself.

Midnight wants me here as backup, but it's hard to imagine a situation where he would actually ask for help. Instead, I have to just sit here, keep an eye on the line at the front counter, and send Midnight a message through my phone if I see Chomp. Midnight is lying in wait in a nearby alley with his own version of the headgear that previously kept Chomp docile.

Once Chomp steps back out of the restaurant, Midnight will ambush him and lock the restraint over his head. Easy. And if anything goes wrong, I'll power up and get Chomp away from here immediately. But of course, Midnight expects nothing to go wrong.

After eight free soda refills, I can't wait any longer and

decide Midnight would never know if I went to the bathroom real quick, even though he's given me explicit instructions not to take my eyes off the front door.

I swear I'm in the bathroom for all of about fifteen seconds, but when I come out, there he is, right at the front counter: Chomp. Even for Seattle in the fall it's too warm to be wearing a scarf tonight, and that's the dead giveaway.

I fumble around in my pocket for my phone, quickly opening the secure messaging app hidden three folders deep and get a message to Midnight right as Chomp grabs his two bags of takeout and heads for the door.

My instinct is to immediately follow him, but Midnight warned me not to come out until he gives me the signal. He doesn't want Chomp spooked, and he doesn't want a fight between two metahumans in the street, so I have no choice but to sit back down and wait.

It feels like an eternity, even though my watch says it's only been thirty seconds. I'm just about to break Midnight's rule and go outside to see for myself what's happening when the text comes through.

Target Captured. Rendezvous at rooftop of 14th and Lincoln.

THIRTY-ONE

The cargo bay door of Midnight's jet unfolds from the body of the plane, making a ramp from the rooftop to the interior. Inside, Chomp sits on one of the parallel benches lining the opposite facing walls. His hands are bound together and attached to a galvanized steel hook bolted to the wall before his back.

His head is completely encased, offering only an obscured view of his face through a steel mesh weave, allowing him to breathe and speak. When he sees me at the bottom of the ramp, I can hear him repeatedly slamming him teeth together in an effort to intimidate me. I almost jump when I first hear how loudly they clap together. My metabands are back on and activated to keep my identity obscured from Chomp. Even if I didn't have to worry about that, I still wouldn't want to be within ten feet of this guy without some kind of protection.

"Keep biting all you want. You're not getting through that," Midnight says as he comes from around the front of the jet and onto the ramp. "I just finished pre-flight checks. We're ready to take this garbage back to a secure facility where he belongs. He's not going to make for much of an engaging travel companion, but I need you to sit back here with him during the flight to make sure he remains detained."

"But he's locked up. There's no way he's getting that helmet off, right?" I say.

Midnight motions for me to step outside the plane.

"Something's not right here," he says.

"What do you mean?"

"I'm not sure yet, but catching him was too easy. I wasn't expecting that much of a fight, but this was almost like he let himself get caught.

"There are over a dozen Hammy Hamburgers in this city.

Why keep coming back to the same one when you know you're a wanted man? He won't tell me how he got the last head guard off, but if I had to guess, I'd say he had help. At top speed, the flight to the New Mexico compound is only fifteen minutes, but I still don't trust him."

"Got it. I'll stay back here."

Midnight turns and walks to the cockpit. Even though being a babysitter is only a little bit less boring than staking out a fast-food place, it's something. I take my seat on the bench opposite Chomp's and buckle up as the cargo bay door rises.

* * *

We're only a few minutes into the ride to the New Mexico facility, but already I don't like it. I can tell Midnight doesn't like it either. Everything is going too smoothly, and nothing ever goes smoothly in this line of work.

I'm seated in the back of the jet, still watching Chomp. He's sitting completely relaxed and motionless, but with his eyes fixated on me. Blinking comes about every minute or so.

"Two minutes out," Midnight says over the two-way earpieces hidden in each of our cowls. The cockpit is sealed off completely from the cargo area for security reasons. It has its own public announcement system, which Midnight could use to communicate with me, but he's playing it safe, using the earpieces instead. No need to give Chomp any more information than he needs.

"I've radioed ahead to the New Mexico facility, and they're preparing a cell. They're aware of his refusal to relinquish his metabands, so they're going to skip the usual formal processing procedure to get him secured and into a cell as quickly as possible. They don't like how easy any of this was either," Midnight says through the radio.

I feel a change in cabin pressure and airspeed. We're close and getting ready to come in for a landing. One of the nicer features of Midnight's jet is that vertical take offs and landings are no problem thanks to the main thrusters being on rotating swivels. This comes in handy when you've often got a roof to take off from instead of a runway.

It also means that we can come in high at close to full speed before rapidly descending into the compound, meaning we don't have to worry as much about an attack from the ground. And once we're near the facility itself, we can partially rely on their radar systems for increased visibility. No one is getting close to this thing without us seeing them coming.

"Do you know what my ability is?" Chomp asks.

It's the first time he's made so much as a peep since we picked him up, and it startles me. The jet is slowing to a stop. We're almost there, and he knows it. He's just trying to rattle me before he's put away forever. I ignore him.

"I asked you a question," he states plainly.

"Shut up," I say back, wishing there were windows back here so I could see how close we are.

"That's not very nice. It's that kind of attitude that's the reason no one's ever fully understood me."

"Yeah, I know what your ability is. You can bite through things. We're all very impressed. Right now the only way your ability is helping you is that it's keeping us from stuffing something into your mouth to shut you up," I say, fidgeting in my seat as though that will somehow make us land sooner.

"But do you know *how* I'm able to bite through anything?"

"How far out are we?" I ask into my earpiece, ignoring Chomp and hoping for an encouraging answer.

The answer doesn't come from Midnight, but rather from the sound of the additional thrusters kicking in, meaning we're preparing to come down for a landing.

"I can bite through anything because I can control the density of my mouth, you see. That means I can make it harder and heavier than any element known to man."

"Fascinating," I reply sarcastically.

"I'm glad you think so. Maybe if someone with your sense of curiosity had caught me in the first place, they would have realized that the ability isn't just limited to my mouth."

I'm not looking at him when it happens, not directly. My gaze is still pointed at the front of the aircraft, where Midnight is, even if I can't see him. At first I almost don't even hear the sound over the jet's engines. It's the sound of straining steel and popping rivets, as if the jet's engines are struggling to keep altitude.

"What's going on back there?" Midnight shouts into my ear over the radio.

I turn back to Chomp, but nothing's out of the ordinary. He's still just sitting there, still staring at me, except now with a smirk on his face. That's when I notice it. The bench he's sitting on, it's bowed, bending underneath his weight.

"Umm, I don't know, but we have to land now!" I shout back to Midnight.

"How about I race you there?" Chomp asks.

Before I can react, the cargo bay is ripped open. Air rushes in, sucking everything not strapped down out into the sky. The lights go out, and flashing red emergency lights come on, along with sirens. The jet tips violently to its right side.

My first thought is that we've been hit by a missile, but there was no explosion. I look back at Chomp again, but just as I do, he sinks through the floor of the jet, leaving only a huge gaping hole in the floor in his place. He's out.

There isn't time to think, only react. I dive through the hole after him amid the wailing emergency sirens and flashing red lights.

Head down, I plunge through the dark night sky with my eyes fixed on my target. He's making himself as aerodynamic as possible, and he has a few seconds' head start on me, but there's no doubt in my mind that I'll catch up with him. It's stopping him that's another story.

"Midnight, are you okay?" I ask into my transponder.

"Don't worry about me. Just stop him," Midnight yells back to me through the noise on his end.

I glance back for a moment to check the condition of his

jet. It's in a tailspin, black smoke pouring out from the hole I just dropped through. I consider turning around and getting Midnight out of there, but stopping Chomp is critical right now.

He must have an ejection seat or something along those lines, I think to myself. That's when I see portions of his jet being jettisoned clear. Two at a time, damaged pieces of the jet are ejected from the core until there's little more than the cockpit left.

A twin pair of blade-like wings shoot out from either side of the cockpit area, and it begins to right itself, no longer plummeting toward earth and instead slowly pulling itself up into a horizontal glide.

He'll be fine, and I feel stupid for even worrying about him in the first place. Now back to the problem at hand.

When I turn back to Chomp, I have to quickly readjust my trajectory. He's changed his in the few seconds since I took my eyes off him, and now he's barreling directly toward the New Mexico facility. This is a new power to me, the ability to change the density of your entire body. I've never dealt with it before, and there are a lot of unknown variables. The faster I can catch up and get in front of him, the better position I'll have.

I yell in Chomp's direction for him to stop, but I'm wasting my breath. The only way to stop him is to get in front of him, so that's what I do. I push myself harder to rocket toward the earth as fast as I can and manage to get past him. I prepare myself as best I can for the impact, hoping that if I'm not strong enough to stop him, I can at least knock him off target. If he misses the facility, he'll be out of other options, and he's not going to want to see how pissed off Midnight is that his plane is broken.

Chomp hits me so fast and so hard that everything goes fuzzy. By the time the few seconds it takes for me to regain my bearings pass, it's already too late. My back smashes through the concrete and steel roof of the New Mexico facility. It sounds like a balloon being popped. There's barely a millisecond in between hitting the roof and hitting the ground. We tear through the facility like it was made out of wet toilet paper.

It isn't over yet, though. We're still falling, down through the Earth itself. I feel dirt and rocks pelting my shoulders, but only for a few seconds before it all turns to rock. I'm wishing I'd paid more attention in Earth science so I'd know what exactly we were hitting and how far down it goes.

I just barely manage to reach over Chomp's shoulder and get a look up at the tunnel the two of us have bored through the ground. At the end of it is a pinhole of light, and it's very far away.

"You have to stop!" I yell into Chomp's ear, but it's no use.

His eyes have gone vacant, and I don't think he can even hear me anymore. More earth pelts me on all sides. The pinhole of light isn't visible over his shoulder at this point.

I need to get out of here.

The rocks and debris smash into the back of my head as I struggle to get around Chomp's body so I'm no longer the one on the receiving end. It's pitch black and hot. Even without having paid much attention in science class, I know we're heading for trouble. I'm pretty sure that we're not just going to pop out on the other side of the planet and go get Chinese food for dinner.

Suddenly, there's light and open space all around us. The air is burning my lungs and smells like rotten eggs. Below me I see where the light is coming from: molten lava. Or is it magma when it's still underground? I always forget. Whatever it is, I'm pretty confident that I won't be able to withstand it.

I shout at Chomp one last time. This time I get his attention, but not in the way I'd like. His eyes snap open and he wraps both of his arms firmly around me, squeezing my body like a vise.

"If I'm not getting out of here, neither are you," he

screams into my ear over the noise waiting for us below.

"Let go of me, and I can help you," I scream back.

"No, thanks," he says before he pulls me in tighter.

We're both heading for the molten rock and whatever's underneath it if I don't think of something quick. In an act of desperation, I twist my body with all my might and turn the tables on Chomp. Now it's his back that's heading straight for the magma. He just laughs, knowing that it won't matter much who hits first when we both splash down, but he forgets how quick I am.

I have to time it perfectly, but the instant Chomp's back hits the liquid fire, his grip loosens. There's only the blink of an eye between the loosening of his grip and when my body will hit the lava too, but I find it and push myself out of Chomp's hold.

Once it's over, I don't look back. There's no need to. And even with my powers, I'm not sure how much time I can spend down here. Better to focus on flying as fast and as high as I can instead of turning around, just in case.

Without light, I can't find the tunnel we made on our way down. I'm kicking toward the surface like I'm at the bottom of a pool rather than miles underground. Luckily, I can still sense which way is up and that's what I'll have to go by.

The rocks give way to rubble, and the rubble turns to dirt before, finally, the dirt turns into dry desert air. I fill my lungs with it, thinking for a minute there that I almost never had the chance to do it again. The fresh air quickly becomes tainted by the smell of smoke, though, and I turn around to find where it's coming from.

The New Mexico facility.

THIRTY-TWO

I'm kicking up a small sandstorm in my wake as I rush back toward the New Mexico facility. The roof looks like it's been ripped apart by a giant can opener. The scene is eerily quiet, and for a moment, I consider the possibility that Chomp's impact may have taken the lives of everyone inside.

Then I realize why it's so quiet: we're in the middle of nowhere. This was by design. This new facility was placed in the desert to correct the mistakes made in Silver Island's original design. The reason there are no screaming ambulances or police sirens is because they're all hundreds of miles away. We're all alone out here.

I make my way inside the building using the only accessible entrance: the giant hole in the roof. Once inside, I find chaos everywhere. Dozens of armed guards are running in every direction possible. The small on-site fire department is struggling to put out fires created by shorted out electronics and spilled chemicals.

Rounding one of the corners, I come upon a small group of guards inspecting the damaged cells. The one closest to me is startled when he sees me and fires a round directly into my chest. The bullet stings but is deflected off and rattles through the grates in the catwalk below.

"Whoa, easy. I'm one of the good guys," I say as I put my hands up in the air.

"How do we know that?" one of the other guards asks.

He has his gun trained on me too, aimed right between my eyes, I think.

"If I wasn't a good guy, I probably wouldn't brush off the fact that you just shot me. Get Halpern. He can vouch for me," I say.

"Stand down, officers," Halpern says as if on cue as he rushes up the nearby stairs.

The guards comply and lower their weapons, then

immediately return to checking cells.

"I'm starting to think you're bad luck," Halpern says to me, motioning for me to walk with him as we talk.

He's peering into cells as we continue down the hallway, double-checking the guards' work and making sure that everyone who's supposed to be in a cell is in a cell.

"How bad is it?" I ask.

"We're not entirely sure yet. We've got an earthmover inbound to fill the crater as quickly as possible and prevent any further damage to the facility. We're not stupid, though. After Silver Island, this place was retrofitted to be fully compartmentalized. In situations like this, where the integrity of the building has been compromised, all the other sections are immediately sealed off. All the detainees should have already been anesthetized via their metaband restriction devices."

"So basically you just knocked everyone out using the same locks you've got over their metabands?"

"That's correct. If it were up to me, I'd keep 'em all like that 24/7, but these human rights activists are all over us nowadays. They say it's *cruel and unusual* to keep them constantly sedated. You see this guy?" Halpern asks me as he motions to a prisoner asleep on the steel floor inside a clear plastic-walled cell.

He's older, maybe in his late 50s and unnaturally skinny with a growing pool of drool collecting under his mouth.

"Called himself Skin. You know why? Because he used his laser vision to skin over a dozen people alive using just his eyes. Did it so quickly and cleanly that most of his victims lived for hours before they finally died from shock. But we're the ones who are cruel and unusual for wanting to make sure this guy doesn't get out again by any means possible."

"Has anyone escaped?" I ask.

"No. All of our systems indicate that the majority of the damage occurred in the dining hall area. None of our cells have been breached and motion sensors indicate that every cell is still currently occupied. We're double checking, of course, but from what we can tell, your buddy didn't hit whatever it was he was aiming for."

"What about Keane?"

"Like I told you, we're checking on everyone."

That isn't the response I want to hear, and somewhere deep in my gut, I know something isn't right. I rush toward the section that holds Keane. As I make my way there, I notice that there are fewer and fewer guards. The ones checking cells haven't made it to this area of the facility yet since it's farthest from the hole Chomp put through their roof.

When I find the area, I approach Keane's cell hesitantly, cautiously, until I can see him and make sure that he's unconscious. Not only is he conscious, he's sitting calmly in his cell with his legs crossed, eyes fixed straight at me and smiling.

I yell for guards.

"Why would you need help from guards, Omni?" Keane asks me. "You know that they're just humans, after all. What could they possibly do that you couldn't?" He stands up and begins to cross the floor of the cell, approaching the plastic wall. "I want to be honest with you, Omni. I think we're close enough that I can be honest, can't I? I mean, I did live inside your little girlfriend's head for quite some time, so I do feel that I know you pretty well, Connor."

He knows who I am. He must have seen it in Iris's mind. This whole time everyone just assumed he could only control others with his abilities but not actually access their thoughts and memories. Stupid! Keane has relied on making everyone believe he is less powerful than he is over and over again.

"I'm sure you've figured out by now that Chomp was under my employ."

"How did you control his mind from that distance?"

"Oh, I didn't control his mind. I might keep some of the things I'm capable of close to the chest, but even I'm not capable of that type of mind control from so far away. No, for that I had to rely on the oldest super power known to man: money. It turns out money can be a fantastic motivator for all sorts of things, even convincing someone to let themselves be caught and then later jump out of a plane, even though all sensible logic should tell you that once you fall you'll never stop.

"But, as I said, unfortunately, I didn't think of everything. I've been funding most of the groups responsible for protesting the use of sedatives on metahuman prisoners of war for quite some time, and I became convinced that they would indeed prevail, or at the very least delay the use of sedatives until I was able to execute my plan.

"Now, however, even if the rest of this prison's population hadn't been knocked out, I doubt I would have had the wherewithal to control them in my current state. It's taking nearly all of my abilities just to keep the sedative from affecting me.

"Of course, it helps that I was able to accurately mimic the negative side effects that occur in a small percentage of the population when they're previously exposed to this particular chemical. After they saw that, they made sure they kept the doses they gave me as low as possible. Not even The Agency wants a lawsuit on their hands if they can prevent it."

"Why tell me all of this?"

"Because the plan didn't work, and I want you to know that. I wanted you to know that something I'd planned for meticulously and spent millions to make happen unfortunately failed, all because of an unexpected variable."

Just then two heavily armored guards enter through a mechanized door on the outer wall of the cellblock.

"Back up against the back of your cell! Show me your hands! Now!" one of them shouts as both aim their rifles at Keane.

"Ah, they must have finally detected the motion in my cell.

I was wondering how long that was going to take."

"Back up, freak!"

"Hmm, I don't think I've seen the two of you in this cellblock before, have I?"

"You're going to be seeing the underside of my boot in about three seconds if you don't comply!"

"The reason why I mention it is because it would appear you gentlemen are unfamiliar with this area of the facility and its particular rules, especially when it comes to outside visitors."

My eyes go wide as I realize what Keane is doing.

"Get out of here!" I scream at them.

"We don't take orders from you clowns."

"You see," Keane says, "the reason I wanted you to know about my plan was so you could also see just how well I'm able to improvise when the unexpected happens. Isn't that right, boys?"

I turn back to look at the two guards. Their expressions have suddenly turned blank, and in the blink of an eye, they've turned their rifles on themselves, each holding the barrel of their own gun with their teeth.

"Stop this right now!" I yell at Keane.

"Oh, I'm not going to kill them, or more accurately, they're not going to kill themselves. Not yet at least. Maybe once all of this is over and they see just what they've done, but that's not on my conscience. That's all on them.

"I know you're fast, Connor, but even you aren't fast enough to stop both of them from pulling the trigger, not if they both do it at the same time. So, I ask you this: Are you going to let me out of here, or would you rather watch these two men die?"

THIRTY-THREE

Everything happens quickly from there. With the New Mexico facility's Faraday cage punctured, it's trivial for a teleporter to get in, and with the money Keane has, it isn't hard to convince one to assist in a jailbreak in exchange for a few million dollars. That's pocket change to Keane, and all I can do is watch.

The teleporter appears and disappears in an instant. It's obvious now that this plan was a long time in the making. Keane would have had to give extremely detailed descriptions of the floor plan to ensure they didn't teleport themselves into a wall or floor. Once Keane found his designated waiting area by a water fountain, all he had to do was check the clock on the wall to know exactly when the teleporter would arrive. In and out. A few seconds after he's gone, the guards begin to regain control over their minds.

"What the hell just happened?" one of them asks me as he pulls the barrel of his rifle back out of his mouth.

"Keane just escaped. I need you to sound whatever alarm you have to," I tell them.

"Uhh, I think we already are," the other guard says over the constant wailing alarms already going off all around the cellblock.

There isn't much more for me to do here, even if they wanted my help, which I'm sure they won't after they hear how Keane just got away. I lift into the air and travel back down the winding hallways of the facility, back to the hole in the roof. The night sky is clear, and I take a position about a thousand feet up so that I can see into the distance, toward the lights of the nearest city. I don't know what I expected to find up here. Keane could have teleported anywhere on Earth, or even off Earth if you want to be technical about it.

"Keane's gone, isn't he?" Midnight asks over my earpiece.

He already knows the answer.

"Yeah. Where are you?" I reply.

"Two o'clock," he replies.

"What happens at two o'clock?" I ask.

There's a sigh at the other end.

"Two o'clock as in slightly to your right. Look up," he says.

Oh. Right. I look in the direction he says and can see the faint shimmer of a heat trail in the sky. It's Midnight's plane, or at least what's left of it, zipping through the sky.

"Meet me in Albuquerque. I'll send coordinates to your device."

* * *

"How many secret hideouts do you have exactly?" I ask as I fly over the city of Albuquerque, trying to keep an eye out for wherever it is I'm going.

I have the exact GPS coordinates, but since I'm not a computer, that doesn't help me as much as something like saying, "Look for the rooftop with a Jola Cola sign on it," would.

I find the building that Midnight gave me coordinates for and land on the roof. There's only one door up here, so I venture a guess that's where I'm heading. The door leading from the roof isn't locked, but there's a second one inside that is. It doesn't matter, though. Once the first door closes, the small space lights up with blue lasers projected from every angle, overlapping and scanning across my body. Once the system is confident that I'm me, the entire room descends a few dozen stories, well below street level.

The elevator slows to a stop, and I exit to find what I've begun to recognize as standard features for Midnight's hideouts: an automated medical bay, computer monitors lining almost every space along the walls, and training simulation areas. Midnight sits at a computer in the center of the room, fixated on the screen.

"What's happening?" I ask as I walk briskly over to him.

"Nothing. Yet," he replies.

"No reports of any eyewitnesses? Someone had to have

seen something. Keane didn't just vanish into thin air. I mean, technically, I guess, he did, but he had to have landed somewhere."

"And I'm sure he did, but unless he's in a public area, we're not going to find him by hacking into red light cameras."

I bite my tongue right before saying something about how we have to try. Of course we have to try. Midnight knows that better than anyone. He doesn't need me reminding him. After a few seconds of silence, there's suddenly an explosion of rage from Midnight like I've never seen before.

He punches the computer monitor in front of him, shattering the screen into a hundred pieces of broken glass. He rips the keyboard from the desk and throws it across the room, smashing another monitor that's hung along the far wall.

I don't say anything, not like I'd know what to say anyway. I've never seen him this frustrated. He pulls off his cowl as though it's suffocating him and stares into space for a long while before he speaks again.

"There's something that I should tell you," he starts.

"Okay ..." I say, not sure what to expect next.

"I think it's only right for you to know now. I'm not sure what Keane has planned next, but the more I learn about him and how he works, the more I'm beginning to expect that this might be the end of the line for me. There are secrets I know that I swore to myself I'd take to the grave, but now that I'm standing in front of it, I'm not sure if it's right to do that anymore. I'm not sure about a lot of things anymore. I'm not even sure where to begin."

More silence follows as Midnight seems to be running through it all in his head, deciding which of the who knows how many secrets is the one he should tell me first. I'm not sure whether he's deciding based on which are the least secretive, or which are the most necessary in order to make sense of the others.

"I know that you have questions about me. About who I am. Where I came from. How it is that I know what I do about metabands. I've done what I can to keep the world from asking those questions of me, and I've gone even further to try to keep you from asking the same, but it's important that you know.

"You know that the metaband that powered my suit belonged to me, but you don't know what happened to the other one."

"There were two?"

"There are always two," he says as he releases an unseen clip from the forearm of his suit. Once unfastened, he removes the lower arm guard, revealing the scarred forearm that I've seen and wondered about once before. "The other was ripped away from me, which is how my arm ended up like this. There was enough residual energy in the other band to regenerate the arm for the most part, but as you can see, it wasn't completely successful before the residual energy was expended."

"I thought it was supposed to be impossible to remove a metaband from its owner once it's linked?"

"It is, nearly. Mine wasn't ripped off by any normal force, though. It was ripped off by the limitations of physics itself."

"I don't think I follow," I say as if the look on my face wasn't making that clear enough.

"What I'm going to tell you is going to seem impossible."

"I'm a teenager that can fly and bend steel thanks to some bracelets. I'll try to keep an open mind," I say, which actually gets him to crack a rare smile.

"The metabands that are currently on Earth aren't from this time. They're from thousands of years in the future."

"How could you know that?"

"Because that's where I'm from too."

THIRTY-FOUR

"A lot of the pieces of this story aren't going to entirely make sense to you. It's not too different than if you tried to explain what happened today to a caveman."

"Thanks," I reply sarcastically.

"I don't mean any offense by that, but it's accurate. In reality, the advances from my time far outweigh the differences between this time and that of the cavemen. I'll try to put what I know and what happened in terms as close to what you'll be able to understand and relate to as possible."

"Okay."

"It happened during an expedition returning to Earth from a few galaxies away. We'd been-"

"We?"

"My team. I'll get to them in a moment. We were returning from an expedition. Metabands at that time were standard issue to all explorers in our position. They were primarily used to help us interface directly with our vessel. It wasn't so much a melding of man and machine as it was allowing the two to simply exist together as one. The metabands connected with their owners at every level of existence. They were incredibly powerful, but to some, there was a belief that their full power had yet to be harnessed.

"The chief scientist aboard my ship was one who believed in this idea, and so he tinkered. He experimented. He was determined to find the limits of this technology. It was technology that had already existed for hundreds of years by my time, but it was still considered a new frontier in many respects.

"I was unaware of the specifics involved in many of these experiments. Part of me just didn't want to know. I didn't want to know how far he would go to find whatever it was he was looking for. I didn't want to know how far he'd go just to prove that he could. By the end, his experiments caused a rupture of energy unlike any the universe had seen before.

"It ripped our ship apart at the molecular level. Our metabands were all that protected us from the harshness of space, but they were all connected. Not only our own, but also the thousands more we were holding onboard as cargo. They were being brought back to Earth for further study from the frontlines of a war being fought in deep space.

"When the experiment caused one to rupture, it opened a hole in the fabric of reality itself. The metabands and my crew were pulled in through that hole. It existed for only a fraction of a second, and when it closed, it took my hand and one of my metabands with it. Luckily, the auxiliary power held in the other kept me alive long enough to make it through the atmosphere and land back on Earth."

"And what about all the other metabands?"

"They were scattered across the solar system, like a sack of potatoes falling out of the back of a truck. The majority of my team landed safely on Earth. It was a few years later when Earth's orbit crossed paths with the first batch of metabands floating in space. They looked like space junk to the untrained eye, but anyone who came upon them after they made it down to Earth would be able to tell right away that there was something unusual about these bracelets."

"And that was the first wave."

"Correct. The second wave was years away still, but I knew it was coming. I'd spent the time in between tracking down metabands as they gravitated back toward Earth's magnetic field. I tried to recover them before anyone else could, but it proved to be an impossible task with the technology available at the time."

"What about the other members of your crew? What happened to them?"

"None of us expected the first wave. We'd all assumed that the metabands had been lost to the vastness of space and time. All we could do was try to go about living normal lives, or as normal as we could make our lives after being displaced this far from our own time.

"I was never able to assimilate. Not fully. I couldn't wrap my head around the concerns of people from this time. I couldn't relate or understand. I spent a long time looking for purpose. I didn't find it until the altered metabands began crashing down to Earth, and that's when I knew I had to do what I could to prevent them from hurting anyone else. That's when I found my purpose.

"But as I said, others were able to adapt. They were able to find their places in this time. They learned to love what were strange customs and technologies to us. They found ways to fit into the current culture and connect with others, even though everyone on earth had been long dead by the time any of us were born.

"Some were even able to make lives for themselves here and families. Connor, your parents were two of those people."

At first, I don't think I heard him right, or I think that he's speaking metaphorically.

"What? What are you talking about?" I ask, shaking my head as if that would make what he's just said go away.

"Your parents. They were colleagues of mine. More than colleagues. They were friends. We were all trapped in this strange time with no one else who could possibly understand what it meant to have gone through what we did. But your parents didn't think that way. They made a purpose and a life for themselves here. A large part of that was you and Derrick, their sons from a time they didn't belong in. But they found purpose in another way too, a way that inspired humanity, by becoming the first two metahumans the world had ever seen."

The room is spinning as all the puzzle pieces I've carried around my entire life begin to fall into place.

"My parents ... they didn't die as innocent bystanders during The Battle."

"No, they didn't. They died as heroes. They died

protecting the city and the time that they'd come to call home."

"My dad ..."

"Your dad was The Governor. Your mom was Silk. She was one of the countless metahumans that died that day trying to stop Jones. The Governor, as you know, was the one who finally did in the end, by throwing him into the sun."

"I think I need to sit down," I mutter as I feel for something behind me to lean up against and luckily find a computer terminal within reach.

"I'm sorry I couldn't tell you any of this sooner, Connor. There wasn't a way to know what the ramifications of anyone finding out the truth would be, which brings me to Jones.

"Jones was a brilliant man. He was obsessed with his work with what are now called metabands in this time, but he was also extremely aware of the potential they had for harm. Despite his work with metabands, he insisted that his family never use them. He worried about the harm, both physical and psychological, that they could have long term. When our craft was torn apart, something strange happened."

"You mean aside from sending all of you through time?"

Midnight actually manages to crack a smile again at that, making me wonder just how literal the mask he wears is.

"Jones's family was on board the ship with him. That was an option available to them since it was a long-haul mission. When the craft was torn apart, his wife, Gillian, and his daughter, Iris, weren't wearing metabands and were presumed dead. For a long time Jones was presumed dead as well.

"But there were things we didn't know at the time that we do know now. The first is obviously that Iris survived. Not only did she survive, but she exhibits metaband-like powers and abilities despite not being linked to a pair of metabands herself. I've been studying her for years, and I'm no closer to an explanation for her abilities than when I started. The tools and materials of this time just aren't adequate to get to the bottom of it. The closest thing I have to a working theory is that when the accident happened, she was still young enough that her genetics were susceptible to manipulation. She was still a newborn, too young to ever safely be exposed to something like metabands, let alone the type of energy caused by Jones's explosion.

"Later, we learned that Jones had survived too, if only technically."

"What do you mean?"

"He didn't go through the same experience the rest of us did. He was too close to the source of energy. After the explosion happened, myself and your parents woke up already plummeting through Earth's atmosphere. We'd traveled back through time centuries, but for us, all of it happened in the blink of an eye.

"Jones wasn't so lucky. He traveled back the same length of time we did, but it didn't happen instantly for him. For him, it was experienced in real time. He spent millennia trapped in a sort of limbo, where time and space didn't exist anywhere except for inside his mind. It's what drove him mad."

"I can imagine thousands of years of solitary confinement would do that."

"When it was finally over and he crashed back to Earth, he was a deeply broken man. He only vaguely remembered and understood what had happened to him. Over time, as he began to recall more and more about his life from before he was trapped in limbo, he began to formulate a theory for setting things right."

"Obviously it didn't work?"

"No, it didn't. And even if it had, the end would have never justified the means."

"So that was the beginning of him becoming a psychopathic murderer?"

"Yes. Time is a lot less flexible than people think. The laws of quantum physics allow for travel through time, but that doesn't mean they allow for time to be changed, at least with any ease. The universe isn't stupid enough to allow itself to become unraveled so easily. Things like the butterfly effect, they're all nonsense. Over a long enough timeline, the universe always finds a way to course correct. It's unconcerned with short-term changes. But long term ... that's a different story.

"When faced with temporal abnormalities, the universe will always attempt to set things back to the way they were heading before the time traveler arrived. But if enough damage to the time line is done, if enough changes happen to significantly alter the known future to the point of no return, then the universe has no choice but to take drastic action.

"Jones's idea was that if he killed enough people, he could alter the entire path of the human race in the future. He believed that if he were able to alter it dramatically enough, metabands would never be invented, or it might mean he would never be born, and in that case, the universe would have no choice but to snap into an alternate path to avoid the paradox. The universe would find a way to prevent him from ever having traveled back in time in the first place in order to prevent the changes that would result, and that's exactly what he wanted.

"He wanted to stop himself from ever coming back in the first place and from ever being trapped in that cage for thousands of years. And as far as he saw the situation, killing random innocents in order to 'save' the universe was not an issue. To him, everyone here had already been dead and buried for a long time. Why should he mourn their deaths any more than you would while studying the bones of a mummy in a museum?"

THIRTY-FIVE

REPORT, the text message from Michelle reads.

Midnight set her up with the same app he uses to securely communicate with me. I was starting to wonder if she couldn't figure out how to use it. The stuff Midnight uses isn't always very user friendly. It's possible she's just testing it out, but something in my gut tells me that isn't the case. Something in my gut tells me that she's finally using it because it's important.

"Hey, did you get this message from Michelle?" Winston asks as he unburies his head from the book he's reading. "Looks like it's important."

Okay, both my gut *and* Winston are telling me that this is something important. I get up from the couch, acknowledging that this nap just isn't going to happen, and grab my bag. Winston closes his book and does the same, and we both head for the door.

"What do you think it could be?" Winston asks as he walks alongside me, looking around beforehand to make sure we're out of range from any eavesdroppers.

"I'm not sure. I checked all the news I could find on my phone but couldn't find anything out of the ordinary happening really. Something about a teleporter getting himself stuck on top of the antenna of some skyscraper in Dubai, but other than that, it seems pretty quiet. I tried calling my brother to see if he'd heard anything that hadn't been reported yet, but I couldn't get through. Usually that means he's busy, so maybe there's something big going on."

"Either way, I guess we'll find out pretty soon."

"What are you guys talking about?" Ellie asks from behind us, so close to our ears that it makes both of us jump.

"Ellie, what are you doing? Didn't Michelle already warn you about not using your abilities on campus, especially when you're using them to startle nice people like us?"

Winston asks her.

"Relax, dummy. I didn't use my powers to sneak up on you. I saw you coming and hid behind that statue over there," she says, gesturing to a statue of a frog, the unfortunate mascot of our school. "Do you guys know what this is about?"

"We were just discussing that before you scared the two of us half to death. No, we don't," I say.

"Jeez, give it a rest already. Some big tough heroes you guys are, practically afraid of your own shadows," Ellie says, giving Winston a jab in his side, causing him to flinch again.

"After you," I say to Ellie as I hold the door open to the Blair Building.

The three of us walk down the empty hallway toward our normal classroom-slash-elevator. Outside the door, there are a few others waiting. I ask them why they aren't inside yet and learn that Michelle wanted them to wait for the rest of us before allowing the elevator down. Whatever it is she wants to tell us, she wants us to all learn about it together.

The ride down to the training area is tense. It can take a little while, so usually people find a place to sit at one of the desks, but not today. Winston is pacing back and forth at the front of the classroom while most of the rest of us stand. We make it past the halfway point, and I can hear the secondary elevator moving out of its resting position to return to the ground floor. Once we're past it, our elevator accelerates its descent.

When we reach the training area and exit the elevator, we see that the halls down here are empty. That's not completely surprising considering there's no training regularly scheduled at this time, but it's still a little eerie. Down the hall, in the distance, I can hear two voices having an argument. Even from this far away I can pick them out as Michelle's and Midnight's. They must hear our collective footsteps because the arguing quiets down as we get closer to the briefing room. Michelle steps outside before we reach the door. The stony look on her face doesn't give me hope or fear about what we're about to learn.

"Come in, everyone," she says as she steps aside from the doorway to make room for us to pass. Midnight has his back to the doorway and is reaffixing his cowl. He almost never takes it off, especially here, where only Michelle and I know his identity. When he does, it's usually serious.

I almost don't notice at first, but all the way in the back of the room, sitting in one of the standard school-style desk-chair combos is Iris. I consider walking to the back of the room and sitting next to her, but the look in her eyes tells me that's a bad idea. There's anger. It's not directed at me, that much I can tell, but it's intense enough that some will undoubtedly spill over onto whoever makes the mistake of trying to talk to her right now.

We find our seats, and Michelle reenters the classroom, closing the door tightly behind her even though there's no one else down here but us, and it's unlikely anyone else is going to accidentally stumble on us a mile beneath the earth.

"Thanks for coming so quickly, everyone. It's important that all of you have time off to rest and do whatever normal things people your age do nowadays, so I hope you understand the circumstances it takes to call you are very serious," Michelle says.

She moves to the front of the room and picks up a remote. Midnight stands with his arms crossed near the door, watching. The screen in the front where a white board would normally be flickers on. On the screen is what looks like a map of Bay View City. It isn't until a plane flies over it that I realize the image is live.

"It hasn't exactly been public knowledge, but we've had a satellite positioned over Bay View City for some time now to monitor the situation there. As you all know, Alpha Team has declared themselves protectors of the city and forbidden any other metahumans within the city limits. This has limited our ability to monitor activity on the ground, but luckily, we do still have some active operatives in the city. This morning we received word from one of those operatives that The Blanks, a vigilante gang who also opposes metahuman activity, have been responsible for a string of disappearances over the last twelve hours. From our analysis, we believe these abductions are connected and that the Alphas are behind them in some way."

"What makes you say that?" Winston asks.

"I was just about to get to that. The reason we believe Alpha Team is involved is because all of the missing people have some tie or connection to the metahuman community. They are either business connections, demonstrated metahuman sympathizers, or have ties to the press," Michelle says.

She looks directly at me when she says that last part, and without having to say a word, I know why. It's Derrick. They have him.

THIRTY-SIX

For a long time it seems like there's nothing we can do except wait. At first I tried to leave. I wanted to go find Derrick. I tried to assure everyone else that I'd be fine. When they warned me about what would happen if I entered the city with my metabands again, I told them I'd leave them behind. Even as the words were leaving my mouth, though, I knew that wasn't a good plan. I don't care if something bad happens to me, but if anything bad happens to Derrick because I wasn't prepared for a fight, I wouldn't be able to live with myself.

So I agreed to wait. We still have no real idea where Derrick and the others are or what Alpha Team even wants with them. At the same time, Michelle has become increasingly concerned with the fact that there are no confirmed sightings of the other members of Alpha Team in at least the past week. It isn't like them to all stay so low when they have an entire city to keep in line. Michelle's sitting on the far end of the room with her phone, pressuring any and every contact she has to try to find more information about what's going on. She's worried, and she's not the type of person who you see that way very often.

The rest of us scour social media for any clues, but nothing promising is found. The quietness of the room starts getting to me. Rationality stops feeling welcome, and I can feel myself getting overwhelmed. My brother, the only family I have left, is missing, along with who knows how many others. I should have fought him harder on staying in Bay View City once the occupation began. I can throw a city bus over a skyscraper, but Derrick's my big brother, which means I still think of him as indestructible. That was stupid of me, and if something happens to him, it'll be my fault.

"Hey," Midnight says as he slaps a hand on my back. "Come with me."

I'm about to protest, tell him that I need to stay on my computer and try to find clues about where Derrick is, but I know that it would be a lie. I've been at it for hours and haven't found anything. I push away from the table and follow Midnight, who didn't wait for my response. He's already in the hallway, walking toward one of the gyms. I follow him to one of the rooms where he's waiting for me next to the punching bags.

"You were looking a little tense in there, and that's understandable. But the time will come for action soon, and that tension and anger can't be what drives you. It can fuel you, it can keep you going when everything else in your body tells you that you can't anymore, but it can't be what you use to make your decisions. That's how people get killed and not just you. The lives of a lot of people might be at stake here."

"I know that, but Derrick's gone and who knows if he's even alive still? What am I supposed to do with that?" I ask.

"There isn't much you can do except try to get rid of some of that anger, because when it's time, there isn't going to be much advance warning. Since you've got nothing else productive to do, you might as well put some time in with one of the heavy bags here. You'll feel better, trust me."

The heavy bags in the gym are all lined up together, far enough apart to make sure you don't bump into the person next to you. They're color-coded to indicate their material composition. At one end hang the heavy bags you might find at a normal boxing gym. At the other are the bags made of iron mesh, filled with steel railroad ties, and held in place with electromagnets that can be adjusted for different intensities.

I flick out my wrists to summon my metabands, intending to try my hardest to knock the iron punching bag across the room, but before I can bring them together, Midnight places his hand on my shoulder.

"Keep 'em off. You'll feel better beating the crap out of something when it's all you doing it," he says.

I hesitate for a moment then realize he's right and dismiss the metabands.

"Plus I don't feel like spending my weekend fixing holes in the drywall around here," Midnight says dryly.

I laugh at the rare joke from him, forgetting how mad I am for a second. He moves around to one of the regular heavy bags and braces up against it with his shoulder. I follow him over and start hitting the bag with my bare fists.

"Sure you don't want to tape your hands up?" he asks.

"No. If I injure anything, I'll just patch it up later with my bands." I take another swing with my right hand.

The truth is that I like feeling the pain in my fists. It's a welcome distraction.

"Keep your head back," Midnight instructs me as I throw a left.

"If Alpha has them, how are we supposed to take on anyone that powerful?" I ask Midnight.

"No one said we're taking on anyone just yet."

"If he has Derrick, then I'm taking him on, even if I have to do it alone."

Midnight doesn't say anything for the next few punches. I can't tell exactly what he's thinking, but I can tell that he's sufficiently convinced that I'm pissed off enough to mean what I said, and he doesn't challenge me on it.

"Did you know I was at The Battle?" he asks.

The question seems to come out of left field, but when he asks, I realize I never really thought about it and that I didn't know he was there. I always assumed I knew everything about it back to front—who was there, who died, and who lived—but now I know that I didn't know the first thing about it. I had no idea that my parents were there for any reason other than lunch. It makes sense to me now that Midnight was there, despite never having heard that reported publicly. I just haven't had enough time to process the information to have even started thinking about his role in all of this back then. Of course he was there, though. That's obvious now.

"I'll take your silence as a negative then," he says. "It never made the papers or anything like that. So many metahumans died that day, and the rest all lost their abilities. That was the big news of the day, not someone like me being there."

"I didn't realize you fought that day."

"I didn't fight. I was there trying to help save people, as many as possible. In the end, I wound up only helping a few and almost getting killed myself. The building I was evacuating a few blocks from midtown collapsed while I was inside of it. Your mother was the one who saved me. If she hadn't swooped in to grab me when she did, I would've been vaporized. There wouldn't have even been a body to identify.

"It was the last time I saw your mother, when she placed me back on the street and told me to run, to find cover. Then she turned and ran back into the fray. I never saw her again."

The story hits me like a punch to the gut. Out of all the things going on today, learning the reality of how my mother died wasn't what I was expecting. The toughest part is the story doesn't even explain how my mom died; it only gives a hint. Moments later, everyone's metabands failed for the last time. Wherever she was when that happened was likely what got her killed. I think back to the images of metahumans literally dropping from the sky that day and a chill runs through my spine thinking that my mother possibly suffered the same fate.

"I think I need some air," I say as I stop hitting the bag.

"There's plenty of air down here," Midnight says.

"Real air. Not this recycled stuff."

"You know that I can't let you go back up to the surface right now."

"Why the hell not?"

"Because Michelle doesn't trust you to be on your own. She's afraid that you'll take off to try to find Derrick on your own."

"Do you think that too?"

"I think I trust you, but you still can't go alone."

THIRTY-SEVEN

"You look absolutely ridiculous," I say to Midnight as we walk out into the unseasonably warm evening air.

The sun is setting on the west side of campus, casting long shadows everywhere. Midnight is dressed as a teacher, or what he thinks a teacher would dress like. He wears a boxy, ill-fitting dress shirt with a clip-on tie. His grayish blond hair is pulled back into a ponytail, and a pair of silver wireframe glasses completes the ridiculous-looking ensemble.

"No one asked you," Midnight growls back at me. "Don't worry about what I look like. Go get your air."

I stick my hands in my pockets and start walking in the general direction of the rest of campus. I don't have any intention of walking that far, but the opposite direction is nothing but woods until the highway.

I'm about fifty yards away when I stop and look at the sky. I'm not sure what I'm looking for, maybe just a metahuman flying through the air to give me a sense that not everyone is scared of Alpha Team, but I know that's not going to happen. We're too close to Bay View City for anyone to even take the chance to fly through here. The skies are completely clear.

After a few minutes of staring into the slowly darkening sky, I decide it's time to turn back. Relaxing for a minute and catching my breath was nice, but I'm already starting to feel anxious that Michelle might have heard something while I'm up here.

When I turn back around, Midnight is nowhere to be seen. Under normal circumstances, this would be expected. He likes to make his exits when no one else is looking, but I'm surprised that he'd do it when everyone else is so concerned that I'll run off. I start walking back toward the Blair Building to find him.

When I round the corner, I can barely believe what I'm

seeing. There, up against the brick wall, suspended by his throat via Midnight's hand, is Keane.

"You've got exactly three seconds to tell me what you're doing here!" Midnight yells at him.

I rush toward the pair, summoning my metabands on the way. Midnight has improvised a disguise for himself out of some kind of lightweight black mask, almost like a mix between a ski mask and the type of pantyhose bank robbers wear on their heads. I assume he must have had it with him this whole time, just in case.

I have no need to pretend I'm not who I really am since Keane already knows.

"What is he doing here?" I ask when I get close enough.

"That's just what he was about to tell us," Midnight says.

"Please, just put me back on the ground, and I can explain," Keane asks.

"Explain from up here," Midnight says.

"I want to talk with you. If I were here to do harm, don't you think I would have already done it? If I wanted to, I could take control over you and just be done with it. I'm refraining from using my powers as a show of good faith," Keane says.

Midnight doesn't move and continues to hold Keane by the throat. He never breaks eye contact with Keane, but he seems to be mulling over what his next move should be. Then he suddenly and abruptly drops Keane to the ground.

"What the hell are you doing?" I ask.

"Talk," Midnight says, ignoring my question. "You've got thirty seconds. If I don't like what I hear, you're going to wish you were back in New Mexico. I know places where even you can't escape, and you wouldn't like them very much."

"I know what Alpha Team is trying to do. I know what their plan is," Keane says.

"And how could you know that?" I ask him.

"In case you've forgotten, I can literally read minds, Mr. Connolly."

"Not theirs you can't. They're too powerful," I reply.

"No, you're correct, but I have been able to search the minds of some of those that they're holding hostage."

"Who?" I ask, immediately thinking of Derrick.

"I'm not at liberty to say, unfortunately."

Before I'm able to open my mouth, Keane is doubled over in pain, clutching his stomach, the result of a knee from Midnight.

"I told you, we're not playing games here," he menacingly whispers into Keane's ear.

"Not anyone you know. People whose minds I've interfaced with previously. That's the only reason I was able to connect from such a long distance. The stress of their kidnapping made them more susceptible. It's the only explanation I can think of, at least.

"How I acquired this information isn't important. It's the information itself that needs to be acted on as quickly as possible."

"And you want us to do your dirty work? We're not your butlers, Keane. You can't just have us do your bidding because you want us to. We can't be bought and sold like that," I snap.

"I have no intention of buying or selling anyone. I just want to see Alpha Team taken down. Saving people is important to you, I understand that, but I'll be honest and say that I imagine saving these people is something you're much more interested in than I am."

"Yeah, I'd imagine that too."

"Yes, well, the problem here is that Alpha Team is surrounded by Bay View City itself. Those people aren't just potential collateral damage to Alpha Team. They're a shield. They know that anyone who dares to try to oppose them and fight will have to do so without harming the citizens, a nearly impossible proposition. Fighting them and costing lives would only prove the point that Alpha Team is trying to make: that metahumans are dangerous."

"Then what's your point?" I ask.

"My point is that I think I might have a way around that for you."

THIRTY-EIGHT

Although we don't discuss it on the way down, Midnight and I both know Michelle isn't going to like this. She doesn't even like the idea of us doing *anything* in regards to Bay View City right now, except waiting for more information. The only reason she might yield is the lack of other options in this situation and the prospect that Derrick may be in danger. That said, the idea of doing something about it is one thing, but bringing Keane into the facility is another.

"I must say, it really is quite a feat you've pulled off here. Were the classrooms retrofitted with the elevator equipment or were they built to be elevators from the very beginning?" Keane asks. The question could be pointed at either Midnight or me, but neither of us is feeling particularly chatty. "I only ask because I'd be quite interested in getting myself something similar after all of this is over."

"After all of this is over, you're going back to prison," Midnight says.

There isn't anger in his voice anymore. He just states it plainly as fact.

"Well, we'll talk about all of that once this is over with. Everything's negotiable," Keane says.

Keane had already been aware of the elevator before we brought him into it. He'd seen into the mind of one of the workers responsible for the original construction of the building all those years ago. Those workers were given specific tasks in relation to very specific pieces of the facility in order to prevent outside knowledge of what was really going on here. Much of the construction was fabricated off-site and assembled later.

After Keane saw bits of what was being built from the memories of the worker, he was able to piece the rest together himself. He figured out what the facility actually was, who had built it, and, most importantly to him, who is here. There isn't much he doesn't already know about all of this.

While it's extremely risky to bring him down here, these are desperate times. As Keane pointed out, if he'd really just wanted access to the facility, it would have been much easier to just take over my or Midnight's mind and make us let him in than try to convince us using logic.

We reach the bottom and the elevator locks into place. Before Midnight or I can reach the door, it opens on its own. Michelle walks in, her eyes looking down at the tablet in her hands.

"Finally. I was starting to think that the two of you got lost somewh ..." she trails off as she sees Keane and, in an instant, lunges for one of the emergency alarms back out in the hallway.

"Michelle, wait," I say. She temporarily freezes. "He's not here to harm us. He's here to help."

"Are you out of your mind! You brought an escaped metahuman convict into our facility!?"

"I know. I know. If we had any other choice, we would have taken it, but we don't, and we're running out of time. He already knew about us and about all of this. All I promised him is that we'd hear him out. That's it. If we don't like what he has to offer, then we send him back out and on his way."

"No, we send him right back to prison where he belongs."

The entire time this argument is happening, Keane stays silent. It's not out of respect or anything even resembling that, though. He's standing there with a smirk on his face, enjoying the argument. He's only staying out of it because he likes to watch the conflict. I'm beginning to doubt bringing him down here was anything other than a stupid idea.

"I only ask for a few moments of your time, Miss ... Adams, is it?" Keane says as he steps forward.

"Stay right where you are, asshole," Michelle says, taking a step back herself as a precaution.

"Miss Adams, as I've explained to your colleagues, if I were here to harm you, I could have done so by now."

"And what if you're just controlling their minds?"

"If I were, why would I not do the same to you? Why even waste the time to explain myself if I wanted to use that shortcut?"

"We're running out of time and options. We should hear him out," Midnight adds.

"Why thank you, Midnight. I never expected someone who spends their nights jumping around on rooftops dressed in their pajamas to be so levelheaded. Maybe all of those people who said you're crazy are wrong after all."

Midnight scowls at Keane, and the look actually seems to work. Keane is momentarily and uncharacteristically flustered.

"Right, so," Keane says as he clears his throat. "The plan ..."

THIRTY-NINE

Keane's proposal relies on him using his powers to control the civilians on the ground and evacuate the city before we go in. With one person controlling everyone, the evacuation can happen incredibly fast. No traffic jams, no pushing and shoving, just a nice orderly line over the bridge and out of harm's way.

Michelle has doubts as to whether Keane is powerful enough to actually pull something like that off, but Midnight believes he is. What Midnight isn't a hundred percent sold on is Keane not having ulterior motives. He lays out his suspicions to Keane directly in front of the entire group, stating that there's no room for any hidden hesitations or doubts. If someone has a problem with any of this, there won't be another chance to speak up.

"I completely understand your ... hesitation, Midnight. All I can offer you as evidence that I'm a man of my word are my past actions."

"You mean like when you used mind control to dupe your colleagues into making lopsided business deals with you or when you paid another metahuman to break you out of prison?"

"Both fair points. In my defense, you have no idea who the men and women I took that money from were actually like. Behind closed doors, they were the kind of monsters who would make your stomach turn. The wealth and power they wielded makes the Alphas look like preschoolers. There are a lot of things you can buy when you're wealthy and a lot of things you're willing to do to become even wealthier. At a certain point, anyone will look the other way if the price is right.

"And as per my escape, I did what was necessary, and I stand behind that. Can any of you say that you would happily sit locked in a cell while your city was overrun by fascists, even though you knew you could do something to stop it? I can answer that question for you: no, you wouldn't. And I admire that. There's a reason why I came to this group with my idea. We may not see eye to eye on everything, but we all would do whatever it takes to ensure the safety of our city. You'll all be breaking the law just by entering Bay View City. How does that make you that much different from me?

"Despite how desperately some of you would like to categorize me as a criminal or a villain, I'm afraid the real world just isn't that simple. You can't just put me in a box so it's easier for you to classify me. It's your right to hold an opinion, and I understand why many of you see me as something less than yourselves, but that doesn't make me a monster."

Everyone in the room is silent.

"If someone has a better idea of how to get everyone else out of the way, I'm all ears," I say.

The room remains silent.

"All right then. That part's taken care of. Now we just have to figure out how we actually beat them," I say.

"The key is separating them," Midnight says from the back of the room as he walks forward to join the rest of the group sitting at the table overlaid with a three-dimensional hologram of Bay View City. "Their metabands are different from all the others, correct? There must be a reason why they're more powerful. We know that all the metabands on Earth are connected to each other. When their metabands bonded to their DNA, it happened in the midst of a nuclear explosion. That nuclear reaction must be what caused the change. Up until now, it'd been assumed that the reaction simply supercharged their metabands to levels previously unseen. The problem with that hypothesis is that's not really how metabands work. You cannot simply create more energy out of energy that didn't previously exist."

"How do you know so much about metabands?" Winston asks.

"Just trust him," I answer.

"The metabands that Alpha Team use aren't more powerful; they're simply connected to each other in a unique way. We know that their previous attempt to destroy Connor's metabands was intended to be self-serving. If Omni's bands had been destroyed, his powers, along with the powers of every metahuman who came after him, would have vanished, but Alpha Team wouldn't have been affected. That's because their energy remains in its own separate loop between the five of them."

"That explains why they're trying to take down other metahumans. They know that with even just a small number of metabands destroyed, most of the rest will stop working, especially if they can get to the earliest people to receive their powers, like me," I say.

"That's not all. I've been watching Alpha Team very closely, and I have another hypothesis that explains why we rarely see them together as a group," Midnight says.

"Well that's easy. If their metabands are all connected, then it'd make sense for them to never be all in the same place at the same time. That would minimize the chances of them all being killed in the same strike," Ellie says.

"That's part of it, but we've seen them act together. They took down Silver Island as a unit, but since then, no one has seen them together, especially not in combat. I believe the reason for this is that they're able to transfer their energy between each other," Midnight says.

"So they're sharing it?" Michelle asks.

"Not exactly. Think of it more like a pool they can all draw from, but when only one of them is drawing power from the pool, it increases that individual's powers exponentially."

"What does that mean?" Winston asks. Midnight looks like he's getting tired of being asked so many questions, and his ire falls on Winston just because he's the last one to have asked. "What? Sorry if I've slept through a few math classes because I've been stuck down here all night."

"It means that when one of them takes power from the others, it's not just the sum of the power added together; it's multiplied."

"So if one of them is taking the power of three, it's like that power gets multiplied by itself."

"And that explains not only how Charlie can seem so much more powerful. It also explains why we rarely see them all fighting at the same time. When Charlie is using their powers, the rest are in the tower, hidden and protected since they're little more than just human at that point."

"So that's when we hit them. We lure Charlie out and go after the others while they're powerless!" Ellie stands up in excitement at the idea.

"That won't work," Midnight says, instantly deflating Ellie's enthusiasm. "Taking down the others while the power is focused inside of Charlie won't change anything since he'll still have all of their power.

"What we need to do is overwhelm them. Force all five to come out fighting so their powers aren't pooled into one unstoppable metahuman anymore. If my predictions are correct, the balance of power is something that they all have control over, meaning that one of them can't simply override the others to take all of the power without the others allowing it. The power has to be relinquished before one of them can take it. That's why Charlie holds the majority of the power most of the time. He was the leader of their squad before all of this, and so he's kept the natural position of leader now as well.

"But they're all still fighters. None of them will lie down and accept defeat just to give someone else their powers. We separate them, beat them until their powers reach reserve levels, and then detain them using Agency restraints."

"It sounds pretty easy. Why hasn't someone tried this before?" I ask.

"Few others understand how their powers really work,

which is obviously intentional on their part. They maintain the illusion that they all have the power of a hundred metahumans and no one dares mess with them.

"But even if someone else did figure it out, there's another reason why no one has tried this yet. It's what makes it risky for us too, and that's the timing. If we don't hit all of them equally as hard in the same timeframe, then they'll be able to transfer their powers away before they hit reserve levels. That's not even taking into account the risk that if one of us doesn't succeed in taking down our target, their powers will be up for grabs for the others. All it takes is one miss on our part and that Alpha Team member will be able to transfer his power to one of the others, who will then easily be able to beat whichever one of us he's up against and so on like dominos until they've won."

"And we're all dead."

"Presumably, yes."

Silence falls over the room again and a few take a long, deep exhale, letting the full gravity of what we're about to try fall on them. There's a million different ways this can all go wrong, and any one of them is enough to take all of us with it.

* * *

Midnight enters the room and the side conversations quickly come to a halt. We've all been waiting for him for over an hour. Some passed the time by sleeping, trying to get in a nap to make up for the rest of the week's lost sleep. Others spent the time training, either running laps around the hundred-mile track or using the heavy lifting room.

Everyone avoids the casualty-prevention room. It's usually one of the busier rooms, and one that the staff encourages us to spend the most time in, but if all goes as planned tonight, we won't need to save anyone. If all goes as planned, our only job will be taking down Alpha Team. If we fail that, then saving innocent lives is going to be next to impossible.

I spend most of the time pacing. It frustrates me that I'm

not invited into the planning. A few months ago, I was the most powerful person on earth, so it's hard not to feel sidelined as "just a kid" right now, even if my powers aren't where they once were.

"Nerves?" Iris asks me.

"A few," I reply.

"That's good. You need some of those. Keep you on your toes," she says back.

"What about you?" I ask.

"I don't get nervous."

"Not even for something as big as this?"

"It's no bigger or smaller than anything else we've done before."

"Yes, it is."

"No, it's not. Not when you consider that every day any of us are out there could be our last. Or could be the last for someone who has the misfortune of standing around taking pictures with their phone on the wrong street corner."

"I guess I never thought of it that way."

"Probably for the best. Might not be the healthiest way to go about trying to live your life."

There's a pause while I consider if I should say what I really want to or not. Before I can say anything, Iris seems to read my mind and says it for me instead.

"Midnight told you about who I really am, didn't he?" she asks.

"Yeah, he did."

"And he told you about who you really are too?"

"I'm always who I've been. What Midnight told me about my parents doesn't change who I am. You shouldn't let it change who you are either."

"That's easy for you to say. Your parents were heroes. The world practically worshiped them. My father was a monster that brought nothing into this world but pain and fear."

"That's not true. He brought you into this world too, and you've saved more lives than you can keep count of."

Iris is quiet, working hard to maintain her exterior and avoid showing anything even resembling an emotion.

"Why don't you hate me?" she asks.

"Why would I hate you?"

"My father killed both of your parents. I almost killed you while at the same time making the world a much more dangerous place by letting so many of these monsters out."

"What your father did isn't what you did. And you didn't do those other things, not really. That wasn't you," I say, my eyes wandering subconsciously toward Keane.

He's sitting in a chair in the corner, reading a book and drinking a cup of tea as though he doesn't have a problem in the world. I don't think I've ever been as relaxed in my life as Keane is right now, a short time before we go into a fight that will put potentially millions of lives at risk. Just seeing him sitting like that, so calm when he's mostly the reason why we're all in this mess, begins to make my blood boil. I move to take a step in his direction, not even sure what I'm going to do or say, when the door opens. The others who had taken a break outside, along with Michelle and Midnight, return to the room.

"All right, everyone. Please take a seat," Michelle begins. "We have a lot of information to disseminate and not a whole lot of time to do it."

She moves to the front of the room as Midnight makes his way to the back, where he prefers standing to sitting and listening to talking. Michelle taps a few buttons on the screen of her tablet. The lights in the room fade down and the screen at the front is illuminated with a map of the world.

"We have intelligence from Bay View City that suggests Alpha Team is gearing up for a public broadcast. While we don't have any specific intelligence about the content of this broadcast, the timing is concerning. With the spate of recent missing journalists and metahuman sympathizers, along with the late hour of this broadcast, we have reason to believe that they may be planning a public demonstration of their power."

"What does that mean?" Winston asks.

"It could mean a few different things, but the one we are obviously most concerned about would be a public form of capital punishment to set an example for the rest of the world."

"Like a beating?"

"Like an execution."

The room quickly fills with murmurs and talk. The blood in my veins turns cold.

"Everyone, please. I understand that there are a lot of emotions in the room, but I need to ask you to put those aside. We have nothing to suggest that anything drastic has taken place yet, and if we do our jobs correctly, tonight we have the potential to end this once and for all. But that can only happen if everyone, and I mean everyone"—Michelle glances at Keane—"has their heads in the game and their hearts in their back pockets for now.

"We'll be launching a coordinated, five-sided attack against Alpha Team this evening before the broadcast is scheduled to occur. The purpose of this five-sided attack is to divide and separate the members of Alpha Team for the purpose of neutralizing them independently without human casualties, as well as preventing the transference of power from one to the next. From our understanding of their abilities, relative distance may play a significant role in the ability for one member to transfer their power to another. Even if this is inaccurate, we believe it will create a substantial tactical advantage if this unit is broken apart.

"We don't like to talk about potential losses, especially in the lead up to something this important, but we also need to make sure that, even in the possibility of defeat, we've made every reasonable effort to at the very least weaken their position. If even one member of Alpha Team is brought down to reserve power and taken into custody, that will be considered an important victory."

As Michelle finishes her speech, I can see her eyes becoming glassy as they fill with tears before her eyelids push them away. She knows how important tonight is to the world, but also to her personally, and despite what she just said, there's no way that a partial victory can be seen as anything other than a catastrophic defeat for us.

"As previously discussed, minimizing civilian casualties is the most important part of this mission. Mr. Keane will be the first one on site with the assistance of August. She'll be teleporting him inside the Bay View City limits and using her invisibility to cloak both Keane and herself while he initiates a mass evacuation of the city.

"At that point, we estimate we have approximately five minutes before Alpha Team either notices the movement or senses that metahumans are inside the city. It'll be important to begin the rest of the attack before this happens while still evacuating as many people as possible beforehand. Timing will be very important here.

"Once the attack begins, we will be separating the Alphas into different areas of the globe as quickly as possible. Ellie, you'll be taking up the first deployment with Jacob and Matt, who'll be harnessed onto you."

"Um, harnessed?" Ellie asks.

"You, Jacob, and Matt will all be attached via carbon fiber harnesses that will be tethered approximately fifteen feet apart. Once inside Bay View City, Jacob and Matt will grab Delta and Echo. Once they have them secured, you'll run toward the west coast of America and over the Pacific Ocean. At three thousand miles off shore, Jacob's harness will detach. He will bring Delta to the bottom of the ocean floor, where we estimate the pressure will significantly reduce Delta's ability to put up a fight.

"Meanwhile, after the leash detaches, you'll head south for Antarctica, where Matt will bring Echo. Again, we are counting on the decreased temperatures to hamper Echo's abilities, but I must warn you that we don't anticipate this to do much. The primary reason for bringing Echo to Antarctica is simply to take him as far away from the others as possible.

"Once both Matt and Jacob are successfully deployed, they'll be joined by other members of the metahuman community to aid in the battle. Ellie, you will return to Bay View City to assist with any collateral damage prevention.

"Concurrently, Foxtrot will be teleported with the aid of Martha to the Sahara Desert. The environment will ensure that his abilities will be diminished at least slightly, while also giving us a sort of home field advantage. We'll be depending on Turner to provide the primary assault against Foxtrot."

"Using the same tactics?" Turner asks.

"No. You'll be using your ability to control projectiles as a primarily offensive technique."

"Um ... so where will I be getting the projectiles?"

"You'll be in the one place on earth that has more potential projectile objects than anywhere else: the desert."

"Ahhh, I get it. Sand."

"Yes ... sand," Michelle says, seemingly thinking twice about how reliable this particular part of the plan is.

"And what about Charlie himself?" Turner asks.

"We anticipate that Charlie will remain steadfast within the city's vicinity and that any attempts to remove him will result in a game of cat and mouse as he fights to return. He's faster than many, if not all of you here, so even if we succeed in bringing him elsewhere, it's extremely unlikely that he will stay there very long. For that reason, we will be deploying Omni and Iris to Bay View City to confront Charlie directly."

The previously quiet room is full of chatter and talk. I'm only able to catch snippets of it as I try to figure out if people agree with this part of the plan or think it's a one-way ticket to getting us all killed. Michelle struggles to regain the attention of the room.

"That's enough. If there are any objections to this plan, now is the time to voice them, because once everyone is out in the field, I expect nothing but one hundred percent commitment. Even with that, we've got a very uphill battle," Michelle says.

"I don't mean to be rude, but is Iris really someone we can trust in there?" one of the girls in the room asks as though Iris isn't sitting five feet away from her.

"I have complete and total faith in Iris's abilities on the battlefield. The reason Omni and Iris have been chosen for this part of the mission is their experience with close-quarter fighting in Bay View City before. They know the city better than anyone else in this room, and we don't have time to have anyone else memorize the layout of the city. In the past, they've admirably reduced or eliminated civilian injuries and deaths.

"Ancillary to that, we believe that these two will provide the most tempting opponents for Charlie. He is more likely to stay inside Bay View City and engage in the fight if it's against two metahumans he sees as his direct rivals. I mean no offense to the others in this room, but we fear that with any other matchup, we run the risk of Charlie potentially fleeing the city to join forces with another member of his team. We're hoping his pride won't let him leave Bay View City if he knows that Omni and Iris are there."

"So basically, we're bait," I say.

"Not if you do what you're supposed to."

"And what is that?"

"Beat him into the ground so hard that no one on earth will ever have to fear him again."

* * *

Getting close to Bay View City proves to be no small task. The media has gotten wind about the public broadcast and have promptly parked themselves all around the perimeter. I know that it's hypocritical for me to get mad at the media for covering the potential execution of my brother when his job is covering this kind of thing too, but it just feels different. He hates this kind of spectacle and has always gone out of his way to make sure that the kinds of metahumans who pulled stunts like this for attention didn't ever get it from him.

Derrick has also fought hard to keep himself out of stories, even when a pair of metabands fell into his own brother's lap, technically wrists, or when his girlfriend turned out to be part of a private organization devoted to training young metahumans. Oh, and his parents were apparently metahumans his entire childhood, but he doesn't even know that yet. All things considered, he's done a pretty good job of not letting his personal life bleed into his work ... until today.

The specifics of the plan have all been hammered out as well as they can be, but even still, a lot of this plan involves improvising as we go. It's the unfortunate side effect of having to react so quickly to something we're not entirely prepared to deal with, but we all have our parts to play in this.

Midnight is the first part of the plan. We're working under the assumption that the hostages are being held in Keane Tower, where the Alphas have been holed up since this began. There's concern that the Alphas are on high alert and paying even more attention than usual to their senses that can pick up on nearby metabands. For this reason, Midnight elected himself to be the first one in, establishing a set of eyes from the building across the way.

My part won't come until the very end, but that's little consolation. It's not easy to relax when you're waiting to jump into a situation practically blind, where it's more than likely you're going to get yourself killed. My brother's life being on the line doesn't help either.

I take up position a mile from the city's "no meta zone" perimeter, hovering a few thousand feet in the air. Even with telescopic vision, there's almost nothing to see. The city looks like it does any other day. There are people going about their regular business, driving home from work, hanging out with their friends. I tell myself that they must have no idea what's going on in their city, because it's too difficult to accept that they know but just don't care.

My earpiece clicks on, and I hear Midnight's voice.

"Midnight to Circle. I have visual confirmation of Delta and Echo on the roof of Keane Tower. They're alone and hostages do not appear to be in the immediate area. Stage one team, acknowledge when ready."

There's a second or two of dead air before there's another click in my ear.

"Ellie to Midnight. Intel received. Prepare for incoming in three ... two ... one."

Before the microphone cuts out, I hear a small sonic boom over the earpiece. A couple of seconds later, the same boom reaches my ears through the air. The rooftop of Keane Tower is blocked from my view and my nerves are racked as I silently wait for something, anything, to come over the radio.

"Targets acquired. En route to first location," Ellie says over the radio.

In the background, I can hear some kind of struggle happening. No one thought it'd be easy to grab those two, but they've done it, so far at least.

"First location reached and target disengaged. En route to second location," Ellie says.

Her voice is strained as she pushes herself faster and faster. In the background, I can hear what at first I think is static before I realize it's the sound of her feet hitting the water over and over again so quickly that the sound has become unrecognizable.

"Foxtrot spotted on the rooftop.. Engage now," Midnight shouts into the microphone.

"Wait, what? We haven't even gotten the all clear from Ellie yet," I say into my earpiece.

"He's on the rooftop looking for the other two. We need to engage now. This may be our only chance before they're all alerted to our presence."

There's nothing but silence for what feels like an eternity

before the earpiece clicks on again.

"Ellie to Circle, location two reached and packages delivered. Returning to home position."

Not what I was waiting to hear, but good news all the same. I consider clicking in to ask what's happening with the other two but stop myself. As soon as there's news, I'll hear. Asking right now will just jam up the channel with uselessness. I can only hope that everything is working and wait. I'm almost up.

"Dammit. They're on to us," Midnight says over the air, "Foxtrot has been teleported away. The rest of the building is going on full lockdown. We're not going to be able to get anywhere close. Blanks are surrounding the building as we speak."

"We'll just have Keane send them away," I suggest.

"Negative. Charlie will see that coming from a mile away and execute the hostages if he knows we're working with Keane."

More silence as everyone thinks the same thing: What the hell are we supposed to do now? I try to think faster and outrun the word that I don't want to hear come out of Midnight's mouth: abort. There has to be another way.

"I have an idea," I say before the idea is even fully formed in my head, but I need to buy time before we give up. "I can get in there. Jim, my friend from Bay View, he's in there. He's a Blank. He's gotta be close to all of this. He can get me in. He can get me close."

"There's no way," Midnight says. "Before you're even over the bay, Charlie will be able to sense you coming."

"What if I don't have my metabands on, though?"

"Then what's the point? Just going in there to get yourself killed?"

"No. We don't know the layout of the interior, which is why we can't just teleport ourselves in, right? But if I went in there and found Charlie, I could relay my coordinates to one of you and you could teleport in with my metabands. It'd happen so quickly that even Charlie wouldn't have time to react before it was too late and I was powered up."

"I don't like it."

"I don't like it either, but we're out of options here. If we give up now, everyone inside that building is as good as dead. We have to at least try."

"I'll teleport him in," Iris says over her earpiece.

"Then you'll both get killed," Midnight growls.

There isn't much time, and Iris's plan sounds as good as anything else I could come up with, meaning one way or another, it's going to be the plan. I push myself down through the air feet first, only easing up from my rapid descent when I'm a few feet from the ground. A few yards away there's a line of cars moving along the road as they pass over the bridge to leave Bay View City. I'm behind a few dense bushes, far enough out of sight that I can power down my metabands without worrying about being seen.

"I'm the fastest teleporter there is. I can have Omni in there and myself out before Charlie even notices. I'm the only one who knows that city well enough to get him close without killing either of us and you know that," Iris says.

"Fi-" I hear through the earpiece. In a literal flash, Iris is in front of me and reaches out to grab my hands. "-ne."

Now we're both standing in an alleyway in Bay View City.

"Power down," Iris whispers to me.

I do as she says, and in another blink, she's gone with my metabands. I almost feel naked without them. Usually, when they're on me, I can't see or feel them if they're in hibernation mode, but somehow in the back of my mind, I always know that they're there, and there's a comfort to that. I just hope wherever Iris is, she's keeping my metabands safe, because I have a feeling I'm going to need them again real soon.

Pulling my phone out of my pocket, I quickly fumble through my recent call log to find Jim's number and hit dial. It rings five times, and I start to worry that he's not going to pick up, but on the sixth ring, I find his voice on the other end.

"What?" he asks, not bothering with any kind of formalities.

"You need to get me into Keane Tower," I say.

"Are you out of your mind?"

"Maybe, but that's not relevant. I need you to get me in so we can stop this once and for all. Can you do it?"

FORTY

The Blank mask is a lot more comfortable than I expected, I think as I walk toward Keane Tower with Jim. The mass evacuation has all but emptied the city streets. A few stragglers walk past us as we climb the steps leading up to the entrance. Their eyes are empty and their gaze is focused straight ahead. I don't turn to look at them, though, mostly out of fear of standing out in any way.

My earpiece is still in place and over the open channel I hear the sounds of a war being waged across multiple continents all over the world. Delta is the first to fall. The crushing pressure of the Pacific Ocean weakened him even faster than we thought it would. Within minutes of being pulled to the ocean floor, he blacked out. Jacob had to work quickly to couple the restraints to his wrists and bring him back up to the surface before he regained consciousness.

Ellie returned to pick up both Jacob and Delta, taking Delta to the New Mexico facility before dropping off Jacob in Antarctica, where the struggle to take down Echo is proving to be tougher than expected. Matt wasn't letting up any of his ground, though, and with Jacob jumping into the fray, it'll only be a matter of time before Echo is going to be put on ice. Pun intended.

FORTY-ONE

I can feel the sweat starting to build underneath the mask where it meets the bridge of my nose. This is about as haphazard of a plan as I've ever been a part of, but it's also completely out of necessity. I can feel my heart beating so hard it feels like it's going to burst out of my chest as I enter the elevator with Jim. The doors close behind us and even though we're alone, you're never *really* alone in Keane Tower. There are cameras everywhere, and I've been warned to not drop the act under any circumstances.

"Omni, status update," Midnight says into my ear through the earpiece. It feels strange to be called Omni when I'm wearing a sweatshirt and jeans. Technically, I'm still masked, even if it isn't the mask that I'm used to. I don't respond, making sure to stick to Jim's rules. After a few seconds, it occurs to Midnight that this is what I must be doing.

"Cough once for everything is going according to plan, twice for complications," he says.

I abide and give one, brief cough. Jim turns his mirrored face to me, his expressionless mask somehow still exuding suspicion. He has just as much, if not more, on the line as I do. If we're caught, I'm at least valuable as a negotiating chip; Jim isn't.

"Ellie is in position and awaiting your signal. Be careful, Connor," Midnight says before temporarily signing off.

There's a small camera underneath my mirrored Blank mask that's feeding a live image to both Midnight and now Ellie. It's there to help Midnight keep an eye on me, but more importantly, it's crucial so Iris can teleport in correctly. Midnight's acquired the floor plan to Keane Tower, but even with that, it would be difficult for Iris to know exactly where I am, and she'll need to be exact. Teleporting into the wrong side of the room could cost seconds, and we might not have those if there's a gun pointed at Derrick's head.

The elevator *dings* and the doors slowly slide open to reveal the penthouse. It's familiar, yet distinctly changed now that Charlie's had a chance to redecorate. Gone are the glass cubicles and six-figure artworks. The penthouse is now sparse and open. Across the room, I see Charlie pacing anxiously back and forth.

In front of him are multiple hostages. All of them are kneeling on the floor with their hands bound behind their backs and black hoods over their heads. I recognize Derrick right away. Something about his posture triggers an immediate recognition. It's confirmed when I also see that he's wearing one of my favorite shirts. I'd been looking for it everywhere, not realizing that he must have stolen it from my closet before I left for the academy. I'd be really pissed off if I wasn't so happy to see that he's still alive.

"What are you doing here?" Charlie barks when he sees us exit the elevator.

There are a few Blanks up here, but only three or four, it looks like. Most of them seem occupied with setting up the camera equipment. I'm temporarily taken aback when I remember that the purpose of this camera is to broadcast a live execution.

"Number thirty-six told us to come up here and help with the equipment," Jim says, thinking quickly on his feet or already having anticipated the question.

The answer seems to satisfy Charlie, and he simply waves us off, indicating that we do whatever we need to as long as we don't bother him. Jim glances over at me and motions for me to follow him. We walk across the wide-open floor as the moonlight streaks in through the full-length windows of the eighty-third floor.

Once we've reached the camera and the other Blanks, Jim opens one of the nearby camera cases and hands me a large coil of electrical cord. He points to the far wall, indicating to me that I need to run it to the outlet there. I'm slightly relieved to have something to occupy my thoughts for a minute, and it gives me a chance to catch my breath.

Midnight, Iris, and I briefly discussed when the best opportunity to strike would be. We all agreed that the moments leading up to the broadcast would likely be best. Charlie will be busy concentrating on his speech, but not concentrating on his surroundings as much as he will be once the camera starts rolling.

I'm supposed to give Iris a sign to indicate that I'm ready, just a simple thumbs up in front of the camera embedded in my mask. She's going to have to trust me completely and teleport in right away, ignoring any hesitation she might have. It's the only way a plan like this will work since even something as simple as a thumbs up could be seen and interpreted by Charlie or one of the Blanks. There won't be any time for second chances.

I reach the far wall and bend over to place the electrical plug into the socket, taking a deep breath before I stand back up. This is going to be it. I'm far enough away from Charlie that the risk to the hostages is minimal, as well as the risk to Iris teleporting in. I might not get a better chance.

When I turn back to the room, I find that my window of surprise is completely gone. There's Charlie, staring right at me, his forearm wrapped tightly around Jim's throat as he holds him in front of his body as a shield.

"Do you really think I'm that stupid? Do you really think that I wouldn't notice a metahuman walking right into my own home? You might not have your metabands with you, but that doesn't mean I can't still sense the residual energy, and the camera I see through your mask just confirmed it. So what do you think we should do with this little traitor?" Charlie asks, tightening his grip around Jim's neck.

I see Derrick's head turn under the black bag. He's just figured out that I must be here. He's silent, but I don't know if that's out of fear or because there's probably half a roll of duct tape wrapped around his mouth.

"Well, if you don't have any ideas, I have one," Charlie

says. There's no time to react before it happens. Charlie's free hand bursts through Jim's torso and his body goes limp and falls to the floor.

"Now!" Midnight screams in my ear. Simultaneously, Iris appears and then disappears in front of me. My metabands are wrapped around my wrists again, and I can feel my body starting to draw in their power like a sponge.

There are tears rolling down my cheeks as I start running and bring my metabands together to activate them. Jim's mortally injured, but there isn't time to help him if I'm going to save anyone else's life here.

The bands collide and the Omni suit spreads across my body. Charlie grins, waving his hand for me to come at him. He won't have to ask twice.

I lunge a few more steps before we meet, me barreling into him head first and breaking through the bulletproof glass window. There's no reaction from Charlie. He waits until we're both floating above the city before casually brushing me aside with his hand, sending me flying clear through a skyscraper three blocks away. I lose control and fall toward the street, sliding and tumbling halfway through downtown before I'm able to grab onto a pothole in the road and slow myself down. The instant I'm back on my feet, I scan the skyline for Charlie, but I can't find him.

Suddenly, my back feels like it's split in two, and I'm moving through the city again at hyper-speed. I look down and see Charlie's arms wrapped around my waist.

"You just couldn't leave well enough alone, could you?" he yells into my ear.

I feel a quick jerk and our momentum changes, diverting the two of us toward the nearest building. Everything goes black as we smash through layer after layer, the sound bordering on deafening before we break through the far wall of the tower, and the moonlight once again illuminates everything around us.

I struggle to turn my head to look behind me and see

what's happened to the building that we both just burst through, but the momentum and wind make it hard to even move as Charlie senses me struggling and tightens his already viselike grip.

"Don't you see what happens when people like you think you're better than the rest of us? When you think that you're above us all? When you think that you're a god who the law doesn't apply to? People get hurt. People die. There are rules to the world. There's an order. Metahumans don't belo-"

His speech is unexpectedly cut off, and I no longer feel his arms wrapped around my waist. I'm decelerating quickly and find that I'm able to get my feet back underneath me and slide to a stop.

But before I even have a chance to see what's happened, I'm already flying backwards in the opposite direction. Whatever stopped Charlie was likely only temporary, and I'll need to take advantage of the momentary upper hand I have.

In the distance, I see Charlie sailing through the night sky until he's only a pinpoint, quickly disappearing out of sight, but it's what is standing right in front of me that's even more surprising: Midnight's mechanized armor. Except it's not. It's different. What was once matte black is now shining white. Details of the armor are highlighted in sky blue, especially around the helmet.

"Midnight?" I ask as I approach cautiously. The last thing I need right now is my clock cleaned by an imposter. The armor turns to face me and lowers its guard.

"Not exactly," says the heavily distorted voice from the inside of this huge metal beast. The visor lifts and various unseen clasps release from the side of the helmet until it's able to lift itself and reveal the identity of its operator: Sarah.

"What?" I'm barely able to stammer out.

"Thought you might be able to use a hand," she says.

"But ... how?"

"When I was injured, Midnight used the suit to save my

life. One of the unforeseen side effects of using it to heal my wounds was that the suit's power supply, its solo metaband, bonded with me."

"And Midnight just gave it to you?"

"It stopped working for him after I was able to bond with it. To be honest, I think he was just going to throw it out before he gave it to me, especially after I had it repainted. I mean, there's only so much black and gray you can take. I didn't think it'd hurt to add a little personality to it if I was going to keep her."

"Her?"

"Yeah, is there a problem with that?"

"Um, no. I've got much bigger problems."

"Damn right you do. That hit just drained my battery almost completely. Keane's got just about everyone out of here, but Charlie's going to be back any second.

"I'm going back to help evacuate the hostages Charlie was holding, but you're going to have to help keep him occupied until we're able to get the city clear and the rest of your team is back."

"Okay."

"Don't look so surprised," Sarah says as the mask's components spring back into action, putting the various pieces back into place to completely cover and protect her face. "This isn't the first time I've had to save your ass."

Blue flames erupt out of the calves of the suit, and she's airborne in an instant, flying through the air toward the bridge where the residents are being evacuated.

I take a moment to check my metabands. They're still intact and powered up, but I don't trust them rely on them right now, especially considering who I'm up against.

It's then that I notice the speck in the night sky. It grows larger and larger as it rapidly approaches. It's Charlie, and he's heading straight for me, but this time I'm ready for him.

I wait until he's almost on top of me, until I can see the rage in his eyes and the muscles pulsing in his jaw as he clenches his teeth. I wait until it's almost too late, and then I quickly step aside, out of the way of his outstretched fist, which I grab with my right hand, creating a small shockwave as his momentum is suddenly stopped.

He's angry, very angry. It can be a very bad thing when someone with this much power is angry, but it can also be the only advantage I have in this fight. Anger makes you sloppy. I can't help Jim, not anymore. The only thing I have a chance at is making sure he didn't die in vain.

"You really think you can beat me?" Charlie asks as he pushes his clenched fist into my hand harder and harder.

"Kinda, yeah."

"You're nothing. You're an anomaly. A nobody who was just in the right place at the right time. You're not special. Without those things around your wrists, you're just a regular person."

"You're right, but that's not a weakness."

I wrap my fingers tightly around his fist, summoning strength I didn't know I still had in me, and pull Charlie over my head, slamming him face first into the pavement so hard that he's buried up to his shoulders.

But he doesn't rise right away. He lies there, laughing. I can hear him through the rubble before he pulls his head back out and takes a seat right there on the pavement.

"You really don't get it, do you? You can't beat me. You can throw me around, punch me, kick me, sure. But you can't beat me. Look at you, with your cracked metabands. Defects. I'm just toying with you, putting on a show, making sure everyone in the world can see what happens if they face me. I'm just trying to make it a little entertaining for me, giving the news crews time to get their drones into the air to cover it all and making sure that they've got every angle covered when I take those metabands off your wrists and crush them in my bare hands. Then everyone will know for sure what I'm capable of and what awaits them if they ever try to defy me.

"It's much better to have one big public fight that puts the fear of God into everyone. That way, I won't have to swat at gnats like you for the rest of my life. Let them all see what happens when someone thinks they can stand up to me and try to destroy a city that doesn't want them."

"It's not up to you to decide what this city wants. They only listen to you because they fear you."

"They fear me? No. They fear you. You and all the other weekend warriors who think just because they found a fancy piece of jewelry that it entitles them to try their hand at being a hero."

"And what makes you any different?"

"I fought for this country, for these people, long before monsters like you came along. I know what's best for them and for everyone else. I'm just the only one who has the balls to stand up to metahumans like you and say that we don't need you or want you. Admit it. The reason why you hate me so badly is that I'm not one of you, and I never will be."

"You've got that right."

"Funny. That's very funny. All right then," Charlie says as he begins rising into the air, still sitting with his legs crossed comfortably in front of him. "I think that's probably enough discussion. These people aren't tuning in to watch a debate. They're tuning in to see a bloodbath. That's the only way they'll pay attention and the only way they'll learn. Time to make an example out of you. Nothing personal, I hope you understand that."

The air around Charlie starts visibly vibrating around him.

"Get out of there, Connor!" Midnight yells into my earpiece, but there's nowhere to go. If I run, he'll just follow. He won't stop until he's gotten what he wants: an example for the rest of the world to see.

FORTY-TWO

Suddenly, a single word echoes through the concrete canyons of downtown Bay View City, a single word coming from a million mouths at the same time.

"Stop."

Charlie holds back his fist, hesitating momentarily. He can see the look of confusion on my face and knows that it's not a trick, or at least, not a trick that I'm any part of. The momentary truce is just long enough for me to break free from his grip and gain some safe distance. If he's going to kill me, I want to at least see it coming.

Both of us scan the skyline, looking for the source of the word, and we both find it. Along the rooftops of buildings throughout the city, there are thousands and thousands of people crowded, all lined up in formation, dangerously close to each other and to the edges of their respective buildings.

"Surrender at once or watch your city kill itself, one person at a time," the unified voice says.

Keane.

"What are you doing, Keane?" I yell into the night sky.

"I'm doing what neither of you have the courage to. I'm ending this, once and for all. Remove your metabands and surrender or people start dying," the bodies reply in unison.

Charlie laughs.

"You really think I care if you kill a few innocent civilians? Collateral damage. The cost of doing business. They won't be the first civilians killed by metahumans, and if people like me were ever to surrender to people like you, they certainly wouldn't be the last," Charlie announces as he addresses the city of mindless drones.

"So be it," they reply.

Without hesitation, the first line of people closest to the edge all take a step forward and all begin their long fall to the street below.

Without thought, I dive toward the nearest building, pulling my arms in close to my body as I pick up speed. My eyes are focused on the falling bodies closest to me.

I collide into the first as gently as possible and still almost snap his neck from the whiplash. Feet first, I continue my flight into the nearest window of the same building, smashing it into a million pieces. Before the last shards have fallen, I have the man I caught safely sprawled out across the office carpeting before I rocket back out of the window.

I'm diving even faster this time, struggling to reach the next victim before she reaches the asphalt below. I grab her just in time, less than fifty feet above the street below, and wince, expecting to hear the sickening thud of the others I couldn't reach as they hit the ground, but the sound doesn't come.

Hesitantly, I turn my head to see what's happened. The street below me flexes and pulsates as person after person falls into it and crosses the street. I see the reason. Winston is standing with his arms outstretched, concentrating. He's changing the molecular structure of the street itself, softening it to save the would-be victims falling from the sky.

"Omni, Winston's not going to be able to hold that up for long. You've got to find Keane and take him down, now!" Midnight says through the earpiece.

I briefly scan the sky for Charlie, even if he's secondary to my worries at this exact second. As I place the woman I caught onto the cushy concrete below, Iris teleports in front of me.

"There's no time," she says as she reaches out for my hands before we instantly materialize in what looks like an abandoned subway station. It's completely empty, except for a television displaying the action above from a live drone feed and Keane.

"We had a deal, Keane. Let go of them!" I scream as I run toward him.

"Not one more step there, Mr. Connolly, unless you want

to see how many people it takes to break your friend's neat little trick. I'm guessing another row or two is all it will take before it'll be impossible to keep the bodies from piling up on themselves. Not much you'll be able to do then, unless Winston wants to start turning the people themselves into jelly, which I strongly advise against if they ever want to live a full life after this is over with."

"Why are you doing this?" I plead.

"To prove that I can to him," Keane says, gesturing toward an unseen Charlie, "and to you. To show everyone that no matter what they think they can do to contain us, put us in little locked boxes that they throw away the keys for, it won't matter. We're what's next, and there's no way to stop the inevitable.

"I think I have a way to show you exactly what I mean. Iris here is a little too immune to my effects now, especially if I want to make sure I'm able to devote enough of my attention to keeping all those people balanced up there.

"But you, Omni. You're a bit of a different story, aren't you? Let's take a little root around inside that head of yours, shall we?"

It feels like a light switch being flicked. That's how fast it happens. In an instant, I'm no longer the driver of my own body; I'm merely a passenger.

"All right, Mr. Connolly, now that you're nice and comfortable, what do you say we go have some fun?"

I try to move my arms, but it's like they belong to someone else. My eyes won't even listen to me. I can't move them or focus them on what I want to. I try to turn my head to look to Iris for help, hoping that she understands what's going on and can stop it, but it's no use. Keane is in complete and total control.

"Why don't we start by having you take flight. Straight up ought to be the quickest way out of here and back into the fray, don't you think?" Keane asks.

Suddenly, my view of Keane is obstructed. My focus

remains on where he stands, but there is a blurry body in front of me now, and it's clad in purple.

I wait for Keane to speak, but no words come. Slowly, I can start to feel the extremities of my body, like when your leg falls asleep and then wakes back up as the blood rushes back in. Keane is losing control, and when the person in front of him steps aside, I understand why.

Iris teleported, just a short distance, less than ten feet. Where she teleported from and the distance isn't important, though. It's where exactly she teleported to that is.

In a flash, she disappeared momentarily before reappearing instantly behind Keane, and I can see what she's done.

There's horror in Keane's eyes as he tries to make sense of the sensation he's feeling, but a moment later, his eyes and hands simultaneously find the cause for concern: a gaping hole straight through his chest. Through it, I can see Iris standing on the other side of him, her right arm covered in blood.

Keane drops to his knees and his eyes close. Tears begin to roll down Iris's white eyes, but her voice shows no sign of sadness.

"I had to, Connor. He was going to use you the same way he used me. He was going to use you to kill. I couldn't let that happen. I just couldn't," she says.

I look back down at Keane, his eyes wide open and unfocused. There's no hope for him.

"There could have been another way, Iris."

"But there wasn't. He's been given chance after chance and we haven't learned. No one has learned. I needed to end this. Not just for me, for everyone. He's not going to hurt anyone ever again. There's nothing you can do now for him. Go stop Charlie."

I look once more at Keane, the life draining from his eyes, before looking back at Iris. He deserved to die, but that's not for people like us to decide. Once we start doing that, we're no different than them.

"I can teleport you back out of here," Iris says.

"I got it," I reply.

"What are you going to do? Blast up through a hundred feet of earth and city infrastructure just because you're mad at me? This isn't your city to destroy either."

"Fine."

Iris reaches out to touch my arm and, in an instant, we're back above the city as though we never left.

I spin in a circle, quickly trying to pin down Charlie's location. I'm glad to see the city is still standing considering how long I was gone. The rooftops are already clearing out of all the people who were under Keane's control as they all retreat back into the relative safety of their office buildings and apartments.

Nearly a mile away from where Iris and I are hovering, I spot the rest of the metahumans from the academy on the street.

"There," I say to Iris before diving through the city toward them. She quickly follows. We land and find a group of confused-looking metas and Sarah, still wearing Midnight's, sorry, *her* mechanized armor.

"What happened?" I ask.

"I'm not sure," Winston says. "One minute we're duking it out with Charlie, holding our own, when all of a sudden, he just ups and takes off on us."

"I'm telling you, he retreated. He got his ass handed to him, saw the writing on the wall, and decided to take off instead of hanging around to face the music after we beat him into submission," Ellie says.

Iris and I trade concerned looks.

"No. Charlie wouldn't quit, not like that. He'd rather go down fighting than run. He can't rally people around the idea that we're all dangerous monsters if he looks afraid of us himself. It doesn't make sense," I say.

My radio earpiece clicks on. At first all I hear is static and no talking. Almost everyone on this channel is here already, everyone except Michelle and Midnight.

"Omni," Midnight says through my earpiece, "we've got a problem."

I step back from the rest of the group who are all now bickering and arguing over what to do next and place my hand up against my ear to try to make sure I can hear him clearly.

"Where are you?" I ask.

"Above you."

I look up but see nothing except for the clear night sky.

"You're not going to be able to see me, even with your vision. I'm miles up in my aircraft. There isn't much time."

"Time?"

"Charlie. He flew past my plane and into the stratosphere approximately ninety seconds ago."

"So he is running away?"

"No. I'm tracking his telemetry. He's outside Earth's gravitational pull and heading for the moon."

"Why would he do that?"

"He's going to try to use it to gain speed. If he can catapult around the moon and back toward Earth, he'll be traveling impossibly fast. Fast enough that his impact could cause an extinction-level event."

"Wait. Slow down. I don't understand."

"I can't slow down, Connor. There's no time. If Charlie returns into Earth's atmosphere at the speed he's traveling, he's going to create a crater the size of the west coast of the United States."

"What do we do? How do we stop him?"

"He's too powerful. Even that strong of a collision might not be enough to kill him. At this point, I don't think he even cares about that. He's up against a wall, and this is the only way he sees out."

"So he's just going to kill everyone on the planet because he lost?"

I'm talking loudly enough that the rest of the group is starting to turn their attention toward me. They murmur back and forth to each other, trying to figure out the other end of the conversation that they can't hear.

"There's one chance, Connor, and I wouldn't even suggest it if it weren't for the fact that we're all dead in a few minutes anyway."

"What is it?"

"Your metabands. They're damaged."

"I know that."

"Listen for a minute. Your metabands are damaged. Metabands aren't supposed to *be* damaged. They were built to withstand literally anything. The reason they were built this way was to protect their power source from ever escaping their confines. Just like how a nuclear power plant has hundreds of safeguards to prevent any type of breach, except times a thousand.

"When the bands, your parents, and I were brought back to this time, it was due to an anomaly we never could have predicted. The bands were damaged in a way they hadn't been designed against. That's what allowed them to tap into the massive amounts of power that they have now. Charlie's bands are unique because they were able to absorb the energy from the nuclear bomb that was meant to destroy them. Your bands, in their damaged state, are open to outside energy now in a similar way."

"I don't understand."

"Your bands can absorb energy the same way Alpha Team's were able to during the explosion."

"That's great, but there's not exactly a nuclear bomb nearby."

"There's not. There's something better. Something with even more energy."

My mind works to figure out what he's getting at when I look up and realize: the other members of the Circle. Their combined energy is greater than any single source of power anywhere in the world.

"Are you getting it yet?" Midnight asks.

"Them. I can take their powers."

"That's my belief, but these bands weren't built for that. The damage will prevent the internal safety systems from blocking the energy input, but you'll be highly unstable."

"The world's about to end anyway. Unstable sounds like a better plan than anything else on the table. How do I do it? Just concentrate or something? That's how I'm able to fly or do anything else with them."

"No, you'll need to tell them to manually enter recharge mode."

"How?"

"By speaking it out loud into either of the bands."

"What? Are you kidding me? These things had voice commands the whole time, and I'm just finding out now?"

"There isn't time for joking around, Connor."

"There's not going to be any time for anything soon so I might as well get it out while I can."

I look down at my shining, cracked silver metabands for what I assume will be the last time. They haven't let me down yet, and I hope they don't now.

"Initiate manual charge," I say.

The others look at me with confusion on their faces when my metabands suddenly start pulsating with a soft white light.

"What are you doing?" Iris asks.

"Charlie didn't quit. He's just stepped back to get a running start. He's catapulting himself around the moon as we speak and planning to slam himself into the city, destroying the entire planet in the process. I might be able to stop him, but I need all the power I can get."

"What do we need to do?" Winston asks.

"They'll need to have physical contact between their metabands and yours for the exchange to work. Once the circuit is complete, the energy should flow into your bands automatically," Midnight says, having heard Winston's question through my microphone.

"Midnight says the metabands need to be touching each other," I relay to the group.

"All right everyone, you heard him. Line up, metabands together with the person to your left and right. We don't have much time," Winston says.

"Wait, what happens to you then?" I hear a heavily distorted voice ask. It belongs to Sarah, or more accurately, to her mechanical suit.

"It doesn't matter. If I don't try this, we're all dead anyway."

"But what if it does work?"

I take a second and glance up into the sky, expecting to see a fiery streak coming through the atmosphere, but it's not there, not yet at least. I turn to Sarah and mentally pull my cowl back into the rest of my suit, revealing my identity.

"What?" the distorted voice asks.

"Protect Derrick for me, okay? He's the only reason I'm still here. He never abandoned me, but now I have to abandon him. Tell him I'm sorry."

Sarah hits a few buttons on her right forearm and the visor to her suit retracts.

"Connor? How are you using Omni's metabands? I don't understand," she says.

Even with all of this, I have to laugh at the question and how she'll feel when she realizes.

"You'll have time to figure it out. I hope."

"Connor, I've got incoming. If you're going to do something, you'd better do it soon."

I pull the cowl back over my head. There's not much need to keep my identity concealed at this point, but it'd feel wrong to go out without the full suit intact. That's how this started, and it's how it'll end.

I lower my forearms to my sides, placing them in front of Winston to my left and Ellie to my right.

"I'm sorry," Iris says through tears.

"Don't ever be sorry. The world can't ask for a better protector."

Winston and Ellie tap their metabands against mine and it begins. What looks like liquid electricity flows from the assembled group, collecting in a pool at my end of the enclosed circle. There's no pain involved, a concern of mine before this started, but their costumes and uniforms retreat back into their respective metabands. Their bands lack the energy even to keep those relatively uncomplicated abilities intact.

At first I don't feel different, but as their power leaves them, I begin to feel it enter me. Everything becomes brighter, clearer. My mind feels like it's running on pure energy, and I can suddenly see everything I have to do laid out in front of me.

I look down at my metabands. They're no longer a silver metallic color. Now they look as though they're made from light itself. My uniform pulses and flows with the same energy, making it appear as though it's alive.

"Go get him, Connor," Iris says to me.

I smile before directing my attention to the sky and take off.

Bay View City shrinks below me as I reach higher and higher, bursting through a lone cloud hanging in the cool autumn sky. I've flown many times by now, but this feels like something else entirely. I'm traveling so quickly it's almost dizzying. The streak that is Charlie waits silently above me. No doubt he's traveling toward me almost as fast as I'm traveling toward him, but he's still far enough away that he remains a blip in the night sky.

The air around me begins to thin and become dark. I'm reaching the edge of Earth's atmosphere. It's higher than I've ever flown before. There's a sudden panic that I won't be able to breathe before I realize that I don't feel the need to. I've become so powerful that even something as critical to life as oxygen isn't necessary for me anymore.

It's now that I start really thinking about what I'm doing, and that that was probably the last time I've stepped foot on earth. There wasn't much of a choice, though, and while the thought of death terrifies me, the thought of what will happen if I don't stop this terrifies me more.

That's what I have to focus on. That's what will get me through this.

The thin atmosphere disappears completely, and I realize that there's no more wind on my face. As if to punctuate the realization that I'm in space, a satellite whizzes past my face only a few feet away. I turn to look at it, but it's already hundreds of miles away by the time I catch a glimpse of it turning around the edge of the Earth.

I turn my attention back toward the moon. Silhouetted against the bright full moon, I pick up sight of him again. Charlie is closer now. Within seconds, he'll be right on top of me.

I take a hard look at him, gauging his angle and direction so I can make my last adjustments. I'll have to hit him with everything I've got. There's no slowing down or second-guessing.

I reach down deep and pull the last reserves of energy I have to push myself as fast as my bands will take me. There's a brief moment when I see Charlie's eyes right as he catches sight of me. There's an instant of confusion followed by an even shorter instant of recognition.

Then we collide.

And then there's nothing.

FORTY-THREE

When I wake up, I'm not sure if I've been out for seconds or weeks. Time itself feels different. The collision, the school, finding my metabands, my parents dying, they all simultaneously feel like they happened impossibly long ago and also like they happened just yesterday.

I'm afraid to open my eyes and find out where I am. If I'm not dead, then I'm likely floating somewhere in space, my metabands barely supplying enough reserve energy to keep me alive, but probably not enough to get me back home.

That worry is short-lived, though. When I finally work up the nerve to open my eyes, all I see is vast, empty white space.

I guess I'm dead after all.

"Hello?" a voice asks.

It sounds scared. I don't know much about religion or ideas about what the afterlife's supposed to be like, but I know enough that hearing the fear in someone else's voice doesn't bode well for me being in the good place instead of the bad place.

I search around for the source of the voice, but find nothing but more empty space.

"Up here," the voice finally says.

I tilt my head and finally see him floating above me: a man, maybe in his thirties. He's wearing a suit that looks almost like the types worn by me and other metahumans, but it's different, plainer, without symbols or colors, just all one white, seamless suit.

The man's gray eyes look terrified. His lower lip is trembling like he's on the verge of bursting into tears.

"Where am I?" the man asks me. "What is this place?"

Well there goes any hope that he was going to be the one to answer that question for me.

"I'm not sure."

"How did you get here?" he asks.

"I'm a metahuman. I was in a ... I'm not sure what you would call it. A collision? When I woke up, I was here."

"A meta ... human? What's a metahuman?" the man asks me.

He says the words as though he's never heard them before in his life. Whoever this person is, he's been here a long time if he's never heard of a metahuman before.

That's when I notice he's wearing metabands around both wrists, which only adds to my confusion.

"I told you how I got here. Why don't you tell me how you got here?"

"I asked you a question," he says, raising his voice with a quick kind of anger that makes me flinch.

"If you tell me how you got here, that would help us both figure out where we are, which I think is probably the most important thing to figure out right now."

The man pauses for a moment, considering what he should, and maybe shouldn't, say to me.

"I was on a vessel. We were inbound back to the Earth relay station when ... there was an accident," he says.

"What kind of accident?"

"The bad kind."

"How long have you been here?"

"I'm not sure. A long time. Nothing changes. Everything stays the same. Every hour of every day. I don't know why I'm even saying 'day.' There are no days here or nights. There's nothing but this. You have to do something. You have to get me out of here. I'm slipping. I'm starting to lose it. I don't know why I'm telling you all of this. I'm not even sure if you're real."

My stomach drops as I start to realize.

"What's your name?" I ask hesitantly.

"John. John Jones. I think. I can barely even remember anymore."

It's him, Jones, the man who killed my parents and

thousands of others, one of the most vile and horrific killers who has ever lived, and he's impossibly standing right here, right in front of me, and ... he's normal.

Maybe he's not normal. He's definitely got a few screws loose still, but he's not the maniac the world watched kill for sport. He's something different. For starters, he can talk. The Jones I knew, before he died, never spoke a word, which only added to the mystery surrounding him.

I begin to open my mouth to ask another question, when my metabands start chirping like crazy. It's a sound I've never heard them make before, something in between a notification sound and an alarm.

"What ... what is that?" Jones asks. "You have them too. You have the same as me." He holds up his wrists to demonstrate that he's wearing metabands as well, as if it wasn't one of the first things I noticed. "What does that sound mean? What are they doing?"

"I'm not sure," I tell him honestly. "They've never done this before."

The chirping becomes more rapid and louder. Jones and I catch each other's glares as we both recognize that the sound is a warning. It's increasing in frequency the same way a bomb would.

Without another word, Jones turns and runs in the opposite direction, far into the never-ending white void. There's nowhere for me to run, not with my metabands still attached. In a panic, I touch the bands together in an effort to deactivate them, hoping that maybe that would stop whatever is about to happen.

It doesn't work. The bands offer no response whatsoever. The beeping continues growing in intensity until it's no longer a beep. It's now one long solid blaring tone.

Then everything white turns black.

FORTY-FOUR

"Welcome back to the land of the living," The Physician says as I open my eyes.

I'm laid out in a hospital bed somewhere deep in the bowels of the facility. I think I've been here for a few days, but it's hard to keep track since I keep fading in and out of consciousness.

"We were all hoping today would be the day you were able to keep those eyelids open for more than a few seconds," he says.

"What happened?" I ask.

"Well, where to begin? For starters, it took about seven hours of searching the entire globe before they found you floating in the middle of the Indian Ocean. A nearby freighter had reported seeing you leaving a flaming trail through the sky as you plummeted back to Earth. Ellie came and found you apparently being nibbled on by a couple of frustrated sharks. Your metabands were in pretty bad shape, but they had enough juice left to keep you alive and prevent the sharks from turning you into lunch. How are we feeling today, Mr. Connolly?" The Physician asks.

"I've felt better."

"Of that, I have no doubt. Your recovery is coming along nicely, though, I must say."

"What can I say? I'm a trooper."

"It can all be directly attributed to the metabands around your wrists, but sure, the positive attitude helps too."

"So when can I get out of here then?"

"You're still going to be laid up for a few days, I'm afraid, but I do have some good news for you. Michelle looked over your charts this morning and deemed you well enough to receive visitors. In fact, I believe your first visitor is already waiting for you."

Derrick walks into the makeshift hospital room, and I can't

believe how happy I am to see him. I immediately try to get out of the bed to give him a hug but find that I'm pretty well secured thanks to all the tubes and wires attached to me.

"Whoa, easy there. These things look expensive," Derrick says.

He leans over to give me a hug.

"I'm so glad you're okay," I say.

"That makes two of us. I guess I really owe you one now, huh?"

"Damn right you do. Don't worry, though. I'm easy to please. The sports package will be fine. I don't want you to have to go out of your way when you shop for my new car."

"Glad to see falling from outer space didn't do anything to your sense of humor."

"How is everyone else?"

"Everyone else is good. In fact, there's actually a few other people who wanted to come say hi to you now that you're awake."

The first face I see come through the door isn't one I expected to see down here, but it's extremely welcome, nevertheless.

"Sarah!"

"You know, you made me feel like a real dummy for not having figured all of this out sooner."

She leans over and gives me a hug, careful not to get tangled in any of the tubes. The next face that I see walk through the door is absolutely one that I never expected to see here or anywhere else. Jim.

"Jim? But how?" I ask.

He doesn't say anything and just leans in to hug me. Unlike Sarah and Derrick, Jim doesn't seem to care about the tubes and cables presumably helping to keep me alive and just goes for it. When he finally pulls back, there are tears in his eyes.

"I don't understand ..." I say.

"I don't completely understand either, but I have your

friend Ellie to thank. She was able to get me to a hospital quickly enough to save my life. Another thirty seconds and I would have been gone for good."

"Jim, I'm so sorry about all of this. I should have told you everything sooner. I should have never gotten you involved in any of this."

"Well, it's a little too late for that, unfortunately."

"What do you mean?"

"Jim's transferring here to the academy," Sarah informs me.

"Technically, I already have, actually. Today was my first day of classes," Jim says.

"And guess what else?" Sarah asks, but she doesn't wait for me to guess. "You're going to have some more company down here soon."

"They're admitting me and Sarah into a new program here. I know we don't have the fancy fashion accessories that you do," Jim says, referring to my metabands, "but considering everything that went down in Bay View City, they want us on board."

"Speak for yourself. I've at least got one metaband," Sarah says.

"Considering these two already know so much about the goings on here now, and because of their work in the field, Michelle thought it would be a good idea to admit them into the program. The world's going to need more people looking out for it than just those who have a pair of metabands," Derrick explains.

"Well now I wish I hadn't gone through all the trouble of making new friends."

"I'm sure they're probably pretty close to being sick of you by now anyway," Sarah jokes.

"Speaking of which, where is everybody else?" I ask.

"I'd love to tell you, but that's classified," Jim says, barely able to contain the smirk on his face.

"They gave this guy security clearance and now that's all

he says about everything. It got old like three days ago," Sarah says.

"It might be old to you, but Connor's been knocked out for a week. I'm sure he thinks it's funny."

"Yup. Hilarious."

"To answer your question without being a smartass, most everyone else is on a mission right now," Sarah says.

"Already?"

"Hey, just because you decided to sleep doesn't mean the rest of the world stops turning. There's still a lotta bad people out there that need straightening out," Sarah says. "Speaking of which, we should probably check on them. We're kinda their support team for this outing, and they should be reaching their target soon. We just had to stop by once we heard you were waking up."

"I should probably get out of here too. They say you still need your rest," Derrick says.

I give each of them one last hug before they leave. On his way out the door, Jim flicks the light switch, and the room darkens. I lie in bed, staring at the ceiling, thinking about how lucky I am to have survived. That's when I see movement in the dark, just out of the corner of my eye.

"I was wondering if you were going to stop by to visit," I say into the darkness.

Out of the shadows, in the far corner of the room, Midnight steps toward my hospital bed.

"You're getting better at that," he says.

"Either that or you're getting worse at hiding."

"Unlikely."

"Why the sneaking around in the first place? You're practically faculty here now."

"I needed to speak with you about what happened, and there's no need to bring anyone else into it. I need to know where you went."

"You saw where I went. You had a better seat than anybody."

"You disappeared from my radar for over nine hours."

I think about what I'm going to say for a few seconds before opening my mouth. I don't have my head fully wrapped around what I experienced yet, and I didn't think I'd have to be explaining it so soon.

"I'm not sure where I went. It was bright. Endless."

"Were you alone?"

"No, there was someone else there."

"Jones."

"How did you know?"

"Where you went is a place that was thought to be only hypothetical, even in my time."

"What is it? Another dimension? Another universe?"

"Not quite, but you're not too far off. The science to explain what that place is doesn't exist in this time yet. The only relevant thing you need to know is that it's where your powers derive from. It's even where your metabands go temporarily when you think you've made them disappear. We call it the Fervor.

"The Jones you met will spend the equivalent of thousands of years alone in that place. It's what will make him into the monster you came to know in this time."

"But he wasn't that yet when I saw him."

"It doesn't matter. It's what he will become."

"But if I was able to leave that place, why couldn't he?"

"I don't know. The energy he was subjected to was much, much higher than what you were."

"If I could get in there and leave, maybe there's a way to get him out of there before he turns into the Jones we know in our time."

"Connor, I'm not even sure how you were able to enter the Fervor in the first place, let alone leave it. Don't count on ever being able to do it again, even if we knew the way."

"So what now then?"

"Now you rest. You just did something no one else in history has ever accomplished, and that includes future history."

"This is starting to get confusing."

"And that's why you need your rest. We're not done. Most of the escapees from Silver Island are still out there. There's a power vacuum right now in Bay View City after the Alphas were defeated, and there are still more metahumans emerging out of the shadows everyday, some good, but a lot of them not.

"Rest up. We're not done yet."

Thank you so much for taking the time read my book. If you enjoyed it and would like to leave a review about it on whatever Internet website you bought it from it would mean the absolute world to me and make sure that there's more. The whole reason this book even exists is due to the amazing readers who supported Meta and The Second Wave with reviews and telling their friends, so thank you!

To stay in the loop on all things 'Meta' and otherwise with me, please sign up for my mailing list at tomreynolds.com/list. You'll get the first chapters of any new books before anyone else and other fun stuff early. No spam either, I promise.

You can find my online elsewhere at the following, or you can email me at tom@tomreynolds.com. Don't be a stranger!

Internet: tomreynolds.com
Twitter: @tomreynolds
Instagram: instagram.com/tomreynolds
Facebook: facebook.com/sometomreynolds
Podcast: tcgte.com

About the Author

Tom Reynolds lives in Brooklyn, NY with a dog named Ginger who despite being illiterate proved to be a really great late night writing partner. The Second Wave is, conveniently, his second book. He wrote this biography in the third person, unlike his books.

Also by Tom Reynolds

Meta (Meta: Book 1)
The Second Wave (Meta: Book 2)

Made in the USA
Las Vegas, NV
28 November 2021